THE FROZEN GOD

Heroes Of The Nine Realms

BOOK 2

ALEX E. MARTIN

DEDICATION PAGE

To my editor Kathy, artist Metakosmian, and to George R. R. Martin, who gave me the courage to put pen to paper and begin my author's journey.

———◈✦◈———

BEFORE YOU BUY

Before You Begin...
     To thank you for continuing this journey across the Nine Realms, I would like to offer some gifts: free colored copies of Svartalfheim and Niflheim. Click here to tell me where to send them or scan the QR Code.

Helheim's First Level

Valley of Shadows

Gjallerbru

Bridge of Judgment

Hrunghorni

Eljudnir

Grapa Cave

Eeterm

Nastrond, the Shore of Corpses

City of the Lost

Yggdrasils Roots

Raven Gjoll

Helheim's Lower Levels

Hraesvelg, the Corpse Eater

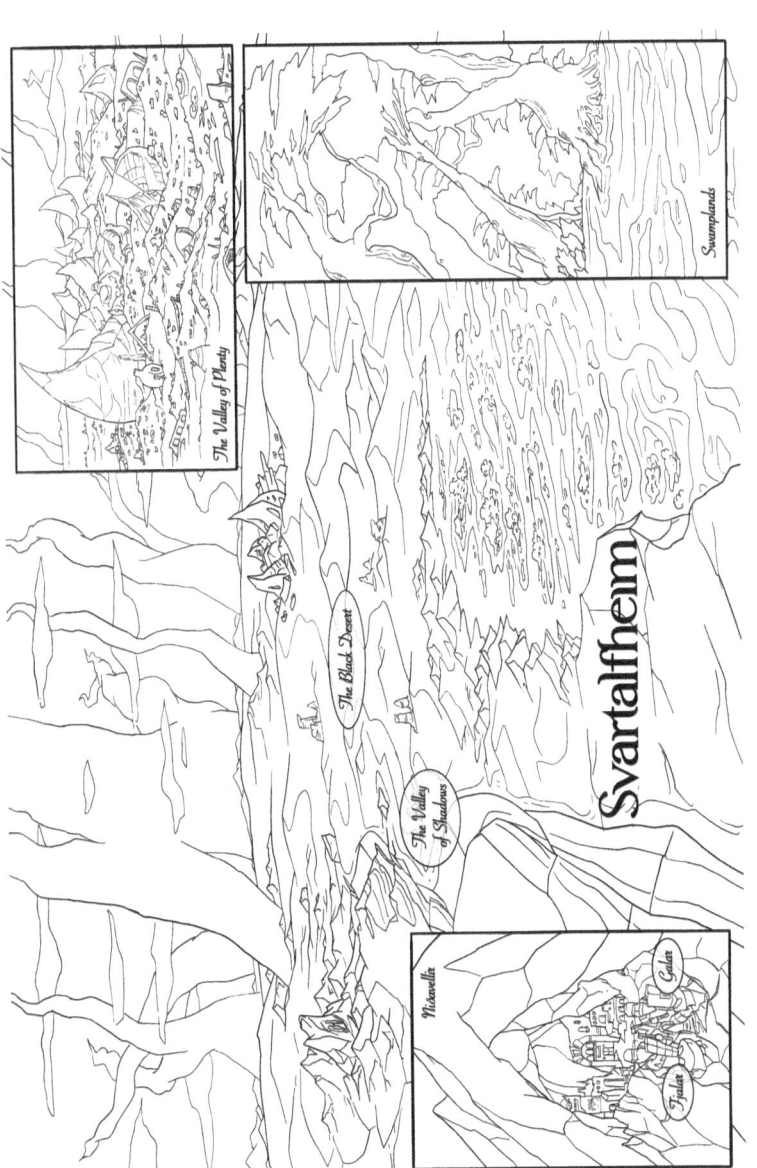

Niflheim

Lake Vid

Mount Isa

The Raven Slick

The Spines

Nidhogg and the Valley of Corpses

NOTE ON PRONUNCIATION

The following notes are intended to clarify some pronunciations of the key names in this series and are by no means exhaustive. Readers can pronounce the names however they choose, but this is how the author pronounces them.

AESIR (Pronounced "A-Seer")

ALGIZ (Pronounced "AHL-giz")

ANDHRÍMNIR (pronounced "An-dree-m-neer.")

ANDVARANAUT (Pronounced "And-var-a-knot")

ÅNDSROSTAVEN (Pronounced "Ands-roh-stah-ven")

ANDVARI (Pronounced "And-var-E" [hard e])

ANGANTYR (Pronounced "AHN-gahn-teer")

ANGRBODA (pronounced "An-gru-boda")

BILLINGR (Pronounced "Bill-ing-er")

BROK (Pronounced "Brock")

BRYNHILD (Pronounced "Brin-hild")

DAGR (Pronounced "DAH-Ger" like the word "Dagger")

DÁINN (Pronounced "Dah-inn")

DRAUPNIR (Pronounced "Drop-near")

DRAUG (Pronounced "DrahG")

DRAUGIR (Pronounced "Drah-Geer")

DURINN (Pronounced "Dur-inn" [hard "in"])

DÚRNIR (Pronounced "Door-near")

DVALINN (Pronounced "Dwah-linn")

EINHERJAR (Pronounced "EYN-hair-yahr")

ELDHRÍMNIR (Pronounced "Elth-ree-m-neer.")

ELUDNIR (Pronounced "e-lud-near")

ELIVAGAR (Pronounced "Eh-lee-vah-gahr")

FAFNIR (Pronounced "FAHF-near")

FAJlAR (Pronounced "FYAH-lahr")

FÁRBAUTI (Pronounced "FAWR-bow-tee")

FENRIR (Pronounced "FEN-rear")

FORNJÓT (Pronounced "Forn-Yatt")[1]

FREKASTEIN (Pronounced "FRE-kah-steyn")

FREYJA (pronounced "Freya" [silent j])

FREYR (Pronounced "Frey-ER")

GALAR (Pronounced "Ga-lear")

GINNUNGAGAP (Pronounced "Gi-noon-gah-gap")

GJALLERBRU (Pronounced "Ya-ler-brew")

GJUKI (Pronounced "GYOO-kee")

GJUKUNG (Pronounced Ga-YOO-koong")

GJÖLL (Pronounced like "Joel")

GULLINKAMBI (Pronounced "GOOL-lin-KAHM-bee")

GULLINBURSTI (Pronounced "Ghoul-in-burst-tee")

GUNNLQÐ (Pronounced "GOON-lohth")

GUTTORM (Pronounced "GOOT-torm")

HÁMUNDR (Pronounced "HA-mun-der")

---

1. In the Norse languages like Old Norse, the letter "j" is typically pronounced like the English "y" as in "yes" or "your", meaning it sounds very similar to an "y" in most words.

HÁVARD (Pronounced "Ha-vArd"

HELHEIM (Pronounced "Hell-Hime")

HERMONDR (Pronounced "Hermond" [silent r])

HJORDIS (Pronounced "YOUR-des")

HLJOD (Pronounced "yold")

HODR (Pronounced "Ho-Der")

HÖGNE (Pronounced "Hog-KNEE")

HJALPREK (Pronounced "HYAHL-prek")

HLIÐSKJÁLF (Pronounced "HLEETH-skyahlf")

HRÆSVELGR (Pronounced "Ha-roth-el-gar")

HREIDMAR (Pronounced "HRAYD-mahr")

HRINGHORNI (Pronounced "Hring-horn-E")

HULDRA (Pronounced "HOOL-drah")

HUGRHEIM (Pronounced "Hue-ger-hime")

HUGINN (Pronounced "HOO-gin")

HYMIR (Pronounced "He-meer")

IDUN (Pronounced "EE-doon")

IVALDI (Pronounced "EE-vahl-dee")

JÁRNGREIPR (Pronounced "YAHRN-greyp-ur")

JONAKR (Pronounced "YON-nah-kr")

JÖRMUNGANDR (pronounced "YOUR-mun-gand-er")

JOTUN (Pronounced "Yo-tun")

KISTFUSKARE (Pronounced "KEEST-foos-KAH-reh")

KVASIR (Pronounced "Ka-Va-Sear")

LITR (Pronounced "Li-tur")

LYNGVI (Pronounced "Ling-vi")

MAGNI (Pronounced "Mag-knee")

MEGINGJÖRD (Pronounced "MEH-ging-yor-d")

MJOLNIR (Pronounced "Myol-neer")

MÓÐGUÐR (Pronounced "Mod-gu-dur")

MODI (Pronounced "Mo-dee")

MÓTSIGNIR (Pronounced "MOHT-sohg-neer.")

MUNDILFARI (Pronounced "Moon-dee-lfah-ree")

MUNINN (Pronounced "MOO-nin")

MUSPELHEIM (Pronounced "Moose-Pell-Heim")

NÁSTRÖND (Pronounced "Na-strond")

NIÐAVELLIR (Pronounced "NEE-dah-vah-leer")

NIFLHEIM (Pronounced "Nif-ill-Hime")

NIDHOGG (Pronounced "Nid-hog")

NJÖRD (Pronounced "Nyord")

OTTR (Pronounced "O-Ter")

RAGNARÖK (Pronounced "RAHG-nah-rock")

RAGR (Pronounced "RAH-gr")

RATATOSKR (Pronounced "Rat-ah-tos-ker")

REKR (Pronounced "REH-Kur")

RERIR (Pronounced "Re-rear")

RÖSKVA (Pronounced Roh-sk-vah")

SÆHRÍMNIR (Pronounced "Sye-rreem-neer.")

SEIDR (Pronounced "See-der")

SIGGIER (Pronounced "Sig-gear")

SIGI (Pronounced "Sig-E")

SIGRÚN (Pronounced "SIG-roohn")

SIGURD ("Sig-urd")

SIGYN (Pronounced "Sig-In")

SIGNY (Pronounced "Sig-knee")

SINDRI (Pronounced "SIN-dree")

SINFJOTLI ("Sin-fot-LEE")

SKADI ("Ska-Dee")

SKULD (Pronounced "Skoold")

SLEIPNIR (Pronounced "Slayp-neer")

SURTR (Pronounced "Surt-er")

SUTTUNGR (Pronounced "SOO-ton-ger")

SVARTALHEIM (Pronounced "Svar-tal-Hime")

SVARBLOOD (Pronounced "SVAHR-blood")

TABLUT (Pronounced "TAH-Bloot")

TANNGNJÓSTR (Pronounced "Tan-ng-yoh-str")

TANNGRISNIR (Pronounced "Tan-gris-neer")

THAIZI (Pronounced "TH-ah-zee")

THIALFI (Pronounced Thee-ahl-fee")

TÝR (Pronounced "Tier")

TYRFING (Pronounced "TEER-fing")

URÐARBRUNNR (Pronounced "Oorth-ar-broonnR")

VANIR (Pronounced "Van-ear")

VERÐANDI (Pronounced "Verrth-ahn-dee")

VÖLSUNG (Pronounced "Vol-sung")

WYRD (Pronounced as "Weird")

YNGLING (Pronounced "EEN-gleeng")

YGGDRASIL (Pronounced "IGG-drah-seel")

YMIR (Pronounced "EE-meer")

PROLOGUE

S igurd's face burned as if tiny needles pierced his skin as the wind whipped around him.

"Hold fast, Sigurd!" Sinfjotli shouted. "Don't give up the ghost yet!"

Sigurd couldn't reply—his teeth chattered too violently. Steam rose from his blue lips like smoke from a chimney as he clutched the giant black wolf's snow-crusted back, desperate for warmth. Another mighty gale descended, a leviathan's howl shaking the air. The wind scoured the snowdrifts, making everything seem so white—it was hard to tell the sky from the snow.

The sun was gone, swallowed by the storm. Snow and ice devoured everything around them, reducing the world to shades of gray and pale blue. Each step felt like a battle. Still, the giant black wolf shuffled forward with Sigurd on his back, paws sliding and scrabbling for purchase on the ice-coated tree root.

Most of Sigurd's body was numb. Ungodly pain ravaged the few areas frostbite hadn't claimed. His heart pounded, each breath escaping in raspy, panicked gasps.

He tried to remember the last time he'd felt warm. Was it after escaping Helheim? The night Guttorm murdered him in his sleep? Or perhaps they *had* already perished and were in Helheim?

No. The Realm of the Dead's frosty blizzards was a cool autumn breeze compared to Niflheim's unforgiving atmosphere. Here, Sigurd's saliva froze between his teeth with every breath. Everywhere he turned was a mist that froze the blood in his veins. The fog and snow seemed to creep through his layers of clothing, under his hauberk and armor, seeping through his skin and wrapping around his bones.

The pain and frostbite became so bad that Sigurd tore off his golden hauberk and plate armor, leaving only the clothes Nanna had gifted him to protect him from the cold. Some might call that foolish, but his armor hurt rather than protected him in this relentless cold.

Even Sinfjotli, despite his thick fur, wasn't immune, moving as though experiencing every winter he'd lived through all at once.

"C-can... y-you... s-smell... an-anything?" Sigurd lisped through chattering teeth.

"The winds are blowing too hard," Sinfjotli growled. "I can't... argh... get a scent."

"W-we... s-should t-turn... b-b-back," Sigurd suggested.

"We've come too far. They're here. They have to be."

Sigurd was too tired and chilled to argue. He buried his face in Sinfjotli's fur, clinging to the only source of warmth. How had it come to this? How had he gone from being a fugitive of Helheim to a scared, frostbitten wreck desperately clinging to his brother's fur? His mind retreated to the recesses of his memories, a feeble distraction from this frigid hell.

Their journey to this realm had been perilous and long but nowhere near as deadly as the situation they were in now. After bidding farewell to Brynhild, Sigurd and Sinfjotli marched north across the World Tree's roots. They trekked across Yggdrasil's twisting roots for two months—or was it longer? It sometimes felt like an eternity. Along the way, they'd been attacked by many creatures: insects the size of barns, toothy worms the size of islands, and other nasty beasts that Sigurd's mind was too weary to recall.

He still bore the scars from those battles. They always walked away from each fight with at least a dozen wounds. Yet the Apples of Idun they'd eaten in Helheim healed their injuries and sustained them throughout that perilous journey devoid of food, water, and sleep.

That felt more like a curse than a blessing. Sigurd had been unable to quench his parched throat for weeks. He wished for food, though his stomach never growled. He craved slumber, but his body buzzed with too much energy to permit that.

But more than anything, he sought guidance from the Norns. That was what brought them to Niflheim, the coldest of the Nine Realms.

From afar, Niflheim had been both foreboding and beautiful. Even hundreds of miles away, standing on the ancient roots of Yggdrasil, Sigurd had felt the mind-numbing chill seep into his bones, making the hairs on the back of his neck stand on end. Niflheim's swirling atmosphere was an ethereal blend of vibrant blues, cerulean, and flecks of white, constantly in motion like the sea. Chunks of ice swirled within its atmosphere, a grim warning of the merciless winter that gripped this realm, where warmth was nothing more than a distant memory.

Sigurd glanced up at Yggdrasil's trunk. High above, his home realm of Midgard shone like a star, flanked by two other bright lights. The distance was so vast that even with his superhuman vision, he couldn't make out Midgard's details.

But he was sure of one thing. Niflheim dwarfed Midgard a dozen times over. Finding three goddesses in that frozen expanse would be like locating three grains of sand at the bottom of the sea. Every instinct screamed at him to avoid this realm at all costs.

But where else could they go? They couldn't hope to climb the World Tree. They couldn't linger on the colossal roots without getting attacked by other creatures that called these lowest echelons of the universe home.

The only other realms they could travel to were Helheim and fiery Muspelheim—realms even deadlier than the one before them.

Sigurd shared a look with Sinfjotli, who shrugged. "We've come this far," his half-brother said. "No sense hesitating. We clawed our way out of Helheim. We can surely handle Niflheim."

Gods above, we were so naïve, Sigurd reflected. *We let the glory of escaping Helheim get to our heads. We should have...* What *could* they have done? What in Ymir's name could they have possibly done to prepare for this journey when all they possessed was a magic sword, a suit of armor, ragged clothes sewn by a goddess, and the ability to transform into a wolf?

Baldur's apples and Sinfjotli's shapeshifting were the only reasons Sigurd clung to life. The snake-eyed warrior had been the first to succumb to the elements after weeks... days... or hours. He didn't know how long they'd been in this forsaken place. The Apple of Idun burned within his stomach like smoldering coals in a furnace as it struggled to heal him. But for each patch of frostbite it repaired on his nose and fingers, another thirteen patches sprang up.

Sigurd collapsed face-first into a deep snowbank. The icy powder enveloped him like a blanket, and to his shame, he wanted nothing more than to let it comfort him, to close his eyes and slip into a sleep from which he would never wake.

But Sinfjotli had other ideas. He abandoned his human form, tearing through the remains of his clothes as he transformed into a wolf, dug Sigurd out of the snow, and hoisted him on his back. The soft fur was the first warm thing Sigurd had felt in ages.

"You won't die like this," Sinfjotli vowed as he sprinted across the snow-covered branch. "Neither of us will."

Sinfjotli always kept his promises. But here, in the unyielding grip of Niflheim, honor and courage meant little.

The further they traveled, the darker and colder the realm grew, as though they were sinking toward the bottom of an ocean that light would never reach.

Sigurd kept himself busy, scanning the darkness, ensuring they stayed on the path. Sinfjotli almost slipped off Yggdrasil's branch more than once. Each time, Sigurd's sharp gaze caught the danger in time to warn his brother, sparing them from falling into a ceaseless abyss below—from which there'd be no return.

As another bone-chilling gale blasted them, Sigurd wondered what his beloved Brynhild was doing now. She'd flown up Yggdrasil's trunk to Asgard after helping them escape Helheim. He didn't know what dangers lurked along the way, but he hoped she was in a warmer, kinder place than this frozen wasteland.

Thinking about her was one of two things that kept him going. The other was their long-lost daughter, Aslaug.

I had another daughter all this time and never knew. The thought stung as sharply as the cold. When Sigurd learned of Svanhild's and Sigmund's murders, his resolve cracked. But Brynhild's revelation—that he still had a living child—convinced him to move forward.

Cruelly, her name was the only thing he knew about her. What sort of life had Aslaug lived? What did she look like? Which of her parents did she resemble more?

Each question consumed him, keeping him tethered to consciousness as Sinfjotli trudged deeper into the darkness.

But soon, even his half-brother succumbed to the elements. A foot of snow had gathered on Sinfjotli's back before the wolf's legs finally buckled. He slumped on his belly, defeated.

The sudden jolt sent Sigurd tumbling, rolling on the ice-covered branch.

It's over, Sigurd knew as he sprawled on his back, listening to Sinfjotli's panting. *We gave it everything, but this is as far as we can go.*

The blizzard relentlessly pounded them, piling an inch of snow every minute.

The snow will become my burial shroud. But I'll feel warm soon.

Regin taught him long ago that everyone feels warm just before death comes. Sigurd clung to that promise, eagerly awaiting that feeling, though it saddened him he wouldn't die bravely on a battlefield.

This would be his second death. His first had been bloody but swift, courtesy of Guttorm. This one, though, wouldn't be glorious, but it would be memorable... if anyone could witness it.

Snow slid off Sigurd's forehead and blond hair as he turned his head to the side and peered further down Yggdrasil's root into the abyss.

We never so much as glimpsed the Norns. All our strife amounted to nothing in the end.

It wasn't as bad as bleeding to death in his bed, he supposed. Besides, Sigurd knew what awaited him. Soon, he'd see Baldur, his aunt, and the others. Maybe he'd see his children, too. He hoped Baldur found them by...

A crunching sound pierced the blizzard's shrieking wails. Three humanoid shadows shifted in the mist. But Sigurd's body gave out, his strength ebbing away, and his eyelids shut before he could wonder if the figures were friend or foe.

CHAPTER ONE

THREADS OF DESTINY

T he air was *too* warm.

That was what woke Sigurd. At first, he assumed he had died and his soul had returned to Helheim. Then he remembered Helheim *had* no warmth, not even on Baldur's ship. And there was no warm air in Niflheim.

He sat up, blinking the sweat from his eyes. A tingling sensation rippled through him, followed by a searing pain. He lay back down as it swept through his body. Many bandages covered his hands, feet, shoulders, and nose. His skin felt icy, numb, and was white with frostbite.

Thankfully, the healing properties of the golden apple Baldur had given him in Helheim activated, and slowly the warmth returned to his limbs, fingers, and toes. But he could tell apple's effects were diminishing because it took much longer for his body to heal than it had in Helheim.

Baldur mentioned that time flowed differently throughout the realms. How much time had passed since then?

The last thing Sigurd remembered clearly was traveling through Niflheim's icy atmosphere with little protection from the cold.

By the gods, that was such a foolish thing to do! Their brave but reckless journey had nearly cost them their lives. They weren't prepared to venture into such unrelenting weather. To say Niflheim had chilled him to the bone didn't do it justice—it felt like his bones had turned to ice. If not for those three shadowy figures, they would have frozen solid and been cast back into Helheim to become Hel's newest playthings.

As he pondered who could have withstood the unforgiving cold and skin-ripping wind and rescued them, Sigurd's throbbing pain finally quieted. As his body finished healing, he sat up and took his bearings. He lay on a giant silken bed, his golden hauberk, the Helmet of Terror, and swords arranged neatly at his feet.

He regretted wearing that outfit on his journey through Niflheim. His golden armor had protected him from many dangers in Midgard and Helheim, but it did *nothing* to protect him from the cold. The frigid air had seeped straight through the metal armor, exacerbating the situation and causing him to get frostbite much faster.

He made a mental note to not make that mistake again as he resumed examining his surroundings. It looked like he was in a large cave, unlike any cave he had seen. The walls, floor, and ceiling were made of wood, not stone. Gnarled roots hung from the ceiling like stalactites, and long golden threads hung from the roof and walls like cobwebs or draperies. It almost resembled the inside of a bird's nest—until he noticed the walls were far too big and solid to be interlocking twigs.

Could we be inside a hollowed-out section of Yggdrasil's root? Sigurd wondered.

In the center of the cave was a large pond, its water overflowing. On the other side, a large ashen tree hung above the well, its branches and roots adorned with glowing spheres. Several manmade channels extended from the well, guiding the trickling water through rivulets to places unknown.

A loud snore echoed to Sigurd's left. He turned to find Sinfjotli lying in the same bed five feet away. Now in his human form, he was covered in even more bandages than himself. Sinfjotli had suffered more frostbite because he had foolishly walked into Niflheim's atmosphere wearing nothing but torn rags. The clothes Nanna gifted him had been torn to shreds during their last stand on the Gjallerbru and couldn't protect him from the elements. Thankfully, his body was also healing, albeit at a much slower rate, thanks to the apples Baldur had given them.

A neatly folded pile of immaculate silken clothes rested on the covers near Sinfjotli's feet. Whoever brought them here had also sewn replacements for the garments he'd had torn to shreds during the battle in Helheim.

As color returned to Sinfjotli's skin, Sigurd took in the sheer size of the bed. It stretched at least twenty or thirty feet long and ten feet wide, and they were covered in a thirty-foot-long quilt emblazoned with innumerous and elaborate designs. Compared to the bed, Sigurd was like an ant. Looking around, he noticed this bed was one of three lining the cave's walls. Each was massive and seemed more suited for sleeping giants than humans.

Sinfjotli stirred awake and sat up. He smiled at Sigurd, then gazed wide-eyed at the cave.

"Where *are* we?" Sinfjotli gasped.

"They're finally awake," a feminine voice remarked.

"They're lucky to be alive," another voice added.

"They have a strong will to live," a third voice said. "They must; otherwise, they'd have never escaped out of Helheim."

Sigurd glanced to the right side of the room, where three women were knitting in a circle. Beside them, an enormous tapestry hung from the ceiling.

One woman operated a spinning wheel, the machine humming loudly, producing copious amounts of thread and yarn at a breakneck pace. A second woman appeared to be measuring and coloring each cord before passing it on to the third, who masterfully knitted each piece of string in its corresponding place. The threads seemed enchanted because they levitated up toward the tapestry.

They worked at astonishing speed, and the tapestry gained fresh layers of detailed and elaborate images every second. Some pictures were large and clear, like the image of a bearded man with a hammer in a rowboat fishing out a sea serpent in the center. But most of the pictures were so microscopic that even Sigurd, with his superhuman vision, had difficulty making out the details.

"W-who are you?" Sigurd rasped, his throat parched.

The women stopped knitting and stood. As they approached the bed, Sigurd realized each woman was ten feet tall, shrouded in silky garments. Around their necks hung golden amulets, each depicting a serpent biting its own tail, that glimmered in the cave's dim light. Their faces were beautiful but unnerving. Their eyes were blank white, lacking pupils, and their skin was so pale it seemed stripped of color. Long, curved fingernails—resembling bird talons—extended from their fingers. Though they were of varying ages—a young maiden, a middle-aged woman, and a crone—it was impossible to peg an exact age on any of them.

The youngest maiden, who wove the strings, wore a dress that reached her ankles, its fabric raven black. The middle-aged woman, who measured and colored each twine, had ashen hair and wore a white dress. The crone, who knitted each thread into the tapestry, was cloaked in a gray hooded gown, her lengthy hair so white it resembled snow as it cascaded from her hood on either side of her neck.

The women regarded them in silence, their blank, pupilless eyes unblinking. After a moment, the middle-aged woman raised a hand and pointed her long, talon-like finger at the piles of clothes resting on the bed. Without a word, the women waited, indifferent, as Sigurd and Sinfjotli slid off the bed and got dressed.

When they finished, the middle-aged woman with ashen hair and a white dress spoke. "Welcome, sons of Sigmund. We are the Norns. You have traversed far and endured much to seek an audience with us. My name is Verðandi."

"I am Skuld," the young maiden with raven black hair and black dress announced.

"And I am Urðr," the crone in the gray hooded dress said.

"Where are we?" Sinfjotli asked.

"In our home, Wyrd's Well," Verðandi answered. "More specifically, you are standing within a hollowed-out section of the root of Yggdrasil. Come, we'll show you."

The Norns led them to the ashen tree on the other side of the pond. It towered fifty feet high, and nine glowing spheres of different colors nested in its branches and roots.

"Is this a miniature version of the World Tree?" Sigurd asked.

"You may think of it that way. You parted with your beloved Brynhild here." Urðr pointed at the central tree root connected to a sickly green-colored sphere. "Then you traveled down the tree root to about here." She traced her finger a quarter of the way down the northernmost tree root, which was connected to an icy blue sphere.

Sigurd stepped back and studied the entire tree. At its center, embedded in the trunk, was a blue-green sphere— Midgard, their home world. Two other spheres were connected to the tree by branches on the same level as Midgard. One was inky black, presumably Svartalfheim. The other, far larger than all the other spheres combined, must represent Jotunheim.

Three more planetoid spheres were connected to several large roots at the tree's base. The sickly green and icy blue spheres Urðr had pointed out were Helheim and Niflheim, respectively. The last root was connected to a giant fiery red sphere, its surface glowing with a dim crimson light. The root itself looked blackened and burned, undoubtedly Muspelheim, the realm of the fire giants.

In the tree's canopy were three more planetoid spheres. One was utterly green, presumably Vanaheim. Another shone bright white sphere, as radiant as a star—Alfheim, the brightest of the Nine Realms. At the very top of the tree's branches, in the center of the canopy, was a golden sphere—Asgard.

"That one root looks sickly compared to the others," Sinfjotli muttered, pointing at the tree root connected to Niflheim.

"Indeed." Verðandi nodded. "It's because of the terrible monster that lives beneath this tree root. He—"

Before she could finish, the cavern convulsed, knocking Sigurd and Sinfjotli to their knees. The water in the pool sloshed wildly, and the miniature ash tree swayed like it was being whipped about by a gale. The root connected to the icy blue orb darkened and started turning a sickly brown.

"Excuse us a moment," Verðandi said. She and her sisters grabbed a watering can and submerged it in the icy pool of water. Once full, they gathered some sand from the floor and mixed it into the can. Then, they sprinkled the water onto the sickly root. After a moment, the tremors stopped, and the tree root regained its ash-white color.

"What was that about?" Sinfjotli demanded as he and Sigurd stood.

"The topic of our conversation," Verðandi replied. "As I was saying, the tree root looks so sickly because of a powerful monster living in Niflheim. Every day, Nidhogg gnaws on the root we're standing in, and every day, we must draw water from the well, mix it with the surrounding sand, and pour the mixture over this miniature Yggdrasil tree so that the actual tree's branches will not rot."

"You want us to slay this creature?" Sinfjotli offered bravely.

"Don't be foolish," Skuld said. "No sane mortal, Aesir, or giant would ever be foolish enough to challenge Nidhogg to a fight. It would be a suicidal endeavor with calamitous results."

"Sinfjotli, son of Sigmund and Signy, you have always been quick to anger and keen to resort to violence," Urðr noted. "You always act on impulse, both on and off the battlefield, rarely considering the repercussions of your actions. That has caused many problems throughout your life and ultimately led to your demise. If you had not killed Brynjar over a mere insult, his sister

Borghild would have had no reason to poison you at Helgi's victory feast. And if you hadn't acted impulsively, you wouldn't have lost Randvi."

Sinfjotli staggered backward as if an arrow had struck him. "You know about that?"

"We know the life stories of everyone who has ever lived," Verðandi said, her voice devoid of emotion. "We were present when you were born, and we have meticulously recorded all the events of your lives."

Urðr and Verðandi walked over to the giant tapestry and pulled on two loose threads. As they tugged, the threads lengthened, expanding until each was the size of a scarf.

"These are your threads of life," Verðandi explained. "They contain every facet of your life, everything that has happened to you, and everything you are experiencing right now. Come and see."

Sigurd stepped forward and examined his thread. Various illustrations were woven into the fabric, showcasing an art style similar to the one used by explorers and shamans when carving their stories onto rune stones. The thread displayed the most significant events of his life—his birth, his intensive training with his mother, his encounter with Grani, his triumph over Lyngvi, his victory over Fafnir, Regin's murder, his fateful meeting with Brynhild atop Hindarfjall, and even his death.

As Sigurd gazed at the image of himself dying in bed, a sword through his chest, he noticed his tapestry didn't end with his death or funeral. The thread continued, showing his bloody duel with Sinfjotli, meeting Baldur, encountering Hel on his ship, fighting Siggeir and the army of the dead on the Gjallerbru, flying toward Hræsvelgr, and even this very moment in Wyrd's Well. He also noticed something else.

"It's not finished," Sigurd observed. "There's still plenty of string left unsewn."

"Correct," Skuld said. "And it's up to you to decide what shape they take."

Sinfjotli frowned. "Excuse me?"

"Your lives are cloth," Verðandi explained, waving her hand over the tapestries, "woven from choice and circumstances. You determine what shape they take based on your choices. Every time you make a decision, it is recorded here on your thread and becomes a part of the greater tapestry."

"Does this tapestry also depict our future?" Sinfjotli asked. "If so, then we've come seeking answers."

"Odin instructed me in a dream to seek your counsel," Sigurd elaborated. "We have many questions. Namely, why were we sent to Helheim? And why did Odin revive us afterward?"

"You *know* why you were both sent to the underworld," Urðr replied in a bored tone. "You both died dishonorable deaths outside of combat, which is a grave offense in the eyes of the Aesir. However, it seems the All-Father Odin has deemed you worthy of a second chance."

She held up Sigurd's and Sinfjotli's strings and pointed to a series of pictures on each one. On Sinfjotli's thread was a picture of their father, Sigmund, carrying his son's body to an old man in a wide-brimmed hat standing on a ferryboat. On Sigurd's string, it showed him lying on a funerary pyre next to Brynhild and his infant son Sigmund as their ship was being launched to sea. As he stared at the image of his funeral, Sigurd noticed the same man with the wide-brimmed hat standing in the background. The following few pictures on both tapestries showed this man riding an eight-legged horse across a golden bridge and meeting with Hel in front of her eponymous city.

"So Odin really was the one who revived us?" Sigurd asked.

"But why?" Sinfjotli inquired. "What's so special about us?"

"Because he's glimpsed the future and decided you are important enough to deserve that honor," Skuld explained. "Ever since he glimpsed Ragnarök, Odin has been obsessed with the future. The knowledge of what he has foreseen guides his every action. The reason he revived you two over countless other souls in Helheim is that he has foreseen that you will both play a pivotal role in the future, a role so important that he's giving you a chance to atone for your sins and the shameful manner of your deaths."

Sigurd wasn't sure what to make of that. It felt flattering that the All-Father valued them so much. But it also felt somewhat overwhelming, as if an enormous weight had been placed on his shoulders. But he could worry about this future pivotal role later. Sigurd had a different goal in mind.

"Please tell us what we must do to reach Valhalla," Sigurd requested.

"We cannot," Skuld said. "It is not for us to decide your path for you."

"I-I don't understand," Sinfjotli said. "You are the Norns, the beings who preside over destiny itself."

The Norns giggled, their laughter barely audible, like the rustling of bird feathers. Yet the sound shook Sigurd to his core.

"You give us far too much credit," Verðandi said. "We may be storytellers, but we three weavers are not divine authors dictating everything that shall happen with absolute, inescapable certainty. Everyone shapes their own fate."

Sinfjotli blinked. "Huh?"

"There is no destiny, Sinfjotli," Skuld said. "Only choices and the knots and patterns they weave."

"History is an enormous tapestry woven through choice and circumstance," Urðr said. "Every mortal, Aesir, Vanir, giant, elf, dwarf, and animal dictates the course of history through their decisions. Everything that's done, for better or worse, becomes a part of your legacy etched in this tapestry."

"And if you cobble together all the choices everyone has ever made, take a step back, and look at the big picture, the tapestry's grand design becomes easy to predict." So saying, Skuld snapped her fingers, and thousands of strings in the baskets levitated and weaved together into a single giant image: a picture of two armies fighting on a golden field.

"Ragnarök," Sigurd whispered.

"It is the only logical ending," Skuld confirmed. "But the ultimate battle is not inevitable because *we* decided long ago that it would happen. It is because all choices have consequences, even those that are not your own. From womb to tomb, we are bound to others' choices, past and present. Everyone adds shape and color to history with every choice we make. Through every crime, mistake, and act of kindness, we collectively shape the future, forming knots that cannot be untied."

Urðr snapped her fingers, and parts of the giant tapestry expanded, enlarging several illustrations. The biggest picture showed three warriors with spears standing over the remains of a bleeding giant. The next showed two armies fighting in plains and a dense forest. The third depicted a man riding an eight-legged horse with a girl, a snakelet, and a wolf pup in his saddle, fleeing from a giantess riding a giant eagle. The fourth showed a much larger snake getting cast into the sea and an enormous wolf being bound with a god sticking his hand in its mouth. The last image showed a glimmering god getting struck by a mistletoe arrow.

"Odin and his brothers slew Ymir, earning the eternal enmity of the giants," Urðr explained. "The bloody war between the Aesir and Vanir pitied the forces of Asgard, Vanaheim, Midgard, Svartalfheim, and Alfheim against each other and eventually resulted in an uneasy alliance between five of the Nine Realms, ensuring that the remaining four realms, Jotunheim, Helheim, Niflheim, and Muspelheim, would eternally be at odds with them. Odin kidnapped Angrboda's children, resulting in Hel being burned and earning the enmity of her brothers Fenrir and Jörmungandr. He and Thor then imprisoned and banished the wolf and serpent, earning their eternal acrimony."

"By that point, Odin could see what direction the realms were heading toward," Skuld interjected. "He realized that all the billions of choices throughout history had twisted together into future knots that cannot be unbound."

"He tried fixing it by making Baldur the lynchpin of the realms, a feeble attempt to stem the tide." Urðr continued. "But Loki arranged Baldur's murder, turning the All-Father's plans into ash, and the ultimate battle became unavoidable."

"Are you two beginning to see the pattern?" Verðandi asked. "Combine those choices and all the other trillions of choices everyone has made throughout history into knots and patterns, and an ultimate battle between the gods and their innumerous foes becomes inevitable."

She studied Sigurd with her pale eyes. "Does that frighten you, knowing that you are the masters of your own fate?"

"A little," Sigurd admitted.

"Don't hide it," Verðandi said. "Knowing you're responsible for your destiny terrifies you far more than you can articulate. That's why it's easier and preferable for the Aesir, Vanir, Jötnar, and mortals to scapegoat three prescient weavers living in a cave instead of taking responsibility for their actions."

Sigurd said nothing for a while after the Norns revealed the truth to him. On the one hand, relief washed over him that the Norns did not predetermine his fate. But that realization brought its own kind of terror. He and everyone else were solely responsible for their destiny. Every decision he made, no matter how big or small, could affect his life and those around him. Contemplating the full ramifications filled him with dread and uncertainty as he wondered if he could make the right choices to ensure a positive outcome.

Sigurd's eyes widened. *'Ensure a positive outcome?'* Yes. That was what Odin instructed him to do in his dream, which was why they'd come seeking the Norns.

"Even if what you say is true, it won't change why we've come. Also, you didn't answer Sinfjotli's question. You may not be almighty, but you're still prescient. If you can make your prophecies by reading a person's past and predicting their future choices, why can't you tell us what we must do to reach Valhalla?"

"It's not that simple." Skuld gestured to the tapestry behind them. "The future is not something that winds down a single road. The future diverges from a single point in time, like loose strands of string in an unfinished quilt. Depending on your choices and circumstances, it can form knots and take on any shape. We sew this tapestry and record your choices, but *you* decide what shapes your threads will take."

"That's why we cannot give you all the answers you seek," Verðandi added. "We can show you the way, but not the destination. That is for you to discover. But you will find the knowledge you seek in this well."

She gestured to the massive pond in the center of the room next to the miniature World Tree. Until now, Sigurd hadn't given the pond much thought. But as he stared into its bottomless, dark blue waters, he realized something was foreboding about this mysterious well.

"This is Urðarbrunnr, the Well of Destiny," Verðandi announced. "The water of this wellspring was the catalyst that gave birth to Ymir and the frost giants. Its waters flow through these channels on the floor, creating the Elivagar, which then travels up the World Tree and becomes the source of all rivers."

As they stared into the bubbling, boiling spring, Sinfjotli narrowed his eyes. "Where are the snakes?"

Sigurd frowned. "What snakes?"

"When I was younger, a traveling bard told me that the Well of Destiny is filled with more snakes than any tongue could enumerate," Sinfjotli explained. "He said their poison created the waters which gave birth to the frost giants."

The Norns chuckled dryly.

"You humans certainly have a creative imagination," Verðandi muttered. "But saying that those waters are poisonous isn't entirely inaccurate. These are the waters that gave birth to Ymir and the frost giants. Yet they are toxic to the living."

"And you would have us drink from it?" Sinfjotli exclaimed. "You aim to poison us!"

The Norns stared at him with their blank eyes.

"You would be wise to learn patience and respect when speaking to beings more powerful than you, son of Sigmund," Skuld cautioned.

Sinfjotli closed his mouth and lowered his head like a scolded child.

"It would be more accurate to say these waters are poison to the weak and the faint of heart," Skuld clarified. "Only the strongest and bravest beings can survive drinking from this well and gain knowledge from the ordeal."

Sigurd glanced at the miniature ash tree hanging above the well with the multicolored spheres nestled amongst its branches and roots. "Odin drank from this well once, didn't he?"

"Indeed." Urðr nodded. "The All-Father was the first person to drink from this well. He came here millennia ago seeking knowledge. But he needed to perform an immense sacrifice to prove his worth before we allowed him to drink from this sacred well. He drove his spear through his own side and then hung himself from this tree by his neck for nine days, bleeding into the well before he could drink from its waters. People called him 'The Lord of the Hanged' afterward."

Sigurd gazed up at the ash tree's branches and swallowed nervously. "Do you expect us to do the same?"

"That won't be necessary," Verðandi assured. "You've already proven your worth in our eyes."

Sigurd blinked. "We have?"

"You, Sinfjotli, and Brynhild fought through a million undead warriors and escaped Helheim, something no human has done before," Urðr said. "And you braved the journey through icy Niflheim to reach us. In our eyes, you've already earned the right to drink from this well."

"That's a relief." Sigurd sighed. He did *not* want to reenact Odin's famous ordeal.

"However, you should know that drinking from the well is still dangerous," Skuld said. "Even if we deem you worthy, the well will make you endure unfathomable pain before it reveals its secrets."

"I'm not afraid," Sinfjotli declared with red-hot anticipation burning in his heart. "My brother and I are no strangers to pain. We'll gladly endure whatever comes."

The Norns seemed pleased with their resolve. Skuld reached inside her hooded gray cloak and produced a single drinking horn.

"Where's the other horn?" Sinfjotli asked. "Shouldn't we each get one?"

"Only one of you needs to drink from the well." Skuld pointed at the two threads hovering behind her. Sigurd noticed his string had now intertwined with Sinfjotli's and merged into a single cord.

"Your threads of fate have intertwined at this pivotal moment," Skuld explained. "Once you drink the waters of destiny, you'll each experience a shared vision, regardless of who drinks from the well."

"But whoever drinks from the well will also experience excruciating pain," Verðandi warned. "So, which one of you will shoulder the burden?"

"In that case, I'll—" Sinfjotli began.

"I'll do it," Sigurd volunteered. "I'll be the one to drink. It *has* to be me."

"Why?" Sinfjotli asked.

"You already died once from drinking poison, brother. I don't want you to die in the same manner a second time."

"What makes you think you'll survive?" Sinfjotli demanded, a hint of worry in his voice.

Sigurd smiled and patted his abdomen. "Father wasn't the only one with a stomach of iron. Back in the day, I could drink anyone under the table. I'll be fine."

The Norns handed him the drinking horn, and Sigurd scooped the icy water from the well. A single water droplet dripped onto Sigurd's hand as he raised the horn above his waist. He winced and nearly spilled the horn's contents all over the floor. The water from the well was so cold it burned his skin. It felt like he was holding a block of solid ice.

"Sigurd?" Sinfjotli asked worriedly.

"I'm fine," Sigurd lied. Putting aside the searing pain burning his palm, unease tightened his chest, his heartbeat erratic. It was as if he were standing back in Helheim, the crushing gravity pushing down on him. Part of him wanted to dump the horn's contents and flee. But another part was compelled to see what truths this well would reveal. The wonder ate away at him like a rat gnawing against the walls of his stomach.

When he was ready, Sigurd raised the drinking horn. "Here's to finding answers." He pressed the horn to his lips and drank deep.

CHAPTER TWO

THROUGH FIRE AND ICE

T he first sip was ice-cold and tasteless. But when Sigurd swallowed it, the freezing water came to life within him. The liquid became burning hot as it traveled down his parched throat. It left an aftertaste on his tongue that tasted sweet like honey, spicy like pepper, salty like nuts, bitter like tea, and sour like lemons. It was all the tastes he had ever known, and none of them. Soon, the horn was empty.

"Through fire and ice, the realms were created," Urðr muttered as Sigurd returned the horn to Skuld.

"And it is in that mixture of opposites that you shall find the answers you seek," Skuld promised. Her voice became distorted and distant with every syllable.

Nausea churned in Sigurd's gut. His mouth went numb from the cold water, yet a burning sensation seared down his esophagus, as if he had just swallowed liquid fire. But that was just the beginning of his agony. Violent tremors racked his body, each nerve aflame with painful tingling. Warm tendrils spread from his stomach through his chest, like fingers of fire coiling around his heart, lungs, and other organs. He collapsed to his knees, drawing sharp breaths as agony laced through his every muscle. His skin turned cold and clammy, yet his limbs felt as if they were being flayed and dipped in hot tar. Darkness swallowed his vision, and silence consumed his ears.

When he opened his eyes, he was adrift in a murky abyss, suspended in nothingness—no solid ground beneath him, no air to fill his lungs, no scents to tickle his nose. Just infinite darkness stretching in all directions. Up, down, everywhere he turned, the darkness was endlessly tall and fathomlessly deep. A place that was nowhere, disconnected from the world, lost in the gaping void of Ginnungagap. No sun, no moon, no stars. No earth, no sky, no sea, no sand. No sense of direction.

But he still existed—had a form. He could turn his head, flex his arms, bend his legs, and wiggle his toes. Yet when he tried to step forward, his forehead slammed into something solid. Frowning, he kicked and punched and struck something impossibly durable. It was as though some barrier was encasing him. But that should have been impossible. There was no height, depth, or width in this gaping abyss, nor any matter to envelop him. Unless... perhaps the dark had closed in on him like a box? Or was something trying to show him something?

As Sigurd's senses heightened, a flicker of something stirred in the darkness. As he looked upward, a single, urgent thought raced through his jumbled mind: *What will emerge from this darkness?*

Two glowing spheres appeared in the void, one dark blue and one fiery red. Sigurd focused his snake eyes, realizing that one sphere burned with roaring flames while the other lay encased in ice. The colors matched those of the spheres on the Norns' tree—Niflheim and Muspelheim.

After a moment, or perhaps forever, the two realms converged. The fires of Muspelheim melted the ice, sending rivers flowing through Niflheim. In the darkness, from a single spring, this water came, branching through the valleys and canyons, forming eleven rivers: the Elivagar. As they drained into Ginnungagap, ice thickened upon the currents, and before long, the void froze over.

But sparks from Muspelheim soon followed, warming the frozen expanse. Heat and flames licked the ice until it melted, sending a warm mist swirling toward the center of the void. And where fire and ice met, where light and darkness, heat and fog entwined, life stirred, roused from the collision of opposing elemental forces.

From the ice, an enormous giant emerged. Soon after, a giant cow appeared, too, licking the salt from a frozen patch. The giant lay down beneath the cow, suckling from its udders. As it fed, life stirred within its massive form. First, a boy and a girl grew from his sweaty armpits. Then his feet pressed together, and a six-headed giant emerged from his sweat. More life forms continued to take shape, birthed from the titan's body as it nursed.

Meanwhile, the cow continued licking until a tuft of hair appeared. With each pass of its tongue, more of a figure was revealed. Eventually, the cow freed the body of a handsome man from the rime. This man differed from the other life forms. He was smaller, but his body radiated with an aura of primordial power. He began to mingle with the giantesses born from the enormous titan's body, and soon, he sired new life. These descendants, in turn, intermingled with the other life forms still emerging from the titan's body, threads of a new lineage.

In time, three hybrid beings rose up and slew the colossal titan with a spear. Blood gushed from its body, a crimson tide flooding all of creation. From the titan's remains, a sapling sprouted and grew until it turned into a towering ash tree with nine planets resting on its branches and roots. But Sigurd had no time to watch—he was swept away in the overwhelming deluge of the giant's blood.

His lungs screamed for air as the flood tossed him about. Just when he thought they would burst, he struck something hard and unyielding. He tumbled across solid stone before landing in a cold snowbank. He inhaled sharply. The flood had vanished. Instead of water, cold, prickly air rushed down his throat.

When he regained his senses, Sigurd stood and took in his surroundings. He was standing on the Gjallerbru, facing south, with the City of the Lost stretching out before him. Towering ice-covered skyscrapers loomed, and he heard the thundering of encroaching hooves. Turning, he spied a hooded figure racing his eight-legged horse across the bridge. The horse carried two wrapped bundles on his back.

Just as Sigurd recognized Odin and Sleipnir, his blood froze in his veins. Hel appeared beside him astride her mount, Helhest. The two riders met at the threshold where the City of the Lost met the Gjallerbru. They dismounted and regarded each other.

"All-Father"—Hel greeted him with a mock bow—"what brings you to my realm? Come to beg me to release your sons again? I thought you learned your lesson last time."

Though Hel's tone was light, Sigurd sensed a cold pressure beneath it, like submerged ice. The politeness in her voice seemed like a challenge, daring Odin to give her a reason to start a brawl.

"Not this time," Odin replied, not taking the bait. "I have come for another soul: Sigurd, son of Sigmund and Hjordis."

Hel raised an eyebrow. "The Dragon Slayer? His soul recently entered my city. He was a mighty warrior when he was alive and lived quite a remarkable life. Sadly, his brother-in-law murdered him in his bed outside of combat. Subsequently, that makes him one of the dishonorable dead. You know the rules, Odin. Not a single soul who dies a dishonorable death may leave this realm unless *I* allow it."

"I think you'll consider it once you hear my offer." Odin dismounted Sleipnir and removed one bundle from his saddle. He uncovered it, revealing a body that Sigurd immediately recognized.

"I present you Sinfjotli, the first-born son of Sigmund."

"You mean the bastard he sired upon his twin sister?" Hel sneered. "That man remorselessly murdered his siblings for the sake of his mother's vengeance. His stepmother poisoned him at a feast, but you stole him before I could collect his soul. Not that it did you much good. His soul can never enter

Valhalla. Its gates will forever be barred to him since he died a dishonorable death."

Hel glanced at the other wrapped bundle on Sleipnir's rump. "The other corpse is Sigurd's body. So, do you intend to trade Sinfjotli's soul for Sigurd's?"

"No. But we can play for both of them."

Hel tilted her head, gaze sharpening. "What kind of 'game' do you propose we play?"

"With your permission, I'll revive them in their bodies, and then we'll each take turns giving them nine impossible tasks across the Nine Realms. If they die at any point along the way, you'll get both their souls. But if they complete the assigned tasks, you'll relinquish your claims to their souls forever, allowing them to enter Valhalla."

A flicker of suspicion crossed Hel's face. She glanced hungrily at Sinfjotli's body, eyeing it as if it were a stolen toy from her doll collection—one she wanted back.

"Why are you so interested in these two warriors, Odin? You've meddled in your descendants' lives before, but never to this extent. Why are these two so special?"

"I have my reasons," he answered cryptically. "But I know you'll accept my challenge."

Hel sneered, baring her pristine and rotten teeth. "Always talking down to me as if you can see through everything and you're in control. I've never liked that about you."

"Come now, Hel, this isn't an unreasonable arrangement. You would be free to pick whatever task you'd like. We could begin here in Helheim if you'd like. You always boasted that Helheim is inescapable. 'Not a single living or dead soul may leave unless you allow it.' But no human has ever had the chance to test that claim while alive. Care to prove the veracity of your boast?"

Before Hel could respond, an emerald fog rolled in from the dark city behind her. It engulfed Sigurd, and the vision of Helheim faded away.

As Sigurd regained his sight, he found himself aboard a giant rowboat in the middle of the ocean. The vessel was so gargantuan that he felt like an ant as he stood on its thwart. At the stern, a giant cast his fishing line into the sea, two freshly caught whales at his feet. At the bow of the ship, the most muscular man Sigurd had ever seen was busy attaching the head of a giant jet-black ox to a heavy hook. Unlike the giant, the red-bearded man dropped his bait off the boat and let it sink to the ocean's depths. Moments later, the line jerked taut. With a mighty heave, the man tugged. The strain was so immense that his feet broke through the strakes at the bottom of the boat. But the beefy man held fast, reeling in the line until, at last, a great serpent reared up out of the water.

Sigurd had never seen a monster so colossal. There was no mistaking it—this was the Midgard Serpent, Jörmungandr, the legendary beast said to be large enough to encircle the earth and bite its own tail.

The snake writhed against the line, thrashing its head back and forth. It reared up, its head rising past the clouds, blocking out the sun. The burly man kept reeling, inch by inch, as the serpent glared at him. They were close enough to touch, separated only by a single, quivering line straining under the tension of the man's grip.

"Are you *mad*?" the giant screamed, bracing himself against the other end of the boat. "You'll destroy everything!"

Sigurd could see his fears were well founded. The ocean trembled, the seabed shook, and the earth groaned. Dragging the Midgard Serpent to the surface was causing the world to unravel.

The red-bearded man ignored the giant's pleas. He drew a hammer from his belt and raised it high above his head. Lighting crackled from its surface, lashing into the clouds above them. The once-picturesque sunny sky blackened, swallowed by a raging storm. Winds howled, waves churned, the thunder roared. The entire sky appeared to synchronize with the red-bearded man's rage.

This must be Thor, Sigurd realized as waterspouts swirled nearby. Amidst the storm and chaos, he noticed something strange—an island had spontaneously appeared in the distance where moments ago there had been nothing but open ocean. But before he could dwell on this, Thor raised his hammer, poised to strike his archenemy.

Suddenly, the giant Hymir lunged forward, fishing knife in hand, and slashed the line with a resounding snap. The serpent plunged back beneath the surface, the ocean calmed, and the clouds dispersed.

But the waves were so large, and the recoil from the snapped line so violent it sent Sigurd hurtling over the side of the boat. He struggled to swim back to the surface, the water churning around him, unrelenting. As the serpent sank beneath the waves, it dragged him down like quicksand, pulling him deeper into the dark abyss.

Sigurd looked down. He caught a glimpse of its monstrous form lunging—jaws wide enough to encircle an island. Before he could react, the World Serpent struck. Down its gullet he went, consumed by darkness.

From there, Sigurd's visions became more fragmentary and random. Somehow, he washed ashore, where a beautiful woman with scarlet hair sat naked on a rock by the sea with a net for clothes, a half-eaten onion at her feet, and a shaggy dog sitting next to her. She was staring at something behind him. He followed her gaze and saw Baldur's giant ship anchored offshore. On its deck, his aunt Signy and his wife Gudrun sat at a table, being healed by Baldur, while his wife Nanna moved between them serving food.

Sigurd turned back but the beautiful woman had vanished.

Now, he stood amid a field of reeds. Above him, rays of light and shadows were battling in the sky above. In the distance, a cornered wolf slayed eleven men and received many wounds. Sigurd followed the bleeding wolf into a dense forest—when suddenly, the trees came alive. Branches, roots, and vines lashed out, wrapping around his body and throat, tightening like iron chains. A murder of ravens descended, their claws raking his flesh.

Suddenly, the foliage and birds crumbled into ash. Sigurd searched around, realizing he was in a volcanic world of fire and brimstone, the air thick with heat and sulfur. A roar like thunder echoed across the scorched land as a conflagration erupted. Flames surged toward him. Sigurd turned and ran, fleeing the oncoming sea of flame.

But then, the blackened lands faded. The heat was gone. Sigurd stopped running, caught his breath, and turned around. He now stood on a rainbow, and before him was the most magnificent city he had ever seen. An instinctive pull urged him toward it. He stepped onto the red stripe. Fire engulfed his leg, racing up his body. As he struggled against the flames, the blaze traveled up the rainbow bridge, consuming the shining city in a raging firestorm. A deep rumble shook the ground. Sigurd turned. Behind him a massive army surged, weapons glinting in the strange light. Suddenly, the rainbow bridge shattered, and he fell into darkness once more.

He landed in the middle of a golden field. The sky above was pitch-black, devoid of sun, moon, or stars. Yet he could see through the darkness thanks to his snake eyes. To his left, an army of giants stretched to the horizon—trolls, ogres, Garm, Fenrir, the most enormous wolf he had ever seen whose back touched the clouds, Jörmungandr and a colossal fire giant with a flaming sword, and Hel herself was standing at the head of an endless sea of undead warriors. To his right, another host assembled—the forces of the gods. Elves, dwarves, valkyries, and warriors of renown. Amongst the ranks were his parents and grandfathers.

"*Which side will you fight for?*" both armies asked synchronously. "*CHOOSE!*"

As they spoke, the fire giant with the flaming sword pressed the tip of his blade against the ground. Flames spread throughout the golden field, engulfing Sigurd's body.

He woke up screaming. Sigurd rolled on the floor and patted himself, trying to extinguish nonexistent flames before he realized he was awake.

He lay on the cave floor next to the pond where he had fallen into his trance-like sleep. Sinfjotli lay nearby and slowly bestirred himself. It looked like the Norns had resumed weaving their tapestry while they slept.

Sinfjotli rose, panicking. The Norns didn't even deign to peer over their shoulders.

"They awaken," Verðandi observed.

Sigurd tried standing up and almost stumbled into the pool behind him. His muscles felt stiff, as if he hadn't moved in hours.

"H-how long were we out?" he croaked.

"About a day," Urðr answered. "Long enough for your threads to take on new patterns."

She rose from her seat and pulled two loose strings from the tapestry that expanded in her hand. Sigurd knew they were his and Sinfjotli's threads. They looked different now, but his vision was still too blurry to make out all the microscopic details.

"Tell us all you have seen, and we will interpret what you saw," Skuld said.

CHAPTER THREE

THE ODYSSEY BEGINS

"Remarkable," Verðandi muttered as Sigurd finished recounting the details of his vision. "Urðarbrunnr revealed many things to you, enough to make the All-Father jealous."

"Now help us make sense of it all," Sigurd demanded in a somewhat insolent tone.

The Norns were unmoved by his impatience. "Aren't you wise enough to figure most of it yourself?" Verðandi challenged.

Sigurd clenched his fists but kept himself in check. Getting angry wouldn't help. He closed his eyes and mulled over everything he'd witnessed... or at least what he could remember.

"That first vision I saw was the birth of creation, wasn't it? The birth of Ymir, of the first god, Buri, and then Ymir's murder at the hands of Odin and his brothers. But why did the well show me that?"

"Perhaps to show the path you must follow," Urðr theorized. "Just as Odin and his brothers slew Ymir to create the world, you two must hack your way to redemption."

"It will be a path paved with hardship and pain," Skuld warned. "And there will be consequences every step of the journey that will benefit and harm the realms in ways you cannot fathom."

Sinfjotli shook his head in disbelief. "You're kidding, right? How could the actions of just two people have that much of a profound impact?"

"Because trying to alter the course of your destiny always has consequences." Verðandi pointed a clawed digit at the image in the tapestry of the bearded man in a boat holding his hammer at the serpent. "Thor proved that years ago during his fishing trip with Hymir."

"He dragged Jörmungandr to the surface," Sinfjotli recalled. "He tried to attack Jörmungandr then and there, but Hymir cut the line."

"But Thor's actions had repercussions," Urðr maintained. "Like you, Thor struggled to change his fate. He attempted to defy destiny and kill the monster he's prophesied to battle at Ragnarök. But in doing so, he disrupted the stability of the realms. Bringing the serpent to the surface weakened the barriers between the worlds, allowing monsters and forces of chaos to invade places they didn't belong. Chaos ensued, and it took the Aesir almost five years to restore order."

"Thor failed to change his fate of battling Jörmungandr at Ragnarök and plunged the realms into chaos," Verðandi said. "And even though both of you can determine your own fates, unlike Thor, the realms will be affected regardless of the outcome. You can create a destiny that will echo throughout eternity."

"And what fate would that be?" Sigurd demanded.

"We'll get there in a moment," Skuld promised. "Before that, there is a misconception I must clear up. What my sister said before you drank from the well was not entirely accurate. You are not the *sole* masters of your fates. Many factors influenced the choices made by you, your half-siblings, and your parents. Sometimes, an invisible hand guides us, subtly influencing our decisions and the course of our lives."

"Do you mean Loki?" Sinfjotli guessed.

"He and Odin have had a hand in the history of the realms in equal parts," Verðandi confirmed. "Although, since Loki's imprisonment, Odin has had to shoulder most of the burden himself."

"Speak plainly!" Sigurd said.

"Now that it's become impossible to prevent the ultimate disaster, Odin has resigned himself to mitigating the damage." Skuld said. "He works tirelessly behind the scenes to control the narrative like an invisible hand guiding others, subtly influencing the choices of them, their siblings, and their parents."

Sinfjotli's eyes widened. "You mean to say that Odin influenced Siggeir to betray our family?"

Verðandi made a tsking sound. "How self-centered you are. Odin has influenced more than just the two of you. He and Loki have influenced the course of hundreds of warriors' lives, working behind the scenes and subtly pushing factors to attain an ideal goal."

"However, sometimes they take a more direct approach." Urðr glanced down at Sigurd's waist. Sigurd followed her gaze and saw she was staring at Tyrfing.

Sigurd remembered the sword's previous owner, Hedrick the Wise. During their duel on the Gjallerbru, Hedrick had told Sigurd his life story when they paused to catch their breath. He claimed on the day he died, Odin visited his hall in disguise and challenged him to a game of riddles, which Hedrick lost by default when Odin asked him, "What did Odin whisper in Baldur's ear at his funeral?" and then attacked the All-Father. Odin turned into a bird and warned Hedrick he would die that night. Later, his servants murdered him in his sleep with Tyrfing.

But was it Hedrick's destiny to perish that night? Or had Odin set it in motion by placing the idea within the servants' heads that their king was as killable as any other man?

How many other destinies and futures had he set in motion? How many people had lived their lives according to his grand designs? Sigurd shook his head, not wanting to ponder all the implications.

"Good call," Verðandi praised as if reading Sigurd's thoughts. "Trying to imagine all the people whose lives Odin has meddled with is like contemplating all the grains of sand on a beach. The mere thought is enough to drive one mad."

Sigurd felt a lump form in his throat as he thought about everything that had been revealed thus far. Knowing Odin had a hand in the destiny of so many warriors, including his own, made a knot form in his stomach. One question raced through his mind faster than any other, but his tongue refused to sound it out.

"Your expression betrays you," Verðandi noted. "It asks the question you dare not voice: Why is Odin so interested in you two? What threat could two warriors with scarcely a drop of the All-Father's blood in their veins possibly pose to the goddess of death? The answer is prophecy. Long ago, a seer had a dream foretelling that mighty warriors would be born from the Maverick Aesir's bloodline who would tip the scales at Ragnarök."

"Is there a word of truth to that, or is it just fantasy born from a dream?" Sinfjotli asked.

"Not all dreams are true," Skuld admitted.

"But Odin certainly treated the prophecy like dogma," Urðr confirmed. "For that reason, he took a special interest in the Volsung dynasty. Odin worked tirelessly behind the scenes, grooming Rerir, Völsung, Sigmund, and the two of you into mighty warriors that could bolster the ranks of the Einherjar. However, after losing Signy and her nine brothers to Helheim because of Siggeir's treachery, Odin vowed not to let another of Sigi's descendants fall into Hel's clutches lest they become one of Hel's draugs and, therefore, a threat to Asgard. Especially not you two."

Sigurd furrowed his brow. "Why would Odin go so far for *us* specifically?"

"Because of this." Skuld gestured to their threads of fate again. Sigurd noticed that the ends of the threads now displayed an image of him and Sinfjotli standing in a golden field between two armies.

"That's the last thing I saw in my vision," he recalled. "That was a glimpse of Ragnarök, wasn't it?"

"Correct." Skuld tapped on the image in the cloth. "And this is precisely why Odin struck a bargain with Hel to play for your souls. During one of Odin's visions of Ragnarök centuries ago, he saw a warrior with snake eyes and a skinchanger fighting and tipping the scales in the great battle between the Einherjar and Hel's army. Odin realized that you two would be instrumental in the battle of Ragnarök."

Skuld let go of the threads and regarded them with her pupilless white eyes. "You two will take part in the battle of Ragnarök and tip the scales in the fight between the Einherjar and the forces of chaos. However, it's still to be determined *which* side you'll fight for. Unlike Thor, your threads have not formed complete knots. Your destinies are far more flexible."

"Ever since Odin foresaw this in one of his visions, he's been helping you throughout your lives, grooming you to become great heroes," Urðr added. "But then you both unexpectedly died inglorious deaths and got sent to Helheim. Hel would have tormented you without end like your nine uncles until you became one of her draugs. That was something Odin could not allow. He rode down to Helheim and made a gamble with Hel to give you a second chance. He wagered that if you could complete nine impossible god-given tasks across the realms, Hel would be forced to relinquish her claim to your souls. Hel agreed, but on the condition that if you die at any point, she will claim both your souls."

"Thus, to fully escape Hel's clutches, you must travel the realms and complete nine tasks," Skuld surmised. "Only then will you be allowed into Valhalla and take your places amongst the Einherjar."

"Escaping from Helheim was merely the first of many labors," Verðandi said. "You must complete eight more epic tasks from the Aesir before you may rest."

Sigurd sat on the root-covered floor, knowing he'd soon collapse from the shock and girth of everything he'd heard if he remained on his feet.

It was a lot to take in. Odin had been grooming him and his brother to become great heroes and went above and beyond to give them a second chance at becoming Einherjar. But even more incomprehensible was that escaping Helheim, something no other soul that died a dishonorable death had achieved, was merely the first of many labors!

Sigurd pulled open the collar of his shirt and examined the ugly scar plastered across his sternum as he pondered just what else the gods expected of them. A wave of phantom pain flashed through his mind as he remembered Guttorm driving Mimung through his chest and seeing that gaping cavity in his sternum as he and Sinfjotli dueled. He'd been wounded many times at the hands of Sinfjotli, Siggeir, and Helheim's undead army, far more than anyone should endure. What further pain was in store for him on this journey?

As he tried to suppress that thought, he looked back at his scar, and a burning question flashed through his head.

"How were our bodies so perfectly preserved? Even if Odin revived us, there should have been some trace of decomposition or rigor mortis, given how long we were deceased. But I felt as if I was waking up from a long nap and could move without impediment, even with that gaping hole in my chest."

"I'd like to know that as well," Sinfjotli said. "Baldur mentioned that time moves differently across the realms, but according to Sigurd's life story that I heard on the *Hringhorni*, I was dead for almost forty or fifty years before he died, but when Odin confronted Hel in the vision, my body was still fresh as a daisy, without a hint of putrefaction. I couldn't smell any trace of rot, and if I concentrated, I could feel traces of our body heat even from a distance. How did Odin arrest the decay?"

"It's thanks to those garments." Urðr pointed a clawed finger at a large basket near the foot of one of their beds. There was nothing special about the oversized garments' design at a glance. But as Sigurd examined the texture, a realization flashed through his mind.

"Those look just like the shrouds in which our bodies were wrapped," he realized.

"As they should," Verðandi confirmed. "The shrouds were woven from our threads with a little help from Mundilfari, the Vanir god of time. When worn by the living, they freeze the wearer's flow of time, preventing disease, aging, or mortal wounds from taking their toll. When wrapped around the dead, they halt decay entirely."

"Odin preserved your bodies in those shrouds until the chance to revive you arose," Urðr added, pointing a clawed finger at Sigurd's sternum. "The clothes he left for you were woven from the same enchanted threads. They were the only reason you remained alive and moving—despite a gaping sword wound inches from your heart and Sinfjotli carrying enough poison in his stomach to kill a bison. At least until Baldur arrived."

Sigurd and Sinfjotli glanced at each other, each silently cursing themselves for recklessly destroying those precious garments during their duel. They wouldn't have risked damaging such precious magical shrouds had they known their clothes had the power to grant humanity's oldest wish.

"Don't think you could have escaped Helheim relying solely on those garments," Urðr corrected, as if sensing their thoughts. "You would have remained stuck in that half-dead state without Baldur's apples, and Hel wouldn't have hesitated to kill you."

"Why *didn't* she just kill us right away?" Sinfjotli blurted. "That's been bugging me for quite a while. If Odin challenged Hel to stop us from escaping her realm, why didn't she just kill us when we woke up in the city?"

"Hubris and curiosity stayed her hand," Urðr explained. "As you rightly observed, Hel could have easily killed you at any point before you met Baldur and received his protective brand. She tried to ensure you couldn't escape from the beginning by using her magic to prevent Odin from fully reviving you. She figured escaping Helheim while in a semi-revived state was impossible. With that in mind, she decided to watch to discern what was so special about you that Odin would go to such lengths to bring you back to his side. And when Sinfjotli fought you to the point of death to see if you truly were Sigmund's son, Hel assumed you would save her the trouble and kill each other without her having to lift a finger. And after Baldur escorted you to the *Hringhorni*, she believed you would elect to remain on his ship for eternity, thus allowing her to win the bet anyway. But when Baldur gifted you those golden apples and fully revived you, Hel realized she could no longer stand by and watch and tried to intervene. But he soon bestowed his blessing on you, preventing her from directly harming you and thus needing to rely on her undead army."

"You should count your lucky stars that her curiosity trumped her sense of duty," Verðandi urged. "But don't think you've fully escaped her. You may have escaped Helheim, but she's still there on your shoulder, waiting for you to perish as you complete eight more tasks across the realms. If you perish during this journey, she will drag you screaming back to the underworld."

Sinfjotli threw his hands up. "This all sounds so overly complicated. Why do we have to go through all this trouble of traveling across the realms and completing these impossible tasks? Why can't we just die in battle like our father and forefathers did?"

"Because you both already died once," Urðr explained. "Normally, a warrior must prove himself by dying bravely in honorable combat to enter Valhalla. But *you* died from being poisoned at a feast, and Sigurd got murdered in his bed. In doing so, you both forfeited your right to enter Valhalla traditionally through a heroic death in battle. More importantly, Hel now has a claim to both of your souls because of the circumstances of your deaths. Thus, the rules have changed."

"Per the wager that Odin struck with Hel, you must travel the realms and complete nine herculean tasks," Verðandi reminded them. "Only then will you be allowed into Valhalla."

"But be warned, sons of Sigmund," Skuld cautioned, "the journey you will make across the Nine Realms is one no mortal has ever walked. If you die a second time, regardless of the circumstances, Hel *will* reclaim both of your souls. There will be no end to your torment. She will break you in both body and mind until you are nothing but her subservient slaves, and you will be forced to slay your father, Sigmund, along with the other members of the Einherjar at Ragnarök."

"That will never happen!" Sinfjotli proclaimed.

"That remains to be seen," Skuld countered, pointing at their threads. "There is still plenty of thread left unsewn. We've given you a basic outline, but your future can still take on any shape."

Sinfjotli glanced at the miniature World Tree with the multicolored realms hanging from its branches and roots. "You said we must travel across the realms and complete eight more tasks. So where must we go first?"

Sigurd stared longingly at the glowing sphere in the tree's center. His first instinct was to head to Midgard to see if he could locate his long-lost daughter, Aslaug, before continuing this quest. But as he stared at the blue-green sphere, he noticed something concerning.

"We're at the bottom of the World Tree right now." He pointed at the tree root. "But Midgard, Svartalfheim, and Jotunheim are higher up the trunk in the center of the tree. How are we supposed to reach the other realms, much less get out of Niflheim?"

The Norns looked past him.

"It seems Odin expected this very predicament," Verðandi remarked.

"What's that supposed to mean?" Sinfjotli asked.

"You're about to find out," Skuld said.

A loud whinny echoed throughout the cavern. Sigurd and Sinfjotli turned toward the entrance as a massive, shadowy creature entered. As it moved into the light, emerging from the gloom of the cave, Sigurd gasped as he beheld the eight-legged stallion.

"It's Sleipnir!" Sigurd gasped.

The mighty stallion stood between twelve and fifteen feet tall at the withers. Its hairy gray coat stretched over a body packed with powerful, sinewy muscles. It had four forelegs and four hind legs.

"Is that really Odin's horse?" Sinfjotli gawked. "Why is he here?"

"Odin sent him to fetch you both and escort you to the next realm," Urðr explained. "You don't need to question it any more than that. As you mortals enjoy saying, 'Don't look a gift horse in the mouth.'"

"I'm not questioning it," Sinfjotli said. "I just feel honored Odin sent us his personal mount! We must be blessed!"

Sinfjotli took a step forward, intending to pet the stallion. But Sleipnir snorted and bared his teeth in warning. Sinfjotli retreated as the stallion pawed the ground with three forelegs.

"Sleipnir won't allow any ordinary vagabond to mount him," Verðandi warned. "You must earn his trust and respect first. Prove that you are worthy to be his riders."

Sigurd knew the Norns weren't exaggerating. Sleipnir was not amenable or welcoming of strangers, let alone just anyone to ride him. Like all stallions, he was strong-willed, but this beast was more than that. Judging from the red stains on his teeth and muzzle, Sigurd suspected he was accustomed to feeding on the flesh of Odin's slain enemies and possibly brazen dolts foolish enough to try riding him without his consent.

That probably should have worried Sigurd, but he couldn't imagine this beautiful horse hurting him. Sigurd felt strangely nostalgic as he gazed at the mighty stallion. A distant and comforting memory resurfaced as he stared at the horse's gray coat.

Without thinking, he stepped forward.

Sleipnir turned and snorted. But as he sniffed, his eyes softened somewhat. There was recognition in his gaze. He didn't protest Sigurd's approach, although he eyed him warily.

"When I was young, I met an unfamiliar old man with a long beard while walking through the woods. I informed him I was heading to my uncle's house to choose a horse and asked if he could come with me to help me decide. The old man proposed that we take the horses down to the River Busiltjörn. He assured me the horse that remained in the water would be my ideal mount. So we drove the horses into the depths of the River Busiltjörn. All the horses swam back to land except for a large, young, handsome gray horse that had never been ridden. After crossing the river, he ran around the opposite meadow and leaped back into the river once more. He traversed it again and returned to his former pasture with no signs of exhaustion. The gray-bearded old man told me, 'That horse is Sleipnir's descendant,' and 'he must be nourished heedfully, for he will be the greatest horse in Midgard.' I turned around to thank him, but the old man vanished. I realize now the old man was your master, Odin."

Sigurd didn't know why he was saying all this out loud. Perhaps he thought it would earn Sleipnir's trust? Or perhaps recounting the story gave him courage? Regardless, Sleipnir never took his eyes off Sigurd as he spoke. Sigurd didn't know if Sleipnir could understand him, but he continued his tale as he inched closer to the eight-legged steed.

"I named that horse Grani. As Odin promised, he was the best and fastest stallion in the Midgard. He was utterly fearless. He never got scared when I rode him into battle or when he heard Fafnir's roar. I loved Grani like a brother. That's why... I have always wanted to thank you, Sleipnir. Thanks to you, I had the greatest horse in Midgard as my companion and best friend."

Sigurd was now face-to-face with the mighty stallion. He nervously lifted his arm and petted Sleipnir's neck. Surprisingly, the stallion didn't protest.

"Remarkable," Urðr said. "The last mortal who tried to pet Sleipnir had his entire arm torn off."

"It's because of Sigurd's bond with Sleipnir's descendant," Verðandi said. "His ancestor, Odin, claimed Sleipnir as his mount ages ago, and he claimed Sleipnir's descendant, Grani, as his own. It seems some friendships are so strong they transcend lifetimes and bloodlines."

Sleipnir jerked his head to the side and nickered impatiently, which was probably his way of telling Sigurd to hop on his back. But when Sigurd tried to mount up, Sleipnir snorted, and Sigurd backed away.

Sleipnir bobbed his head to the side again, his mane swaying in the cave's draft as if trying to tell Sigurd something. Sigurd looked at the mighty steed, wondering what it was trying to convey. Then he noticed the saddlebags attached to Sleipnir's saddle. Could Sleipnir want him to take a peek inside? Sigurd cautiously approached again, opened the saddlebags, and rummaged through them until his fingers brushed against something smooth and rectangular. Pulling it out, he saw it was a scroll made of parchment. He carefully unrolled it, studying the neat handwriting and intricate drawings.

"What is it?" Sinfjotli asked.

"It's a message from Odin." Sigurd cleared his throat and read aloud:

Sons of Sigmund,

Congratulations on clawing your way out of Helheim. You both show great promise. But escaping Helheim was merely the beginning. You won't last long on this great peregrination if all you have between you is a sword, a golden hauberk, and a magical helmet. You must redress this if you are to have even the slightest chance of surviving this journey. For your second task, travel to Svartalfheim with Sleipnir and convince the dwarves to craft weapons and armor of immense power for you.

Do not fail to impress me.

Odin, King of Asgard, All-Father, Protector of the Realms.

Sigurd furrowed his brow as he finished reading and turned to the Norns. "Odin wants us to commission the dwarves to forge weapons and armor as our second task? That hardly seems like a challenge after escaping Helheim."

Verðandi shook her head. "You have no idea how wrong you are."

Sigurd froze. He stared at her, scanning her heart for an answer, but could discern nothing through his clairvoyance. The Norns were probably the only people whose hearts he couldn't read.

"What's that supposed to mean?" Sinfjotli demanded.

"This next task will be the most excruciating thing you've ever done. You'll learn there is a price to pay for everything you gain in this world." Skuld looked at Sigurd with pity in her pure white eyes.

Her words sent a chill through Sigurd's blood. But he cast off his fear and focused on the task at hand as Sleipnir nickered impatiently. This time, Sigurd was sure the stallion was beckoning him to mount. He swung himself onto Sleipnir's broad back, then reached down and helped his brother into the saddle.

"Thank you for everything." Sigurd bowed.

"Farewell, sons of Sigmund," Skuld replied. "We look forward to recording the events of your journey. And Sigurd, I wish you good fortune in the trial to come."

As the Norns resumed working on their tapestry, Sleipnir turned and cantered through the cave.

As they made their way to the exit, Sigurd looked ahead with his telescopic vision at the howling wind outside the Norns' cave. He wondered how they were supposed to travel to Svartalfheim and escape this icy realm without freezing to death.

Sigurd got his answer when Sleipnir stepped outside into the freezing blizzard. The mighty stallion reared on his hind legs and broke into a gallop.

He ran so blindingly fast across the root of the World Tree that Sigurd nearly fell out of the saddle.

Within mere seconds, Sleipnir emerged from Niflheim's atmosphere. The eight-legged horse continued sprinting across the root of the World Tree and galloped straight up the trunk of Yggdrasil like a spider scurrying up a wall.

CHAPTER FOUR

PLAINS OF DARKNESS

As Sigurd clung to Sleipnir's saddle, he had no way of knowing just how long or far they had traveled across the vast expanse of the World Tree. Sleipnir was moving with such staggering speed that it was impossible to gauge either distance or time. The wind howled past him, tearing at his skin as if peeling it away. Sleipnir's eight powerful legs thundered across the trunk of Yggdrasil. The world spun in a dizzying blur, flipping upside down and sideways simultaneously. All Sigurd could do was hold on to the saddle for dear life, keep his eyes shut against the stinging dust, and pray he didn't black out before they reached their destination.

Their terrifying voyage ended as Sleipnir slowed down and came to a halt. Sigurd opened his eyes to discover they were standing in a vast desert.

The sand beneath Sleipnir's hooves was blacker than obsidian. In the distance, jagged rock formations jutted from the dunes like towering obelisks. Overhead, pitch-black clouds choked the sky, shrouding the dim red sun. Only a few feeble rays pierced the gloom. Everything in this desolate landscape was steeped in darkness—the sand, the rocks, and even the sky itself seemed to drink in the light, leaving the entire landscape bleak and lifeless.

"This must be Svartalfheim," Sigurd thought aloud. "No wonder Regin often called this realm 'The Dark Fields.'"

Heavy panting came from behind. Sigurd glanced over his shoulder. Sinfjotli's knuckles were white from gripping the saddle, his hair wild and standing on end. He looked on the verge of toppling—yet his expression was a whirlwind of emotions. Excitement, elation, and fear flickered across his face as if he had just experienced the most exhilarating ride of his entire life.

"You alright?" Sigurd asked.

Sinfjotli nodded weakly. "Never been more grateful to be alive."

"Got that right." Sigurd's heart fluttered like a bird inside a cage in his chest. He felt more alert and alive than he had ever been.

Sinfjotli looked around at the black desert. "So this is Svartalfheim? Where are we supposed to...? Whoa!"

Without warning, Sleipnir launched into a gallop, tearing across the rocky desert. He had paused only as a courtesy, granting Sigurd and his brother a moment to catch their breath—but his patience was as short-lived as a snowflake in hot sand. The mighty stallion needed no guidance. He sprinted across dunes and twisting rock formations that would have left Sigurd wandering in circles if he were traveling on foot.

As they raced through Svartalfheim, Sigurd marveled at Sleipnir's speed. His former mount, Grani, had been the fasted horse in Midgard, but compared to his legendary ancestor, he was a mere shadow. The mighty stallion thundered across deserts, sprinted over lakes as if they were solid ground, and climbed mountains with the speed and force of a lightning strike.

After traversing an entire stony desert and scaling a mountain range, Sleipnir galloped into a dark aperture between towering cliffs so steep that the canyon that ran beneath them was perpetually in shadow.

To most, traveling through this valley of shadows would be like riding into an abyss, but Sigurd's snake eyes allowed him to see in the dark. As Sleipnir galloped through the shadowy pass, he studied the holes and hollow caves littering the canyon's steep walls. The wind whistled through some of them, producing an eerie humming sound. It was the perfect place for dragons to make their lair, and as if on cue, a majestic dragon glided overhead and disappeared into one cave, confirming Sigurd's suspicion.

After a thrilling thirty-minute ride through the cleft of darkness, Sleipnir emerged into a vast stone valley bathed in dim sunlight. At the base of the largest mountain stood a colossal fortress, its walls carved into the rocky cliff and flanked by two towering stone statues. Sleipnir skidded to a stop right in front of the imposing figures.

"I guess this is where we get off," Sigurd said as he dismounted. However, as soon as his feet touched the ground, a strange discomfort settled over him. It wasn't the usual soreness from riding for days. It was something else entirely. An icy chill shot up from his feet, coiling around his spine. It slithered through him, cold and insidious, reaching for his heart.

As Sigurd looked down, he discovered he was standing on a mesmerizing, glossy black road. The stone gleamed like polished marble, its surface strangely decorative given the desolate surroundings. He couldn't resist the urge to touch it. The moment his fingers brushed the stone, the chill in his spine flared. He recognized the feeling. He had felt the same sensation back in Helheim. The City of the Lost was constructed from this same oily black stone. And now he recalled seeing it littered throughout Svartalfheim as Sleipnir carried them across the landscape. Perhaps Svartalfheim was where it originated from?

Sigurd set aside his curiosity—he had more important matters to attend to. He took a moment to stretch, easing the stiffness from their grueling ride, then thanked Sleipnir for his aid. The stallion reared onto his hind legs and galloped away, presumably bound for Asgard.

As Sleipnir disappeared from view, Sigurd turned and gazed at the massive stone fortress behind them. Its architecture was unlike anything he had ever seen, towering so high they had to tilt their heads back to take it all in. Flanking the fortress were two massive statues of dwarves, each standing sixty feet tall and brandishing formidable weapons. One, painted a pale blue, gripped a giant axe, while the other, hued in purplish pink, held a fearsome war hammer.

The fortress's walls bristled with countless openings and murder holes, a testament to its impenetrability. No army could hope to break through its gates. Any foolish enough to try would be met with a deadly barrage of arrows and scalding oil. The skeletal remains littering the ground told the story of past attempts—invaders and rock trolls who had dared breach the stronghold, only to be cut down by arrows, boiling oil, and other merciless devices. At the entrance, two large stone doors stood, engraved with the image of a giant dwarf wielding a war hammer. Intricate carvings depicted scenes of war: the clash of sword and shield and spear, arrows in flight, and heroes at battle.

"There's no way we can open that gate by ourselves," Sigurd said, shaking his head. "Each door must weigh at least seventy-five tons. Since the dwarves built it, it will be locked up tighter than a drum with many fancy mechanisms."

"Do you see any other way in?" Sinfjotli asked. "We might as well get a closer look."

Sinfjotli took a step forward. Before he could take another, a giant stone axe struck the ground before them. The earth quaked beneath their feet, and Sigurd and Sinfjotli stumbled back as a cloud of dust billowed around them. When it finally settled, Sigurd saw the truth—the two stone statues flanking the fortress had sprung to life, their massive form now blocking their path to the gate.

"Who approaches Niðavellir?" the blue statue demanded in an earthy voice. "Are you friend or foe?"

Sigurd hesitated before answering. "We stand before you with cordial intentions."

"That remains to be seen," the purple statue retorted.

Sigurd gazed at the purple statue, amazed that it was moving and talking. As he stared at it, he noticed something through his clairvoyant vision. The statue had a heart in its chest. The other statue did as well. Although their hearts had turned to stone, Sigurd realized these statues were once living beings.

"Who are you?" Sigurd demanded.

"I am Fjalar," the blue statue announced. "And this is my brother Galar."

"Why are you statues attacking us?" Sinfjotli demanded.

Galar scowled. "We were not always statues. Long ago, we were once wicked dwarves who captured the god Kvasir, drained his body of blood, and turned it into the mead of poetry. On our way back to Svartalfheim, we also murdered a giant named Gilling and his wife. Their son Suttungr captured and imprisoned us on a rock that the rising tide would submerge. Fearing for our lives, we offered him the magical mead if he'd spare us."

"Odin found us as we returned to Svartalfheim," Fjalar added. "With him was the god Kvasir, who had been revitalized after having his blood replaced with new blood Ivaldi had made for him. For murdering Kvasir and giving away the mead of poetry to Suttungr, Odin turned us into giant stone statues and condemned us to guard the gates of Niðavellir. Our duty is to ensure that only the dwarves, Aesir, and their allies can enter the subterranean city."

Fjalar hefted his war hammer. "Now state your intentions. What business do you have in Niðavellir?"

"And do not lie," Galar warned, his eyes flashing red. "We will know if you do."

"We're customers seeking to purchase weapons and armor. My name is Sigurd, and this is my brother, Sinfjotli."

When Sigurd announced his name, something about the statues' demeanors changed. They seemed taken aback and... startled.

"Sigurd?" Galar repeated. "Are you perchance Sigurd the Dragon Slayer?"

"That's me." Sigurd nodded.

The stone statues looked at each other, then brandished their weapons. For a moment, Sigurd worried they were about to attack him and Sinfjotli. Instead, they walked to their previous posts and jammed the butts of their weapons into the ground and turned them. Sigurd heard mechanisms grinding away beneath the soil as Fjalar and Galar twisted their weapons. The ground rocked as the colossal gates of Niðavellir parted.

"Ivaldi has summoned you for adjudication," Galar announced. "Don't keep the king waiting."

The statues assumed their original positions on both sides of the fortress and returned to their stone form.

As the gates of Niðavellir swung open, Sigurd and Sinfjotli shared a furtive glance, their hearts pounding.

"I have a bad feeling about this," Sigurd muttered.

"Whatever happens, we'll face it together," Sinfjotli promised. But before he could take a step forward, Sigurd grabbed his shoulder.

"Promise me something before we set foot in there. No matter what happens, do *not* kill anyone. If we are going to convince these dwarves to forge us anything, we need to be in their favor."

"You have my solemn word. I won't spill any dwarven blood," Sinfjotli vowed.

Sigurd relaxed. Sinfjotli was a man of many faults—impetuous, crass, and belligerent—but his convictions were impeccable. Once he gave his word, he'd see the promise fulfilled, no matter the cost.

Satisfied his brother wouldn't provoke an altercation, Sigurd removed his hand, nodded, and they entered the dwarven fortress side by side. Soon, the doors shut behind them, sealing off all light from the outside world and leaving them in darkness. However, it posed no problem to Sigurd, whose snake eyes let him see in the dark.

Sinfjotli, meanwhile, moved with caution, staying close as he followed the sound of Sigurd's footsteps and his scent.

They walked along a marble pathway lined by statues of dwarves standing guard with arraying weapons. The path led them into a vast chamber, where they were met with a breathtaking sight—the ceiling opened up, allowing natural light to illuminate the area. Giant statues of dwarves towered above them, etched out of colossal pillars of stone that seemed to hold up the ceiling itself. The sculptors had crafted them masterfully, shaping the pillars into mighty dwarves holding the weight of the ceiling on their sturdy shoulders.

In the center of the circular open-air room was a colossal bronze statue of a giant bearded blacksmith hammering a flaming sword. Beyond it, Sigurd glimpsed what looked like the residential area of a city with long rows of dull buildings roughly two stories tall. Scattered throughout the landscape, enormous abysses yawned, their depths occasionally erupting with magma as lava geysers spewed molten rock into the air.

Sinfjotli grabbed Sigurd's shoulder while sniffing the air.

Sigurd's senses kicked into high gear as he inhaled deeply, his hand reaching for the hilt of his trusty sword. The air was thick with the acrid scent of coal fires, mingling with the metallic tang of heated metal and the damp mustiness of mildew. Then he caught a whiff of ripe sweat in the air.

"How many?" Sigurd ventured.

"Too many," Sinfjotli warned.

As if on cue, a crowd of dwarves emerged from the shadows behind the statues and converged on them from all sides. They were heavy, broad-shouldered, and broad-chested people. The dwarves were all short in stature, seldom reaching a height of over four and a half feet. Each dwarf was about as tall as a human male's chest. However, given Sigurd's lanky stature, they barely reached his waist. They were shorter than the average man and had stubby legs but were much tougher and more muscular. Sigurd figured all of them were strong enough to bend steel bars with their bare hands.

"Seize them!" a loud voice boomed. The army of angry dwarves brandished their axes and war hammers and converged on them from all sides.

At least two hundred dwarves were attacking them, each stronger than the average man. But their strength was pitiful compared to the draugir of Helheim, whom Sigurd and Sinfjotli had recently battled. Usually, they would have easily defeated this army in minutes. But they purposefully held back. They had not come here to fight. The dwarves had attacked without provocation, but they wouldn't spill blood, even in self-defense.

Sigurd never drew his swords; instead, he relied on his hands and the power of his magic helmet to strike terror into their ranks. Whenever a dwarf lunged too close, Sigurd turned toward them, and the Tarnhelm would take on the shape of the dwarf's greatest fear. One by one, dwarves backed away in fear, letting his brethren take his place.

Beside him, Sinfjotli used his brute strength, shoving back wave after wave of attackers, fighting valiantly alongside Sigurd. They fought for an hour, dodging and deflecting blows, consciously avoiding spilling dwarven blood. Then, at last, a commanding voice cut through the chaos.

"Step aside," the voice boomed. "I'll handle this."

Sigurd turned, and his eyes widened. A dwarf clad in dark steel armor was pushing through the crowds of fellow dwarves. But 'dwarf' was perhaps a misnomer in this case. Unlike the other dwarves, this one was as big as a troll, easily ten or twelve feet tall!

Sigurd was so stunned by the dwarf's sheer size that he failed to notice the giant dual-handled war hammer swinging toward him. The blow struck him square in the face. Everything faded to black.

The next time Sigurd opened his eyes, he was lying naked on a cold stone floor. His weapons and armor were gone, probably pilfered by those wretched, thieving dwarves.

He attempted to stand but found it impossible. Despite his efforts, he could only raise himself to his knees and no further. Cold steel manacles shackled his wrists to the floor. Sigurd resigned himself to kneeling, straightened his back as much as possible, and took in his surroundings.

He was in the middle of a vast underground amphitheater, chained to a dais. Rows upon rows of seats stretched around him, filled with over fifty thousand dwarves. The cavernous space loomed above, with towering stalagmites hanging from the ceiling like the spires of a buried city. Glancing down, he saw a mural beneath his feet—an image of a blacksmith hammering a blazing sword emblazoned on the stone. His chains were fastened to metal anchors at opposite ends of the artwork, binding him in place. Helpless amid this massive gathering, he could do nothing but wait.

"You're finally awake," a booming voice said. "Good. Now we can begin."

Sigurd turned toward the sound and saw a gargantuan dwarf slouched upon a giant throne made of platinum. Piercing blue eyes locked onto him, holding him captive in their intensity. The dwarf's meticulously groomed beard cascaded down his chest like a waterfall of hair. The triangular decorative shapes woven into his beard reminded Sigurd of majestic mountain peaks. He wore a suit of shining gold armor beneath an ornate fur outfit, exuding both wealth and power. Atop his head rested a crown with jagged peaks, its surface embellished with engravings of ravens on both sides, signifying his status as a king.

However, what intrigued Sigurd most was the king's immense size. The dwarf who had knocked him out earlier was the size of a troll, but this dwarf king was the size of a small giant, at least twenty-five feet tall!

"Sigurd, son of Sigmund, you stand accused of the murder of my grandsons," the dwarf king announced. "How do you plead?"

Chapter Five

Blood Price

"'Murder of your grandsons?'" Sigurd repeated groggily. "There must be some mistake. I have killed no dwarves since I arrived here. I consciously avoided killing anyone, even though I could have easily cut through them like a knife through cake. I'm afraid you're mistaken... um... I'm sorry I didn't catch your name."

"Cretin!" Another giant dwarf seated to the right of the platinum throne rose to his feet, brandishing a massive red war hammer tipped with a spike. Sigurd recognized him instantly. It was the same warrior who had him unconscious earlier.

At least ten feet tall, everything about him hinted at royalty and savagery. An impressive fur outfit draped over strong, square shoulders. Scars carved deep into flesh ran back into his beard and hairline. Though his head was bald, a receding hairline trailed down the back of his skull. Warding runes and ancient symbols were tattooed across his scalp and hands. Everything about him looked formidable, and his scars spoke of a warrior who had been in plenty of scrapes.

"You address Ivaldi, the father of all dwarves, and king of Svartalfheim," The dwarf growled. "Show some respect!"

"At ease, Mótsignir," Ivaldi urged, holding up a hand. "There's no need to get nettled over formalities. The lad has done nothing to offend me yet

48

and meant no disrespect. He's probably still recovering from the blow you inflicted earlier and trying to make sense of the situation."

Mótsignir sat back in his seat, glowering at Sigurd like every other dwarf in the assembly. The tiered rows filled with watching eyes. Behind him, Sinfjotli hung naked inside a golden crow cage. The large lump on his forehead made it clear—Mótsignir's hammer had knocked his brother unconscious as well.

"You haven't murdered anyone in Svartalfheim," Ivaldi conceded. "At least not *yet*. To clarify, you stand accused of murdering my grandsons Regin and Fafnir. How do you plead?"

For a moment, Sigurd was stunned. Hearing Ivaldi refer to Fafnir as his grandson was baffling—until he remembered. Fafnir had once been a dwarf before his greed and lust for gold turned him into a dragon. He and his brothers, Regin and Ottr, were the sons of the dwarf Hreidmar, who was apparently Ivaldi's son.

"I ask again," Ivaldi warned in a nettled tone, snapping Sigurd back to reality, "how do you plead?"

"Just wait a minute!" Sigurd pleaded. "I understand why you'd want justice for Regin's death. But why Fafnir? From what I understand, you disowned him after his greed drove him to murder his father and later turned him into a dragon. And Regin." Sigurd grimaced. "Regin was cut from the same cloth as Fafnir. He lusted after the treasure as much as his brother. He planned to murder me after everything I'd done for him."

"You heard him!" a dwarf shouted. "He just confessed!"

"Insolent human!" the dwarven assembly roared. "Murderer! Cut out his tongue. Flay him alive!"

"SILENCE!" Ivaldi roared. He grabbed a gigantic war hammer leaning against his platinum throne and slammed the butt of the weapon against the floor. The impact sent a shockwave across the ground, knocking Sigurd off his feet. The dwarves hushed and sat back in their seats.

"I won't deny that Fafnir was a reprehensible monster," Ivaldi said. "But he was a dwarf once, and he and Regin were my grandsons. Since time immemorial, it has been the law that the families of murdered victims must seek justice for their kins' deaths. Regardless of your motivations and their repugnant character, the blood of my kin still stains your hands. Honor demands I seek justice for their deaths. It's as simple as that."

Sigurd glanced around the dwarven assembly. Their eyes gleamed with hunger—not for food, but for something else. Their gaze reminded him of how Regin used to study trees and rocks. When Sigurd had once asked what he was doing, Regin had replied he was imagining everything he could craft from their base components. The dwarves were looking at him the same way now, eyeing his body and imagining the trophies or trinkets they could make from his remains.

Sigurd looked back at Ivaldi. Through his clairvoyance, he couldn't detect any prejudice or avarice from the old dwarf king. But he could see one thing clearly—his resolve. The dwarf king was adamant about executing him.

Sigurd weighed his options. He was stark naked and weaponless. The heavy chains that bound his wrists to the ground were engraved with many runes. One glance told him they were enchanted—unbreakable even with his strength. But even if he could break free of his bonds, escape seemed impossible. Thousands of dwarves filled the assembly, each twice as strong as an ordinary human. He had no way to get to Sinfjotli, let alone break him out of that crow cage. And even if he managed to flee the amphitheater, the labyrinthine underground city would swallow him whole. He wouldn't get far before they captured him.

"If you have nothing else to say, then I shall pass summary judgement," Ivaldi announced. "Sigurd, son of Sigmund, I sentence you to death for the murders of my grandsons. Mótsignir, you and Gandalf may proceed."

Mótsignir and another ten-foot-tall dwarf grabbed their hammers, vaulted over the walls, and made their way toward him. They took their positions on either side and prepared to swing their war hammers down on his head.

Sigurd fought with all his might against the chains that bound him. As he struggled, something caught his attention—Andvari's ring on his left ring finger. The thieving dwarves purloined everything else while he was out cold. Why had they let him keep an invaluable and beautiful ring?

As he stared at the glittering band, a memory surfaced—Regin's tale of how Fafnir had come to possess the ring and his cursed hoard. It all began when Odin and Loki accidentally slew Ottr and were forced to pay the blood price to atone for his death.

That's it! Sigurd realized. "I offer to pay the blood price!" he shouted as the dwarven executioners raised their war hammers. The enormous dwarves paused and looked back at their king for instructions.

"He doesn't deserve the chance!" the crowd shouted. "Kill him and be done with it. Bash his head in! We want to see his brains caved in! I want to craft trinkets from his bones!"

"SILENCE!" Ivaldi roared, tapping the ground with his war hammer, cowing them to quiet. "You were saying, Sigurd?"

"I offer to pay the blood price," Sigurd reiterated. "Regin once told me that Odin and Loki accidentally killed his brother Ottr while he was sunbathing as an otter. His father, Hreidmar, was so angry that he, Fafnir, and Regin confiscated their weapons and refused to return them until they paid the blood price for his death. They covered Ottr's entire body in a layer of gold to atone for their mistake. I offer to do the same."

Ivaldi stroked his long, ashen beard, contemplating the desperate offer. "Very well. I accept your offer. However, you'll have to pay the blood price for both Regin *and* Fafnir. Bring me enough wealth to completely cover their weight in gold, and I will absolve you of the blood debt. Out of courtesy, I'll give you two months to gather enough wealth. But if you cannot deliver on your promise, I'll have you eaten alive by a dragon."

CHAPTER SIX

A HELPFUL HAND

Sigurd's arms burned with fatigue as he swung his pickaxe against the stone wall, the sharp crack echoing throughout the mineshaft. After a few more swings, the rock splintered, revealing hidden treasure. He chipped away at the remaining stone until his prize lay fully exposed.

A rough diamond of exceptional quality, approximately four inches long, two inches wide, two and a half inches deep, weighing around one and a half pounds. It was the largest he had uncovered so far, although he wagered even bigger ones lay buried in the mine of Svartalfheim.

As he studied the precious gem, his thoughts drifted to the events that had led to his enslavement.

Weeks earlier, after Ivaldi had accepted his offer to pay the blood price, his sons had escorted him out of the amphitheater and into the mines of Svartalfheim. The dwarves had given Sigurd a thrall's garb—brown breeches, a rough-spun tunic, and horsehide boots—before pressing a pickaxe into his hands and telling him to mine. Yet, even in servitude, one thing remained untouched. Andvari's ring still sat on his finger. The only possession the dwarves hadn't taken from him.

Sigurd didn't know how much time had passed in the gloomy, dark mines. Weeks? Maybe a month? But he was making progress. He had already mined three mineshafts and amassed a fortune in gold and gemstones. Finding enough wealth to cover Regin and Fafnir's weight in gold was daunting, but thankfully, the mines of Svartalfheim were full to bursting with gemstones and valuable ore.

Andvari's ring helped to expedite the mining process. That was the only silver lining about Sigurd's situation. According to legend, whoever wore Andvaranaut would always be wealthy, as the ring would guide the wearer to wealth. It was like a prospector's greatest dream come true.

However, the ring also carried a curse—to bring misfortune and destruction to whoever possessed it. Perhaps that was why the greedy dwarves hadn't taken the ring when they'd confiscated Sigurd's weapons and armor. In his first life, the ring had brought Sigurd and his family nothing but misfortune, yet it was proving useful to him in the mines of Svartalfheim. Every time he swung his axe into a wall, he struck it rich.

Svartalfheim seemed like a limitless supply of ore and precious metals. When Sigurd asked what he'd find in these mineshafts, the dwarves escorting him boasted: "In Svartalfheim, you'll find every precious gemstone you have ever heard of and many you haven't. The wealth of Svartalfheim continues to reveal itself, like a meadow in bloom."

And they were right. Sigurd had already unearthed thousands of multicolored diamonds, a thousand rubies, two thousand azure sapphires, five thousand emeralds, ten thousand veins of silver, and tons of veins of gold ore. It was a miner's wildest dream come true. If a hundred prospectors spent a hundred nights dreaming of riches, their fantasies couldn't compare to the reality of these mines. The dwarves claimed that some shafts had been mined for over a thousand years and still hadn't run out of resources. They also claimed Sigurd had only scratched the surface. Deeper shafts remained unexplored, teeming with unknown dangers and wonders.

Once, Sigurd stumbled upon a hidden chamber filled with the largest crystals he had ever seen. Gargantuan beams of milky-white selenite, some stretching forty feet long and over thirteen feet thick, crisscrossed the underground chamber in mesmerizing formations. Its beauty so enraptured Sigurd that he resolved to leave the treasure untouched for others to discover and admire.

But that discovery had been the only bright moment in his task. The mine shafts were cold, lonely, and pitch-black. The dwarves hadn't given him a lantern, but visibility wasn't an issue—his snake eyes allowed him to see clearly in the dark. He also never needed to take a break to eat or sleep; the Apple of Idun he had eaten in Helheim kept him nourished and energized.

Still, it was lonely, tiring work. Sigurd couldn't remember the last time he had interacted with another person. Then, one day, a bright light flared in the mineshaft. It was so dazzling that it felt like a miniature sun had appeared, its glow reflecting off the countless diamonds, emeralds, rubies, and other riches lining the walls.

"So, you're the warrior that's got ol' Ivaldi throwing a hissy fit and calling maledictions down?" a gruff voice remarked.

Sigurd turned to the two dwarves who had appeared behind him.

The dwarf to the right, holding a lantern, wasn't particularly remarkable. He wore a gilded dwarven chest plate over a green undershirt underneath and red gloves. His long-braided beard was impeccably groomed, exuding a sweet smell like lavender or soap. Aside from that, he looked like every other dwarf in Svartalfheim, though he seemed more polite, well-meaning, and erudite than the rest.

But the dwarf to the left was bizarre-looking. Nearly bald, with a broken nose and a long, unruly, dirty brown beard, he looked as if he hadn't seen a comb—or a bath—in years. His pox-scarred face was half-hidden beneath the tangled mass of hair, and a foul stench clung to him, thick with sweat and soot. He wore a sleeveless chest plate, blackened with grime, and gripped a sheathed sword in his filthy, unwashed hands. But the most remarkable thing about him was his skin. His eyes, nails, gums, and most of the skin from his fingertips to shoulders were a mottled blue-gray, with only a few patches of pale, blackened skin. The dwarf must've suffered from Argyria, a rare skin condition caused by prolonged exposure to silver. Sigurd had heard stories of miners who developed this affliction, their bodies forever stained by the very metal they unearthed. But he had never seen it with his own eyes.

"What's the matter?" the smelly dwarf asked after a minute of Sigurd rudely gawking at his blue arms. "Cat got your fucking tongue? You want me to tie a rope around your testicles and the other end to a goat to loosen it for you?"

The dwarves burst out laughing. But they stopped when Sigurd thrust his pickaxe at them, pointing the sharp tip at the blue dwarf's neck.

"Watch. Your. *Tone*," Sigurd warned as he glared at them with his snake eyes. A glare that could send any predator or ruffian into submission. But the blue dwarf casually met Sigurd's gaze, finding his snake eyes more curious than terrifying.

"Oh, don't mind his crassness," the other dwarf said, nuzzling aside Sigurd's pickaxe. "Brok has always been foul-mouthed, slovenly, and ill-mannered. But he's mostly harmless and good-natured. I can't say the same for his prurient jokes."

Sigurd blinked several times. "Wait a minute! Did you say his name is Brok?"

"That's right. And I'm Sindri. We're..."

"The Huldra Brothers!" Sigurd interrupted giddily. "You're the dwarves who forged Freyr's boar Gullinbursti, Odin's golden ring Draupnir, and Thor's hammer Mjolnir!"

"Gah ha ha ha ha! I suppose our reputation precedes us." Brok laughed while scratching his head.

"Of course it does!" Sigurd exclaimed. "Your craftsman skills are legendary in Midgard. Regin always claimed you two were the greatest smiths in Svartalfheim!"

"I don't know about that." Sindri giggled, shyly scratching his head. "The Sons of Ivaldi might contest that honor. After all, they're the ones who forged Sif's hair, Freyr's ship *Skidbladnir*, and Odin's spear Gungnir."

"I-I never dreamed I'd be able to meet you." Sigurd grinned. "To what do I owe the pleasure of meeting such legendary craftsmen?"

"You're the talk of Svartalfheim," Brok said. "Your name is on the mouth of every dwarf here. We decided to meet you in person and see if the rumors about you were true."

He removed a drinking flask from his belt and offered it to Sigurd. "You've been down in these mines a whole month. You must have worked up quite the thirst."

"It's been that long, huh?" Sigurd muttered as he took the flask and drank deeply. Within was a mead so thick and potent that it made his eyes water and sent tendrils of fire snaking through his chest.

"That's not mead!" Sigurd coughed.

"No, that's a proper dwarven drink." Brok laughed. "Not like that *juice* you humans drink in Midgard."

Sigurd took a deep breath and then took another deep swig. He'd had nothing to drink since he drank from the Well of Destiny. The Apple of Idun he'd eaten in Helheim still kept him nourished and energized, but it couldn't ease his parched throat. It didn't matter if this brew tasted like day-old cock cheese. As long as it quenched his parched throat, it would suffice.

When he handed the flask back, Brok stepped back and gave Sigurd a cursory glance before looking him straight in the eyes.

"You killed Fafnir and Regin?" Brok asked, though it wasn't a question.

"Yes," Sigurd admitted.

Brok seemed to detect the slight shame in Sigurd's voice and held up his hands. "It's alright. I'd never hold *that* against you. Regin was a greedy cunt, and Fafnir was an even bigger cunt. Ivaldi will never admit this to your face, but those two were disgraces in the eyes of all dwarves. The Nine Realms are a lot cleaner without them around."

"If you say so." Sigurd sighed sadly. Their words couldn't assuage his guilt. Even if he was a scoundrel, Regin's death still weighed on Sigurd to this day.

Sindri smiled. "He doesn't seem so bad. He seems quite humble to me."

"More like a dejected puppy," Brok disagreed. "I find it hard to believe a whining pup like you slew Fafnir. Speaking of which..."

He stepped back and unsheathed the sword he was carrying. After a moment, Sigurd realized it was Gram.

"This is your sword, isn't it?" Brok asked. "Is this the same one you used to slay Fafnir?"

"Yes." Sigurd nodded. "But why do you have it?"

"The dwarves who incapacitated you gave it to us for safekeeping after they confiscated all your armor and weapons," Sindri explained. "We also have your helmet and armor back at our shop, along with your... *other* sword."

"We repaired your armor and upgraded the design," Brok added. "It's made of meta-aramid fibers now, designed to withstand burning heat and freezing cold."

"Thank you," Sigurd muttered. "What compelled you to do that, if you don't mind me asking?"

"Sheer fucking principle," Brok answered. "We couldn't stand the state of it. The armor was dented, and the chain links in the mail were torn. Just what the fuck were you fighting against for it to get so badly damaged?"

"Helheim's undead army," Sigurd answered. "My brother, Brynhild, and I had to cut down thousands of draugirs and slay two draugs before clawing our way out of Helheim. According to the Norns, we slew over a million draugirs before we escaped. I didn't realize the kill count was that high, but I'll take their word for it."

Brok and Sindri stared at him with newfound respect. They regained their composure and gestured back to the sword.

"Does it have a name?" Brok asked.

"Gram," Sigurd answered.

"Gram?" Sindri repeated with a hint of derision. "That's not a very majestic name."

Sigurd shrugged. "I wasn't the one who picked it. My father, Sigmund, named it as he died in my mother's arms. Sinfjotli claims our father never called the sword anything before that point. I saw no reason to rename it."

"So you're not one of those vainglorious heroes who give fancy names on every sword they use?" Brok nodded. "I respect that."

He examined the fuller of the blade. "Hmmm. The blade broke previously! You mentioned Regin fixed it for you?"

"That's right." Sigurd nodded. "After he reforged it, he handed it to me and said: 'If this sword doesn't fit the bill, then I am no blacksmith.' When I tested it by striking the anvil, the blade cut clean through the heavy iron and its oak stand right to the floor. Then, to test its edge, I threw a tuft of wool into a river and held the blade downstream. The wool got cut cleanly in two. Afterward, we went to a waterfall, and I waited in the plunge pool as Regin took a large bundle of logs upriver and sent them tumbling down the waterfall at me. I chopped through each log as they fell. By the end, I had chopped almost thirty logs in half, but Gram hadn't suffered a single nick."

"Regin may have been a greedy cunt like his brother, but at least the son of a bitch could forge." Brok kept admiring the handiwork of the sword and then frowned. "Still, there's room for improvement. You carved these runes into the fuller yourself, didn't you?"

"Yes," Sigurd admitted. "Brynhild instructed me—"

"That's what I thought," Brok interrupted with a wave of his hand. "No dwarf, not even Regin, would carve runes this sloppily into a blade." He brought out some tools from his belt and began tinkering with the runes on the sword. The runes glowed as he worked, and Gram seemed to illuminate slightly.

"Look, unless you came to give me back my sword, I need to get back to work." Sigurd turned and swung his pickaxe at a nearby amethyst crystal while Brok continued chiseling into Gram.

"I remember when Odin commissioned us to forge this sword," Sindri muttered as he watched his brother work.

That got Sigurd's attention. "*You* forged it?"

"That's right." Sindri nodded. "See here. That's our brand."

He pointed to a slight indentation on the hilt, which depicted two interlocking serpents twined around a dark sun.

"I thought Regin made that when he reforged the sword," Sigurd remarked.

"As if." Brok snorted derisively. "Regin's brand wouldn't be worth the paper I need after a shit."

"Odin commissioned us to forge this sword," Sindri continued, trying to move the conversation along. "He promised us that someday, the greatest hero in the north would wield it. We all thought it was meant for your father, Sigmund. But it was really meant for you."

"This sword is meant for great and valiant tasks, just like you," Brok added while glancing up from his work. "You want to spend the remainder of your life working like a thrall?"

"No," Sigurd admitted as he swung his pickaxe on a dazzling diamond. "Nor do I plan to. I only need to gather enough riches to pay the blood price. Then my brother and I will be free to leave this place."

Brok shook his head. "You misunderstand. Ivaldi is playing you, kid. The deal was you must get enough gold to completely cover Regin's and Fafnir's bodies to pay the blood price within two months."

"What of it?" Sigurd asked. "Is there some kind of catch here?"

"Have you forgotten?" Sindri rolled his eyes, as if Sigurd was missing something obvious. "Fafnir was a *dragon*, and an enormous one at that! The last time I saw him, he was a hundred and fifty feet long, and I imagine he was ten times that size when you killed him. I reckon it would take a human like you fifty years to amass enough riches to completely cover his weight in gold. But you only have a single month left. You'll run out of time before you mine anywhere near that much wealth."

Sigurd felt his stomach tighten. "But that's... he... Ivaldi gave me his word. Why would...?"

"You see," Brok chimed in, "Ivaldi is planning to avenge his grandsons by making you work like a slave until you die. He thinks it's an appropriate humiliation for someone as renowned as you. When you cannot get enough gold in the allotted time, Ivaldi will execute you as promised. And your brother will die as well. Have no doubt about that. Once he's dead, Ivaldi's sons will dismember his corpse piece by piece and craft trinkets from his body, the same way Odin and his brothers formed Midgard out of Ymir's flesh."

Sigurd could tell from the look in their eyes that they were speaking the truth. He glanced at the pile of wealth he'd amassed so far. There were enough riches to pay Regin's weight in gold ten times over. But Fafnir was a much trickier matter. Sigurd remembered how big Fafnir had been. Every step the dragon took caused the earth to shake, and every time he flapped his wings, it was like a hurricane.

Sigurd thought about all the treasure he'd taken from Hindarfjall. Every night, Fafnir buried himself beneath his giant hoard like a blanket. There had been enough gold and riches in that cave to make Sigurd the envy of the entire world after he had killed Fafnir and taken it for himself. There was no conceivable way Sigurd could gain *that* much gold in another month, even with Andvari's ring aiding him.

"What should I do?" Sigurd asked in desperation. "If I cannot deliver, Ivaldi will kill me and my brother."

Brok and Sindri finished tinkering with Gram. The blade looked sharper now, and the multicolored runes glowed in the dark. The dwarves examined the massive shimmering pile of gold, gems, and other precious minerals Sigurd had accumulated so far on the nearby mine cart.

"Your options aren't ideal," Sindri admitted. "If you try to run away, you and your brother will die, and when you inevitably cannot mine enough gold, you'll die. It seems there's no way to avoid dying."

"Well, there is *one way* he could survive," Brok thought out loud.

"How?" Sindri stared at his brother until his eyes widened with horror. "Wait... No! You want him to... But he'd have to... Oh, gods!"

"What?" Sigurd inquired, looking back and forth between the two.

"There *might* be a way to outsmart Ivaldi, absolve the blood debt he placed on your head, and gain extraordinary power," Brok replied. "And it will all come from a dragon."

"A dragon?" Sigurd repeated.

"That's right." Brok nodded. "You remember how much power you gained after you killed Fafnir?"

Sigurd examined the palm of his hand and thought back to the day he killed Fafnir. Although he'd been swinging a pickaxe for an entire month, his hands weren't callused or blistered. It was thanks to his invulnerable skin.

"When I killed Fafnir, I bathed in his blood, which made my skin invulnerable to most threats," Sigurd recalled aloud.

"Oh, gross!" Sindri squealed squeamishly.

"And after I tasted the juices from his heart, I gained the ability to understand birds and to read the hearts of men," Sigurd continued. "And when I devoured the heart, I gained snake eyes that could see in the dark and spot things from miles away."

"Please stop," Sindri pleaded, as his face rapidly turned green. "I—I can't take this!" Sindri ran to a nearby bucket and began vomiting into it.

Sigurd frowned. "What's his problem?"

"Oh, don't mind Sindri." Brok laughed. "He's a germaphobe and gets nauseous whenever he hears someone talking about doing 'unclean things.'

Just be glad you're not covered in blood right now, or else you'd probably have to pay the blood price for Sindri, too. But as you pointed out, when you killed Fafnir, you gained invulnerability, snake eyes that could see miles away, and the ability to understand birds. All those abilities are impressive. But you've only scratched the surface of what you can achieve. If you want to attain true power and beat Ivaldi at his own game, you must undergo the Trial of Svarblood."

"Trial of Svarblood?" Sigurd repeated. "What's that?"

"Ask your brother about it," Brok instructed. "He's undergone it before. He'll know how it works. But don't be surprised if he's not forthcoming. The Trial is your family's darkest secret, a skeleton in the closet blacker even than Sinfjotli's incestuous origins. You might have to twist his arm to get the information you need."

"I'll keep that in mind," Sigurd vowed. "But I doubt he'll give me much trouble. Sinfjotli rarely lies, especially not to me."

"We'll see," Brok demurred. "Now listen closely. If you want to leave this realm alive, take the wealth you've mined so far and use it to pay only for Regin's blood price. As for Fafnir, you'll trick Ivaldi into letting you undergo the Trial of Svarblood to pay for his blood debt. If it succeeds, you'll be free to leave the realm. And if you play your cards right, you might even trick Ivaldi into forging something useful for your brother as well."

"Thank you." Sigurd bowed as he set his pickaxe down. "I'll go see Sinfjotli now."

Brok held out a hand. "Not so fast, kid. That information isn't for free. You can't get something for nothing in Svartalfheim. What'll you offer us in return?"

"Help yourself to all the gold I've mined," Sigurd offered. "As you said, there's more than enough here to pay Regin's blood price."

Brok shook his head. "Gold isn't as valuable to Sindri and me as it is to other dwarves and humans. We have an almost limitless supply of it and other riches and metals here in Svartalfheim. Sindri and I already have all the treasure we need. After all, we *make* treasure for a living. My brother and I prefer to receive more... exotic forms of payment for our services."

"Well, what *do* you want?" Sigurd asked.

Brok crossed his arms and stared intently at Sigurd while Sindri continued hurling his lunch into his bucket. Sigurd shuddered. There was something very unnerving about Brok's gaze. It reminded him of how a carpenter studies a tall tree, imagining all the wonderful knickknacks he could make from the lumber. The blue dwarf was probably imagining what trinkets he could make from Sigurd's corpse.

"You ever heard of the time Loki almost lost his head to us in a bet?" Brok asked.

"Yes, but it's been a while since I heard that story," Sigurd admitted.

"Well, the short version is that we forged Gullinbursti, Draupnir, and Thor's hammer Mjolnir because Loki bet his head that we couldn't forge treasure that matched the Sons of Ivaldi's masterpieces. But when the time came to collect, the sneaky bastard cheated me out of my payment by pointing out that he hadn't promised me his neck. That's more or less the type of payment we expect for our services."

Brok looked Sigurd in the eyes and cocked his head to the side. "Maybe you could offer me one of your eyes. I hear your eyesight is second only to Heimdall's and Odin's. I reckon I could craft something useful from one of your eyeballs, like a magic telescope."

"That is out of the question!" Sigurd yelled. His voice echoed through the mineshaft like a blast of thunder.

Brok held his hands up. "Alright, calm down. I didn't mean to startle you. I'm just giving you an option. But that's the type of payment we expect for our services. So, what are you prepared to offer?"

"I have already offered you all the treasure I have," Sigurd insisted. "All I have left is my ring and the clothes off my back..."

"Ring?" Brok interrupted. "What ring?" He stopped studying Sigurd with hungry eyes and glanced at the shiny ring on Sigurd's hand. The dwarf frowned. "Is this a joke? There's nothing there."

"Are you blind?" Sigurd bellowed. He waved his left hand emphatically and tapped the cursed ring multiple times. "It's right here on my left ring finger. This ring was the only possession the dwarves *didn't* confiscate when they captured me."

Brok arched an eyebrow. He looked closer at Sigurd's hand and scratched his beard in deep thought. "By any chance, is there a rune carved into this ring?"

Sigurd glanced at the Andvaranaut. After a moment, he noticed a faint green symbol chiseled into the gemstone. It was barely noticeable amidst the dark green color of the emerald.

"It's faint, but I think the Perthro rune is engraved onto the gemstone," Sigurd reported.

"That explains it," Brok decided. "That rune means 'secret.' It can obscure whatever item it's been chiseled into from unsavory eyes. Its previous owner must have enchanted it so no dwarf could see it. That's why my brethren didn't confiscate it from you after you got captured."

"That makes sense," Sigurd agreed. He twisted the ring on his finger. "This ring was Andvari's prized possession. He *really* didn't want anyone to take it from him."

Brok eyes widened. "Andvari?"

"That's right." Sigurd nodded. "This was his ring once upon a time."

Brok looked skeptically at Sigurd and then shook his head. "Hold out your left hand for a moment."

Sigurd obliged. Brok held his hand in front of Sigurd's hand and traced a magical symbol in the air.

"Krasa," he muttered. A sound like glass breaking rippled through the air and echoed throughout the mineshaft. The glowing symbol on the gemstone faded. The ring shined brighter than before in the light of Brok's lantern.

Now that he could clearly see the ring, Brok got a good look at it. His eyes became as wide as dinner plates.

"Shut your mouth!" Brok exclaimed. "Is that really...? Sindri! Hey, Sindri, come and have a look at this!"

"What is it?" Sindri groaned groggily as he stood up from his bucket. When he turned and saw the glimmering ring on Sigurd's finger, he also became wide-eyed. "Holy shit! Is that the Andvaranaut? Where did you get that?"

"I found it in Fafnir's cave," Sigurd answered while uncomfortably twisting the ring on his finger. "Actually, I recently got it back from my wife in Helheim. But I originally found it amongst the treasure in Fafnir's hoard at Gnitaheath. The dragon warned me not to take it, or it'd bring me misfortune... but I took it anyway."

That was another mistake Sigurd deeply regretted. So many tragedies could have been avoided if he hadn't taken the cursed treasure. His forced marriage to Gudrun, his betrayal of Brynhild, his death at Guttorm's hands, Brynhild's suicide, and the deaths of Gudrun's entire family could have all been prevented if he hadn't taken the cursed hoard.

But Brok and Sindri didn't seem concerned that the ring was cursed. They kept staring at it in wonder.

"It really is the Andvaranaut," Brok muttered. He smiled hungrily. "That'll do. Give it here, and we'll call it even."

"No." He pulled back his hand and caressed the ring. "This was my wife's last gift to me before we parted ways forever. It means a lot to me. You would have me trade a ring as valuable as this over some paltry advice and information?"

Sigurd's attachment to his ring was just an act. In truth, Sigurd despised the Andvaranaut because it had brought him, Brynhild, and his wife Gudrun nothing but misfortune throughout their lives. Frankly, he would have traded it away for a cup of sufficiently strong mead. But these dwarves seemed to covet it despite Andvari's curse. That gave him an excellent bargaining position.

Sadly, Sigurd had never been the best at acting, and his feigned attachment to the ring did not fool Brok. But the dwarf was quick on the uptake and grasped Sigurd's unspoken message.

"You're right," the blue dwarf conceded. "That wouldn't be a fair trade. So what *else* do you want in exchange for the ring?"

Sigurd thought long and hard for a few moments. He glanced at his sword dangling from Brok's belt, and an idea formed. "The Norns warned us we must travel the Nine Realms and face foes and challenges beyond the imagination of men to reach Valhalla, and Odin tasked us with gaining weapons from your people. You two forged some of the Aesir's greatest weapons and treasures, including Mjolnir. My brother lacks weapons or armor, and I have only two swords, armor, and a helmet, which are all currently in your possession. So, in exchange for this ring, I want you to return all of my possessions and forge weapons and armor to aid us in this journey."

CHAPTER SEVEN

A BROTHER'S DESPERATE PLEA

Niðavellir's main prison was unique from the jails Sigurd had seen on his travels throughout the wide world. Imprisonment had been a foreign concept to him growing up. In the Norse culture, crimes were punished through fines, death, slavery, or exile. It made no sense to him to waste time and resources keeping a felon locked up in a cage like livestock. But Sigurd had visited many places that opted to do precisely that. Lords, kings, and dukes locked criminals in underground dungeons without windows, filled with squalor, and infested with rats, and then just left them there to rot for years.

During his travels through Midgard, he had seen various types of prisons. The cruelest ones had been oubliettes—prison cells that could only be accessed from above and were impossible to escape without aid. Some lords might leave a prisoner in one and toss away the key, leaving them to starve to death.

But the prison of Niðavellir was different. It was a vast underground chamber. Previously, it had been a source of valuable minerals until the dwarves mined it dry and converted it into a vast prison. It seemed excessively big since there were only a handful of prisoners. Sigurd counted less than two dozen dwarves. Under Ivaldi's strict rule, most dwarves seldom committed crimes. Any that did were executed or given draconian punishments. Only a handful of criminals were ever sent here.

There weren't many guards, and the prisoners were treated leniently. They could roam around and converse with one another, but the bleak setting, lack of activity, and boredom drove many to madness. Though there were no cells to confine them, they remained trapped all the same, free to roam within the prison walls, but they could never set foot outside them.

The only exception was Sinfjotli, who was caged inside a cell. His cell was large and unexpectedly comfortable; Sigurd thought it may once have been an affluent dwarf's bedchamber. A hearth large enough to hold a kettle sat in one corner, a privy was tucked into a nook, and an iron-and-oak cot rested against a wall. The dwarves had even given him a tallow candle, a stack of firewood, and furs for his bed. Yet, for all its comforts, his cell remained a cell.

The walls were solid stone, and the iron doors and bars were reinforced with powerful runes. No man or beast could hope to break them. Two pairs of long, heavy iron fetters dangled from the ceiling, but the dwarves hadn't shackled Sinfjotli. There was no need.

Sigurd had heard that after the dwarves tossed him in, Sinfjotli had tried breaking out by shifting into a wolf and ramming the door. He stopped once he realized all he was doing was giving himself a concussion.

At least Sinfjotli has a bed, Sigurd thought with a hint of envy as he gazed at the small cot draped with furs. When he wasn't mining, the dwarves kept him sealed in a dark room with nothing but a stone slab to rest on.

Sigurd didn't waste any time telling Sinfjotli the Huldra Brothers' plan and inquired about the Trial of Svarblood.

It went off to a terrible start, just like Brok forewarned.

"Where did you hear about that?" Sinfjotli demanded angrily. "Who told you about the Trial of Svarblood?"

"Brok and Sindri," Sigurd answered.

Sinfjotli blinked. His rage, boiling within him moments ago, subsided into total surprise. "You mean the Huldra Brothers? Aren't they the dwarves who forged Thor's hammer?"

"That's them."

Sinfjotli narrowed his eyes. "And you trust them?"

"They've agreed to help me in exchange for Andvari's ring. The Huldra Brothers are reputed to be men of their word. Once they take a contract, they always deliver."

"I've heard the same thing said about many men who turned out to be traitors in the end," Sinfjotli scoffed dismissively. "You're supposed to be able to read people's hearts and glean their intentions. Tell me truthfully. Can we trust them?"

Sigurd shrugged. "More than any other dwarf here, though that's not saying much. The rest just call me an 'oath breaker,' 'murderer,' or spit in my face whenever they walk by me. Have they been treating you well?"

"I can't complain." Sinfjotli gestured around the cell he was locked in. "The dwarves don't love me, but they don't hate me, either. They give me food, water, wood for the hearth, and a warm bed, but naught else."

So much for that "dwarven hospitality" Regin always boasted about, Sigurd thought. "So what *is* the Trial of Svarblood? How does it work? Do I need to find a magic pelt?"

Sinfjotli arched an eyebrow. "A magic pelt?"

"Back on Baldur's ship, you claimed that you and Father once came across enchanted wolf pelts during your years of training while hiding in the wilderness from Siggeir's forces. When you put them on, the pelts transformed you both into wolves, but you could not remove them. For ten days, you and Father lived as wolves running through the forest, killing many men. On the eleventh day, you removed the pelts and promptly burned them in a fire. But because of the ordeal, you were now skinchangers able to transform into wolves at will. That's how you became a skinchanger, isn't it?"

Sinfjotli remained silent for a while. His face was unreadable, but he almost looked happy.

"So you really knew nothing after all?" He heaved a heavy sigh. "That's a relief."

Sigurd's eyes widened. "Wait... that's... not what happened? But back on Baldur's ship, you..."

"I lied. That story about Father and me finding magic wolf pelts is the one and only lie of my life." Sinfjotli held up a hand and gestured to a scar on his palm. "Father made me swear a blood oath to tell that story to anyone who asked how we became skinchangers. He wanted the truth buried and forgotten so that no one would follow in our footsteps and subject themselves to the same horror. If you truly knew nothing, then our plan succeeded."

Sinfjotli regarded the scar on his palm. "I told a single lie, and the poets, skalds, and the entire world believed it. How poetic. That all that's needed to change the course of history: for one honest person to tell a single lie."

"So then what *really* happened?" Sigurd pressed. "Why are you able to turn into a wolf?"

"Sigurd." Sinfjotli reached through the bars of his cell and placed his hand on Sigurd's shoulder. "You are my brother. I accepted that truth long ago. That is why, as your brother, I must ask you not to walk this path. The chalice you wish to drink from will bring unimaginable pain and horror. Please don't go through with this. Find another way."

"Your concern is touching, but I'm afraid there isn't time to find an alternative," Sigurd persisted as he shook off Sinfjotli's hand. "I already told Ivaldi's servant to fetch him."

"You did what?" Sinfjotli staggered backward. "Why? It hasn't been two months yet."

"To force your hand. I figured you wouldn't want to tell me about the Trial. So, I set everything in motion before I came here. I chucked my pickaxe at the dwarf standing guard at the mine and told him: 'Fetch your master because I am done working as his slave.' Ivaldi will summon court tomorrow. Once the old king sees that I haven't mined enough gold, he will definitely execute me. According to Brok and Sindri, this 'Trial of Svarblood' may be the only way to pay the blood price, outwit Ivaldi, and fulfill Odin's second task. I'll kill three birds with one stone."

"You don't know what you've done." Sinfjotli sagged onto his cot and nervously ran his hands through his hair. "You utter fool. You have no clue how much pain you'll endure!"

"I'm sorry to force your hand like this and make you break your promise to Father, but we're running out of time. The guards will be here soon to put me in chains and throw me in a cell for tomorrow's assembly. If you don't tell me everything now, I'll die a pointless death at Ivaldi's hands. Please tell me about the Trial of Svarblood before it's too late."

"So be it." Sinfjotli sighed with a steady yet sorrowful voice. He rose to his feet and gazed at Sigurd with pity and remorse. "Before I get into the specifics, there is something you must know: In order for the Trial of Svarblood to succeed, you must die one more time."

Sigurd furrowed his brow. "'I must die one more time?' What do you mean?"

Sinfjotli took a deep breath, steeling himself. "To become a skinchanger, you must allow yourself to be eaten alive by an animal of your choice."

CHAPTER EIGHT

THE HORRID TRUTH

Sigurd stumbled backward from the cell and nearly tripped over a crate as the full import of Sinfjotli's words registered in his mind. "You mean that... you and Father... you were... no! NO!"

"The Trial of Svarblood is an ancient ritual that transfers your soul into an animal of your choice," Sinfjotli explained while ignoring Sigurd's growing horror. "You seem to think I'm a human who can transform into a wolf at will. But it's the other way around. The reality is you *become* the animal that devours you."

"No!" Sigurd yelled. "You're not... you can't be... you're human! I can see it in your eyes and heart. You are a human being like me!"

Sinfjotli shook his head. "Only in appearance. And even that's just for show. Physiologically, I'm a wolf. You could say that the Trial turned me into a wolf that now wears a man's skin."

Sigurd felt nauseous. He didn't want to believe it. But he knew Sinfjotli was telling the truth. He could see it with his clairvoyance. So many things made sense. When they fought each other in Helheim, Sigurd noticed Sinfjotli was much more robust and heavier than he appeared. The many scars covering his neck and body were the kind only a savage beast could inflict. Whenever Sinfjotli transformed, it looked like a beast emerging from his skin, like how a man might tear off his heavy garments on a sweltering day.

Sigurd tried to regain his composure as the stormy sea of fear, disgust, and horror flooded his mind. But the abyss only deepened as the memories of the Norns' warning came flooding back.

"The Norns claimed if we die a second time on this journey, Hel will claim our souls." Sigurd looked intently at Sinfjotli. "If I go through with this, then…"

"She won't be able to claim your soul because the Trial doesn't count as a true death," Sinfjotli assured. "It's an all-or-nothing gamble. If you pass, you'll be reborn and keep living your life and will still get the chance to go to Valhalla."

"But the Norns said—"

"Did you forget our father is in Valhalla?" Sinfjotli interrupted. "We both underwent the Trial, but he didn't wind up in Helheim for it. The only reason I got sent to the underworld was because that scheming bitch Borghild poisoned me at the feast. But Father got the chance to die fighting and go to Valhalla."

As Sigurd contemplated those words, he sighed, feeling the storm within his mind calm somewhat. "So even though I'll perish a second time, Hel can't claim my soul."

"You shouldn't find comfort in that! The stakes are incredibly high. Only three in ten people survive this ritual. Those who don't pass the Trial not only die. Their souls are destroyed! Do you understand what that entails? If you fail the Trial, not only will you die, there won't even be an afterlife for you! The dragon that eats you will take your body and live on."

Sigurd frowned. "'Take my body?'"

Sinfjotli bit his lower lip. "Remember how I said in Helheim that Siggeir's mother was a wolf who fell madly in love with his father and took on a human form to become his bride? The thing is, that wasn't an exaggeration or a calumny to further blacken Siggeir's name. Long ago, a sorceress in Gautland underwent the Trial, hoping to gain more power and let herself be devoured by a wolf. Unfortunately, she didn't have what it took to survive. The she-wolf's soul subsumed the sorceress's body, mind, and intellect, and she lived as a human from that day on, free to switch between her new human and old wolf bodies as she pleased."

Sinfjotli stared intently at Sigurd. "And if you fail, the same thing will happen to you. The dragon will take your body, memories, and sense of self. You're risking every facet of yourself in this all-or-nothing gamble."

"You and Father survived," Sigurd pointed out.

"Just barely. We had my mother's help as a practitioner of magic. She learned about the Trial from the sorceress in the Scandinavian Mountains, who had prophesied Siggeir's doom and prepared the potion necessary to start the ritual. We survived the ordeal thanks to her efforts, but the cost was... so high."

Sinfjotli ran his fingers over the scars along his neck and shoulder and shuddered. "I will never forget that day. The wolf that ate me... didn't kill me right away. It *toyed* with me for over an hour, devouring me piece by bloody piece until I screamed and begged for death. Its fangs were like icy spears. I can still feel its frigid teeth tearing into my flesh. And I'll never forget what happened afterward."

"What do you mean?" Sigurd ventured.

"There's another grave risk that comes with the Trial. Even if you pass the Trial of Svarblood, your soul needs around ten days to adjust to its new body. During that time, your mind is trapped in a feral state, and you threaten everything around you. After Father and I passed the Trial, we scoured the forest for ten days in a blood rage, indiscriminately killing everything we came across. Men, women, children, livestock, wild animals; no one was safe from our rampage. Not even me. On the tenth day, Father attacked me in a murderous rage and nearly killed me. I still don't know how I survived that vicious assault."

He's not lying, Sigurd knew. He could see it in Sinfjotli's eyes. This part of the story was no fabrication.

"When we regained our sanity and human forms, we beheld all the destruction we had wrought," Sinfjotli continued. "We had killed scores of people, destroyed entire farms, butchered livestock, slaughtered the beasts of the forest, massacred several villages, and nearly killed each other. That rampant destruction was merely what *two* reincarnated wolves gone mad with bloodlust were capable of."

Sinfjotli stared at Sigurd with terror in his eyes. After a moment, Sigurd's eyes widened as he grasped the full implications of his brother's words. "You're saying that once I pass the Trial—"

"*Assuming* you pass the Trial," Sinfjotli corrected sharply. "There's no guarantee you'll survive. But if you did... it's terrifying to imagine the rampant destruction you would inflict as a dragon during the ten days you're mad with bloodlust and unable to revert to your human form."

Sinfjotli stared at the stone floor. "If I'm being honest, I'm not even sure if the Trial of Svarblood will work in this situation. The Trial is typically used to transform humans into bears, wolves, lions, or other predators. You're planning to use it to become a *dragon*! As far as I know, that has never been attempted! Frankly, I'm not even sure it's possible. There's a good chance it won't even activate, and you'll die a pointless and painful death. But let's be generous and assume for a moment that it works and you pass. The side effects... Sigurd, I can't even remember what it was like to live as a human before the Trial, like not having a nose that could detect a scent from miles away or overwhelm my brain when I'm in a crowd. I salivate whenever I smell the scent of blood. I am quick to anger, willing to kill anyone over the slightest insult or provocation, and when I snap and give in to rage... I hurt people. When I get angry... I lose my mind, and everything goes red. The world around me just... fades away. Then all I can see is the person I want to kill. It doesn't matter if they're my enemy, friend, or family."

Sinfjotli touched the scars on his neck and shoulder again and shivered. "I've had to endure all this because of transforming into a wolf. I can't even imagine what would happen to *you* if you became a dragon or how it might change you. If you lose control or cannot maintain your sense of self, you'll lash out at friends and foes alike. Are you still sure you want to go through with this?"

As Sigurd stood outside his brother's cell shaking in fear and disgust, something the Norn Skuld had said before they departed Wyrd's Well echoed in his mind. *"I wish you good fortune in the trial to come."*

Did they know *this would happen?* Sigurd wondered. They claimed choices shape destiny, and yet...?

Sigurd's eyes widened. As he thought about the Norns, he recalled something else. When Odin visited him in the dream he'd had after escaping Helheim, there was a moment when Fafnir's corpse devoured him. During his prophetic dream in the Norn's cave, he was swallowed by the Midgard Serpent. Then he remembered something else and closed his eyes.

"I saw Father," he muttered abruptly.

"What?" Sinfjotli asked. "When?"

"During the vision I had after I drank from the Well of Destiny. I saw Ragnarök. I stood in the middle of a golden field. It was pitch-black. There was no sun, moon, or star in the sky. But I could still see everything. Father was there amongst the ranks of the warriors in Valhalla, and so was my mother. They asked me, 'Which side will you fight for? Choose!' And during that dream... I kept witnessing myself being devoured alive by a dragon and even the Midgard Serpent. I don't know why, but I just *know* this is something that *will* happen. Somehow... I've always known that someday I would be consumed by a dragon."

"Sigurd, the risks—"

"I know the risks!" Sigurd exploded. "I realize what's at stake here. But I swear by the gods that no matter what it takes when Ragnarök comes, I *will* stand alongside Father and the rest of the Einherjar! I won't let Brynhild damn herself to Helheim because of me. I won't let Hel win and turn us into her mindless servants. If I must become a dragon to fulfill that vow, I'll gladly do it. Now, tell me how to start the Trial."

"Very well..." Sinfjotli sighed.

CHAPTER NINE

THE DRAGON SLAYER'S FINAL BOW

"I warned you I'd execute you if you failed to gather enough gold," Ivaldi bellowed from his throne.

Sigurd was again on his knees, chained to the arena in the dwarven amphitheater. All the wealth he'd mined lay in a gigantic pile before him. He had mined enough gold and precious metals to make him one of the wealthiest men alive in Midgard. But it still wasn't enough to cover Fafnir's weight in gold.

"I know well what you said, Ivaldi." Sigurd looked the king dead in the eyes. "So do it."

Ivaldi shot him a raised eyebrow. "Excuse me?"

"Execute me! Feed me to a dragon, as you threatened. But before you do, grant me four last requests." Sigurd gestured to the pile of wealth. "I've gathered enough treasure to pay Regin's weight in gold ten times over. Surely, that's enough for you to grant me some last requests."

Ivaldi leaned forward on his throne, intrigued by Sigurd's audacious request. Around him, the other dwarves raged, shouting accusations of murder and saying he didn't deserve the chance. But Ivaldi silenced them with his booming voice.

"That depends on what you ask for," Ivaldi warned. "But by all means, speak. I'm curious what someone like you would ask for on their day of reckoning."

"First, let me be eaten alive by a dragon of my choice. I was lauded my whole life as Sigurd the Dragon Slayer. I know that singers and poets will sing praises of this day. It'll make for a better song if I am slain by a beast of my choice. Second, release my brother. Fafnir's and Regin's deaths were my responsibility alone. Sinfjotli is entirely innocent of that crime. Third, I ask that you craft my brother a suit of armor that will put all else to shame. You can accept the gold I've collected so far to atone for Regin's death as payment for this task."

Ivaldi leaned back on his throne and stroked his long beard as he contemplated his requests. "Sigurd the Dragon Slayer, eaten by a dragon of his own choice," he mused. "That would be quite poetic. As for your second request..."

Ivaldi glanced beyond Sigurd and regarded Sinfjotli, who was being restrained in an unyielding grip by two giant armored dwarves at the opposite side of the amphitheater.

"Calling him 'innocent' is a bit of a stretch. Your brother is guilty of many heinous crimes. Even here in Svartalfheim, we've heard of his wicked deeds. However, I suppose he hasn't done anything to personally offend us dwarves."

Ivaldi scratched his beard and then nodded. "Billingr, Dúrnir, release the other prisoner, but keep a close eye on him!"

Ivaldi's two sons obeyed. They unshackled Sinfjotli from his chains and escorted him away from the arena. They wisely kept their weapons brandished in case he tried something foolish, like trying to rescue Sigurd.

"Your third request is quite presumptuous, Sigurd," Ivaldi noted disapprovingly. "However, since you're willing to pay on your brother's behalf, I suppose some arrangements could be made. Now, what about your fourth request?"

Sigurd fought the urge to smile at how well everything was unfolding and kept his face a mask of quiet despair. "Oh, my last request is a simple matter. I request you swear a blood oath that once the dragon has devoured me, you'll forgive me for killing Regin and Fafnir and absolve me of the blood debt."

Ivaldi raised a curious eyebrow. "That is a very unusual last request. How could that possibly benefit you or your brother after you're dead?"

"It will clear my name. I—I've done... many things I'm not proud of. But one of the few things I truly regret is killing Regin. Even though it was in self-defense, it has haunted me for years that I killed him after everything he did for me. If I'm going to perish, I want to die knowing I restored some small shred of honor to my name."

"Is that what this is about?" Ivaldi chuckled. "Very well."

Sigurd almost squealed with joy but wisely kept his face a meek mask. The dwarf king obviously thought there was no way this could backfire on him.

Ivaldi rose from his throne and drew a knife from his belt. The blade had a unique texture and wavy pattern, almost like looking at flowing water. The design reminded Sigurd of a crucible steel dagger, and it was just as sharp as one as Ivaldi sliced open his left palm. He then held his clenched fist over a nearby brazier, letting his blood drip into the flames below.

"I, Ivaldi, solemnly swear that once you are devoured, I will absolve you of the blood debt and forgive you for murdering my grandsons."

After sheathing his dagger, Ivaldi traced a healing rune on his left hand. There was a burst of light, and the wound healed itself. With that done, Ivaldi turned and summoned his eldest son. "Mótsignir, go take this malefactor to the Dragon Pit so we can fulfill his first request."

"Yes, Father." Mótsignir hopped into the arena, unshackled Sigurd from the dais, and roughly escorted him through the cavernous halls of Svartalfheim, warning him not to do anything stupid along the way.

As they walked through the darkness of the underground dwarven city, Sigurd couldn't help but be awed. It was the first time he'd been allowed to travel around Niðavellir. The walls shimmered with glittering gems and precious metals, catching the dim light of their torches. The air was heavy with the scent of molten metal and the sounds of dwarven smiths hammering away at their forges, eager to finish their work in time for the execution. As they made their way deeper into the city, he marveled at the intricate carvings and architecture surrounding them. Although his time was limited, and Mótsignir kept impatiently shoving and warning him to keep moving, Sigurd couldn't stop himself from stopping dead in his tracks to admire the splendor surrounding him.

After traversing through labyrinth-like passageways, Sigurd and Mótsignir traveled down a long, wide tunnel that seemed to stretch on for miles. The walls were adorned with intricate carvings of dragons and other mythical creatures. Sigurd couldn't help but halt and voice his respect and admiration for the artistry of the ancient craftsmen. Mótsignir, however, had little patience. With shoved Sigurd forward, warning him to stay focused.

At the end of the corridor was an enormous gate, its iron doors so big that fifty horsemen could ride through abreast. At Mótsignir's command, the two dwarven guards unlocked the gate and heaved open the doors. The sight waiting on the other side took Sigurd's breath away.

The Dragon Pit was a vast crater-like quarry, its depths carved with countless shafts that had been hollowed out and repurposed as dragon lairs. There was no roof—far above, the open sky stretched a mile overhead. Majestic dragons soared in and out, gliding to their nests where hatchlings lay waiting. Dragons of all shapes and sizes filled the air, weaving through the space in a magnificent spectacle.

"Why is there no dome?" Sigurd asked. "The dragons could leave whenever they want."

"That's the point," Mótsignir replied, rolling his eyes. "Dragons aren't horses. You can't just pen them up in stables, or they will stop growing and wither. They need to be free, able to spread their wings, soar through the air, and grow and hunt at their leisure."

"What if they don't return to this pit?"

"That's their choice. We dwarves are not their owners or their masters. We are their allies and partners. They sometimes help us transport gold and riches, temper our steel with their flame, and help defend our realm from invaders. In exchange, we give them a place to return to rest and raise their young."

Mótsignir looked like he was about to say more, but at that moment, a young hatchling landed on his shoulder. It was about the size of a small dog. Soon, another hatchling, probably its elder sibling, landed nearby. The hatchling was as big as a newborn colt at around twenty-nine inches tall and two feet long. It had cream and gold-colored scales, and its wings were reddish orange.

Intrigued, Sigurd stepped forward to get a better look at the hatchling. Half a heartbeat later, its parent slammed into the ground in front of him. The impact was so forceful that Sigurd stumbled off his feet. When he opened his eyes, he found himself staring into the angry eyes of an adult dragon. It was massive—at least fifty long from tail to snout, its shiny silver scales glinting.

The dragon fixed him with a baleful glare, flames dancing across its teeth as it hissed a warning.

Undaunted, Mótsignir stepped in between Sigurd and the beast. Dwarf prince and dragon locked eyes in a silent standoff. After a moment, the dragon turned away and took to the air. Its two hatchlings soon followed.

"Incredible." Sigurd clambered to his feet and gazed in awe at all the dragons soaring about the pit. Some randomly spewed fire, each fireball a different color than the last.

It was beautiful.

But dangerous.

A mighty roar shattered the moment.

Sigurd's gaze snapped upward, where two mastodonic dragons clashed in the open sky.

"Males fighting over a female." Mótsignir muttered.

One was covered in black, round scales decorated with spiraling blue markings. Its bready white eyes gleamed with aggression, and his head—broad and blunt—was crowned with four large, elongated plates extending backward. Rows of razor-sharp teeth lined its powerful jaws. Its vast wings, feathery, akin to a bird's, spread wide, and its long tail trailed behind it, ending in a stinger-like shape made for bashing foes.

Its opponent was cloaked in dark red scales streaked with beige markings. Scars marred its body—deep slashes along its stomach and neck, the largest forming an X-shape at its center. A line of jagged black spikes ran from the base of its skull down its back to the end of its tail. Unlike his opponent, this dragon had a sharply angular head with horns and a single, upward-pointing spike just above his nose. Its dark round eyes burned with intensity, the yellow sclerae stark against its crimson. It bared its fangs, and rows of sharp canine teeth glistened, complemented by deadly claws, each tipped with long, serrated, red nails. Its enormous, bony wings resembled a bat's, with rippled tips built for power and speed.

Sigurd stood transfixed, watching the epic battle unfold above him. The two males were locked in fierce combat, fighting tooth and claw for the chance to mate with a female. Sparks flew as their horns locked in a deadly dance. Flames erupted from their mouths, illuminating the pit below with a fiery glow.

The red dragon let out a deafening roar as he hurled a blazing red fireball toward his opponent, so bright it lit the pit like a second sun. The black dragon countered with a furnace blast of cobalt flames, the heat of which could be felt even from where Sigurd stood. Wings beat furiously as the two behemoths grappled in midair, each vying for dominance.

As the fight escalated, the dwarven guards at the gate scrambled for cover, and the other dragons took to the sky to avoid being caught in the crossfire. Sigurd watched in awe and terror as the two males tumbled toward him in a tangled heap of wings and claws. At the last moment, they disengaged, soared to opposite ends of the pit, and landed. They glowered at each other, hissing angrily, poised to strike again.

Just when it seemed their battle was to enter an even more aggressive stage, a thunderous roar echoed from the lowest levels of the Dragon Pit, shaking the very ground beneath their feet. Even Mótsignir quailed before the sound. It was the sort of roar an alpha wolf would unleash to assert its dominance over its rowdy packmates.

The red and black dragons immediately lowered their heads, cowed by the ferocity of whatever fearsome beast dwelled at the bottom of the pit. Without a second thought, they took to the air and fled in opposite directions. As the tension faded, the other dragons soon returned, filling the pit with a vibrant display of colors as they soared, a beautiful contrast to the darkened sky above.

Sigurd began coughing. He'd been so captivated by the breathtaking display of power that he'd neglected to breathe. As he steadied his breath and watched the dragons swoop and spiral, Mótsignir turned and looked at Sigurd, his expression unreadable.

"Do you know why you humans are so fascinated and terrified of dragons?" Mótsignir asked.

"I couldn't say." Sigurd shrugged. "Dragons are the most famous mythical beasts. If you asked a hundred people what constitutes a dragon or what makes them fascinating, you'd likely get a hundred different answers."

"Not inaccurate," Mótsignir agreed. "But what makes the creatures flying around this pit so mesmerizing to your Nordic culture? Why have poets, skalds, and storytellers given so much attention to dragons over birds, snakes, lizards, bears, wolves, and other creatures? What unique abilities do dragons possess that no other animal does?"

"They breathe fire," Sigurd stated simply.

Mótsignir nodded. "Fire is power in its most primal state. It is the most fascinating and awe-inspiring element of nature to humans. Fire burns. It destroys. It can burn down entire forests or raze cities to the ground if used recklessly. In war, soldiers often do precisely that to destroy and demoralize their enemies. But conversely, fire is also life-giving. It nourishes you, providing light and warmth. You use it to cook food, warm your homes, and light your way at night. Blacksmiths use fire to heat their forges and work metal. Farmers use fire to burn away old vegetation to make room for fresh growth. When a great warrior or hero dies valiantly, they place his body on a ship and set it alight to hasten his journey to paradise. Fire is a catalyst for life, destruction, creation, and rebirth. Thus, to humans, a creature that spews fire from its mouth must be terrifying and awe-inspiring, for it commands the very power of creation and destruction. Subsequently, any human who tames or slays such a fearsome beast should be given honor, fame, and glory because, in a sense, they have conquered the most dangerous element in nature. This is partly why dragons are hunted, exploited, and slaughtered everywhere in Midgard. They are just so impressive that it's no surprise that humanity's first instinct is to slaughter them. Many men kill them for no better reason than to name themselves *dragon slayer*."

"What about you 'civilized' dwarves? What do you see when you look at these majestic creatures we ignoramus humans don't?"

"We view them more pragmatically. We don't see dragons as good or evil. They are merely useful creatures with which we share a symbiotic relationship. We give them a place to roost, lay their eggs, and raise their young in peace. We also heal their injuries and nurse them back to health if needed. In return, they provide us with fire to heat our forges and other precious treasures and defend Svartalfheim from any who might try to conquer us. We are not their masters; merely their friends, partners, and equals."

"And did that same attitude apply to Fafnir as well? He was a dragon, too."

"Of course not!" Mótsignir scowled. "Fafnir was a despicable, avaricious creature reviled by dwarves and dragons alike!"

"And yet you're going to execute me for slaying him and Regin. That hardly seems fair."

Mótsignir glowered at Sigurd. "Murder is still murder, even if the victim was a monster. My father harbors no affection whatsoever for Fafnir or Regin. We are doing this simply because it's the law. You murdered our kin and must be punished for it."

"How admirable," Sigurd smirked insolently. "But the realms aren't black and white. You should try exercising some independent thought instead of doing everything *Daddy* tells you to. Ivaldi has got his hand so far up your ass that he's playing your vocal cords like a lyre."

This time, he'd poked the bear too hard. Mótsignir seized Sigurd by the throat and lifted him into the air. Slamming him back against a stone pillar, he squeezed till Sigurd's face turned black. He kicked and writhed for a while, trying fruitlessly to pry the dwarf's grip loose. Even if his wrists weren't manacled, Sigurd would not have been able to break the dwarf's iron grip.

Soon, Mótsignir's rage cooled. He opened his hand, and Sigurd flopped to the stone floor, gasping greedily for air like a fish on dry land.

"You didn't come here to sightsee," Mótsignir warned. "Nor did you come here to trade japes or have a philosophical discussion about the human and dwarven perceptions of dragons. Now hurry and pick the creature of your doom. Don't test our patience."

Sigurd studied the many dragons flying about and resting in the caves. Each one was more magnificent than the last. One dragon stood out with its blood-red scales and vermillion wings, while its mate had stunning scarlet skin and pink membranes. A third was pale blue, adorned with silver markings and sapphire wings, and was flying around the pit alongside a more petite, slender green dragon with pearl horns, crests, and wings in a captivating mating ritual.

The silvery dragon Sigurd had encountered earlier was in its lair teaching its hatchling how to breathe fire and shooting white fireballs from its mouth as a demonstration. Two dragons slept curled up next to each other like cats in a nearby cave. They were a stunning sight with dark blue scales, pale white underbellies, sky-blue wing membranes, purple hair, and black horns and talons. But unlike the others, they seemed to be frost dragons because whenever they exhaled, their breath coated the walls of their lair with ice.

But one particular dragon caught Sigurd's eye as he peered over the edge into the abyss. It slept alone in a vast cave in the lowest echelons of the pit. It was bigger than the others, with golden scales, horns, and pink membranes in its wings. Half of its right horn was chipped off, while the left was unscratched. Sigurd knew at once this was the beast that had cowed the two fighting males and ended their battle with just one roar. This dragon seemed to exude a sense of age, might, and power compared to the others.

"I choose the golden one at the bottom of the pit." Sigurd pointed.

"You picked Old One Horn," Mótsignir noted with approval. "Golden dragons are the largest and most powerful species here in Svartalfheim, and he is one of our oldest and greatest dragons. A worthy choice."

Mótsignir commanded the guards to rouse the golden dragon and escort it to the amphitheater. Afterward, he dragged Sigurd out of the pit and into the tunnel. Sigurd didn't resist but took his time. He relished the feeling of stone beneath his feet, knowing deep down this would be the last time he would ever experience it. He savored each step, a quiet farewell, his toes against the cold ground, the faint breeze stirring his hair. It was bittersweet, knowing he would never feel this with the body he was born with. But for now, he let himself live in the moment, savoring the simple pleasure of walking through the underground city for as long as it lasted.

The stillness was almost palpable as they walked. It seemed every dwarf had flocked to the amphitheater to witness Sigurd's execution, leaving the streets, shops, and homes eerily deserted. But as the silence threatened to become unbearable, a gruff voice shattered the peace. From the shadows of an alley, Brok and Sindri emerged, much to the surprise of Sigurd and Mótsignir. Sindri flashed a mischievous grin at Sigurd before turning his attention to the towering dwarf behind him.

"Mótsignir, you old son of a bitch! How are you?" Brok greeted.

Sigurd cast a wary glance at Mótsignir. He was known as the Bear of Svartalfheim—renowned for his size, prowess, and fiery temper. Ivaldi's eldest son and right-hand man was a stern and humorless being who took offense to any slight. Had Sigurd spoken to him with such disrespect, Mótsignir would have smacked him with enough force to rupture an eardrum, punched him through a wall, or crushed his throat with one hand. Instead, the hulking dwarf smiled back.

"Well met, Brok and Sindri." Mótsignir nodded politely.

Sigurd couldn't believe his eyes. Mótsignir habitually wore an expression as though he were determined to drive his head through a brick wall. But his attitude and demeanor softened as he conversed with the Huldra Brothers.

"Are you... friends?" Sigurd ventured.

"I wouldn't go that far," Mótsignir said. "More like rivals. My brothers and I often compete with them to see who can forge the best items for the Aesir and Vanir. The Huldra Brothers' craftsmanship skills are legendary, enough to rival me and all my brothers put together."

"That's high praise coming from you," Sindri humored.

Mótsignir looked at him, and his smile faded. He looked back at Sigurd. "As much as I enjoy conversing with you both, I'm busy escorting the prisoner."

"We know," Brok acknowledged. "That's why we're here. We wanted to see him before the big execution."

Mótsignir furrowed his brow. "I heard a report from the guards stationed at the mines that you two went in there and met with Sigurd two days ago. They claimed you brought one of his swords with you."

"Oh, that? We just wanted to meet him in person and ask a couple of questions about the sword," Brok explained. "Gram is one of the best swords we ever forged. We wanted to glean all the juicy details of its exploits for our chronicles. We also struck up a contract and came to give him something."

Brok nodded at Sindri. His brother reached into his pouch and produced a corked vial.

"What is that?" Mótsignir demanded.

"It's our homemade brew," Sindri claimed. "Sigurd has been working in the mines for two months without food or water. He paid us a large share of his treasure so we would make him one last brew before he dies."

"This is absurd." Mótsignir scowled. "I won't allow—"

"Would you unclench your anus and get that coal-turned diamond out of your ass!" Brok exclaimed. "The lad is about to be eaten alive by a dragon. I wouldn't wish that on my worst enemy. The least you can do is let him have this last drink. It might help ease the pain he's about to endure."

Mótsignir ground his teeth but sighed and waved his hand. "Make it quick. We're on a tight schedule."

"See, Brok, the Bear of Svartalfheim has a heart, after all." Sindri stepped forward and uncorked the vial. The rancid smell hit Sigurd at once. It smelled like putrid, rotten flesh, and the liquid within had an oily, thick texture like slime. Sigurd almost turned away and gagged as Sindri handed him the ceramic vial. But he kept his disgust and bile in check when he saw Sindri's dour expression.

"You must drink it all," he whispered. "*Every* drop."

Sigurd nodded and took a deep swig. His face reflexively scrounged up at the acrid taste, and he almost spat it back out. The potion was the most rancid thing he had ever tasted. The cold water from the Well of Destiny had tasted like all the best things Sigurd had known. But this potion tasted like all the *worst* things condensed into liquid form. Salty like urine, earthy like mud, slimy like a hagfish, and tasted like a rancid, maggot-infested carcass left to rot in the sun.

His taste buds screamed at him to stop ingesting the vile sludge and spit it out. His innards twisted and begged for mercy with every sip. Yet he forced himself to drink. He drained the vial and dropped it, doubling over, coughing and wheezing as tendrils of fire spread throughout his chest and coiled around his organs.

"What's going on?" Mótsignir demanded. "What have you done?"

"He's fine," Brok said. "The lad's just a lightweight. He's too accustomed to that *juice* they drink in Midgard. He can't handle a true dwarven drink. Here, I'll help him stand."

Brok kneeled and helped Sigurd to his feet. He grabbed Sigurd's manacled hands and pressed something into his right palm. Without looking down, Sigurd closed his fingers around it. He glanced questioningly at Brok. The dwarf met his eyes and nodded encouragingly as he shook Sigurd's manacled hand.

"Take care, Sigurd," Brok said as he stepped away.

Mótsignir watched as the Huldra Brothers walked away. Sigurd sighed. *He hasn't noticed.* He ran his fingers over the white mushroom hidden in his right hand. If it was as bad as the potion had been, he might retch, but there was no turning back now. As Mótsignir looked away to bid farewell to the Huldra Brothers, Sigurd feigned a cough, covered his mouth with his hands, and consumed the mushroom.

The mushroom didn't taste as terrible as he thought it would. Its potent, earthy flavor was tolerable, but its rubbery texture made it difficult to chew and swallow. After a while, Sigurd felt the mushroom reacting to the potion in his stomach. Gradually, the tendrils of fire coursing throughout his body cooled and dissipated. But they weren't entirely gone.

When the Huldra Brothers had vanished from sight down an alley, Mótsignir ordered Sigurd to resume moving. Sigurd felt the potion's effects as they walked to the amphitheater. A wave of weakness crashed over him, leaving him numb and dizzy. He staggered drunkenly against a nearby stone wall. His limbs felt unnaturally cold, as if all his body's strength, energy, and warmth were being siphoned toward a single point in his abdomen.

"Keep moving!" Mótsignir shoved Sigurd's shoulder. Sigurd staggered forward and stopped himself from tripping.

The crippling feeling soon passed. "Yes, sir," Sigurd replied.

***

They quietly returned to the amphitheater, and Sigurd dutifully took his place upon the mural in the center of the arena. Mótsignir gathered the chains, but Ivaldi called out to him before he could shackle Sigurd.

"That won't be necessary," Ivaldi said.

Mótsignir looked questioningly at the dwarf king. "But, Father, what if he—"

"He won't run away," Ivaldi assured. "Take a gander at his face. Those aren't the eyes of a man who's afraid to die. Remove the manacles from his wrists as well. Those won't be necessary, either."

"As you wish, Father." Mótsignir reached into his pocket, brought out the key, and unshackled the manacles from Sigurd's wrists. The metal restraints fell to the floor with a satisfying clank.

Sigurd turned and bowed to the dwarf king. "Thank you, Ivaldi."

"For what?" Ivaldi asked. "I'm just making sure that the dragon that eats you won't have metal in its stomach for the next few weeks."

"How considerate," Sigurd said sarcastically while rubbing his chaffed wrists. He turned his back to the dwarf king and his court and kneeled on the mural, ignoring the mocking and jeering from the dwarves. Although he was about to endure an unlawful and unfair execution, Sigurd behaved with dignity. He would meet the gaze of these raucous dwarves with composure and a stoic face. He wouldn't display an ounce of fear.

As Sigurd closed his eyes, waiting for the dragon to arrive, he reminisced about his visit to Sinfjotli in prison yesterday, mulling over everything he'd told him. He'd told Sinfjotli he'd do whatever it would take to attain Valhalla. But now that he was here waiting for the cup of agony he had requested, his resolve crumbled. The rational part of his brain told him to run. But there was no backing out now.

Sigurd squeezed his fists and tried to quell the fear by reminding himself he wasn't the first to face this harrowing ordeal or even the first member of his family to do it.

You and Sinfjotli survived this ordeal, Father. But there's no guarantee that I will. Or that I'll still be me afterward.

His thoughts drifted to his dear friends in the underworld. *"I think you both have what it takes to become the first to escape Helheim,"* Baldur had told them. *"You are skilled warriors and have won battles that lesser men have called unwinnable."*

He found little solace in that. He wondered if Baldur had found his children yet in the underworld. Then he thought of his long-lost daughter, Aslaug.

I never got to hold her. I never even knew she existed until after I died. Sigurd grimaced. *Just once would have been enough. I wish I'd had the chance to see you just once.*

THOOM! THOOM! THOOM!

The ground quaked. Sigurd cracked open his eyes, and his heart raced as he beheld the creature of his impending doom enter the amphitheater.

Up close, Old One Horn was even more impressive than Sigurd had imagined. He easily outclassed all the other dragons in the Dragon Pit. His size and weight were simply staggering, with a length of two hundred feet from tail to snout. As he strode into the amphitheater, his massive frame cast a formidable shadow upon the ground that enveloped every onlooker. Awe and terror gripped Sigurd. The sword-like teeth gleamed menacingly; his massive reptilian head alone must have been thirty feet. But it was his eyes—piercing blue and glowing with an otherworldly light that unsettled him the most—they seemed to stare right through him. Dark brown claws, each large enough to easily crush boulders, dug into the ground with each step. His red wings unfurled like banners of war, stark against his light underbelly. Tufts of red fur adorned the dragon's elbows and tail, a contrast to his otherwise imposing form.

Age had left its mark on him. Scales were missing in places, and old battle scars crisscrossed his neck and limbs. His once-mighty horns bore the proof he was a veteran of many fights—chipped, cracked, broken. One of the two enormous horns jutting from the back of his head had been shattered entirely, earning him his nickname. Yet, even with these signs of wear and tear, Old One Horn remained a terrifying force of nature, a battle-worn titan.

The dragon sniffed the air, then looked Sigurd straight in the eyes. As its jaws parted, revealing rows of teeth, Sigurd felt like a snake's prey staring into the gaping maw of oblivion. The dwarves roared as the golden behemoth advanced. Out of the corner of his eyes, Sigurd noticed Sinfjotli standing amongst the crowd, flanked by Brok and Sindri. He couldn't hear anything over the raucous dwarven assembly and the approaching dragon, but he could see their lips moving. Perhaps they were praying or chanting some unknown verse that was part of the Trial.

Odin, please make this work, Sigurd prayed as the dragon drew nearer. The beast lunged forward, and Sigurd closed his eyes as its jaws closed around him.

He tried not to scream. He wanted to remain calm and as motionless as a statue as the dragon devoured him piecemeal. But being eaten alive was not something *anyone* could endure. The pain of having his left arm torn from his shoulder, teeth sinking deep into his flesh, and his organs spilling out of his abdomen was too much to bear. His mind was ablaze with pain, unlike anything he had felt before. A raw, piercing wail ripped from his throat, a banshee's cry of agony, fear, and fury mingled in one dreadful shriek. It swelled louder and louder, a hoarse yell of pain.

The incomprehensible pain wasn't even the worst part. The worst part was that Sigurd couldn't faint. He'd hoped the blood loss, the sheer agony, would send him into shock, granting him the mercy of losing consciousness. But the dragon's bites had the opposite effect. The maddening sensations were too intense to allow Sigurd such an escape. Thus, he remained aware through it all. Every waking moment. Every vicious tear of flesh. Every ripped muscle from bone.

As the dragon feasted on his body, Sigurd clung to Sinfjotli's instructions from yesterday, if only to distract himself from the pain: *"For the Trial of Svarblood to activate, you must first eat a Psilocybe mushroom and drink a potion made from hazel bark, shavings of amber, and a subterranean variety of purple foxglove. Obtaining them all here in Svartalfheim should be easy enough if the Huldra Brothers are helping us. Next, you must devour a heart belonging to the species you wish to be reborn as. Since you already bathed in Fafnir's blood and ate his heart long ago, I suppose this condition has already been met. After that, all that's left to do is let yourself be devoured. From there, it's a battle between your soul and the dragon's. I can't say what you'll experience. Every person has their own unique experience. Just know that if it works, you will be reborn."*

Those words proved to be of little comfort to Sigurd as the dragon bit off his legs just below his knees. Old One Horn struck again, higher this time. Everything below his ribs was gone in an instant; his entrails dangled from within his torn belly like burned black snakes. Blood sprayed everywhere. Shock and blood loss consumed him. And with the last of his strength, he whispered Brynhild's name.

The last thing Sigurd felt was the dragon's jaws closing around his head, enveloping him in darkness as its teeth sank into his neck and shoulders.

Chapter Ten

An Old Friend

Sigurd's senses came alive as he awoke to the feeling of something cool and wet enveloping his bare skin. As he sat up, he discovered he was submerged naked in a pool of knee-deep water.

Sigurd emerged from the pool, gasping for air like a desperate fish. He had been submerged for what felt like an eternity, and his lungs burned with the need for oxygen. As he crawled out of the water, cool air rushed into his chest, and he heaved a deep sigh of relief as he inhaled. His heart was beating wildly in his chest, and he felt disoriented as he looked around, trying to make sense of his surroundings.

"Where am I?" Sigurd wondered aloud as water trickled down his neck and back. He was inside a vast limestone cavern filled with jagged stalagmites and stalactites. But it wasn't the cavernous amphitheater he had been executed in moments ago. This cavern looked old and uninhabited.

A glimmer of light caught Sigurd's eye.

He turned, and his jaw dropped. Piles upon piles of gold and treasure sprawled across the floor of the cave—gold, silver, and bronze trinkets, ornately decorated jugs, emerald necklaces, sapphires the size of a man's fist, a diamond and ruby encrusted crown, ornate pieces of armor, swords with bejeweled pommels, crucible steel daggers, jade animal statues, and a sea of golden coins and trinkets everywhere he turned. By his estimate, at least three thousand tons of gold and treasure lay before him.

"Wait a minute!" Sigurd gasped. "I know this gold. I remember this cave!"

There was no doubt about it. He was standing inside the Cavern of Gnitaheath!

"Oh, what delicious irony," a voice snickered in the gloom. "You slew me, bathed in my blood, ate my heart, and became renowned throughout the land as 'Sigurd the Dragon Slayer.' And now here you are after being devoured piecemeal by another dragon."

Sigurd's blood turned to ice in his veins. "That voice. I—I remember that voice!"

He turned around slowly. Sure enough, the mighty dragon he had slain long ago lay sprawled beside his golden hoard. He looked exactly as Sigurd remembered with his long, scaly, and stocky reptilian body. Four scaly legs anchored its frame, the front two shaped as hands. Two enormous bat-like wings jutted from his back while a sinuous, snake-like tail coiled beside him. A crest of spurs adorned his head, flanked by two prominent six-foot horns. His scales were a reddish-black, fading to a dark underside. Black spines and spikes lined the ridge of his back and the length of his serpentine neck.

But his most distinguishing feature was his gleaming orange-yellow eyes. They were colored like fire, with slit pupils with intricate, keyhole-like shapes. Sigurd could never forget those fearsome eyes.

"Fafnir." Sigurd gasped in disbelief and disgust. "This isn't... you can't be real. You're dead! You've been dead for years."

Fafnir let out a chuckle that was as smooth as silk, contrasting with his monstrous size. "Am I dead in your memory? In your heart? Because if the answer to either question is no, then I am not dead. People truly die when everyone forgets them. But thanks to you killing me, both our names shall live eternally across the Nine Realms."

Sigurd shook his head. "This must be a dream. I'm just imagining this. Unless... is this part of the Trial of Svarblood?"

The dragon nodded ever so slightly. "This place, Hugrheim, is the world of your inner mind. You can think of it as the space between reality and the afterlife."

"Then why are you here?" Sigurd pressed. "Are you supposed to be the physical manifestation of Old One Horn's soul?"

"Perhaps," Fafnir answered with a hint of playful mystery. "Or maybe I've been here all along. Perhaps eating my heart all those years ago allowed part of my essence to live on within you, just waiting for a chance to resurface. But who am I to look a gift horse in the mouth? We *finally* get to see each other again after all this time!"

Fafnir leaned in with his long serpentine neck to get a better look at Sigurd. His pink meaty tongue dangled out the side of his snout through jagged teeth as he examined Sigurd with mute appeal.

"You've fallen quite far, Sigurd." Fafnir gestured to the ugly scar on Sigurd's chest with his tongue. "Imagine what your epitaph must say. 'Sigurd the Dragon Slayer, killed because of the scheming machinations of a vengeful valkyrie, a jealous brother-in-law, and an avaricious mother-in-law.' Tell me, was taking my hoard of treasure worth it? In the end, it got you, your beloved Brynhild, your son, and your treacherous whore of a wife killed."

"Be silent, Fafnir!" Sigurd jerked to his feet, sending a wash of cool water across the pool, and gestured to the mountains of gold and treasure beside the dragon. "You murdered your father for this treasure and allowed your greed to turn you into a dragon! You have no right to chastise me, monster!"

"Oh, I don't know, Sigurd." Fafnir snickered. "*You* killed *me*, remember? You took my life, my heart, and my treasure. Now you're trying to take over the body of another dragon to cheat death and weasel your way out of a blood debt to my grandfather. It seems like you're the actual monster here."

Sigurd grimaced.

"And if you shelved your indignation for a moment, you'd realize I have every right to reprimand you," Fafnir continued in a harsher tone. "The very reason you're in this sticky situation and on this quest for redemption is that you disregarded my final warning."

He rose on all four legs and walked toward the mountains of treasure. Fafnir scooped up a pile of wealth, letting the gold and jewels slip through his clawed fingers like water droplets.

"As I died, I warned you that although there was enough gold in my hoard to make your wealth the envy of the entire world, this same gold would lead to your death and the deaths of all who owned it. I also warned you that Regin was planning to kill you now that you had served your purpose and that you'd be better off riding away on your horse and never setting eyes on Andvari's cursed hoard or his ring, Andvaranaut. But you defied my warning, slew my brother, and took the gold and my cursed ring, anyway. Given all that ensued, I'd argue I have every right to condemn you for being an utter fool."

His venomous words stung deeper than any blade could. If Sigurd hadn't taken the gold, then perhaps Gudrun's mother, that damnable sorceress Grimhild, wouldn't have forced Sigurd into marrying into their family by erasing his memories of Brynhild. He might have been able to keep his vows to return to Brynhild, live out the rest of his days peacefully with her and their daughter, and eventually die fighting heroically for a noble cause. In that scenario, Gudrun, her brothers, and the rest of the Gjukungs might not have suffered their sad fates. Their bloodlines wouldn't have been extinguished, and their kingdoms wouldn't have been obliterated by King Atli.

But alas, Sigurd hadn't listened. He had taken Fafnir's cursed gold and brought with it all the tragedy that followed. Fafnir was absolutely right. He was a fool.

As Sigurd hung his head in shame, he noticed a glimmer of light in the rippling water. Gram lay near his feet beneath the water's surface. The blade glowed bright blue.

Sigurd stared at it in abject confusion and then smiled. Even in death, his trusty sword remained by his side.

"I killed you once, Fafnir," he said as he retrieved Gram from the pool. "I will gladly do it again."

"The only reason you slew me last time was that you caught me off guard!" Fafnir showed his underbelly and gestured to a scar on his left breast, nearest his heart. "Instead of facing me like a true warrior, you dug a pit and waited inside it like a gopher until I walked right over you and then stabbed me in the heart. Then you waited until I was too weak from blood loss to defend myself before you landed the killing blow. But this time will be different, Sigurd. You have nowhere to hide or any old men to provide you with sage advice. More importantly, this time, you have my full attention!"

Fafnir unfurled his wings and reared on his hind legs in an intimidating battle stance. The dragon towered over Sigurd like one of the City of the Lost's skyscrapers, enveloping him in an enormous shadow. Fafnir's body looked almost humanoid from this angle, like a giant man who had grown scales, sprouted wings, and a tail.

"The rules of the Trial of Svarblood are simple, Sigurd. It's a fight to the death between souls to decide which soul keeps Old One Horn's body. If you die, your soul will be destroyed, and there won't be an afterlife. But if you win, then you *might* be reborn and become this dragon!"

Sigurd grinned. "Good! Nothing simpler."

CHAPTER ELEVEN

THE BATTLE THAT NEVER WAS

As man and dragon clashed, Sigurd's heart surged with joy and excitement. Slaying Fafnir had been his most celebrated and significant accomplishment in life. But deep down, Sigurd felt the glory was unearned. He knew his victory had been tainted by a dirty sneak attack and often wondered what might have happened had he faced Fafnir head-on like a true warrior. Late at night, as he lay awake, lost in thought, Sigurd couldn't help but imagine how their battle might've unfolded if he had fought Fafnir properly.

He got his answer in his second death.

Fafnir tried to crush Sigurd beneath his clawed hand. Sigurd pirouetted out of danger and slashed the dragon's scaly palm. As Fafnir hissed, Sigurd disengaged and rushed toward the dragon's chest, hoping to strike the scar on its haunches. But in one lightning-quick motion, Fafnir outstretched his wings and, with a single flap, generated a blast of air that slammed into Sigurd like a battering ram, sending him flying into the stone wall of the cave.

His lower back howled in pain, but it couldn't stop Sigurd from laughing gleefully. He was terrified. The stakes were incredibly high. If he died here, there wouldn't be an afterlife. But he also felt so happy. Because now, he got to experience the battle he'd dreamed of.

As Sigurd scrambled to his feet and closed the distance, Fafnir tried to bite him, rearing his neck back and striking like a viper. But Sigurd evaded the dragon's teeth. Frustrated, Fafnir tried to eviscerate Sigurd with his claws. Sigurd sidestepped the attack. He then rushed forward, vaulted off the dragon's left arm, and slashed the dragon's head in a powerful downward strike with Gram.

Fafnir roared. He whipped his long neck to the right and then bashed the left side of his head into Sigurd, sending him flying across the cave. Sigurd clambered to his feet as Fafnir hissed. His left eye was gone. One of his horns had been sliced off, and the dragon had a jagged rent down the left side of his head almost three feet long. Fresh blood poured from the wound and his empty eye socket, hot and smoking.

"You will pay for that!" Fafnir hissed. He spread his wings and took to the air. Hovering forty feet above the ground, Fafnir reared his head back and spewed a purple gas from his mouth.

Poisonous gas! Sigurd realized. He had mere seconds to take a deep breath before the poison cloud enveloped him.

Unfortunately, holding his breath wouldn't be enough because the gas was highly acidic. Sigurd's eyes began burning, and his skin felt like it was melting as it sizzled and smoked. The foul odor overwhelmed his nose even though he was covering his face and holding his breath. At first, it smelled like rotten eggs. Then it became sickeningly sweet, like oil.

The gas is flammable! Sigurd remembered. He snapped open his eyes. Fafnir was now hovering near the cave's ceiling, soaring high above the gas. His belly and throat glowed with red light from within. Panic seized Sigurd as he realized Fafnir was about to ignite the gas.

"BURN!" Fafnir roared. He reared his head back and unleashed a mastodonic column of flame.

Out of sheer desperation, Sigurd dove into the pool of water he had emerged from just as the gas ignited into a massive explosion. The fire cloud spread through the cave, singeing the limestone walls and melting some of the gold trinkets in Fafnir's hoard. The blast brought the pool water to a boil and the heat turned his skin red like a boiled lobster in a pot.

Better to be boiled than roasted outside, Sigurd told himself as he held his breath under the steaming hot water, waiting for the explosion to subside.

When it was over, Fafnir landed on the cave floor and began searching for Sigurd. Sigurd was about to emerge and resume their fight when an idea formed in his mind. He had a golden opportunity to catch Fafnir off guard. So he compelled himself to remain underwater even as his lungs began screaming at him for air. He ignored the pain and waited as Fafnir prowled the cave.

"Where are you?" the dragon hissed angrily.

Sigurd watched from beneath the water's surface as the dragon scanned the cave, waiting for his chance and praying that Fafnir didn't notice him. He held his breath until Fafnir stepped over the pool, the dragon's underbelly and haunches directly above.

Now! Sigurd burst from the water and thrust Gram deep into Fafnir's belly just as he had done long ago at Gnitaheath. Blood splashed across Sigurd's face and blinded him as Fafnir roared.

Something hard and sharp slammed into Sigurd's chest, sending him tumbling backward onto the limestone floor. Fafnir laughed as Sigurd clambered to his feet. He wiped the steaming dragon blood from his eyes and discovered why.

Sigurd hadn't stabbed Fafnir in his underbelly! He had missed and thrust Gram into the thick muscle of the dragon's left haunch.

Sigurd wondered what had happened. Had the refraction in the water thrown off his aim? No, that wasn't it. Fafnir *expected* that sneak attack.

"Didn't I tell you things would be different this time?" The dragon hissed. "You can't kill me with the same dirty trick twice!"

Fafnir whipped his tail as fast as a thunderbolt, slamming it against Sigurd's chest, and sending him crashing into the mountain of treasure on the other side of the cave.

Stabbing pains surged throughout Sigurd's body. Crashing into the mountain of treasure was like slamming into a solid gold block. Worse, the gold was still steaming hot from Fafnir's earlier explosion. The searing metal scorched Sigurd's bare skin as if freshly smelted in a forge. Gold coins stuck to his arms and back, branding him with their blistering heat.

Sigurd bit his lips to stifle a cry as he clambered to his feet. He brushed off several gold coins still sticking to his skin and rubbed the painful second-degree burns they left behind. The gold beneath his feet felt smoking hot and seared the soles of his bare feet. He swallowed the pain as he clambered down the mountain of treasure and stepped onto the much cooler limestone floor. He couldn't afford to lose focus.

Fafnir was still standing at the other end of the cave. The dragon's wounds were hot and smoking. His left eye was now an empty hole crusted over with black blood, but his smoldering right eye burned orangey-yellow like a fiery pit as he glowered at Sigurd.

Fafnir reared up on all four legs and charged. But the dragon abruptly stumbled and collapsed when he was only halfway across the cave. Sigurd saw why—Gram was still embedded in Fafnir's left hind leg. The wound wasn't lethal, but it was enough to cripple the dragon's mobility.

Frustrated, Fafnir unleashed a torrent of flames. Sigurd narrowly evaded the blast by diving behind a large boulder near the mountain of treasure. But he knew he wasn't safe. Fafnir's flames were hot enough to melt the limestone walls and reduced the stalagmites jutting from the surrounding ground into puddles of slag. Soon, even the basalt rock he hid behind began to liquefy.

As the rock melted like a wax candle, Sigurd saw Fafnir's belly and throat glowing red. He dashed for cover as the dragon unleashed another furnace blast of red flame so bright it lit up the cavern like a second sun. Sigurd frantically scurried along the cavern's wall as the torrent of fire chased after him.

He made it to the other side of the cavern, saw a large boulder almost ten feet tall and weighing three tons, and dove behind it just as Fafnir unleashed another torrent of flame. The boulder held, shielding him from the inferno—at least for now.

The air grew thick with smoke and brimstone. As Sigurd pressed his back against the boulder, he cursed how this battle had taken a turn for the worse. He was naked, both literally and figuratively. He had no armor to protect him from the flames. No weapon to strike back. He knew from experience that Fafnir's scales were tougher than steel. Gram was the only blade sharp enough to wound the beast, but it was still lodged in Fafnir's leg. Retrieving it wasn't an option. Fafnir had secured the perfect vantage point. He loomed in the center of the cave, where he could see Sigurd's approach and would reduce him to ashes in seconds with his flames.

Sigurd considered leaving the cave and taking the fight elsewhere. But there was no way to escape this place. Most caverns of this size had a series of twisty passageways that either led deeper underground or connected to the surface. But this cavern seemed to be a vast, sealed chamber. There was no trace of an entrance or an exit anywhere to be found along the smooth limestone walls.

With no way to escape or fight back, all Sigurd could do was scurry along the walls and duck for cover as the dragon continued blasting flames at him. He knew he couldn't do this forever. Fafnir's flames had already reduced half the stalagmites and rock formations in the cavern into puddles of slag. Sigurd was running out of shelter. Soon, he'd have nowhere to hide.

Sigurd paused. There was still one place untouched by the flames. He glanced at the towering mountains of gold and treasure on the far side of the cave. In life, Fafnir had jealously guarded that famous hoard like a rabid watchdog. He slept upon it every night and killed anyone who strayed too close to Gnitaheath. Would he risk destroying his precious treasure to kill

Sigurd? Was Fafnir's greed greater than his bloodlust, greater than his desire for revenge?

Sigurd didn't have time to consider. An enormous serpentine shadow loomed over him. He glanced up—Fafnir was there, looking down on him with a gleam in his eye. The dragon had stealthily approached the boulder while he was still spewing his flames. His roars and the fiery explosions had masked his footsteps, preventing Sigurd from noticing. In the smoldering orange pit of Fafnir's remaining eye, Sigurd saw his own reflection—small, weak, scared. He cast aside his fear, scrambled to his feet, and bolted for the treasure just as the dragon swiped its claws.

Sigurd had reacted too late. The dragon's claws shredded through the stone boulder like knives slicing through wet clay and raked Sigurd's lower back. He stumbled, collapsing face-first onto the stone ground.

A tsunami of blinding pain crashed over him as he struggled to rise. Fafnir's claws had missed Sigurd's spine by a mere inch as they shredded the muscles of his lower back and left hip. The wounds felt deep; when Sigurd removed his hand, it was slick with blood.

He was severely hurt, but he knew he had to get up. The stakes of this battle were too high. If he died here, then that was it. There wouldn't be an afterlife, and Sinfjotli would have to fend for himself.

By force of will alone, Sigurd lifted himself off the ground. His left hip and leg were numb and weak. So he shifted all his weight onto his right leg and staggered to one knee.

He didn't have time to fully stand up. A massive shadow rippled across his face. Sigurd glanced up. Fafnir loomed above him, his long serpentine neck bent back like an archer's bow.

Realizing what was about to happen, Sigurd summoned all the strength he could muster and leaped to the right just as Fafnir snapped shut. The dragon's teeth missed his left foot by an inch.

Sigurd hit the ground rolling. He looked up. Gram was sticking out from Fafnir's leg mere feet away. His heart filled with hope. But Fafnir veered around before he could reach for his trusty weapon, and Sigurd had to retreat even further when the dragon's claws came slashing toward him once more.

Fafnir hissed angrily and lashed his tail sideways. But Sigurd was ready. He jumped as high as he could manage with his injuries, and the tail zipped harmlessly beneath his feet.

The dragon roared with black fury. That single evasion seemed to infuriate Fafnir more than any other wound Sigurd had dealt.

"I'm sick of you scrambling around like a rat!" Fafnir bellowed. "No more running away!"

Fafnir spread his wings, took to the air, and unleashed a torrent of flames. But he wasn't aiming at Sigurd. Sigurd's eyes followed the inferno—straight to the mountains of treasure. A massive fireball engulfed the hoard, its intense heat liquefying gold, silver, and jewels into a molten flood. The searing tide of gold poured down the mound, racing across the limestone like an unstoppable avalanche, consuming everything in its fiery path.

Panic clawed at Sigurd's chest. Fafnir clearly intended to turn the entire cave floor into a lake of molten gold, leaving Sigurd nowhere to run.

Or so he thought. Before Fafnir could fly higher to safety, Sigurd dashed forward, grabbing hold of the dragon's tail just as the tidal wave barreled toward him. The sharp reptilian scales burned and tore into Sigurd's fingers. But he held fast, gripping them so firmly that his palms started bleeding. Fafnir thrashed, whipping his tail violently in midair, trying to shake him off. Sigurd reached out and yanked Gram free from the dragon's hind leg. With renewed determination, he scrambled up the tail and sprinted across the dragon's back. With a powerful strike, he severed one of Fafnir's wings. As the dragon roared, Sigurd jumped with all his might, grabbed hold of a large limestone stalactite hanging from the ceiling, and watched the dragon plummet.

Fafnir crashed into the pool of molten gold with such force that the entire cavern trembled. Stalactites shattered and rained down like spears. The dragon roared as he sank beneath the sea of gold and vanished from sight. Sigurd watched as the golden flood spread throughout the cave and began to cool and solidify into a gleaming polished floor.

Half a heartbeat later, Fafnir burst from the molten pool, wailing in agony. Scolding gold clung to his scales like liquid fire, hardening in jagged burning patches. "It burns!" he wailed, voice raw with torment. "Argh, it burns!"

As the dragon writhed, Sigurd saw his chance. He released his hold of the stalactite and plummeted headlong toward Fafnir. He channeled all his remaining strength into a single slash. Gram sliced through molten gold, scales, flesh, and bone, ripping deep into the dragon's body, carving through internal organs, leaving a jagged twenty-foot rent down Fafnir's underbelly.

It was a devastating attack, but as Sigurd crashed headlong into the solidified golden floor, he realized he hadn't thoroughly thought his plan through.

The next time Sigurd opened his eyes, he found himself sprawled on his back on the warm gold floor. He almost blacked out from the pain—every inch of him screamed. His ribs, limbs, his entire body felt broken. Heat pulsed from his skin, his vision tinged red. A hazy memory surfaced—Fafnir's jagged wound erupting like a geyser, boiling dragon blood splattering him in right before he slammed into the ground.

The dragon lay nearby, disemboweled and bleeding from scores of wounds. Despite his injuries, Fafnir noticed Sigurd writhing and slowly lifted his head off the ground. His orange-yellow eye gleamed, but not with malice—with something that looked almost like pride and admiration.

"That was a splendid attack, Sigurd. I expected nothing less from you. It's a shame we never got to fight like this long ago."

Sigurd didn't reply. He was exhausted, badly wounded, and covered head to toe in the dragon's steaming blood. His legs felt broken. His vision blurred as steaming blood burned his eyes like thousands of tiny molten blades.

With great effort, Sigurd rolled onto his stomach. Through his blurry red vision, he spotted the pool of water he'd emerged from. The only section of the cave floor that hadn't been covered in liquid gold. Dragging his broken body, he crawled toward it, desperate to clean his eyes.

He plunged his hands in, splashing the cool liquid onto his face and washed out his stinging eyes. His reflection changed shape in the ripples of the water. When the water settled and became still, the reflection staring back at him was not his own. It looked scaley and reptilian.

"Is... is it over?" Sigurd turned back to Fafnir and stumbled. His movements were sluggish, almost like he was trying to move through deep water, and his voice sounded slurred.

"Almost," Fafnir assured. "There is one last step left. Hold still." With that as his only warning, Fafnir lunged from the ground where he lay defeated, grabbed Sigurd with his claws, and began devouring him.

"What are you doing?" Sigurd screamed. "STOP! Nnngggghh!!" He tried to struggle but found himself unable to move.

"Don't struggle," Fafnir said. "The pain you feel... is merely the agony... of birth."

CHAPTER TWELVE

A WORD ONCE GIVEN

"Hghhghhgghh!" Sigurd gasped, awake.

He was back in the dwarven amphitheater in Svartalfheim, lying naked on the cold stone floor. He was covered head to toe in steaming blood. His skin burned, and steam billowed from every pore. About twenty feet away, Sigurd could see the mural where the dragon had devoured him, now painted in a puddle of his blood.

"Sigurd!" a voice called joyfully. Sinfjotli was pushing his way through the dwarven assembly. He vaulted over the front row and dashed across the arena. He helped Sigurd to sit up straight and wrapped his shoulders with a cloak.

"B-Brother, what... what happened?" Sigurd asked between ragged breaths.

"I won't sugarcoat this," Sinfjotli forewarned. "You were eaten alive by Old One Horn. The dragon left no trace of you behind, aside from that puddle of blood over yonder. Then it started walking back to the Dragon Pit. At first, I feared the Trial hadn't worked and you had just died a pointless death. I thought about how I would make Ivaldi pay for this when the dragon roared in pain. It started flying, then collapsed to the ground and began writhing in agony. It clawed at its belly as if something was tearing it apart from the inside. Then its head started changing shape during its death throes, and I could see a human face forming in its snout. After that, the dragon stopped moving. Its

111

body shrank, its wings receded into its body, and it morphed into a humanoid form. And now here you are."

"I remember!" Sigurd shrieked as he clutched the shoulder the dragon had torn off. "Gods, I remember everything!"

"I know," Sinfjotli said. "But the important thing is you survived."

Sinfjotli paused and then burst out laughing as if he had only now grasped the full reality of the situation.

"You did it!" Sinfjotli laughed in disbelief and joy. "You crazy son of a bitch, you actually did it! You passed the Trial of Svarblood!"

But at what cost? Sigurd wondered as he clutched the scars on his shoulders and neck where the dragon had bitten him. There was nothing physically wrong with him. His body was completely whole again, and all his limbs were intact. But he would never forget how it felt being eaten alive. Those phantom pains would haunt him for the rest of his days, and the scars he had received from the ordeal would never fade.

The amphitheater was eerily quiet. The dwarves had cheered raucously as the dragon devoured him piecemeal. But all the smiles had died. Every dwarf in the assembly stared at him with wide eyes and gaping mouths. Even Ivaldi and Mótsignir were dumbfounded by what they had just witnessed.

Meanwhile, Brok dragged Sindri's limp body through the assembly toward an exit. Sindri had presumably fainted from watching the grizzly execution. Brok winked at Sigurd and gave a congratulatory smile before dragging his brother's unconscious body out of the amphitheater.

As he stared at the assembly of stunned dwarves, Sigurd noticed Sinfjotli was standing a few feet away from him. His eyes were full of concern, but he looked nervous and wary.

"What's wrong?" Sigurd asked. "Why are you standing so far from me?"

"It's just a precaution," Sinfjotli replied. "Forgive me. It's just that even if someone passes the Trial of Svarblood, it normally takes their soul several days to adjust to their new body. At first, it feels like your brain's full of bugs.

You can't think. You just want to lash out. I expected you to go on a bloody rampage and kill every dwarf here. Instead, you instantly regained your sanity along with your human form."

"I don't plan on killing anyone yet," Sigurd assured.

Sinfjotli sighed, and his body became more relaxed. "How are you feeling overall?"

Sigurd examined the steaming palm of his right hand. "I feel... hot. It feels like a fire is burning beneath my skin and a bonfire raging inside my chest. But it doesn't hurt. Aside from that, I don't feel any different from before."

"What about your senses?" Sinfjotli inquired.

Sigurd concentrated. His vision was as sharp as ever. His hearing felt more acute. But more importantly, his sense of smell had radically intensified. As Sigurd inhaled through his nostrils, he noticed he could smell things much better.

Unfortunately, he came to rue that new heightened sense when he noticed the dwarves' musk.

"By the gods!" Sigurd gasped, covering his nose. "Those dwarves smell rancid! One smells like someone vomited a week-old corpse and then took a shit on it!"

"You'll get used to it." Sinfjotli chuckled. "Let's get you some help. You need a bath and possibly a potent drink."

"No!" Sigurd refused. "No, I'm okay. Before anything, I will collect on the debt I'm owed."

Sigurd stood up and pointed at Ivaldi, who, along with the rest of the dwarves, had remained wide-eyed and speechless.

"A deal's a deal, Ivaldi," Sigurd shouted. "I allowed myself to be eaten by a dragon. Now, keep your word and fulfill your end of the agreement! Absolve me of the blood debt!"

Ivaldi's shocked expression turned to rage, and for a tense moment, it looked like he was on the verge of ordering his sons to kill Sigurd anyway. Instead, he closed his eyes and sighed.

"A word once given," Ivaldi grumbled. He rose from his throne and hoisted his gigantic hammer high above him. "Sigurd, son of Sigmund, on behalf of all dwarves, I, Ivaldi, king of Svartalfheim, forgive the blood debt for the deaths of Regin and Fafnir!"

Ivaldi slammed the butt of his hammer down with a loud THUMP that caused the ground to shake and a stalactite from the ceiling to crash to the floor.

"You're not finished," Sigurd reminded him. "You still have my third request to fulfill."

Ivaldi shot him a murderous look for his insolent tone, but Sigurd knew the dwarf king could do nothing but pout. Morally, he was in checkmate. He'd given his word without fathoming that it could backfire, and he was now honor-bound to keep his promises. Ivaldi tapped the butt of his hammer to the ground twice. "Mótsignir, Billingr, Dáinn, Durinn, Dúrnir, Gandalf, and Dvalinn. Come with me, my sons. We have much work to do."

CHAPTER THIRTEEN

❖◆❖

A "PERFECT" WEAPON

"**A**re you finished yet?" Sinfjotli asked.

"Not yet," Sindri replied.

"You've been forging nonstop for two consecutive days! You haven't even taken a break to eat, drink, or piss. Surely it's ready by now?"

"It'll be ready when we *decide* it's ready," Brok replied sharply. "For dwarves, forging a weapon is a sacred event, like a marriage or a child's birth. You can't rush these things."

"Hmm," Sinfjotli grumbled.

This was the most Brok and Sindri had spoken since they started forging. The dwarves took their work that seriously.

After the Trial of Svarblood, the Huldra Brothers brought them to their workshop. They promised Sinfjotli they'd make him a mighty weapon and got straight to work. They had spent two whole days and nights single-mindedly smelting metal ingots without taking a break to eat or sleep. If Sinfjotli tried speaking to them, they would give him brief and laconic replies and never look away from their work.

Sinfjotli had observed the smelting process more out of boredom than genuine interest. It seemed interesting enough. Brok and Sindri created an alloy made from several substances, including obsidian, dark steel ingots, and bronze, to make the metal for this unique weapon. They used some kind of chemical to break down each hard substance into a liquid form and used runic magic to blend them. Brok then infused fires from Muspelheim into the combined liquid before it was rendered solid again with another strange chemical and water the dwarves claimed came from the Vimur, the largest of the Elivagar Rivers. Sindri promised him this process would imbue the metal with magic.

It was now the third day of the forging process. While Brok melted down the ingots and smelted them into what Sinfjotli assumed was an axe head, Sindri was busy crafting an ornate wooden handle.

Sinfjotli grew restless. Watching them work had lost its appeal, and he started pacing back and forth impatiently through Brok and Sindri's enormous smithy. Their workshop was a vast arsenal, its walls lined with every kind of tool Sinfjotli could imagine, alongside an impressive assortment of knives, swords, and other weapons. Shelves overflowed with jars containing some of the most bizarre ingredients Sinfjotli had ever seen.

Dozens of tables were scattered throughout the workshop, each cluttered with half-finished projects. One held a partially dismantled automaton. Another displayed a chariot made entirely of flames. Resting in one corner of the workshop was a mechanical falcon crafted from silver and bronze. Unlike the other creations, this one moved. The sentient metal bird often flew around the room. Sometimes, it landed on Sindri's shoulder and affectionately nipped his ear.

Several impressive weapons were on display, including several sets of crucible steel swords and enchanted blades that remained as hot as the moment they were forged—for hundreds of years.

The smithy itself was divided almost perfectly in half, almost as if an invisible line ran through the center of the room. Brok and Sindri were polar opposites, and their workstations made that abundantly clear. Brok's side was a complete mess. Tools weren't where they were supposed to be; a workbench overflowed with heaps of scrap metal and junk, and the floor and walls were covered in grease, soot, and dirt.

Sindri's side of the workshop was a stark contrast—tidier, cleaner, organized. Sinfjotli figured Sindri's neatness bordered on ritualistic. Every tool had its place, neat outlines drawn on the wall, clearly showing where everything was supposed to be. Gilded mail coats, polished to perfection hung on mannequins, and the floor was cleaned so well Sindri could have eaten off it. But Sinfjotli doubted the dwarf would do something so 'unclean.'

Against one wall stood an enormous furnace and anvil—neutral ground between the brothers—where they worked in rare harmony, forging this new weapon.

Sinfjotli had had enough. The billowing smoke and grease-laden air churned his stomach, and the pacing had done nothing to ease his restlessness. He decided he ought to check on Sigurd. He grabbed a crate full of bottles of mead from a nearby table and walked to the workshop's entrance. The doorway was no simple threshold—it was a massive iron vault door, circular and thick as a fortress wall. As Sinfjotli approached, brass gears turned, hydraulic pistons hissed, and the door automatically opened with lots of blowing steam.

Outside, a deep, seemingly bottomless chasm stretched, one of many that could be found in Svartalfheim. Several stone bridges spanned the void, linking the workshop to a cluster of dwarven houses on the other side. He could hear the rhythmic clang of hammers striking anvils, other dwarves hammering away in their smithies.

The Huldra Brothers' workshop was isolated from the rest of the dwarves' smithies. Their mastery of the craft was unmatched, earning them prestige and affluence in Svartalfheim—a status few could rival. Unlike the common forges crowded together, they had earned the right to operate their shop on their own isolated plot of land.

Brok and Sindri stand apart from the other dwarves like kings from their serfs, Sinfjotli thought as he walked by several armor stands and weapons racks in front of the workshop.

He turned a corner and found Sigurd sitting on a pile of crates outside the forge. His brother still wore the wool garments Brok and Sindri had given him after they all left the amphitheater two days ago. The dwarves had also returned Sigurd's swords and armor to him, but Sigurd had yet to put them on. He was still, sitting in a fetal position on the crate, wrapped in a blanket and clutching his shoulders. His eyes were wide open, and he was panting. Sigurd touched one scar where the dragon had sunk its teeth into his flesh and trembled.

Normally, Sinfjotli would have considered the sight of a mighty warrior like Sigurd curled up in fear pitiful, disgraceful even. But this was an exception. Sigurd had been eaten alive by a dragon. A death few could imagine, and even fewer could survive. That kind of pain, that kind of horror, wasn't something someone could easily forget or overcome.

Not even Sigurd.

The Trial had visibly changed Sigurd. He'd grown four inches taller, standing at least seven feet tall, and his golden hair was now a metallic platinum. Ugly scars marred his torso, left shoulder, and limbs—marks where Old One Horn had sunk its teeth into his flesh.

His eyes were different, too. Sigurd's golden pupils were still vertical slits, like a cat's, but the sclerae were a darker hue. His eyes no longer resembled a serpent's. Now, they reminded Sinfjotli of a different kind of reptile altogether. A dragon.

Sinfjotli lowered himself onto a nearby crate. "How are you feeling?"

"I can still feel it." Sigurd quivered. He touched the scars on his left shoulder. "I can still *feel* the dragon's teeth sinking deep into my flesh, ripping off my arm, tearing off my legs, and biting off my neck!"

"I get how you feel," Sinfjotli said as he handed Sigurd a bottle of mead.

Sigurd grasped the bottle and drank it all in one swig without stopping for a breath of air. Sinfjotli picked up another bottle from the crate he'd brought and uncorked it just as Sigurd finished drinking his own.

"I still have nightmares from when I underwent the Trial of Svarblood," Sinfjotli admitted after taking a swig. "To be honest, I envy you right now."

"Why would you?" Sigurd demanded, as he wiped the sticky mead from his lips.

Sinfjotli squeezed his eyes shut. "My trial went much worse than yours did. The dragon devoured you quickly. I reckon you lost consciousness after the fifth bite. But the wolf that devoured me wasn't as merciful. It toyed with me for nearly half an hour, biting off my fingers, hands, feet, and genitals before tearing out my throat. Like you, I screamed and howled in pain. But that's not why I'm jealous. It's because you immediately regained your human form after passing the Trial."

"W-what do you mean?" Sigurd stuttered.

"Remember the aftereffects I warned you about? Even if someone passes the Trial of Svarblood, it normally takes their soul several days to adjust to their new body. During that time, the person is in a savage state of mind and is dangerous to everyone around them."

Sinfjotli paused, taking another long swig of mead. "After I passed the Trial of Svarblood, I was struck with madness and spent ten days running through the woods, living like a mad beast and killing many men before I regained sanity. No one was safe from me. I still have nightmares about that bloody rampage. I was certain you'd go on an even more destructive rampage and kill every dwarf in the assembly after you passed the Trial. Instead, you regained your human form with your sanity intact."

"Do you think I got lucky?" Sigurd asked.

"No clue," Sinfjotli admitted. "Nobody has ever attempted to become a dragon through the Trial of Svarblood, as far as I know. Also, you consumed the heart and bathed in the blood of a sentient dragon, who used to be a dwarf, many years prior. There were too many factors at play here. Just be thankful you survived and didn't go on a violent rampage. The dwarves wouldn't be helping us now if you had."

Sigurd took little solace in that. He snatched another bottle of mead from the crate and downed the whole thing without pause. Sinfjotli watched as Sigurd greedily chugged the bottle.

Sigurd had an increased appetite and thirst since undergoing the Trial. But Sinfjotli knew that wasn't why his brother was drinking so much. He was trying to forget, to flee into a mist of alcohol to escape the traumatic memories of what he had endured.

"It's no use!" Sigurd smashed the empty bottle against the ground, sending shards of glass everywhere. "I can't get drunk, no matter how much alcohol I consume."

"That must be a side effect of becoming a dragon," Sinfjotli muttered. "Your metabolism probably increased tenfold. But getting so irresponsibly drunk that you can hardly feel anything isn't the way to handle your trauma."

"Then how did *you* overcome it?" Sigurd demanded with a hint of hope and desperation. "How did you forget the horror of being devoured alive by a wolf?"

"I never did." Sinfjotli traced his fingers over the scars on his neck and shoulder. "I still have nightmares about that dreadful day. The darkness never leaves you, Sigurd. It only recedes. After a while... I stopped thinking about the Trial, and the nightmares became less frequent. The same will happen to you, given enough time."

"I don't think I can *stop* thinking about it!" Sigurd moaned.

"Then think of something else," Sinfjotli suggested. "Whenever the phantom pains haunt you, just think of something comforting. Focus on that one thing and nothing else."

Sinfjotli gestured to the scars on his wrists and forearms. "When I was younger, I'd distract myself from the trauma of the Trial of Svarblood by looking at these scars. I'd remember my promise to my mother on my tenth birthday to punish Siggeir for all the evil he'd wrought on our family. That had been my sole reason for living and it was the reason I volunteered to undergo the Trial. As I stared at these scars and thought about my mission, the phantom pains subsided. Try finding a similar totem to focus on to distract yourself from the trauma."

Sigurd remained silent for a long while. He picked up Gram from the pile of armor Sinfjotli had left beside him, unsheathed the sword, and stared intently at the blade.

Sinfjotli studied the runes along the fuller. He had held Gram three times throughout his life. The first time was when he was eleven years old. His father lent it to him to practice his swordsmanship. However, he promptly took the blade back after Sinfjotli nearly sliced off his hand when he tried sharpening the weapon with a whetstone, not knowing how sharp it was. The second time was during his battle against his wicked stepfather in Helheim, and the third had been his last stand on the Gjallerbru. Sinfjotli knew how light and sharp it was. The sword felt good in his hand, but it looked even better in Sigurd's, almost as if the weapon had been forged specifically to fit his hand.

"After Old One Horn devoured me, I woke up inside the Cave of Gnitaheath," Sigurd recalled. "Fafnir was there, and we fought. I had no armor or clothes, but I still had this sword. Even in death, Gram was by my side."

"That'll do," Sinfjotli said. "Whenever the trauma of the Trial overwhelms you, you need only draw that sword to remind yourself of your purpose. It'll remind you why you underwent the Trial and why we're on this journey."

Sigurd stared at him. They might have spoken more, but Brok called out to them. "Hey, mutt, we're almost finished. Come back inside."

They entered the shop, and Brok motioned them to the forge. Resting on a large anvil was the weapon they'd been forging. It was definitely an axe. Brok and Sindri had already attached the axe head to the handle even though the metal was still white-hot. Sinfjotli found that odd, but he decided not to question professionals.

"Is it done?" Sinfjotli asked.

"Almost." Brok nodded. "There's just one last step left. Come here and hold out your hand."

Sinfjotli did as he was told and reached for the axe.

"Oh, I can never watch this part," Sindri muttered.

"Wait, what?" Sinfjotli asked.

Brok seized his right forearm in an iron grip that could bend steel. Sindri turned away as Brok drew his knife from his belt and carved it into Sinfjotli's palm in three fast strokes. Brok sheathed his dagger while still holding Sinfjotli's wrist in an unbreakable hold with one hand. With his free hand, he squeezed Sinfjotli's right hand so hard blood trickled out and poured onto the axe.

"There, finished," Brok announced merrily as the axe head steamed. He released his death grip, and Sinfjotli backed away, clutching his bleeding palm.

"Was that really necessary?" Sinfjotli complained. Despite its bronze appearance, Brok's dagger was incredibly sharp. It could have easily cut him straight to the bone if Brok didn't know what he was doing.

"Course," Brok replied, chiseling a symbol into the smoking axe head. "As a matter of fact, that there was the most important step in the whole forging process."

Brok finished chiseling a shape into the axe, and the blade glowed bright blue. Sinfjotli's right hand also glowed blue, and his wound magically healed itself. When the light subsided, Sinfjotli found he had a glowing arrow-shaped scar on his right palm.

"If you needed my blood, you could have just asked," Sinfjotli complained. "Why'd you carve an arrow into my palm?"

"That's not an arrow," Sigurd corrected. "It's the rune Tiwaz. I have that same rune etched in my sword."

Sigurd drew Gram and pointed out a set of runes carved along the fuller. "When Brynhild taught me the runes on Hindarfjall, she instructed me to carve these symbols onto the blade. She said if I wanted to achieve victory in battle, I had to carve 'victory runes' on my sword and think of the name 'Tiwaz' twice every time I drew my sword. But this rune is versatile and can also mean several other things. I think, in this case, it means, 'Return.'"

"That's enough showing off, 'rune expert.'" Brok snorted, rolling his eyes as he and Sindri dunked the axe into a vat of coolant. "Anyway, we're finished. Here you are."

With a flamboyant gesture, Brok presented the finished weapon. It was a two-handed double-blade axe. The ebony shaft was at least three feet long, just the right length for Sinfjotli. The axe head had glowing runes etched along its blade and handle.

Sinfjotli grabbed the axe in his right hand. Immediately, he felt a surge of power and energy course through his arm. He swung it about several times, testing its weight.

"Oh, and I whipped up something special for you, too, Sigurd," Sindri announced. He pointed at the belt wrapped around Sigurd's waist. "I tinkered with your belt and armor and enchanted them so they'll shift with you, vanishing and reappearing whenever you transform. This will allow you to always retain both your swords and armor when you transform into a dragon."

Sigurd gave a forced smile. "Thanks, but I don't think I'll need to do that for a long time."

"Of course," Sindri agreed. "Anyway, let's head outside. Brok and I will set up a few training dummies for Sinfjotli to test his new axe."

The training dummies of Svartalfheim differed from what Sinfjotli was accustomed to. In Midgard, a warrior usually trained with mannequins made from straw, wood, and cloth that they could stab and slash at their leisure. But here in Svartalfheim, the dummies were enchanted straw and clay golems that could move and fight back.

The three golems the Huldra Brothers summoned from a nearby storage facility wore lamellar armor and helmets. One wielded a shield, the other a metal spear, and the last one wielded an axe and shield emblazoned with the image of a serpent biting its own tail.

"They're just straw dolls underneath the armor, so hack and slash to your heart's content," Sindri invited.

"But don't get too cocky," Brok warned. "Their weapons are made of crucible steel. We wouldn't want to make this too easy for you."

"Thanks." Sinfjotli smiled eagerly. "I'll take you at your word and show no restraint."

The first golem with the sword attacked Sinfjotli. He blocked three strikes, then stepped in close and chopped off its right leg in a downward swing. As it collapsed, the second golem charged. It swung its axe down in a brutal charge, but Sinfjotli was faster. He took a slight step back, dodging the blow, then brought his own axe down and locked its head around the golem's weapon. He tugged, throwing the creature off balance, then sidestepped to the left and swung his axe, splitting the golem in half at the waist.

The third golem charged, spear poised to strike. Sinfjotli caught the shaft with his axe head, redirecting the strike to his right. He changed grip and swung, his blade cleaving through the golem's shoulder, severing its arm.

The remaining golems put up a decent fight, but it took little effort for Sinfjotli to dispatch them as Sigurd and the Huldra Brothers watched with mute appeal. Once defeated, the golems stood up, reattached their missing parts, and walked away.

"The axe suits you." Sigurd applauded as the golems returned to their storage facility.

"It has a good balance and grip," Sinfjotli agreed. But there was still something else he wanted to test out. Sinfjotli noticed a large anvil resting outside the smithy near a window. He reared his arm back and hurled his axe at it. The weapon spun through the air and struck the anvil. The axe cut clean through the heavy iron and its oak stand, splitting the anvil cleanly in half.

"It's extremely sharp too!" Sinfjotli smiled.

"So is any other battle axe." Sindri sighed, rolling his eyes. "But this one is special. It was forged with your blood; thus, it's permanently bonded to you. Once thrown, it'll always return to your hand whenever you want it to."

"Watch and learn!" Brok pulled the axe from the bisected anvil and hurled it into the nearby chasm. The axe vanished into the abyss.

"Now go on and try it," Brok urged. "Hold out your arm and call it back to your hand."

Sinfjotli stretched out his right arm. *Return*, he thought. A tingle sparked in his palm. From the depths of the chasm, a spinning blur shot upward. His axe was magically levitating itself out of the abyss! It streaked through the air and within five seconds, the spinning axe landed comfortably in Sinfjotli's right hand.

"Amazing." Sinfjotli laughed. He continued throwing with his new weapon and calling it back to his hand. "This axe is perfect."

"Perfect?" Brok burst out laughing. "Don't be ridiculous, boy. There's no such thing as a 'perfect weapon.' Know why? Because every weapon's greatest weakness is its user. A weapon is only as good as the hand that wields it. A master wielding a stick has a sharp blade, while an amateur with a weapon of mass destruction like Mjolnir reduces it to scrap."

Brok reached up and caught the axe midair as it was returning to Sinfjotli's hand without losing any fingers. "This axe is just a tool, like any other. You decide how it's used. You're responsible for your victory or defeat in battle. Not this axe."

"It's still a fine weapon," Sigurd commended. "And the best weapons have names. What will yours be?"

Sinfjotli thought for a moment and then answered: "Wolfsbane."

Sigurd nodded with approval. But Brok and Sindri seemed less impressed.

"Meh, I've heard worse names." Sindri shrugged.

"Anyways, that's enough practicing," Brok decided. "Sigurd, we repaired your armor for you. Once you get dressed, we'll head out. Ivaldi and his sons should be finished forging your last gift soon. A set of armor forged from pure legend!"

"Let's get going," Sindri agreed. "We don't want to keep the ol' bastard waiting. The only thing Ivaldi hates more than criminals are lollygaggers who show up late."

Chapter Fourteen

Unexpected Guests

They arrived while Ivaldi, Mótsignir, and his other sons were hammering the finishing touches on the armor. Ivaldi's private forge took up an entire underground chamber large enough to fit the dwarven amphitheater. The forge housed towering vats and containers, an anvil as tall as a two-story house, and countless tools neatly stacked on the walls. Some instruments even hung from the ceiling on hooks drilled into stalactites.

"Let's hang back and watch," Sindri proposed. "It's not every day mortals get to witness Ivaldi and his sons at work."

It appeared they had just finished submerging the metal in a vat of black sludge. As Ivaldi's son Gandalf carried the vat away, Brok informed them it contained water from the River Ván, adding, "Metal tempered with pure hatred is the strongest in the realms."

Ivaldi and his sons carefully placed the sizzling armor on a stand in the center of the room. Mótsignir pulled a lever, and a vat opened, unleashing a blazing heat that left Sinfjotli's face covered in burns and blisters. As the flames and heat enveloped the metal, Ivaldi hefted his hammer high in the air and brought it down on the raw metal with so much force that sixteen stalactites broke off the ceiling and crashed to the ground. He and his sons took turns beating the metal, shaping it how they liked. When they finished hammering, they cooled the blazing metal in a giant vat of water.

"That blast of heat came directly from Muspelheim," Sindri explained as steam and fog filled the chamber. "And that vat contains water straight from the well of Hvergelmir in Niflheim. The first being, Ymir, was born from the merging of the fires of Muspelheim and the frost of Niflheim. It's astounding what can be achieved when two polar opposite forces combine."

Ivaldi and his sons worked the metal for ten more minutes. Eventually, they stopped and turned around, as if only now noticing the four of them standing there.

"Good, you've arrived." Ivaldi sighed as he wiped the sweat from his brow. "Now that you're here, Sinfjotli, we can add the final touches."

Sinfjotli blinked. "Me? What do you need me for?"

Brok reached up and tapped the butt of Sinfjotli's axe. "The same reason we needed you in our workshop to finish forging this beauty."

A surge of phantom pain flashed through Sinfjotli's mind as he remembered Brok carving his knife deep into his palm. "But you've already done this to me!" He held up his hand, showing off the glowing scar on his palm. "Why do I need to go through it again?"

"The Tiwaz rune won't cut it," Sindri explained. "Besides, they need your blood to complete the forging process." He swallowed nervously. "It's an... unsanitary but mandatory step."

"Well, what are you waiting for?" Brok urged. "Get going. Time is money."

Sinfjotli sighed as he walked over to the other smiths and extended his left hand so they could carve another rune.

One of Ivaldi's sons snickered. "Ha, you wish."

Ivaldi's sons swarmed him, shoved him to the ground, and tore off his shirt. Four of them pinned his limbs to the stone ground while the fifth drew his bronze knife, pressed the tip against Sinfjotli's bare chest, and thrust deep. He twisted the knife as he carved it into Sinfjotli's flesh, pushing the blade far deeper than he had any right to.

Before he could carve deeper, Sinfjotli forced himself up and flung the dwarf and his brothers headlong into the limestone walls on the other side of the forge.

"No, Sinfjotli!" Gandalf pleaded. "Please, just calm down and let us—"

"I'm sick of your sadistic antics!" Sinfjotli snarled as he sprang to his feet. His teeth elongated into fangs as his body began shapeshifting. "You were about to plunge that knife between my ribs and let me bleed out like a stuck pig! You think I'll just lie there and let you shrimps carve me up like a turkey!"

"ENOUGH!" Ivaldi slammed the butt of his hammer against the ground. The force of the impact and his deafening tone were enough to cow his sons and make Sinfjotli halt his transformation. The dwarf king looked at him, and Sinfjotli relaxed when he saw the regretful look in Ivaldi's eyes as he bowed his head.

"My sincerest apologies for not adequately explaining everything. My sons get overzealous with their work and act inconsiderately toward our clients. To finish forging the armor and binding to you, we need your blood and must carve a powerful rune into your flesh." He pointed to Sinfjotli's right hand. "Brok and Sindri carved the Tiwaz rune into your palm to permanently bind that axe to you. As painful as it may be, we must do the same to complete the forging process. Please don't make this any harder for us than it needs to be."

Sinfjotli glared at the dwarf king, then sighed. His teeth and claws receded into his flesh as he lay down on the stone ground. "Get on with it."

Ivaldi's sons didn't dawdle. They placed two silver bowls between Sinfjotli's arms and chest and got to work. Their small, meaty hands expertly carved a gigantic runic tattoo into his chest and collected his blood in the two bowls as it trickled down the skin on either side of his chest. As the blade sliced into his flesh, Sinfjotli winced but didn't scream. He'd endured far worse than this before, like when his mother had torn the flesh from his forearms on his tenth birthday.

Still, something was very unsettling about this. Although Sinfjotli knew his life wasn't in any real danger, the macabre scene of the dwarves chanting in a guttural language he couldn't comprehend as they jabbed their daggers into his flesh made him feel like a human sacrifice about to be harvested by vultures. It felt as if something other than blood was being siphoned from him with every cut. Despite the unease crawling beneath his skin, Sinfjotli remained stoic, allowing the dwarves to continue their work until the tattoo was complete.

When the ritual was complete, the chanting stopped, and the dwarf Gandalf handed the two bowls of blood to their father. Sinfjotli sat up as Ivaldi walked over to the still-steaming armor and poured the blood onto the raw metal. The armor glowed, as did the runic symbol on Sinfjotli's chest. When the light dimmed and his cuts sealed, Sinfjotli stood up and walked to the nearest bronze brazier, which was as bright and clean as a stainless mirror. He examined the glowing symbol on his chest, taking in all the details.

"That's the vegvísir rune, a powerful symbol designed to help the bearer find their way through turbulent times," Ivaldi's son Durinn explained. "It's also meant to protect warriors and give them courage and strength, assuring their victory against enemies. It allowed us to permanently bind the armor to you. Even if the armor is removed, that symbol will always guide it back to you so it can protect you."

Sinfjotli's brows furrowed as he gazed at the intricate design. It almost looked like a snowflake, which didn't suit his tastes. "Was this necessary?"

"What are you so upset about?" Billingr asked. "I thought you Norse warriors loved body art and tattoos. Aren't scars something you warriors take pride in? I heard warriors wear the scars from their battles like medals of valor to show their history as fighters." He pointed at the scars on Sinfjotli's wrists, shoulders, and torso. "You've already got enough scars to make your torso look like a jigsaw puzzle. What's the harm in adding another to the collection?"

Sinfjotli looked down at the glowing scar and frowned. "I get what you're saying. But having a huge glowing snowflake-shaped scar on my chest is a bit... distasteful."

"Regardless of how you feel about that, it was a crucial step in the forging process," Dúrnir insisted. "And thanks to that, we're finished. Have a look."

All eyes trained on Ivaldi as he rose to his full height. He gestured for his sons to come to lift the armor from its stand, then turned and presented the completed work with a flamboyant gesture.

"Behold the Kistfuskare!" he proclaimed. "Or in your tongue, 'the Coffin Cheater.'"

Sinfjotli's eyes widened as he examined the suit of black scale armor Ivaldi's sons placed before him. He'd never had much interest in armor, but he wasn't foolish enough to run into battle without protection. Speed and maneuverability mattered more to him than plate armor; it was too heavy, too restrictive. That's why he'd always favored fur, boiled leather, or chain mail—anything that let him move freely.

Still, Sinfjotli couldn't deny that the armor on the rack before him was unquestionably the finest, most beautiful set he had ever seen. Dark as smoke, its scales shimmered in the torchlight, edged in red gold. Patterns inscribed in the metal, runes and arcane symbols folded into the steel.

"It's gorgeous!" Sinfjotli gasped.

Ivaldi stepped forward. "On my honor as the father of the dwarves and king of Svartalfheim, I promise you that no mortal has ever had, nor will ever have, a set of armor as strong, adaptable, or powerful as this one." He nodded toward the suit. "Now that it's bonded to you, it will always protect you, even in death. You don't even have to go through the trouble of putting it on. Just strip naked, extend your hand, and the armor will do the rest."

Despite his skepticism, Sinfjotli did as he was told, tearing off the remnants of his torn shirt, removing his pants and shoes. His grip tightened. The Norns had sewn these clothes for him. Discarding them felt wrong. But after everything they'd endured, the garments were little more than tattered rags. With a deep breath, he tossed them into a nearby brazier; the flames swallowed them whole. Sinfjotli ignored the uncouth comments from the dwarves about the "small size of his pecker" and reached out with his right hand toward the suit.

The runes carved into his hand and chest glowed blue. The armor sprang to life. Its right gauntlet grabbed his wrist. Then it—moved. A step forward. A tightening grip. The armor proceeded to wrap itself around Sinfjotli's body as if... No. Not as if... for this was the truth of it. The armor had a *mind of its own!*

It slithered and coiled around Sinfjotli's body like a serpent, automatically setting and clasping itself into place without a single hand needing to fasten it. In less than ten seconds, the process was complete. He blinked; he realized he was looking through the helmet's visor.

"How does it feel?" Sigurd asked.

Sinfjotli stretched, moved his limbs, and then broke into a run. The armor appeared durable and heavy, like the sturdy chitinous exoskeleton covering an insect's soft innards. But he wore it as if it was the thinnest silk. He even executed a backward somersault, movements fluid, unrestrained. It placed no burden on his maneuverability, defying every expectation.

"It's so light!" Sinfjotli exclaimed. "It doesn't even feel like I'm wearing armor. It feels like another layer of my skin."

"That's because the armor adapts to its user's body," Ivaldi explained. "Actually, it's more accurate to say that the armor adapts to whatever situation its wearer is in. Observe."

Ivaldi raised his war hammer and swung it down on Sinfjotli's head before he could protest or even raise his hands in defense. The hammer struck Sinfjotli's helmet so hard it split the ground, creating a massive crater where Sinfjotli stood. But when the dust settled, Sinfjotli still stood. Upright at the bottom of the hole with the hammer still pressing against his helmet.

"I—I should be dead," Sinfjotli panted after Ivaldi retrieved his hammer and he stepped out of the crater. "I should be nothing but a bloody smear. But I barely felt that!"

"The armor adapts to whatever danger its user is in," Ivaldi said. "It'll adapt to whatever environment you're in and even allow you to breathe underwater should the need arise. It will also enhance all your current physical abilities, and whenever you transform into a wolf, the armor will morph with you as you change shape and envelop your wolf form. But please don't attempt that yet. The armor needs time to adjust to your body's physiology before you can try a feat like that."

Sinfjotli examined the gauntlets, imagining how fearsome he'd look on the battlefield as an armored wolf. "How did you make something like this?"

"It wasn't easy," Ivaldi admitted. "The recipe for the armor required items rarer than hen's teeth." He began listing them off, counting on his fingers. "Scales from the World Serpent. A berserker's cowardice. A bucket of a fire giant's sweat—collected in summer. Two armpits from a snake. To name but a few. But thanks to your brother's... ordeal... we secured the two most important ingredients: The rage of a dragon and the screams of the innocent. We mixed them all together and tempered the raw metal in the pure hatred of the River Ván."

Sinfjotli frowned. "Armpits of a serpent? Fire giant's sweat? Screams of the innocent? What kind of nonsense is that?"

"It's far from nonsense!" Sindri scowled. "Our people have a saying: 'Rarity paves the way for opportunity.' The rarer something is, the more valuable it is. When you combine the rarest ingredients, you can create things beyond imagination."

"But how do you acquire them?" Sigurd asked. "For that matter, how do you capture the rage of a dragon or screams?"

"Tchah! There'd be no point explaining it to you," Brok scoffed. "The words would go right over your noggins."

Sigurd crossed his arms and stared defiantly at the dwarves. "Try us."

The Huldra Brothers glanced up at Ivaldi.

"Can we really tell them?" Brok asked. "It's our trade secret."

Ivaldi shrugged. "They're not elves, and they're no craftsmen, either. I doubt they could comprehend the nuanced secret of our craft."

"Alright then." Sindri dramatically cleared his throat. "To put this as simplistically as possible, dwarven craftsmanship is all about understanding intangibles. Something's *nature* is more important than its *form*. Any third-rate blacksmith can forge a lump of iron into a sword with heat from a furnace. However, a genuine master blacksmith who understands fire's nature can infuse his furnace's flames into the metal, creating a magic weapon that remains as hot as the moment it was forged for hundreds of years. Understanding the nature of intangibles like fire, wind, sound, or emotion is crucial to harness them."

"Okaaay..." Sinfjotli frowned. "But how do you harvest those intangibles?"

Every dwarf in the smithy burst out laughing.

"See!" Brok chortled. "What did I tell y'all? Sindri's words went in one ear and straight out the other like a wind tunnel!"

Suddenly, a booming sound like thunder reverberated throughout the cavernous room, drowning out the laughter. Everyone turned toward the entrance of the smithy, where two tall, muscular men stood clapping. Whenever their hands clapped, the sound boomed throughout the hall like thunder.

"Good show, as always, Ivaldi," one remarked. "You and your boys never fail to impress."

"Lord Magni! Lord Modi! What a surprise!" Ivaldi exclaimed. "What brings you two to Svartalfheim?"

Sinfjotli's eyes widened. *Magni and Modi? Aren't they the Sons of Thor and the gods of strength and courage?*

They certainly *looked* like they could be Thor's offspring from their towering size and well-toned physiques. Both gods were exceptionally tall with very muscular builds. Magni, the god still clapping, stood seven feet nine inches tall with an extremely robust shape. His body was adorned with scars from previous battles and several runic tattoos covered his chest, back, and face. He had sharp yet handsome features. His eyes were an icy shade of blue, his blond hair separated into three braids, and he had two smaller braids in his beard. He radiated power and the air around him burned with energy.

His brother wasn't as tall, but he still dwarfed Sigurd by half a foot. Modi was just as muscular as Magni but looked very different. His eyes were ice blue, but his hair was red, and a reddish, forked beard covered half his face. He smelled of rain and clean wind.

Sinfjotli figured they were probably half-brothers, just like him and Sigurd. As the ringing in his ears subsided, Modi stepped forth and gazed at the towering dwarf king.

"We're here to collect our weapons," he announced.

"I—I see," Ivaldi muttered. "Your weapons are ready, of course. But you've come very early. I thought you planned to retrieve them in the spring?"

"That was our original agreement, but we urgently need them now," Magni explained.

"Of course." Ivaldi nodded. "Say no more. Brok, Sindri, Dáinn, go fetch their weapons."

Sindri nodded and bowed. Brok gave a slight nod, probably the closest thing to a respectful gesture he could make. The third dwarf, Dáinn, rose from his bench and bowed respectfully to Ivaldi and then to Magni and Modi. He looked like most other dwarves, except for the fact his mouth was wired shut. The three vanished into a nearby corridor.

"They'll return shortly," Ivaldi assured. "In the meantime, allow me to serve you a few tankards of ale."

"Thank you for the offer, but we must discuss an urgent matter with these two." Modi jerked his head slightly toward Sinfjotli and Sigurd.

Ivaldi's polite smile faded. "I see. So you're here on behalf of your grandfather? In that case, shall I have my sons prepare the Gauntlet? I'm sure you'll want to test out your weapons afterward."

"That sounds good to me." Magni smiled eagerly.

"I'll see to it right away." Ivaldi bowed politely to the two gods, then turned to Sinfjotli and Sigurd. He stopped himself short of scowling as he locked eyes with Sigurd. "I've kept my word to the letter and forged your brother the ultimate armor as you requested. With this, our business has concluded. I'll give you until sunrise tomorrow to depart Niðavellir. I do not wish to see you again."

The king turned his back on them and walked away with his sons. Sinfjotli clenched his armored fists as he reflected on everything the king had put them through. But surprisingly, Sigurd was the one who called out. "Ivaldi!"

The king paused and peered over his left shoulder as Sigurd trembled with rage. "I won't condemn you for the pain I recently endured, as most of it was of my own volition," he admitted. "But what you put me through when we arrived here was unjust! You ambushed us, then made me endure a rigged trial and summarily declared I was guilty without giving me a chance to defend myself properly and cruelly led me along with the false promise of amnesty. Someday, you will answer for that affront! It won't be by my hand, but you shall reap what you've sown!"

As Sigurd finished venting, Ivaldi lowered his left eye. Sinfjotli couldn't read people's hearts like Sigurd could, but he detected a hint of shame in the king's gaze.

"I might," Ivaldi admitted as he looked away. "Even a king isn't above the law. I may have to atone for my conduct someday, but you definitely won't be the one to judge me. Regardless, I wish you both luck in the ordeals ahead. Farewell."

With that, Ivaldi and his sons departed. As they exited the forge, the Sons of Thor approached Sigurd and Sinfjotli and gave them a cursory inspection. This wasn't the first time they'd met the Aesir. But unlike in Helheim, being in the presence of two *living* Aesir was a little intimidating. Sinfjotli and Sigurd were at least six foot four and seven feet tall, respectively. But Magni and Modi were at least a foot taller than them. Their blue eyes looked stormy, as if lightning could shoot from them at any moment. Sinfjotli's hair stood on end as if reacting to the power and electricity coursing through Magni's and Modi's bodies.

"So, these are the two warriors who are the talk of Asgard," Magni remarked. "Word is you two clawed your way out of Helheim."

"We had help," Sigurd said. "Baldur helped guide us through the city and stopped Hel from harming us directly. Brynhild appeared when our situation seemed hopeless and helped us fend off her vicious army, and we never would have escaped if I hadn't convinced Hræsvelgr to help us."

Modi chuckled. "That'll make for a queer song, won't it, Magni? Sigurd and Sinfjotli fought their way out of Helheim but only escaped after enlisting a giant eagle to their cause."

"It does sound ridiculous in hindsight." Sinfjotli chuckled. He noticed his unease was gone. Magni and Modi might've looked and felt intimidating, but they were as friendly as Baldur and Hodr. *Are all Aesir this easy to talk to, or have we just been lucky so far?*

"How long have you two been here?" Sigurd asked.

"We arrived in Svartalfheim just as your... ordeal was happening in the amphitheater." Modi placed a hand on Sigurd's shoulder. "You've got balls, lad. I've never seen a man willingly let himself be eaten by a dragon just to outwit a dwarf and fulfill a task from our grandfather."

His words of praise didn't have the intended effect. Sigurd winced, pushed Magni's hand away, and impulsively clutched his left shoulder. "That... that wasn't the only reason," Sigurd managed as he continued trembling from phantom pains.

"You paid a grievous price," Magni said. "But you both gained much from it. You fulfilled your second task, which is fortunate, as you'll need everything you've gained to survive your third task."

Sinfjotli frowned. "Our third task?"

"We came to Svartalfheim to collect our weapons," Magni explained. "But we're also here to deliver you a message from our grandfather. Now that you've fulfilled your second task, the All-Father has decreed that you must return to Niflheim and slay an ancient giant."

Niflheim. Just hearing the name made Sinfjotli shiver. They'd barely survived their brief journey through that icy realm months ago. They'd both been at the point of death when the Norns found them, and they hadn't even made it halfway through the realm's frigid atmosphere before collapsing. Now Odin had tasked them with returning to that frozen realm? It seemed too cruel.

"My lords?" a nervous voice called. Everyone turned as Sindri, Brok, and Dain returned carrying two newly forged weapons.

"Here you are, Magni." Sindri presented one weapon. "A broadsword tempered in cyclonic thunder."

Magni held up the mighty blade. A large golden-and-white metal sword. When Magni grasped the hilt, bluish energy hues brimmed through and around it.

"Very impressive," Magni remarked. "I reckon I could cleave a mountain in half."

"Indeed, but please don't do so here in Svartalfheim," Sindri requested. "Our mountains are quite valuable and filled with many resources. No sense destroying one just to test your sword's sharpness."

"Don't worry, I won't." Magni chuckled.

"And for you, Modi, a war hammer forged from the heavens and the earth," Brok announced. He and Dain hoisted the weapon over their heads, which was so heavy it required both of them to lift it.

The war hammer had a six-foot shaft and an elaborately decorated hammer with a spike attached to the head. It looked like it weighed over a hundred pounds, but Modi effortlessly lifted it over his shoulder with one arm. As he grasped the weapon, there was a sudden surge of energy, and Sinfjotli's ears popped. Modi held the war hammer aloft and stared at it in wonder. Then he frowned.

"I—Is something the matter, Modi?" Sindri asked nervously.

"This hammer," Modi muttered. "It... reminds me of Mjolnir in a way."

"It should," Brok agreed. "This is what we originally envisioned for Mjolnir. Unfortunately, Loki sabotaged the forging process, and the handle ended up being too short. A minor cosmetic problem in the end, but this is how Thor's hammer was meant to look."

Modi grinned. He clapped, and thunder echoed across Svartalfheim. "Wait until our family sees this! It'll make our father green with envy as I smite frost giants and protect Asgard."

"You shouldn't boast or make assumptions like that," Sindri warned. "This hammer is nowhere *near* as powerful as Mjolnir."

"*What?*" Modi blinked. "Why? You said this is what Mjolnir was supposed to look like. How could it not be more powerful?"

"Mjolnir is one of a kind, lad," Brok explained. "The ingredients we used to forge it were so rare that they no longer exist. We'll never be able to replicate that masterpiece again or make another hammer as powerful as it."

Modi looked disheartened.

"Oh, don't look so dour," Sindri urged. "It might be a far cry from Mjolnir, but that war hammer is a formidable weapon in its own right. I reckon it contains about a tenth of Mjolnir's destructive capability."

Modi smiled. "It'll do then."

"Alright then." Sindri nodded. "I imagine you'd like to test out your weapons right away. I figure Ivaldi has finished setting things up for you by now. Let's head over to the Gauntlet."

Brok patted Sinfjotli on the back. "Consider yourself fortunate. It's rare for a mortal to witness two gods in action."

CHAPTER FIFTEEN

THE GAUNTLET

Sigurd sat on the edge of his seat as the portcullis rose swiftly, vanishing into the ceiling. An army of a million golems and automatons marched into the circular arena. In the center of the stadium, Magni and Modi stood ready, surrounded by tier upon tier of audience seats.

The Gauntlet was an enormous coliseum, far larger than the amphitheater where Sigurd had faced the Trial of Svarblood. Its oval expanse measured one thousand two hundred feet along its long axis and about a thousand feet across the short. Towering at one hundred and fifty feet tall, the arena could seat up to one hundred thousand dwarves across its multi-tiered seating.

Glowing crystals adorned the place, illuminating the area with bright white light. Most of the crystals in the tiered seats were located along the stairs, their glow intentionally dimmed to keep the audience in relative darkness. In contrast, the crystals embedded in the arena floor burned bright, ensuring the battlefield remained the focal point. Even though they were several hundred feet below ground, the main arena was as bright as day.

That said, Sigurd, Sinfjotli, Brok, and Sindri were the only ones present in the audience. Ivaldi and the rest of the dwarves had politely abstained. Sinfjotli proposed sitting at the edge to view the ring below, but Brok and Sindri disagreed, stating it was unsafe and they should sit at least twenty rows back.

They were right to be cautious. Although they were up against over a million opponents, Magni and Modi began effortlessly decimating their foes. Electricity flashed through the air whenever Modi swung his hammer or Magni swung his great sword. Fragments, severed limbs, and torsos of golems and automatons went flying in every direction every time they attacked. The air became sultry and stinging. Goosebumps sprang up on Sigurd's arm, and his long platinum hair stood up as if drawn toward the gods' energy.

"Better get used to this intense feeling!" Brok jested as he patted Sigurd's back. "You'll face many powerful monsters like them on your journey! Just be glad you're on friendly terms with these two."

A familiar chill raced up Sigurd's spine, and he noticed that Brok was wearing Andvari's ring on his right ring finger.

"Are you sure you want to keep the ring?" he asked.

"Why," Brok asked. "Do you want it back?"

"Of course not!" Sigurd exclaimed. "That cursed ring brought my family and me nothing but misery, tragedy, and—"

"We know," Sindri interjected. "But that's *precisely* why we want the ring."

Sigurd blinked several times and stared at Sindri, unsure if he'd heard him right. "Excuse me?"

"We're not interested in the ring so much as the curse Andvari placed upon it," Sindri explained. "The ability to bring misfortune upon whoever wears it is a powerful curse that can even shape the future. If we disenchant this ring, we could use this magic to craft something extraordinary."

That's why they wanted the ring! Sigurd thought. It made sense, in a way. Unlike the other dwarves and humans, the Huldra Brothers shunned gold and precious metals, preferring more exotic forms of payment. Magic like this would certainly fit the bill.

"What about the ring?" Sigurd asked curiously. "What'll happen to it?"

"It'll still be able to locate gold like it was designed to after we disenchant it," Sindri assured. "So it'll still prove a valuable asset to us."

Sigurd raised an eyebrow. "I thought you had no interest in treasure or gold?"

"We don't," Brok affirmed. "But plenty of gullible people out there would trade rare ingredients for a valuable magical item like this. Until then, we'll hang onto it as a memento until the right opportunity presents itself."

"Do as you will," Sigurd muttered as he turned away and watched the two gods make mincemeat of a crowd of golems.

Modi's war hammer shattered them like wet clay; Magni's great sword cleaved through their ranks like a fiery sword slicing through columns of butter. The gods' onslaught was mesmerizing, but Sigurd's mind was elsewhere, contemplating the next task the gods demanded from them.

"Brok, will this armor really protect me in Niflheim?" Sinfjotli asked as they watched Magni and Modi smash an entire legion of automatons.

Brok shot him an indignant look. "You took a hit from Ivaldi's hammer and walked away without a scratch. That wasn't proof enough for you?"

"Of its durability," Sinfjotli conceded. "But that alone might not be enough. I know what Ivaldi said in his forge and how the armor will adapt to my environment. But I've been to Niflheim before. The cold—"

"You know nothing of coldness," Brok interrupted sharply. "You have yet to see how vicious Niflheim is. You made it less than halfway through the upper echelons of its atmosphere. Compared to the primordial realm's surface, what you endured is like a gentle winter's kiss. The storms on Niflheim's surface are so strong the wind can shred through metal like butter and strip flesh from bones."

Sigurd's worry and unease deepened. The thought of facing the harsh and unforgiving realm of ice again made him feel like an ant about to get whipped around by a blizzard.

"Don't fret," Sindri assured. "The Kistfuskare can, without a doubt, protect you from Niflheim's elements. However, I wouldn't vouch for your survival on that armor alone. Niflheim is not a realm that gods or mortals are meant to inhabit. It is the darkest and coldest of the Nine Realms. The shadowy lands of Svartalfheim are nothing compared to the pitch-blackness of Niflheim. The winds there are so strong and cold they'd freeze most men solid in moments. The rivers that flow from its center are poisonous. Standing in the realm won't kill you if you wear the armor, but your journey still might."

Sigurd shuddered, remembering how close he'd come to dying the last time they'd visited that dreaded realm. They'd only been traveling in the realm's upper atmosphere. If Brok wasn't exaggerating, Niflheim's surface was exponentially colder!

"What about Sigurd?" Sinfjotli asked. "Will he be alright? You did some upgrades to his hauberk and armor. Can it protect him from the cold like mine?"

"No," Sindri answered. "We've made some improvements so it won't give him frostbite like before, and it'll shift with him whenever he transforms. But Sigurd's armor won't adapt to his environment like yours can, Sinfjotli." Sindri glanced up at Sigurd. "That said, Sigurd doesn't need any special protection from the cold. He'll be fine on his own."

Sigurd raised an eyebrow. "Why's that?"

The ground quaked before Sindri could elaborate. Everyone turned toward the arena as Modi leaped into the air, his powerful muscles propelling him higher and higher until he soared a hundred feet above the arena. As he twirled his war hammer in circles above his head, its whistling dance echoed throughout the coliseum. Modi brought the hammer down with a fierce cry, smashing it upon a battalion of automatons with a thunderous impact. The ground shook from the blow, and debris and weapons flew everywhere.

Several of those came spinning right at them. Brok and Sindri ducked as broken bits of blades and gears sailed overhead. Meanwhile, Sinfjotli got struck head-on by a spinning sword, which shattered as it crashed into the

Coffin Cheater. One of those pieces flung toward Sigurd and struck his right cheek before he could react.

Suddenly, a battle axe plummeted from the sky and struck Sigurd on the head. Given its size and weight, it should have cleaved him in two. Instead, the axe bounced off his forehead like a mere pebble, leaving no wound, no blood, not even a scratch. Sigurd rubbed his forehead and cheek in amazement, his fingers searching for an injury that wasn't there.

"I barely felt that," he muttered.

Brok poked the back of Sigurd's left hand. "Didja already forget you're a dragon? This fleshy humanoid appearance is just for show."

Sigurd grimaced. "I'm trying not to think about that."

Brok continued as if he hadn't heard. "Your flesh is harder than a diamond now. It'll take a truly formidable weapon to leave a scratch on you. As a bonus, you shouldn't feel cold in Niflheim."

"So we'll be fine?" Sinfjotli pressed.

"Whether you survive is up to you," Sindri warned. "But should you survive your journey through Niflheim, I promise you that the Kistfuskare will protect you from many of the dangers you encounter in seven of the other realms."

Sigurd frowned. "Only *seven* realms?"

Sindri rubbed his mouth and nervously ran a hand through his braided beard. "Muspelheim is the exception. The fires in that realm burn so hot that they burn through magic! As far as we know, the fire giants are the only living creatures that can survive in that hellish realm. Pray you don't encounter any. The weapons they wield... they're beyond anything you can imagine. Muspelheim's heat alone can set someone ablaze in seconds! That primordial realm would push the Kistfuskare to its limits."

Sigurd shuddered. He vaguely recalled Baldur telling them that half of Hel's body was permanently burned when Odin rode Sleipnir too close to

Muspelheim as he fled from her mother. That alone was a testament to how dangerous the other primordial realm was.

Suddenly, a deafening explosion blasted them all with hot air. Tendrils of electricity undulated through the air, blinding them with white light brighter than the sun's rays.

When the explosion subsided, Sigurd saw Magni and Modi standing in the center of the arena, surrounded by the shattered and smoldering remains of thousands of golems and automatons.

Sigurd's anxiety subsided, and his jaw hit the floor. There had been over a million automatons and golems in this arena, and Magni and Modi had defeated this fast?

So this is the power of the Aesir, Sigurd thought as Magni and Modi left the arena and made their way to the bleachers.

"You've outdone yourselves," Magni praised as he hefted his great sword over one shoulder. "These weapons are outstanding!"

"Thank you." Sindri smiled. He held out his hand expectantly. "Now, there's the small matter of our fee?"

Modi reached down and removed a bag from his belt. "As promised, here's a lock of my sister Thrúd's hair and some we snipped from Idun. I hope you craft something special from it."

"Oh, you can count on that!" Brok laughed, seizing the bag. "I've got so many ideas in the works!"

"Let us know how that works out," Modi requested.

"We will," Brok promised as he pocked the bag. He turned to Sigurd and gave a big, toothy grin.

"Well, lad, it looks like this is where we part ways," Brok announced. "It's been fun."

"I don't know if 'fun' is the right word," Sigurd said. His relationship with the Huldra Brothers was unique. He'd met them in the mines about a week ago when he was at rock bottom. They had given him unusual but sage advice, which included the outlandish suggestion that he be consumed by a dragon to strong-arm Ivaldi into absolving Sigurd and forging them magic equipment. They had even suggested he offer one of his eyes or internal organs as payment for their help. But Andvari's ring had proven more valuable to them. They had helped him survive the execution by brewing the potion that allowed him to undergo the Trial of Svarblood. They then forged Sinfjotli's axe and crafted Sigurd a magic belt.

"You two are good friends," Sigurd admitted. "I'll miss you both."

"Aw, don't make it sound so final," Sindri urged. "I'm sure we'll see each other again."

Sigurd grinned. "In that case, I won't say goodbye."

"Gah ha ha ha ha! That's the spirit, lad!" Brok laughed. "Anyway, it's high time Sindri and I take our leave. We've got some serious forging to do."

With that, the Huldra Brothers left the coliseum.

"Alright, let's go," Magni said once the dwarves were out of sight. "The four of us have a *long* adventure ahead of us."

"Wait, you're coming with us to Niflheim as well?" Sinfjotli blurted out.

"Aye." Modi nodded. "That's not a problem, is it?"

"N-no, of course not," Sinfjotli stammered. "It's just... I wasn't expecting the Sons of Thor to volunteer to join us."

The air pressure in the arena plummeted, and Sigurd's ears popped. Magni's and Modi's eyes crackled with electricity, and their weapons hummed with power. Sigurd worried his brother had somehow enraged them and they were about to smite him. But after a moment, he realized they were just peeved.

"Sons of Thor," Magni grumbled, his voice laced with irritation. "That's all anyone calls us. All these years, and we're still known as Thor's little boys. Never mind that we're the gods of strength and courage." He gestured at the mountains of automaton corpses in the arena behind them. "You saw how much power we possess, but no. Nobody ever takes us seriously. Whenever someone speaks of 'Mighty Magni' or 'Brave Modi,' it is always as 'the Sons of Thor.' We're perpetually stuck in our old man's shadow."

"That's partly why we want to join you on your journey through Niflheim," Modi explained. "Since no one has ever slain a primordial giant in that frigid realm, we figure it will give us a chance to pull one over on our father and step into the limelight."

"And according to Uncle Heimdall, this giant is supposed to be one of the most powerful in the realms," Magni added, his eyes sparkling. "It's an ancient giant purportedly on par with Surtr, capable of drinking oceans, splitting the earth asunder, and uprooting mountains with a single step. As strong as you are, it would be unwise for you two to face such a mighty foe alone."

"And without our help, you'll have a hard time traveling across the World Tree to Niflheim, much less getting out of Svartalfheim," Modi added. "So, do you have any objections?"

"None at all!" Sigurd beamed. "I'm looking forward to working with you two. It's not every day someone gets to go on a quest alongside the Aesir."

Modi smiled. "Well said, lad. Alright, let's go."

CHAPTER SIXTEEN

THE LAST SUNRISE

P assing through Niðavellir's towering gates, Sigurd and his companions were hit with a breathtaking sight.

The surface of Svartalfheim was exactly as Sigurd remembered. He had been underground for months, never returning to the surface even once. It felt refreshing to breathe fresh air again, even though oily black stone mountains and the barren road gave the entrance to Niðavellir a gloomy atmosphere.

However, it wasn't the landscape that left Sigurd awestruck. Standing between the towering stone statues of Fjalar and Galar, he stood beside his companions, quietly surveying the sight before him. Sunrise. The golden light spilled over the mountaintops. Sigurd couldn't remember the last time he'd seen the sun. Its rays reminded him of the Apple of Idun he'd eaten in Helheim. His legs gave out. He fell to his knees, overcome, as tears streamed freely down his cheeks. Sinfjotli was also on his knees, weeping tears of joy. They had endured death, darkness, the abyss itself, and now, at last, they had returned to the light.

Admittedly, this wasn't the prettiest sunrise Sigurd had seen. The sun, veiled behind dark clouds and the black mountains of Svartalfheim, was little more than a pale glow, no brighter than the moon in Midgard's night sky. Yet it was everything. After spending so much time underground, the sight of the sun filled Sigurd with a quiet, aching joy. It was like reuniting with an old friend after years apart.

"How long have you two been underground in Niðavellir?" Modi asked.

"I—I don't know," Sinfjotli admitted, his voice cracked and heavy with emotion. "It's so dark down there. I... I never saw daylight... until now."

"Sindri mentioned I worked in the mines for a full month," Sigurd recalled. "I think it's been a week since they approached me, and I... underwent the Trial." He shivered slightly. "I could see clearly in the dark tunnels and underground city, unlike Sinfjotli. But still... we went all that time without seeing the sun."

"You should savor this moment and burn the sight into your memory," Magni advised. "This might be the last time you see a sunrise."

That sucked the joy out of Sigurd. He thought about the cold journey that lay ahead of them. Niflheim was purportedly the coldest and *darkest* of the Nine Realms, darker than even Svartalfheim's bleak black landscape. The sun's warm rays could not penetrate through Niflheim's thick atmosphere. Sigurd and his brother had only made it halfway through the realm's frigid atmosphere before succumbing to the elements. Sigurd was barely conscious by the time the Norns rescued them. But he vividly remembered how cold and dark it had become. The sun was as distant and dim as a star by that point.

Now, they would have to venture even further into that frigid realm. They wouldn't be able to see the sun, the moon, or the stars once they were on the surface. And only the Norns would know for certain how long they would be in that icy hell.

Sigurd took Magni's advice. He stared at the rising sun until his eyes stung. When a black cloud passed over it, Sigurd decided he was ready. He stood up and wiped the tears from his face.

"We'd better get moving," Sigurd announced. "It took us about a month to travel across the roots of World Tree to reach Niflheim by foot."

"Well then, it's fortunate that you got two gods to expedite the journey." Modi held his fingers to his mouth and whistled loudly. After a moment, a chariot pulled by two enormous goats appeared before them.

"Sigurd and Sinfjotli, meet Tanngrisnir and Tanngnjóstr." Modi gestured flamboyantly.

The goats cast a cursory glance at Sigurd and Sinfjotli. Each goat was as big and bulky as a bison. Their horns were about six feet in length. They looked to be the same age, but there were too many rings on their horns to gauge an accurate age.

Tanngnjóstr, the goat on the left, seemed to have a calm and laid-back attitude. His horns were long and curved like an ibex's, his fur was white as snow, and he kept grinding his teeth. His brother Tanngrisnir was a bit more aggressive and bleated angrily every other minute. His horns were twisted like a ram's, and his coat was brownish gray.

As Sigurd stared into the goats' eyes, he noticed something. They initially seemed happy as Magni and Modi petted them. Yet he also detected fear and frustration as they gazed at their masters. They also looked traumatized, but Sigurd couldn't fathom why.

The chariot's design was simple but elegant and emblazoned with gold. The prow and sideboards were covered in runes and magical enchantments. A battering ram jutted from the front of the yoke holding Tanngrisnir and Tanngnjóstr. The two wheels bore razor-sharp blades, reminiscent of the Persian scythed chariots Sigurd had seen illustrated in books as a child. Sigurd couldn't tell if the blades were supposed to cut down enemies or slice up clouds.

Inside, the chariot was surprisingly spacious and big enough to fit all four of them. At Magni's and Modi's command, the chariot could alter its shape to adapt to their current needs, as demonstrated when they created two extra seats for Sigurd and Sinfjotli from the floorboards once they were all on board.

As Sigurd stood at the prow of the chariot, his gaze drifted to the goat on the right, Tanngrisnir. It had a lame leg. The goat bleated angrily whenever he shifted his weight onto his left hind leg as if it was causing him immense pain.

That jogged Sigurd's memory. Where had he heard about a goat with a lame leg pulling a chariot?

And then it dawned on him. "This... is Thor's chariot, isn't it?"

"Y-yes, it is," Magni stuttered while exchanging a worried glance with Modi.

Sigurd found the slight hesitation in Magni's answer curious. He was the god of strength, and Modi was the god of courage. Sigurd's first impression was that they were utterly fearless and men who could never back down from a challenge. They were both powerful as well. Sigurd had felt their immense energy when Modi placed his hand on his shoulder earlier. So what could they possibly be nervous about?

"Hang on." Sigurd slowly realized as he glanced back and forth between the chariot and the Sons of Thor. "You didn't steal this, did you?"

"Maaaybe," Modi replied in a sheepish voice.

"You did!" Sigurd burst out laughing. "Ha! You stole your father's chariot! Oh, I can already see how Thor is going to react..." He paused, and his mirth faded as he let the scenario play out in his head. "Oh. That's why you're worried. Thor will murder both of you when you return to Asgard, won't he?"

"Maaaybe," Modi said again in that same sheepish voice. "But I doubt he'll go *that* far. Oh, he'll definitely punish us. He's always had a short fuse. But we'll survive whatever beating he puts us through. Who knows? Once we succeed, he might feel proud enough to let us off lightly."

"That's only *if* we succeed," Magni corrected. "Strength and courage won't be enough to survive where we're going." He and Modi picked up the reins, shouted a command, and Tanngrisnir and Tanngnjóstr bolted forward.

The chariot wheels roared like thunder beneath their feet as they rocketed across the rocky landscape. Soon, everything became a blur as they reached the branch of Yggdrasil and left Svartalfheim behind them.

CHAPTER SEVENTEEN

BEFORE THE PLUNGE

This is taking too long, Sigurd thought as Magni and Modi brought the chariot to another needless stop.

They had spent days riding down the trunk of Yggdrasil, and at night (or whatever passed for a night on the trunk of the World Tree), they stopped to rest upon one of the many enormous branches. Perhaps their progress was slowed because one goat had a lame leg. Or perhaps Thor's sons weren't used to controlling their father's goats. But it was mainly because Magni and Modi kept annoyingly taking meal breaks.

Every time the sun completed a circle around the World Tree, Magni and Modi brought the chariot to a stop and made camp on one of the many secondary branches sprouting from the World Tree's trunk. None of these branches were as big as the two scaffolding branches Svartalfheim and Jotunheim existed on. But each one was as big as a continent, so there was never any worry of falling off.

After they made camp, they'd have their meals. Magni and Modi had voracious appetites! They boasted they could each devour an entire bison! Despite their insatiable appetites, Thor's sons showed surprising foresight and restraint. They insisted on conserving supplies for the treacherous journey through Niflheim. So instead, they ate the goats Tanngrisnir and Tanngnjóstr whenever hunger struck!

Sigurd couldn't help feeling bad for the goats, especially since he got the impression Thor and his sons did this often. After making camp, Magni and Modi slaughtered Tanngrisnir and Tanngnjóstr and placed their meat inside an enormous cooking pot. At first, Sigurd found it disturbing that they were devouring their mounts. But Magni explained the goats were magical. As long as they saved the bones and wrapped them inside the skins overnight, the goats would be fully resurrected in the morning.

"Just don't break any bones," Magni warned. "Pops won't forgive you if you give one of his goats another lame leg. One poor lad, Thialfi, made that mistake years ago, and he and his sister Röskva have remained our old man's servants as penance to this day."

Sigurd had heard the story before but still listened intently as Magni recounted the details while nibbling on one of the roasted goat legs.

"Long ago, Loki and our father were sent on a mission into Jotunheim," Magni recounted. "Along the way, they stopped by a peasant's house in Midgard to rest for the night. The peasant family who lived there welcomed them with open arms but warned they had no meat to offer for supper. So our father graciously slaughtered Tanngrisnir and Tanngnjóstr and let the family partake in his and Loki's dinner as gratitude for their hospitality. When they finished, he told everyone to pile the bones on the goatskins. Despite their generous offer, Pops and Loki devoured the lion's share of the meal, so the peasant's son, Thialfi, was still hungry. While everyone was asleep that night, Thialfi snuck downstairs, took one goat's ham bone, and split it open to get to the marrow. The next morning, Pops resurrected his goats, but when they stood up, he discovered that Tanngrisnir now had a lame hind leg. He was livid! Terrified of his wrath, the peasants offered him their children as compensation. Thialfi and Röskva have been our old man's servants ever since."

"A just but lenient punishment," Sinfjotli commended. "There are worse fates."

"Indeed," Sigurd concurred. He stared at Tanngrisnir's skull, now understanding why the goat was so aggressive.

Eventually, after eighteen days and nights and many more unnecessary meal breaks, they reached the bottom of the World Tree and traveled along the northernmost root of Yggdrasil. Right before they rode toward the icy blue realm, Magni brought the goats to a halt and pointed at the sun, moon, and stars shimmering high above them.

"You should burn this sight into your minds," Magni suggested. "This could be the last time any of us see the sun's light and feel its warmth on our skin."

Sigurd gazed up in awe at the magnificent World Tree towering over them. Its branches stretched out in all directions. He could see glimpses of the other eight realms nestled among the tree's branches and roots, each one a world of its own. As he looked up at the tree's canopy, he noticed the moon circling Midgard, the realm of humans, and the stars shimmering above. But it was the sun he savored most. Even from this distance at the base of the World Tree, its radiant light shone down upon him, illuminating everything around him with a warm, golden glow.

He wanted to burn the sun's image into his memory, to remember every detail of this moment forever. As he gazed up at the World Tree and the sun, Sigurd felt a sense of peace wash over him. All his worries and fears faded away for a moment, and he was filled with a sense of joy and wonder.

But he knew he couldn't remain here forever. He nodded when he'd had his fill. Magni and Modi whipped the reins, and Tanngrisnir and Tanngnjóstr bolted into the darkness of Niflheim's atmosphere.

Sigurd didn't feel as chilled traveling through Niflheim's frigid atmosphere as he had the first time he and Sinfjotli ventured into the realm of ice. The air was still cold enough to snap teeth, and the omnipresent wind constantly bombarded them, whipping across snowdrifts and making everything seem so white that it was hard to tell the sky from snow. But Sigurd didn't feel like his life was in mortal danger this time. In fact, his skin and armor felt hot. Sinfjotli's armor was protecting him from the extreme cold. Magni and Modi didn't seem to mind the powerful winds, but even they occasionally complained about the cold air and how their beards were getting crusted with ice.

As they rode down the tree root through the icy clouds, Sigurd wondered if they'd come across the Norns again. But then he realized he had no clue where their cave was along the tree root. He and Sinfjotli had been unconscious and at the point of death when the Norns found them and brought them back to their cave. Later, when they departed, Sleipnir had galloped so fast that Sigurd could not discern where they had left from. Not that it mattered much. Sigurd had no wish to speak with those fickle witches after what he'd endured in Svartalfheim.

After riding down the root of Yggdrasil for what felt like an hour, Magni and Modi abruptly stopped driving and dismounted.

"Why have we stopped?" Sigurd asked as he stepped off the chariot.

Magni and Modi didn't reply. They walked to the edge of the root and peered over the side. Sigurd didn't know what they were looking at. There was nothing to see here. The clouds and fog of Niflheim were so thick he could cut them with his sword. He'd literally done that very thing as they rode down the giant tree root out of boredom.

"Sigurd, come here and tell us how far we are from the ground," Modi requested.

Sigurd frowned but did as they asked and veered over the side of the root.

"Well?" Modi asked. "Can you gauge how far we are from the ground?"

"It's no good," Sigurd replied. "The clouds are too thick. Not even my superhuman eyesight can pierce the veil."

"Let's try something to remedy that," Magni said. "Stand back for a moment."

Magni and Modi closed their eyes and concentrated. They clenched their fists so hard their muscles tensed up, and their veins bulged through their skin. Electricity crackled from their bodies and channeled into the thick clouds around them. Then, a small opening in the clouds emerged.

"Well?" Magni groaned under immense strain. "How far... is it... to the surface?"

Sigurd glanced over. The small opening in the clouds Magni and Modi had created was barely eleven feet in diameter, but it was just big enough for him to see through.

"We're still a thousand miles from the surface," he estimated.

"Alright, that's good enough," Modi said. He and his brother relaxed and opened their eyes. They walked over to the chariot and unhitched Tanngrisnir and Tanngnjóstr from its yoke. Magni picked up the goats in his arms and hoisted them onto his shoulders. Meanwhile, Modi lifted the entire chariot over his head.

"What the hell are you doing?" Sinfjotli demanded.

"Taking necessary precautions," Modi replied. "We're going to jump off from here. We wouldn't want the chariot to get damaged by the impact."

"Have you gone mad?" Sinfjotli yelled. "Sigurd just said we're still a thousand miles above the surface, and you want to jump off?"

"It's quicker this way," Modi insisted. "We're currently a quarter of the way through Niflheim's atmosphere. If we continue traveling down the root of Yggdrasil like this, we'll be continuously exposed to Niflheim's atmosphere. From here onwards, the atmosphere is six thousand miles thick. It's too thick for the goats."

"Bullshit!" Sigurd exclaimed. "Sleipnir rode through these clouds without issue. Tanngrisnir and Tanngnjóstr should easily make it through with no problem, too. What's the real reason?"

As he waited for the gods of strength and courage to explain themselves, Sigurd noticed something peculiar. They were sweating, their pupils were dilated, and Modi's left hand was shaking. But it wasn't because of the strain of holding the chariot over his head. Modi was too strong for that to bother him. And every few seconds, Magni glanced nervously down the giant tree root as if he expected something to emerge from the dark clouds.

"You're afraid," Sigurd said. "There's something at the bottom of this root that you're terrified of. You would rather jump off and plummet a thousand miles to the ground than face whatever awaits us at the base of this tree root?"

Magni and Modi glared at him. Sigurd's ears popped. He wondered if they were about to smite him for having the gall to suggest that they, the gods of strength and courage, were afraid.

"Uncle Heimdall mentioned you have the clairvoyant ability to read the hearts of others." Magni sighed. "I suppose there's no point skirting around the truth with you." He set the goats down while Modi gingerly lowered the chariot.

"There is a monster that dwells at the bottom of this root that puts all others to shame," Modi admitted. He hesitated for a moment. "Its name... is Nidhogg, the dragon of the apocalypse. It is a monster so large and powerful that it can gnaw upon the root of the World Tree. It gnaws on one of the roots of creation! Do you understand how powerful such a creature is? The mere act of conversing with this beast... is akin to walking on a tightrope over boiling magma. It poses too much of a risk. Please, just trust us on this. Jumping off the root of the World Tree now would be a much safer option than confronting Nidhogg."

"Alright," Sigurd relented. "I'll take your word for it."

Sinfjotli stared incredulously at him.

"Don't look at me like that, brother." Sigurd scowled. "I've already been devoured by a dragon once. I have no intention of reliving the experience."

Sinfjotli looked like he wanted to say more, but he held his tongue. He gave a slight nod, offering his consent to the plan.

Now they were all in agreement, Magni and Modi picked up the goats and chariot again as Sigurd and Sinfjotli braced themselves for what they were about to do. Time seemed to slow as Sigurd inched his way toward the edge, his legs shaking uncontrollably. The giant tree root beneath his feet grew colder as his toes neared the drop. His heart was beating inside his chest like a trapped bird in a cage, desperate to escape.

Gazing down the tunnel Magni and Modi had created in the freezing dark clouds, Sigurd almost fainted. To the average person, there was nothing but darkness in that gaping hole. But with his telescopic vision, Sigurd could see everything, including what awaited them at the bottom. His entire life flashed before his eyes. Then, a brawny hand grasped his shoulder.

"Don't think," Modi advised. "Just take the plunge."

Sigurd took a deep breath, perhaps his last, and jumped off the root of Yggdrasil, plunging into the abyss.

CHAPTER EIGHTEEN

THE ONLY ONE IN THE WORLD

Brynhild was exhausted and frustrated after months of non-stop flying. She had traversed the towering World Tree for what seemed like an eternity. However, at long last, her arduous journey ended as she reached the pinnacle of Yggdrasil, where she found herself on the outskirts of Asgard.

An enormous golden watchtower rose before her. It was connected to the Bifröst, the glimmering rainbow bridge that led to the City of Gladsheim. The glimmering city shone in the distance like the radiant sun.

Brynhild flapped her wings and landed on the edge of the rainbow bridge. She stumbled several times as her legs were as stiff as twigs from disuse. But she soon got a hold of herself and relished the feeling of the shimmering light beneath her soles. After flying for so long, it felt good to be on her feet again.

Heimdall's Watchtower, Himinbjörg, was just as majestic as she remembered. The extremely tall, circular-shaped stone building towered over everything, including the Walls of Asgard. The tower was over eight hundred feet. She could see an enormous balcony that jutted from the top if she stretched her neck back. Purportedly, Heimdall could gaze from the top of his tower and perceive every facet of the Nine Realms with his impressive vision.

"Greetings, Brynhild," a voice called.

Brynhild turned. A familiar face stood in front of the massive door at the base of the watchtower: Heimdall, the Watchman of the Gods, the god of vigilance, foresight, and order, and the Guardian of the Bifröst. His skin shimmered and glowed in the bright sun. He held the bottom of his massive great sword, Hofund, in his hands, and the legendary Gjallarhorn dangled from his belt.

Heimdall's lips parted into a smile, showing off his golden teeth. "It has been a long time, my dear."

Brynhild warmly returned the smile. "Lord Heimdall. How long have I…"

"Six months. You've been traveling up the World Tree for about six months."

"I see. So half a year has already passed?"

It was shorter than Brynhild expected. Time flowed differently across the realms, but her journey up the World Tree had been long, perilous, and tedious. She'd been attacked by giant insects and other nasty creatures thriving on Yggdrasil's trunk at least fifteen times. She'd been injured dozens of times in those skirmishes, though not as bad as the wounds she'd suffered in Helheim. Neither time nor her runic magic had healed those injuries.

But Brynhild hadn't travelled alone. She encountered Ratatoskr after bypassing Midgard and battling a giant beetle the size of an island. The Messenger Squirrel was on his way to Niflheim to deliver a message to Nidhogg from Gullinkambi. They struck up a pleasant conversation before each went their separate ways.

But when Ratatoskr climbed back up the World Tree eighteen days later with a message from Nidhogg to Gullinkambi and discovered she was no closer to Asgard, he offered to let her ride on his shoulder to expedite the journey to Yggdrasil's upper echelons. Brynhild gladly accepted, having grown weary of the incessant attacks.

The attacks stopped after that. Most creatures avoided Ratatoskr, and he proved too quick for the belligerent fools who didn't mind their business.

The valkyrie and giant squirrel shared many sparkling conversations before parting ways near Yggdrasil's canopy. Ratatoskr eagerly gleaned every juicy detail he could glean from her while also catching her up to speed on what had happened while she was struggling for years to enter Helheim.

Sadly, Ratatoskr couldn't divulge much about what transpired in Midgard since her death, nor did he have any clue what became of her long-lost daughter.

That soured the journey. Her daughter still lived, but she had no idea what became of her nor her father.

Brynhild wondered how Sigurd was doing. Every fiber of her being had wanted to accompany him and Sinfjotli on their journey to Niflheim. But she had to leave them because Freyja had summoned her. Brynhild was a valkyrie, and her queen's orders could not be ignored. She'd learned the hard way what happens when the gods' servants disobeyed them.

"Why was I summoned to Asgard?" she inquired.

"Odin plans to put you on trial for your role in Sigurd's death," Heimdall informed her. "He still holds you accountable for Sigurd's demise and has called an assembly to decide your fate."

Brynhild blinked several times, unsure if she'd heard him right. Rage boiled inside her as she kept repeating his words in her head. "Is this some kind of joke? I got summoned away from Helheim and spent six months traveling up the World Tree for this?"

"The All-Father, Freyja, and several other Aesir are already waiting in Valhalla," Heimdall continued, indifferent to her anger. "They will decide your fate."

"My fate isn't theirs to decide!" Brynhild declared.

"They might disagree," Heimdall countered calmly.

Brynhild wanted to say more, but she wisely held her tongue. She decided just to accept it. The sooner this mummer's farce was done with, the better. As she stepped onto the Bifröst, intending to walk the rest of the way to Asgard, Heimdall appeared before her, placing a firm hand on her shoulder and halting her in her tracks.

"I've been monitoring Sigurd's and Sinfjotli's progress," he said. "They've both come quite far since you parted outside Helheim. They survived their trip to Niflheim and had an audience with the Norns. Then Sleipnir took them to Svartalfheim. They gained weapons and armor of supreme quality, and Sigurd underwent the Trial of Svarblood."

"He did *what*?" Brynhild screamed. "Why would he *do* that to himself?"

"I couldn't say." Heimdall shrugged. "I can observe and hear everyone from this watchtower, but I seldom know what they're thinking or why people make their choices. You'll have to ask him yourself when you next meet. *Assuming* you meet again, that is."

"We will," Brynhild said. "We made a promise."

Heimdall withdrew his hand from her shoulder and scrutinized her, one eye fixed on her, while the other remained trained on the horizon, checking for potential dangers to Asgard. His eyes moved independently, both admirable and unsettling. Supposedly, even in battle or on missions to Midgard or the other realms, he always kept one eye on Asgard's borders, ever mindful of his duty.

"Why are you so devoted to Sigurd?" he asked.

Brynhild raised an eyebrow. "Why do you want to know that?"

"I'm curious." Heimdall gestured to the horizon. "I can see and hear everything that happens across the realms from this vantage point. I've observed countless relationships. But I've never seen one like yours. You flew headlong into Helheim and battled Hel's army of death for..."

"...for a man who betrayed me and tricked me into marrying a man I hated," Brynhild finished. She ground her teeth. "Lord Heimdall, you and I both know that what happened was ultimately the result of my treacherous husband Gunnar and his damnable mother's machinations!"

"I am well aware. But what makes Sigurd so special that you would go so far for him?"

Brynhild rolled her eyes. "Don't you already *know* why he's special? Aren't you able to see everything with your all-seeing eyes?"

"I'm fully aware of Sigurd's skills, prowess, and power. I know just how special he is and why my father has taken an interest in him and his brother. But why is he special to *you*? What has he done to deserve such devotion from you?"

"It's... complicated. Are you sure you want to know? It'll take a long time to help you understand."

"I won't let you pass into Asgard until I'm satisfied with an answer," Heimdall informed her sternly. "The All-Father and the others have waited six months for you to arrive. They can wait a little longer."

Brynhild let out a deep sigh, her shoulders slumping slightly as she resigned herself to the situation. Arguing with Heimdall would only make matters worse.

"Do you have anything to drink?" she ventured. "I'm parched after traveling up the World Tree."

Heimdall pointed to his watchtower. "You'll find a barrel of mead inside. Help yourself."

Brynhild gladly took up the offer. She gulped down over two horns' worth of mead before she was satisfied and then returned to Heimdall. She found that the Watchman of the Gods had brought a chair for her and invited her to sit.

Brynhild sank down onto the cushioned seat with a deep sigh of relief. After spending six long months flying up the World Tree, her body was sore and exhausted. But now, she could relax and let the soft cushion cradle her weary body. It felt like heaven to sit still for just a moment, to be free from the endless flying and the constant strain on her muscles. She closed her eyes and let out a contented sigh, feeling all the tension drain from her body.

Heimdall hadn't brought a chair for himself and stood by, waiting as Brynhild got comfortable. But that wasn't surprising at all since sitting was beneath him. Supposedly, the Watchman of the Gods never once rested his back on the ground and spent all his time standing. Brynhild had never seen him sit on his throne in Asgard and wondered if he had ever taken a break or sat down in his entire life.

"To understand why Sigurd means so much to me, you must know more about my life," Brynhild began. "Like several other valkyries, I was once a mortal woman favored by the Aesir from the moment I was born. But an onlooker wouldn't get the impression that the gods blessed me. My mortal years were full of pain and heartbreak.

"I was born over a thousand years ago. My parents were Buthli, a powerful Germanic chieftain, and Thora, a famed shield maiden. We lived in a modest but strategically important village along the coast of the North Sea. Our land was rich in resources, the soil was fertile, and our access to the sea provided us with a steady food supply. My parents were the leaders of the village. My mother, Thora, was our village's best warrior and sailor. But one terrible day, her ship sank, and she drowned at sea."

Brynhild paused. "I... I have very few memories of my mother. I remember her wielding an enormous double-bladed battle axe and her thickly braided, bow-adorned, scarlet hair flowing beneath an antlered helmet. But that's all I can recall. Father assured me that Mother loved me and my younger brother, Atli, dearly and would never stop doing so, even in death.

"However, my father was left devastated over his wife's death. He often wished that he would have died in her place instead. Despair, rage, and a sense of failure overcame him, leaving us vulnerable. Many neighboring tribes coveted our village for its wealth and resources. In the past, my parents had repelled every attack. But after my mother's death, my father was devastated. He had lost his wife, closest advisor, and his greatest ally. Without her strength and tactical genius, we could not withstand the other tribes' countless attacks. I was forced to watch as they trampled our homes, plundered our stores, burned our ships, and destroyed our fields.

"The final blow came when I was sixteen. One fateful night, my father's mortal enemy, Merikh, came and sacked our village for the last time. As Merikh's men set the village ablaze and began killing the wounded, a raider apprehended me as I tried to escape the village with my brother. With Atli and my lives as leverage, Merikh offered our father a chance to spare the village if he defied Viking tradition to die honorably in battle. Seeing no other way out, my father kneeled in submission and tossed aside his axe, allowing Merikh to pick it up and execute him with it. Merikh then broke his deal with my father and ordered the entire village massacred, anyway.

"It was at that moment that something awakened within me," Brynhild recalled. "Seeing Merikh murder my father and then break his oath filled me with immense rage. I wretched my captor's sword from his hand and slew him with it. Then, I retrieved my father's axe and cut down every warrior in my wake as I carved a bloody path to Merikh. I was eventually overwhelmed and subdued, but not before slaying over sixty men. Many of Merikh's surviving men fearfully advised him to slit my throat. But Merikh had other ideas. He had never seen a warrior with such potential and wanted to use it.

"Merikh brought Atli and me back to his village and presented me with an ultimatum. He offered to make me the general of his army and grant me the honor of leading his men into battle. If I refused, he would kill my brother. I agreed to his terms, but not before making him swear a blood oath not to harm Atli so long as I served him."

Brynhild bit her lip. "I spent many years serving Merikh, leading his men into battle and bringing them glorious victories. Many claimed I was blessed by the war goddess Freyja and had been given the power to decide who lived and died in battle. Merikh's village grew fat off my conquests, and he eventually became the tyrannical leader of an enormous confederation after I subjugated many of the surrounding tribes.

"Throughout all that time, I never once saw my brother. Merikh had sent Atli to a secret remote location to ensure my continued loyalty. He assured me he was being treated well. But he never missed an opportunity to remind me what would happen to him if I rebelled.

"After thirteen bloody years, Merikh decided to 'reward' me for my service by making me his concubine. He warned me not to refuse or do anything stupid, or he would kill Atli. Biting my tongue, I agreed but asked for time to prepare.

"On the day I was to surrender myself to Merikh's lust, I went to the river to bathe and scrubbed my skin until I started bleeding, disgusted by what I had agreed to do. However, as I left the river, I encountered Sven, a devoted and righteous servant who was among the few in Merikh's kingdom who truly embodied these qualities. He informed me that Merikh murdered Atli thirteen years ago on the day after I agreed to be his general.

"Words cannot even begin to describe the black rage I felt that morning. I had spent the past thirteen years of my life killing and pillaging for my little brother's sake. Yet, it had all been for naught! Merikh had betrayed his word and murdered my last remaining family member. Worst of all, he lied to ensure my continued loyalty. I spent years destroying villages and towns and slaughtering thousands in the service of a liar, a murderer, and a traitor!

"That night, I donned my armor and exacted my bloody revenge. I stormed Merikh's castle with fire and steel, butchered his entire army, captured the king, and carved the blood eagle onto the wicked oath breaker's back. Afterward, I set all the captive slaves free. But I didn't flee the castle as it burned down. I had committed too many wicked deeds and resolved myself to perishing in the flames and facing judgement in Helheim for all I had wrought."

"But my family had other plans," Heimdall inferred.

Brynhild nodded. "Lady Freyja appeared before me amidst the flames and escorted me to Vanaheim. She made me into a valkyrie, granted me my metallic wings, bestowed me extraordinary power, and tasked me with choosing who lived and died in battle and escorting the heroes to Fólkvangr."

Brynhild smiled bittersweetly. "For a time, I was happy. Freyja was a wise and compassionate master. But everything changed one day when I got reassigned to serve the All-Father. Odin proved to be a more demanding and ruthless master. He wanted me to use my power to influence those who died in a battle ahead of time to ensure that Valhalla and Fólkvangr received a steady supply of formidable warriors and heroes that he deemed worthy."

She took a deep breath. "One particular assignment changed everything. Odin tasked me with ensuring that Hjalmgunnar, the King of the Goths, triumphed in a battle over his enemy, King Agnarr. The All-Father had given me this sort of order many times. But on this occasion, I visited King Agnarr's camp in the guise of a mortal woman for several days to discern what was so special about this king and why Odin wanted him in Valhalla. While wandering around his camp, I chanced upon a young boy who looked exactly like my slain brother. He even shared the same name, Atli. I grew fond of the youth and spent many days with him. He started looking up to me as an older sister."

Brynhild paused, her eyes glistening with a mix of sadness and relief. "That reawakened something within me. After the death of Atli, something withered in me. But that feeling, that capacity for love and compassion, had returned. I realized that if I obeyed Odin's command and helped Hjalmgunnar win, this young boy and all of King Agnarr's forces would perish in the ensuing battle. I couldn't bear the thought of it, so I made the fateful decision to disobey Odin and let King Agnarr triumph instead."

"That's why you did it?" Heimdall questioned skeptically. "You disobeyed my father for the sake of a young boy who was a memento of your brother?"

"I... I don't know," Brynhild admitted. "There might have been more to it than that. Perhaps I felt guilty over how many warriors I had sent to their deaths to appease the All-Father. Or maybe I was sick of Odin's incessant demands and wanted to rebel against him. Regardless, Odin was livid at my insubordination. He stripped me of my wings and power, made me mortal, and placed a curse on me that ensured I could never harm another living creature. Then he imprisoned me on top of Hindarfjall in a deep slumber surrounded by a ring of flames until a man without fear awakened me."

Brynhild smiled warmly. "That man ended up being Sigurd. He came to Hindarfjall after slaying Fafnir and taking the dragon's hoard. He easily passed through the ring of fire, found me sleeping in the fortress beneath a wall of shields, and used Gram to cut open my chain mail, which awoke me from my deep slumber.

"I'll never forget that moment. I opened my eyes and addressed Sigurd by his name. Even though Odin had made me mortal, I still had a hint of valkyrie abilities, allowing me to tell who my liberator was and how much time had passed since I was last conscious. I then asked Sigurd why he had come.

"Sigurd explained how a pair of nuthatches had advised him to come to Hindarfjall. He then got to one knee and asked to receive my wisdom. I spent many weeks teaching Sigurd what I knew. I taught him about the origins of runes and how they could be used. I taught him how to read and write runes and how to use them to heal and cure illness, and I had him carve several runes on Gram to improve his prowess. I told him to guard his wine cup against poison. I warned him never to trust the child of a man he killed. I advised him to always choose his words carefully so that he could never be hurt by what he did not say. Days passed into weeks, and we grew closer.

"Then, one fateful day, Sigurd proposed to me out of the blue while I was in the middle of advising him to be careful not to provoke his in-laws—if, of course, he was ever to marry. Then he said, 'I believe the woman I've set my heart upon is sitting right here next to me.'

"I was astounded by his sudden proposal. But Sigurd told me there was nothing sudden about it. Over the past few weeks, he had grown quite fond of me. I had given him sagacious advice, and we'd had many insightful conversations. I'd taught him about the runes and how to perform attacks he had never known before. Above all else, he declared I was the most beautiful woman he had ever seen.

"I was flustered but not impressed. I told Sigurd I was a warrior and a valkyrie first and foremost and I would never give up wearing a helmet or ignore the call to battle to become a mere housewife.

"Sigurd told me he had no intention of ever treating me like that. He claimed I was his equal, and if Odin's curse preventing me from harming living creatures were ever lifted, he would want me by his side in battle.

"Sigurd vowed he would marry me or no one, and as proof of his pledge, he handed me Andvari's ring, the greatest treasure from Fafnir's hoard. He then got to one knee and asked me if I would marry him."

Brynhild couldn't help but smile as she continued. "I cried tears of joy for the very first time that day. Every man I had known until that point had treated me the same way. They looked at me, but they didn't *see* me. To them, I was just an object, a weapon of mass destruction, a childbearing tool, or a useful pawn in a grand scheme. But Sigurd was different. He was the only one in the world who ever treated me like a real person... and a woman. We spent many beautiful days on Hindarfjall training, learning, and making love. I... I experienced joy unlike anything I had ever known."

Brynhild sighed as her mirth faded. "But it wasn't fated to last. Even though I had become mortal, I still retained a hint of my valkyrie power. I could sense death as it happened or when it was coming. When a person close to me, like Sigurd or his loved ones, died, it came as a ringing in my ears. One day, I sensed that a great battle had been fought in Denmark and that Sigurd's mother had perished. When I told him, he headed home immediately to investigate what had happened. But before he left, he vowed he would return to me. The next day, I experienced morning sickness and realized I was pregnant. I was overjoyed and prayed to Freyja that Sigurd would return in time to see the birth of our child. But he never did. Weeks passed, and then months. I eventually gave birth to our daughter, Aslaug, on a chilly winter morning. I considered that an ill omen. As I held my daughter, I wondered what had happened to Sigurd and resolved to find him. I traveled to a nearby village and entrusted Aslaug to Heimer, a close friend I knew to be a righteous man. I kissed Aslaug goodbye and promised to return once I found her father."

"But you never did," Heimdall said. "More accurately, you never left?"

Brynhild nodded sadly. "I returned to Hindarfjall to prepare for the trip. But at that moment, Sigurd drank the potion Grimhild had prepared for him. This potion erased all of Sigurd's memories of me. The spell also affected me, and I forgot about everything related to Sigurd, including the fact we had a daughter.

"I spent over... half a year on Hindarfjall just waiting idly inside the fortress wreathed by flames." Brynhild continued. "I... I wasn't sure what I was doing there. The only thing I knew for certain was that someday, someone would come through the ring of fire. I could feel it in my bones. Eventually, Sigurd returned to me. But..."

"...it wasn't for the right reason," Heimdall said.

Brynhild squeezed her eyes shut. "Sigurd had already married Gudrun by then. But his mother-in-law, Grimhild, was unconvinced that the potion had affected me. She knew I was a valkyrie and, more importantly, that Sigurd and I had been betrothed. He had proudly announced that detail when he politely refused to marry Gudrun at the feast her husband held for him. Grimhild feared more than anything else what would happen if I should come to their kingdom and tell Sigurd the truth. She knew about Sigurd's draconian disposition toward traitors and feared that if the truth came to light, Sigurd wouldn't hesitate to butcher her and all her children for turning him into an adulterer and oath breaker. She decided the only way to ensure that never came to pass was to have me married off to her son Gunnar. But he couldn't pass through the ring of flames being an unworthy man. So Sigurd made the ill-fated decision to pose as him and court me on his brother-in-law's behalf. And then—"

"That's enough," Heimdall interrupted. "I already heard what happened next and why you orchestrated Sigurd's death."

Brynhild faltered. "You... heard?"

He nodded. "I listened to you explain it all to Sigurd on the roots of Yggdrasil after you escaped Helheim."

"Oh... right."

Heimdall's keen senses weren't limited to his sight. His hearing was also quite sharp despite having only one ear. He could hear grass as it grew on the earth, wool as it grew on sheep, and even sounds beyond the pale of human ears. From this watchtower, he could see and hear everything unfold across the Nine Realms.

Brynhild almost blushed as she considered the implications of that. How many embarrassing moments had Heimdall watched or overheard over the years? Had he seen her and Sigurd on the nights they...?

"You've shed light on many things," Heimdall announced, snapping her back to reality. "So you remain devoted to Sigurd because he was the first man to treat you like a person?"

"It's more than that," she assured. "Since I met him, Sigurd has brought light back into my life in so many ways. He reminded me what freedom is, reminded me I'm not a weapon of mass destruction, and he's given me a reason to fight for what I believe in and cherish. He made me feel like a woman again and instilled within me how to desire and dream like one. The reason I saved Sigurd in Helheim and remain so devoted to him is that... I love him. I don't say that lightly, Heimdall. It's as if we are a single soul in two bodies. Sigurd and I are bound to each other. Once the threads of fate are tangled, they cannot be undone. If Asgard, Midgard, and all the realms perished at Ragnarök, and Sigurd alone remained, I would be content to keep living. But if it were the opposite, if the Nine Realms all else remained intact, and he alone was annihilated, I would rather recede into oblivion with him. That's why... I won't ever stop loving him. If he is allowed into Valhalla, then that is where I will stay. If he returns to Helheim, I am fully prepared to leap into the underworld to be with him without a second thought. I will *always* be with him wherever his soul resides. That is our destiny."

Heimdall smiled, revealing his golden teeth. "Well spoken, my dear. Whatever the outcome of your trial, you and Sigurd will meet again. The Norns have deemed it." He jerked his head slightly, inviting Brynhild to travel across the rainbow bridge.

With a thankful nod, Brynhild rose from her seat and strode across the Bifröst toward Gladsheim. As she crossed the rainbow bridge, she thought about the Trial of Svarblood, the ancient forbidden ritual used to create skinchangers. She shuddered as she thought about the awful pain Sigurd must have endured.

"Sigurd," Brynhild thought aloud, "I don't know why you did such a horrid thing to yourself, but please don't lose heart. Escaping Helheim and undergoing that horrid trial was only the beginning. From now on, you must walk down a long, dark path, one that's filled with even more pain and suffering than you recently experienced in Svartalfheim. I'm sorry I can't be with you through it all. Still, I pray... no. I *know* you won't falter from the path you've chosen. No matter what happens, keep moving forward!"

CHAPTER NINETEEN

A HARD LANDING

Five hours. They fell for over *five hours* before breaking through Niflheim's dense atmosphere. As they plummeted, the chute Magni and Modi had created began closing, and the thick clouds slowed their descent. It was like sinking through a giant ocean of freezing water. The deeper they fell, the darker it became, as if the sun's light was forbidden from ever reaching this depth.

They finally broke through the clouds and plunged into an ocean of utter darkness. Sinfjotli didn't even register they'd broken through the atmosphere—not until the whistling in his ears turned into a roar, and he realized the icy grip of the clouds was gone.

Panic surged through Sinfjotli as he frantically tried to think of a way to land safely, only to slam into the ground a moment later. The shockwave sent tremors through his entire body. When he noticed he wasn't feeling any pain, Sinfjotli worried he'd been paralyzed from the impact. But as he breathed in the cold air and felt the dampness against his skin, he realized he was completely uninjured. His armor had absorbed the entire force of the impact.

This armor's durability is outstanding, Sinfjotli thought. *I just fell a thousand miles and didn't break a single bone!*

After further admiring the brilliant design of the armor, Sinfjotli looked around to get his bearings; he couldn't see anything. He tried glancing up at the chute Magni and Modi had made in the clouds, but there was nothing there. No sun, moon, or a single star or light source existed in the sky.

"Sigurd?" he called out.

"I'm here," a voice replied from behind amidst the howling winds. "So are Magni and Modi."

"I can't see you," Sinfjotli said, turning toward the direction of the voice.

"But I can see you." A firm hand grasped Sinfjotli's shoulder. He sniffed the frigid air and realized Sigurd was standing in front of him. Judging from the foul smell of goat hide and cheese, Magni and Modi were also standing beside him.

"Welcome to Niflheim, the coldest and darkest of the Nine Realms," Magni announced.

The word "darkest" didn't do it justice. This entire realm was gripped in complete darkness. Even the dreary, desolate landscape of Svartalfheim and its sunless mines paled in comparison to the absolute darkness of Niflheim. If Sinfjotli was standing at the bottom of the deepest, most sunless mineshaft in Svartalfheim, it could not have been blacker. He was engulfed in absolute darkness, making him lose all sense of what was left, right, up, or down. He might as well have been blind.

"Ivaldi wasn't exaggerating when he spoke of Niflheim," Sinfjotli remarked. "I can't see a bloody thing!"

"Aye," Magni agreed. "The clouds above us are so thick that light can't reach the surface. Luckily, we came prepared for this."

Sinfjotli heard the goats bleat as Magni set them down and fidgeted around his pack, searching for something. Suddenly, a flash of bright light blinded him.

It took a few moments for Sinfjotli's eyes to adjust. When they did, he saw Magni had set the goats down and was now holding a glowing multicolored crystal in his hand. It glittered as he moved it, and rays of white light sprang from his hand.

"Sorry about that," Magni said as Sinfjotli rubbed his eyes. "This is a light crystal from Alfheim. Freyr gave it to us before we left for Svartalfheim. He claims it glows with the light of a star."

There may have been some truth to that. The luminescent crystal shone much like a star in the darkness, projecting rays of white light and illuminating their surroundings.

Now he could see, Sinfjotli got his bearings. They were standing at the bottom of a massive bowl-shaped crater. It looked like they had landed on top of a giant ice cap that had caved in under their immense weight and the velocity of their fall. Thick fog and darkness obscured everything beyond the rims of the crater. Mist hung in the air like hazy shreds of white that coiled and undulated as if they were alive. Sinfjotli noticed that the light crystal only illuminated a limited area around them. Everything beyond the rim of the crater was still shrouded in thick mist.

Magni and Modi looked completely unfazed after hitting the ground after jumping off the World Tree and plummeting a thousand miles. But that wasn't surprising. Their uncle Baldur frequently jumped off the Bridge of Judgement and crash-landed onto his ship whenever he returned from scouring the City of the Lost. Even without his divine protection, Sinfjotli suspected Baldur could do that without suffering much harm. Like him, Magni and Modi were both Aesir and the Sons of Thor to boot. They came from tough stock.

Sigurd also looked unharmed. Sinfjotli figured Modi must have grabbed him with his free hand during the fall and held onto him when they landed, which spared Sigurd from becoming a bloody smear on the ice. It was the same trick Baldur had used in Helheim to prevent him and Sinfjotli from getting hurt after he jumped off the Bridge of Judgement and crash-landed on the *Hringhorni*.

"That crystal will be useful," Sinfjotli noted. "But it looks like it can only illuminate a limited area."

"Aye," Magni grumbled. "Even if we can see our immediate surroundings, we're still functionally blind."

"No, we're not," Sigurd announced. "*I* can see just fine in this darkness."

Sigurd glanced around. His snake eyes dilated and constricted as he peered into the darkness.

"It looks like we're standing on a large ice cap," Sigurd reported. "There's a wide chain of mountains bisected by an enormous glacier about eight miles away. I wager the mountain range is about two hundred and twenty miles long and thirty miles wide. I can also see the root of the World Tree far in the distance. It travels through the clouds and eventually touches the ground somewhere far to the north."

Sinfjotli could only stare, utterly gobsmacked. "How can you see *anything* in this darkness and mist?"

Sigurd grinned and pointed at his golden slit eyes. "It's another gift of mine. I can see clearly in the dark. I suppose that's another ability you didn't hear me mention on Baldur's ship."

"Well, this makes things decidedly easier!" Magni laughed. "Sigurd, we'll rely on you to see long distances and guide us through Niflheim."

"Where are we headed?" Sinfjotli asked. "We're supposed to slay a frost giant, but do you have any inkling where it is exactly?"

"Uncle Heimdall promised we'd find the most powerful giant in the realm at Mount Isa," Modi explained. "It's the largest mountain in all the Nine Realms according to... to... him." Modi frowned and focused intently on something in the distance. "Something is generating massive amounts of electricity in the south. That could be our quarry. Sigurd, can you see a mountain that's bigger than the rest?"

Sigurd stared intently at where Modi was pointing. His serpentine pupils became more distinct, and the veins near his temples bulged from increased blood flow to his eyes as he peered even further into the darkness. His golden eyes dilated so much that Sinfjotli worried they were about to pop out of Sigurd's sockets.

"There is a mountain to the southeast that's so big that it obscures the horizon," Sigurd reported.

"How big is it?" Sinfjotli ventured.

Sigurd chuckled dryly, a hint of awe and disbelief under his breath. "'Big' doesn't do it justice. The base alone must be three hundred miles in diameter! But I don't know how tall it is. Impenetrable clouds completely obscure the peak. It's very far away, with many mountain ranges, ice caps, and other obstacles between it and us."

"It's nothing Tanngrisnir and Tanngnjóstr can't overcome," Magni boasted. "Now that we have our heading, we best get going."

They hitched the goats to the chariot yoke, mounted up, and began riding across the icy realm, with Sigurd acting as the guide, telling them where to go.

CHAPTER TWENTY

THE ETERNAL WINTER

S now, snow, everywhere, as far as he could see. Everywhere he looked, all was dark, with nothing to break up the monotony of it. Sinfjotli had seen such unbroken vistas before, like the black deserts of Svartalfheim, the boundless oceans he had crossed with his father, and Norway's endless mountain ranges. But nothing could compare to the desolate emptiness he now experienced in Niflheim. As the chariot thundered across the icy plains and through the fog like a blind man shuffling through an unfamiliar hall, Sinfjotli could not see one sign of life anywhere in this dark, frozen wasteland.

Tanngrisnir and Tanngnjóstr valiantly trudged into the gloomy darkness and through the thick snow. In Svartalfheim, their hooves had made a sound like thunder as they raced across the dark plains. But in Niflheim, the deep snow banks and mist muffled the sound, making it seem small and hushed. Magni and Modi continued driving Tanngrisnir and Tanngnjóstr while Sigurd acted as their guide, telling them where to go. Sinfjotli prayed they didn't accidentally drive off a cliff.

They weren't totally blind. Magni and Modi had attached their light crystals to the rimes of each side of the chariot, allowing everyone to walk around without stumbling over their supplies or falling off the vehicle. But the fog was so thick that the crystals barely illuminated the interior of the chariot. All Sinfjotli could see was a dim light to his left and another shining to his right. He could scarcely see his own feet in front of him as the goats trekked through Niflheim's raging blizzards.

The snow and wind dampened sounds, making it hard to hear anything approaching. Assuming there *was* anything living here. Magni and Modi claimed Niflheim was home to many mysterious lifeforms, but Sinfjotli doubted anything could thrive in this icy wasteland.

As the chariot thundered across the icy plains, Sinfjotli stared out into the misty darkness. He wondered how much time had passed since they first landed here. It felt like they'd been traveling for days or weeks. It was hard to tell. Then again, they had no way to accurately discern the passage of time with the sun, moon, and stars obscured.

Even Magni and Modi couldn't give an accurate answer when asked. "Time flows differently throughout each realm," Magni explained. "For instance, time flows much slower in Helheim than it does in Midgard. One minute in Midgard could last about an hour in Helheim."

Great, Sinfjotli thought. So for all that they knew, a single day could have passed in Midgard while they spent years wandering through Niflheim's icy darkness, or a decade had gone by in Midgard while they were trekking through this maddening darkness and ice for only a week.

Niflheim was definitely not a realm for the weak-willed. The ground was much colder than the skies above. The thick atmosphere prevented any sunlight from reaching the ground, ensuring the surface of Niflheim remained pitch-black and at a temperature cold enough to snap bone. Their breath turned to ice before the air even left their lungs. If they remained exposed to the elements for too long, their saliva froze, causing frost to form in between their teeth. At one point, Magni and Modi had to use their knives as toothpicks.

They primarily relied on the chariot to travel because walking was much more challenging. But this wasn't just because the snowdrifts and ice were extremely deep. Sinfjotli felt heavier in this realm, as if he weighed twice as much as usual. Magni told him it was because the gravity of Niflheim was much stronger than what they were accustomed to in Midgard.

For Sinfjotli, the worst part about Niflheim was the wind. It blew so violently that it could easily send an ordinary man flying off his feet like a leaf in a storm. It reminded him of when Hræsvelgr blasted him and Sigurd with hurricane-force winds that sent them flying. All four of them were heavy enough to prevent that from happening in this frigid realm. But the wind still felt like their skin was being assaulted by thousands of sharp needles.

Thankfully, the Coffin Cheater protected Sinfjotli from the cold, just as Ivaldi promised. The armor acted like a layer of blubber, protecting Sinfjotli from the elements and trapping all his body heat inside, keeping him nice and toasty—sometimes a little too well.

Magni and Modi appeared to be managing well in the extreme cold. They wore layers of thick fur over their leather jerkins and channeled electricity through their bodies, generating heat from within. Sigurd had discovered this the hard way when he touched Modi and received a very nasty static shock. He claimed afterward it felt like he had been struck by lightning.

Surprisingly, Sigurd seemed the least affected by the cold. He shivered as much as any of them and had bundled himself in heavy layers, but he didn't seem as bothered by the extreme cold. In fact, when Sinfjotli had placed his hand on Sigurd's shoulder for support after stumbling in the chariot, he recoiled; his brother's skin was burning hot, just like the day he passed the Trial of Svarblood.

But even the mighty Aesir had their limits. After about three days of consecutive riding since their last break, the Sons of Thor eventually needed to rest and find refuge from the elements. They halted their journey at the foot of a massive mountain and dismounted. The gods of strength and courage smashed their weapons against the mountain's base, creating a narrow cave deep enough to provide refuge from the bitter cold.

They had done this several times already in this realm. As always, the goats bore the brunt of their survival. Magni and Modi butchered, ate, and resurrected Tanngrisnir and Tanngnjóstr for the thirty-seventh time since leaving Svartalfheim. Sinfjotli pitied the poor beasts, but the Aesir needed constant sustenance—not just to stay strong, but to fuel the electric currents coursing through their bodies that kept them warm.

At every stop, Magni and Modi devoured most of the meat, leaving just a fraction for Sigurd and Sinfjotli. Thankfully, the goats were the size of bison, so there was always enough to go around.

Cooking was challenging in Niflheim. Since fire couldn't burn here, the brothers relied on electricity from their weapons to sear the meat, forcing Sinfjotli and Sigurd to keep their distance to avoid stray bolts.

Sinfjotli and Sigurd stood near the cave entrance, waiting for Magni and Modi to finish cooking. They stared into the pitch-snowy blackness stretching out before them, the fog so thick Sinfjotli couldn't see his nose in front of his face.

"Sinfjotli, what was our father like?" Sigurd asked.

"Our father," Sinfjotli repeated with a frown that twisted into a smile. "He was the greatest warrior I knew until I met you. He had a stomach of iron and was immune to poison. He could drink anyone under the table. I could never beat him in a drinking contest."

"But what was he like?" Sigurd pressed. "As a king? As a father?"

"Strict," Sinfjotli answered right away. "He never hesitated to punish me, Helgi, or Hámundr when we got out of line. But his punishments were always fair and just. Once, the three of us got so drunk we killed two men in a bar fight and burned down the whole tavern. Father paid wergilds to the families as recompense, granted the tavern's owner all the resources he'd need to build another, and made the three of us build it ourselves as punishment."

"It sounds like he was very generous and openhanded," Sigurd muttered.

"Aye, but he'd never forget an insult. He once razed an aristocrat's castle to the ground when he learned the noble had called me 'a bastard born of incest.' But he was also quick to forgive. When the noble's son pleaded for mercy for his own wife and children, Father granted it and let him keep his lands and titles. I've never seen the type of loyalty Father could inspire."

Sinfjotli sighed. "When we returned to Hunaland, both chivalrous and vile men alike flocked to swear us fealty and join the grand army we assembled to take back our homeland. The nobles and peasants, the chivalrous and vile, and men and women all grew to love my father. Ah... I remember everything about our father."

"But I never knew him," Sigurd lamented. "I never got the chance. He perished in my mother's arms before I was born. The only things I know about him are based on stories my mother and others told me. Until that vision in Helheim, I didn't even know what Father looked like. You're lucky, Sinfjotli. You knew him before he died. He gave you everything. But all he left behind for me was my name and a broken sword."

Sigurd drew Gram and regarded the fuller. "Gram has been a support for my heart. From this sword, I learned of a 'father's love,' duty, and honor. But no matter how much comfort I've found in holding it, it can never compare to a genuine parent's love. It wasn't until I had children of my own and held Svanhild in my arms for the first time that I realized that. I wish I'd gotten to experience it with our father. Just once would have been enough."

As the wind outside the cave shrilled like a mother mourning her slain children and Sigurd sheathed his sword, Sinfjotli reflected on the vision they had experienced in Helheim of their father's final battle. Sigmund had received dozens of grievous injuries but kept fighting until he slew Hávard. When he collapsed, his face looked so peaceful and content.

"Do you think that's the last thing Father remembered?" Sinfjotli asked. "The pain? Dying in your mother's arms, regretting that he'd never see his son grow up? Or do you think he was proud that he had fought a meaningful duel and avenged your grandfather with everything he had, knowing that was his last battle and Odin himself would soon come to escort him to Valhalla?"

"Oh, he was definitely proud," Magni confirmed as he and Modi joined them at the cave entrance. "But not just for the reasons you mentioned. When he got to Asgard, he boasted that the All-Father himself had to personally ensure this would be his final battle. Your grandfather, Völsung, claimed it was a testament to his son's skill as a warrior."

"You know our father?" Sinfjotli asked.

Sigurd sighed and rolled his eyes. After a moment, Sinfjotli realized just how redundant and obtuse his question was. Magni and Modi were gods who lived in Asgard. Obviously, they would have met Sigmund at some point.

Thankfully, Magni and Modi didn't mind his tactlessness.

"We know him quite well." Modi grinned. "We met him when Odin escorted him to Valhalla after he died."

"Your father is quite the character." Magni laughed. "Sigmund once challenged us both to arm wrestling contents, and he challenged our father to a drinking contest. Sigmund lost, obviously, but he lasted far longer than most challengers. Thor was so impressed that he allowed Sigmund to accompany him on an adventure into Jotunheim. We can tell you more about it inside."

Tonight (or whatever passed for a night in this sunless realm), Magni and Modi had made a stew of broiled broth, complete with wild beans, peppers, and simmered goat meat. Although they were frugally conserving their supplies, the ingredients blended well. And the main course was, of course, the simmering tender meat from the slaughtered goats.

"Your mother is quite the character as well, Sigurd," Modi added as he helped himself to another bowl of pottage. "I can see why Sigmund was so taken by her. She is a capable warrior. She once challenged Týr to a duel and lasted a full minute against the god of war. Only a handful of mortals have persisted that long against our uncle."

Sigurd smiled proudly as he feasted on the cooked goat meat.

"How did your mother die?" Sinfjotli wondered aloud as he took a bite out of Tanngrisnir's leg.

"She perished in a stupid war." Sigurd took a swig of mead and then grinned. "But she died a glorious and meaningful death."

CHAPTER TWENTY-ONE

THE IRON QUEEN

"**M**y mother's death played out like a chapter right of Volsung history," Sigurd began. "I told you on Baldur's ship that my stepfather's family, the house of Yngling, was the mightiest dynasty in Danish history. Unfortunately, as is often the case with monarchs, their greatest enemies were their kin.

"After I defeated Lyngvi and obliterated his entire army, some of my friends and allies elected to remain behind and establish their own kingdoms within Lyngvi's former territory. After I left with Regin to face Fafnir, my stepfather also left Denmark to help my friends and allies consolidate their hold on Lyngvi's territory and set up multiple client kingdoms loyal to him. During his year-long absence, a powerful army led by Alf's jealous twin brother Yngvi invaded Denmark, hoping to conquer the kingdom and seize the throne in his absence."

Sigurd grimaced. "Yngvi was filled with all the spite and envy that often accompanies second sons in dynastic families. Coming second from his mother's womb, a few heartbeats after his twin brother, Alf, had denied him the glory of kingship and the wealth of house Yngling. And he coveted the throne more than anything else.

"I already told you that my stepfather was an accomplished king. Alf was a great warrior who always won his battles, and as a ruler, he was generous, happy, and sociable. But Yngvi was everything Alf was not. He was unsociable and harsh and stayed home instead of pillaging in other countries. But he was also quite cunning and shrewd. Whenever my stepfather was out raiding or on business, Yngvi secretly struck up alliances with minor lords who disliked Alf for justified or ill reasons. He spent years forging secret pacts until he felt the time was ready.

"While my stepfather consolidated his hold on Lyngvi's former empire and I was still at Hindarfjall with Brynhild, Yngvi and his forces invaded our home. Only my mother and several warriors stood against them. She had a sizeable army with her. But she did not meet Yngvi in an open battle. Instead, she and her men scoured the countryside and helped farmers, peasants, and other civilians evacuate to Alf's castle as Yngvi's army approached."

"Why didn't she just attack him?" Sinfjotli interrupted. "That would have seemed more sensible than letting him lay siege to the castle. I remember you boasting that Hjordis was one of the greatest warriors of her day. I reckon she could have had a better chance of vanquishing him in battle."

"Mother cared more about protecting the lives of her people than vanquishing her traitorous brother-in-law in battle," Sigurd explained. "In war, the people who suffer the most are often common folk. Farmers, fishers, tanners, millers, and other simple folks who have never held a weapon before are always the first to suffer the wrath of invading armies."

"Careful," Modi cautioned. "You make it sound like everyone in Yngvi's army was a bloodthirsty villain driven by greed and malice. But you shouldn't generalize like that, Sigurd. Very few people go to war to fight for an evil cause. Almost everyone fights for what they perceive is right, no matter how misguided it may be."

"Yngvi undoubtedly had many righteous and misguided warriors in his army," Sigurd conceded. "Not everyone in Yngvi's army was a monster, and not everyone in my army was a hero. War brings out the worst in people. Even the best warriors can succumb to greed, bloodlust, and worse vices once they get a taste of battle. I've seen it happen often, even to some of my comrades. When we first landed on Lyngvi's lands, I announced our war was with Lyngvi and all the men who had sacked Hunaland. Then I gave everyone two simple restrictions: spare the children and anyone who might've been taken captive from Hunaland years ago, and rape no women! I warned that if anyone broke this order, they would hang. I ended up having to hang a hundred of my comrades before the war was over. Regin once said there's a monster within every man that awakens during war, and that is especially true for men and boys who lived their entire lives devoted to revenge. Worse, when an uncaring leader commands them and doesn't punish his soldiers for committing heinous war crimes, many men can slip further into villainy. Men will plunder and burn the countryside bare to fill their starving bellies. They'll sate their lust on the daughters and wives of farmers, millers, fishermen, and other innocent country folks, and if their husbands, fathers, or brothers try to stop it, they'll get murdered. Then they'll butcher the wailing babies and children because they can't stand the sound of their wailing. Then they'll burn their entire house down and sow their fields with saltpeter out of sheer spite. I've seen it happen far too many times. So did my mother. And that's why she chose not to face Yngvi in battle.

"A monarch must serve their nation, their people, and above all else, keep them safe. Over the years, my mother grew fond of Alf and the people who had taken her in. Thus, she and her forces gathered as many men, women, and children as they could rescue from the nearby villages and towns into my stepfather's castle as Yngvi's army approached and barred the gates. She sent messengers to my stepfather, warning him to return to Denmark immediately. But Alf was far away in Lyngvi's former territory, and a brutal siege ensued as they waited for aid.

"Because of its strategic location and cultural significance, Yngvi needed to take Alf's castle to conquer the rest of Denmark. He tried many times to breach the fortress. But Mother and her forces repelled no less than a dozen assaults. Every morning, his army sent volleys of arrows over the castle walls, then my mother's forces collected the arrows and fired them back. Toward the end of the siege, Yngvi resorted to flinging the rotting carcasses of livestock over the walls.

"Thankfully, the siege ended before any diseases could spread. When my stepfather learned about his brother's rebellion, Alf rushed back to Denmark with as many men as he could muster. It took him less than three days to return to Denmark, and he sent word to my mother that he was coming and urged her to hold out until he arrived. But the messenger was intercepted by Yngvi's forces before he could reach the castle. When Yngvi learned his brother had returned, he knew he had to take the fortress now or risk losing everything. He split his army in half and attacked the castle in an out-pincer maneuver. He sent half his army to harass the south side of the castle while the rest of his men attacked the main gate on the northern side.

"My mother knew she didn't have enough men to adequately counter the pincer maneuver. So, she sent most of the able-fighting men available to her to counter Yngvi's attack from the south. Meanwhile, she stationed herself at the main northern gate of the castle with a handful of her best soldiers. My uncle Grípir and friends Folan, Vafi the Loon, and Birna Bloodtusk were among those who joined her. As Yngvi's forces battered the gate, she gave a rousing speech to her warriors and vowed she wouldn't let a single enemy soldier set one foot inside the castle's inner yard. Then, the enemy broke through the gate.

"Against all odds, my mother and her forces held out against the vicious pincer maneuver until nightfall when King Alf finally arrived and fell upon Yngvi's rear guard with all his strength. That horrible night was filled with blood, screams, and death. When the sun rose the following day, the grass around the castle was dyed red with blood, and the moat was choked with corpses. Ten thousand men lay dead, but Yngvi's army had suffered the worst casualties. The entire army was annihilated, and Yngvi perished in the battle.

When his corpse was found, it was drawn, quartered, and his head was placed on a pike above the main gate. Some disgruntled nobles claimed my stepfather slew his traitorous brother in glorious single combat and proclaimed him a kinslayer. But when I asked him about it, Alf told me he had no recollection of the event. The night had been very cloudy. Only the dim light of the torches and campfires of Yngvi's army allowed Alf's army to see enough to avoid friendly fire. He might have slain his brother during the charge. But more likely, his twin was slain by some unknown soldier who likely didn't even realize who he killed.

"In the end, Mother's strategy succeeded. Yngvi and everyone who supported him had been slain, and my stepfather's castle and all the refugees housed within had been spared.

"But it had come at a grievous price. As crows and wild dogs feasted upon the bodies of the slain, my stepfather and his men made their way through bloodstained grass toward the castle's main gate. There, he found mounds of bodies strewn across the ground. My best friends, Folan, Vafi, and Birna, were amongst the slain, and a single person still stood upright in the center of the gate.

"When my stepfather saw the sword Lady Misery still clutched in the corpse's bloody hands, he realized it was my mother standing dead on her feet before him. He was aghast at how battered and bloody his wife looked. Her torso and face were bruised and mutilated to where she was unrecognizable. But he also felt proud. Even in death, her body stubbornly refused to fall and remained upright. Amazingly, she hadn't taken a single wound to her back. When Alf gazed past her, he saw there wasn't a single corpse lying in the castle's inner yard. Throughout that bloody battle, she never once turned her back on her opponents or took a single step backward. She had kept her word and defended the gate at the cost of her own life.

"My stepfather waited until I arrived before giving my mother, my friends, and everyone who fought alongside her a hero's funeral. Alf erected a statue of my mother outside his main hall, and everyone in Denmark hailed my mother as 'The Iron Wall of Denmark.'

"What a heroine." Sinfjotli whistled. "Besides our ancestor Sigi's last stand, your mother's last stand is the most courageous story I've heard."

"We thought so as well," Modi agreed. "Everyone in Asgard was impressed by her valiant last stand. Freyja was so amazed that she personally escorted Hjordis's soul to Asgard along with all the souls of her comrades who died alongside her. She even offered her a special place of honor in Fólkvangr, but Hjordis elected to remain in Valhalla with your father, Sigmund."

Sigurd smiled. "Mother often said her time with Father was brief. But during that one year together, they had loved a lifetime. I'm happy they're together again and that all my friends got to take their places in Valhalla alongside her."

A tear of joy trickled down Sigurd's face. He noticed Sinfjotli staring and wiped it away.

"I was just remembering the dream I had right after we escaped Helheim," Sigurd explained. "Odin showed me a glimpse of Valhalla. I saw our family and my friends Folan, Vafi, and Birna seated at a table. I'm so happy that part wasn't a dream, and they really are in Valhalla. Given how fickle and picky the valkyries can be, I always feared they wouldn't be chosen."

Suddenly, Sigurd's smile melted into a scowl. He turned to Magni and Modi. "Why are the rules of the afterlife so stringent? Why must someone die in battle to go to Valhalla, and everyone who doesn't is automatically sent to Helheim?"

"It's just the way things are," Modi replied.

"*Why?*" Sigurd said. "Why are the rules of the afterlife so draconian?"

Modi sighed. "It's a product of the Jötnar's and Aesir's blood-soaked destiny of hate. A curse of hate that began generations ago when Odin slew Ymir."

"Sigurd, you need to understand just how bloody and violent things were in the beginning," Magni explained. "The frost giants never forgave our grandfather for slaying Ymir and bringing their race to the brink of extinction in the deluge of blood that flowed from the progenitor's wound. This grudge fueled the Jötnar throughout history, driving them to take up arms against the Aesir. The wars we fought against Bergelmir's descendants and, later, the Vanir were extremely ferocious. Millions died on all sides. The battles were on scales beyond anything you can imagine. If a single person hesitated, lost heart, or took a just single step backward, an entire battle would be lost. So our grandfather decreed that only the bravest warriors who wouldn't hesitate to sacrifice their lives in battle would be granted the honor of fighting alongside the Aesir. In his view, the measure of a man's life ought to be determined by the circumstances of his death."

"Things cooled down after the Aesir-Vanir War ended," Modi added. "We brokered peace with the Vanir and reached an uneasy stalemate with the giants. There weren't any more all-out wars between the realms, and any battles fought were nowhere near as destructive as before. However, the tradition of measuring a person's life by the circumstances of their death remained in place. Grandfather claims that when Ragnarök comes, it will be a war unlike anything ever seen. That's why he remains adamant that only those who prove themselves by dying bravely can earn a place in Valhalla since they will not hesitate in the final battle. In his eyes, only battle can decide a person's true worth."

"It's still a flawed system," Sinfjotli grumbled.

Magni looked at him and then sighed before taking a sip from his drinking horn. He did not refute Sinfjotli's remark, and Sinfjotli knew it was because he was right.

The problem with such a draconian system is that not everyone dies in battle. His father often said, "The weak don't get to choose how they die." But the strong rarely did, either. Anyone could die at any moment, in countless ways, from disease, famine, injuries, accident, or even assassination. Even the bravest and most righteous warriors had no guarantee of a glorious end. Baldur was proof of that. The best and most virtuous Aesir, yet condemned to Helheim simply because he hadn't died in combat.

Sinfjotli and his brother were no exception. He was poisoned by his vengeful stepmother, and Sigurd was murdered by his jealous brother-in-law. They'd both lived checkered lives, committed many wicked deeds, but in the eyes of Hel and the Aesir, their most unforgivable crime would always be not dying bravely in battle, something neither of them had any say in. And now they were on a quest, traveling across the realms, atoning for a fate that had never been in their hands.

Sinfjotli sighed as he drained his horn of mead. When it was empty, he stood up and went to the chariot to refill it. As he rummaged through the supplies, he noticed a wisp of light out of the corner of his eye. He turned toward the cave entrance. In the darkness beyond, multicolored lights flickered on and off. He dropped his horn and rushed to the entrance to see what it was.

He stepped out into the freezing darkness and gazed up. At first, there was nothing. Then, a long streak of crystal-blue light appeared. Then another, a sapphire streak across the sky. It was shaped like a comet, except this comet had several tails attached to the head instead of one.

No. Those weren't tails. They were tentacles!

All at once, the lights shone brightly, illuminating the darkness. A school of flying bioluminescent jellyfish dancing in the wind. They floated gracefully through the open air as if swimming in the water.

Sigurd appeared next to Sinfjotli, and Magni and Modi soon joined them as they stared in awe at the majestic light show.

"Even in the darkest realm, there is still beautiful life," Sigurd noted.

The wind picked up, and the jellyfish scattered. Their bioluminescent lights vanished, leaving Sinfjotli and his companions in pitch darkness. The air outside the cave felt even colder than before. Sinfjotli could feel the temperature change, even though the interior of his armor was as hot as an oven.

As Sinfjotli wondered what was happening, he noticed a foul scent in the wind. "Something's approaching." He reached for his axe.

"We sense it too," Magni affirmed. The god of strength scanned the darkness. "There are at least ten of them from the—"

"Incoming!" Sigurd shouted, shoving Sinfjotli aside as an enormous chunk of ice barreled out of the darkness. Magni and Modi stepped forward. Sword and hammer struck in unison, smashing the icy projectile to pieces. Electricity crackled from their weapons, briefly illuminating the darkness. As Sinfjotli rose to his feet, he saw it had been a two-ton chunk of ice.

What could have thrown something that heavy? Sinfjotli pondered.

He soon found the answer when loud, crunching footsteps approached. Magni unfastened the light crystal from his belt and held it over his head, sending rays of light in all directions. In the thick mist and raging blizzard, it was only as bright as a lantern. Through the shifting veil of snow, ten humanoid creatures emerged. Each stood nearly fifteen feet tall, their hulking forms covered with white furry hides. Beneath, sinewy blue skin the color of permafrost, stretched over powerful limbs, legs as tall as trees, splayed padded feet for traction on the ice. Clawed hands flexed, while bestial faces twisted into snarls beneath heavy brows. Several of them, clearly male, had two ram-like tusks jutting from the sides of their heads and shaggy white beards caked with blood.

"A pack of hungry frost trolls," Magni growled. "They must have been drawn here by the smell of cooked goat meat."

"We picked a bad time to eat Tanngrisnir and Tanngnjóstr," Sinfjotli grumbled. Without the goats, they couldn't run away through this waist-deep snow. They'd have to wait an entire night, or whatever passed for a night in this sunless realm, before they could magically revive the goats and travel again.

But Sinfjotli had no intention of fleeing. He had Sigurd and the gods of strength and courage by his side. Fighting in this raging blizzard and total darkness wouldn't be ideal, but it was not impossible. Sinfjotli felt no fear. Not even as he stared at the trolls' bestial faces and their glowing blue eyes. Instead, he felt angry. Angry that they had interrupted such a beautiful spectacle. Furious they had interrupted their dinner, and enraged he was stuck in absolute darkness on a quest to atone for an insignificant "crime."

The Aesir value courage in battle above all else, Sinfjotli thought. *Let there be blood, then!*

The most enormous frost troll, the pack's leader, stepped forward. It towered over Sinfjotli and its comrades with its massive size and brawn. It raised its primitive war club fashioned out of animal bones and skulls and bellowed.

"RRRRRRREEEEEEEEEGH!" Its voice was baneful, a scream of pain and fury that burned Sinfjotli's ears. The cry lingered in the misty air as the rest of the pack charged.

Sinfjotli summoned Wolfsbane to his hand and bravely charged at the nearest troll.

But his confidence soon turned to ash. As Magni and Modi clashed against four trolls, their battle pushed them further away from Sinfjotli and Sigurd. The Sons of Thor soon vanished into misty darkness, taking the light crystal with them. As the dim light faded into darkness, so did Sinfjotli's courage.

CHAPTER TWENTY-TWO

A WOLF'S CHAGRIN

S now crunched to Sinfjotli's left—too late. The troll's club slammed into Sinfjotli's side. He went flying back, the power of the blow carrying him through the air. He landed on his back, barely able to breathe. Pain shot up his left side like fire. He cringed as a fresh jolt exploded in his head with blinding whiteness. He felt another tight, sharp pain in his chest as he struggled to breathe.

Crap, Sinfjotli thought. *That one got my ribs.* He ran his hand over his left side. There was a deep indentation in his chest plate where the armor had caved in.

Get up! Sinfjotli staggered to his knees, but the pain kept him from standing. As he struggled to breathe, he looked around, wondering where the troll was. Was it approaching him? Was it alone? Were there more trolls amassing around him? He had no way of knowing. All he saw was pitch-black in every direction.

Sinfjotli cursed his luck. He was fighting utterly blind in the total darkness of Niflheim. That presented a significant issue. The sense most used in battle is sight. Everyone fights based on visual information. Any warrior would be severely disadvantaged in total darkness like this, especially against a savage beast three times his size.

Sinfjotli was utterly helpless. His father had once prepared him for a situation like this, forcing him to spar while blindfolded to sharpen his other senses. But that training was useless here. The wind would howl like a roaring beast every few seconds, and the shrieking sound masked the frost trolls' approaching footsteps. Sinfjotli could smell the trolls' putrid musk, but the wind was blowing to his back, so he couldn't tell how close they were, when they were about to strike, or from which direction.

Out of desperation, Sinfjotli threw his axe blindly in the trolls' general direction. Sometimes, he got lucky, and Wolfsbane would return to his hand with the scent of blood on its axe head. But he could not confirm if he'd done any significant damage.

Sinfjotli also had no inkling of how the battle was progressing. He'd been separated from Sigurd and had no clue where his brother was now. Magni and Modi were fighting far away in the distance. Sometimes, they'd generate bolts of lightning, momentarily illuminating the landscape and providing Sinfjotli brief glimpses of the trolls' hideous forms. But this proved more of a hindrance than a boon. After spending so long in pitch-blackness, Sinfjotli's eyes had adjusted to the darkness. He could probably see the trolls' silhouettes if it wasn't so misty. But whenever Magni or Modi channeled electricity, the bright flash blinded Sinfjotli, leaving him disoriented and even more vulnerable to the savage frost trolls' attacks.

The only silver lining about this unfavorable situation was that the frost trolls couldn't seriously injure him, thanks to the Coffin Cheater. Sinfjotli's magic armor protected him from whatever the trolls threw at him.

Unfortunately, that protection sometimes came at a painful cost. These frost trolls were much stronger than the undead ones Sinfjotli and Sigurd had faced in Helheim. Whenever they landed a hit, the blow was powerful enough to dent his armor. The Coffin Cheater would magically repair itself given enough time, but the sudden strikes always made Sinfjotli gasp, as if Modi's war hammer had struck him. The armor could soften the below but couldn't disperse the blows entirely. The most recent strike had left a crater-like dent in the armor. Sinfjotli's left side burned as if two of his ribs had cracked under the pressure.

As he recovered his breath and considered how to turn this disadvantageous situation around, he heard a troll bellow in the darkness. This wasn't their usual war cry. It was a scream full of shock and pain.

Sinfjotli smelled blood to his right. He stood up and swung his axe. But his attack got interrupted mid-swing when something grabbed his wrist.

"Take it easy," a familiar voice warned. "It's just me."

"Sigurd?"

"Yes, it's me." His brother released his grip on his arm. Sinfjotli turned toward the direction of Sigurd's voice, but he couldn't see anything in the misty darkness. But he knew Sigurd could see him clearly with his superhuman eyes.

"You're holding on by a thread here, brother," Sigurd observed. "You've barely scored a couple of hits. You don't have to push yourself so hard."

Sinfjotli scowled. "Are you suggesting I sit this fight out?"

"That's not what I meant. You're not fighting alone. You have me, Magni, and Modi to back you up."

Sinfjotli scowled.

"Reaching out for help isn't a sign of weakness," Sigurd continued. "Sometimes it takes great strength and courage to admit when you're in over your head."

Sinfjotli considered his words before Sigurd suddenly shoved him aside. There was a loud crunch, presumably a troll burying his club in the deep snow after missing Sinfjotli. He scrambled to his feet and then detected Sigurd's scent next to him.

"What's the status of the battle?" Sinfjotli inquired. "How many trolls remain?"

"Magni and Modi are dealing with five of them further away," Sigurd reported. "I already dealt with three of them and just slew a fourth. It's just the pack leader left."

He's already killed that many? Sinfjotli thought with a twinge of envy. *And I haven't slain a single one yet.*

"This doesn't make you weak," Sigurd assured as if reading Sinfjotli's' mind. "These trolls are just too strong. They're even tougher than those trolls we fought back in Helheim, and *they* were already dead."

That last detail both intrigued and reassured Sinfjotli. It also filled him with renewed purpose. He was determined to prove himself by slaying at least one troll.

"Where exactly is the last troll?" Sinfjotli demanded.

"He's standing in front of us about thirty feet away," Sigurd said. "But be careful. This pack leader is the toughest son of a bitch in the pack. We should handle him together."

"Thanks for the offer, but I'll pass." Sinfjotli dropped Wolfsbane and doubled over, his hands and knees on the ground. "Could you step back for a moment? There's something I want to test out."

"What are you planning?" Sigurd inquired.

"Ivaldi said the Coffin Cheater will adapt to protect me from any situation," Sinfjotli recalled aloud. "I've wondered what would happen if I tried transforming while wearing it."

He closed his eyes and concentrated as his flesh began to twitch and change shape. The Coffin Cheater instantly responded. He heard the metal twisting and felt the armor's gauntlets, boots, breastplate, and helmet adapting to his changing body shape. Within seconds, he stood up as a giant armored wolf.

He must have looked quite fearsome because he heard Sigurd take a few steps backward. Sinfjotli was about to ask if the troll had moved away when he remembered something else. Coffin Cheater was supposed to obey his every command. Could it guide him to the frost troll? It was worth a shot.

"Kistfuskare, hunt!"

The armor immediately began moving on its own accord, forcing Sinfjotli's body to lunge forward. Soon, he noticed the troll's putrid stench directly in front of him. He leaped off the ground.

The next thing he knew, he had knocked the troll on its back and began tearing out its throat. The beast stopped struggling after the twelfth bite. It was probably dead, but Sinfjotli took no chances and continued ravaging the troll's body. He might have continued mauling the corpse until it was nothing but a bloody smear had a loud crash and blinding flash of light not jolted him from his frenzy.

Disoriented, Sinfjotli staggered back, blinking rapidly. As his vision adjusted to the light, the scene sharpened. Magni stood over another frost troll, the light crystal on his belt illuminating the area. The troll beneath him twitched, grasping weakly at the god of strength. With effortless brutality, Magni swatted away its grasping hands, seized its head, and twisted sharply. The sickening snap echoed in the icy air.

"Those were some tough sons of bitches!" Magni remarked as he hopped off the corpse. He held out his hand, and his greatsword magically returned to him, thick with troll blood. As Magni wiped the blade clean, Sinfjotli caught his reflection in the sword's fuller. He looked every bit the monstrous predator, an armored wolf; a surge of pride coursed through him.

Magni holstered his sword across his back and turned, smiling. But his smile faded as he stared at the bloody corpse Sinfjotli had ravaged.

The pack leader's corpse was a bloody mess. Its torso lay scattered in chunks; it was missing a leg. Its arms and head had been ripped off, jagged stumps still gushing blood, painting the snow red.

"Bor's breath, you didn't show any mercy!" Magni remarked.

"He couldn't afford to," Sigurd said as he emerged from the darkness. "These frost trolls were unnaturally tenacious. I cut off one troll's arm, and it still kept fighting. It even picked up its detached limb and used it like a club."

"Yeah, we had trouble on our end as well," Modi reported as he emerged from the darkness and stepped into the light. "It took us about twenty minutes just to kill a single one."

Sinfjotli could only stare. "They gave you that much trouble? You should have easily wiped the floor with them. I mean, you're both gods!"

"That made little a difference against the trolls." Modi shrugged. "We blasted those whoresons with lightning no less than seven times, and they still kept fighting."

Sinfjotli was speechless. These frost trolls had been some of the most formidable creatures he'd faced. He and Sigurd had fought many undead trolls during their last stand on the Gjallerbru. After the draugs and the undead giants, the trolls had been the strongest soldiers in Hel's army. But these frost trolls were at least ten or twenty times more powerful than their undead counterparts.

"Those were some very tough foes," Sinfjotli muttered. "They were even tougher than the trolls we fought in Helheim."

"How could there be such a discrepancy in power between living trolls and dead ones?" Sigurd asked. "Was it because these trolls were still alive?"

"No, it's because of Niflheim's extreme cold," Modi replied.

"The cold weather caused this?" Sinfjotli asked skeptically.

"Creatures of frost draw their strength from cold weather, which allows them to reach their physical peak," Magni explained. "And since Niflheim is the coldest realm, this amplified their power to its maximum potential. That's why these frost trolls were twenty times stronger than the ones you're accustomed to fighting. It's also why the beast damaged Kistfuskare."

Sigurd looked at the dent in the side of Sinfjotli's armor as if only now noticing it. "Ivaldi said it would protect him."

"It has its limits," Magni said. "Considering how much the trolls' strength was amplified, Sinfjotli might as well have been receiving punches from Modi and me."

"That aside, you both did well," Modi said. "Slaying even one of those monsters is quite the achievement. And Sigurd slew four of them!"

"Aye. Well done, both of you." Magni clapped Sigurd's shoulder. But he winced and stepped back, clutching his hand. First-degree burns covered his palm.

"Fuck me! Sigurd, you're burning hot right now!"

Sigurd blinked. "I am?"

"Yes!" Magni yelled. "It feels like I thrust my hand into a vat of boiling oil."

Sigurd looked puzzled. "But... I don't feel hot. I don't feel cold, either. I don't feel any different from when this fight began."

As Sigurd examined his hands and chest, Sinfjotli noticed that the falling snowflakes sizzled and evaporated when they touched Sigurd's helmet and shoulders. The ground beneath his feet was steaming.

Magni and Modi shared a worried look. Something was amiss. But they took Sigurd at his word and headed back to the cave.

CHAPTER TWENTY-THREE

SVARBLOOD THE SKINCHANGER

They finished dinner and tried to get some shut-eye, but sleep eluded Sinfjotli as it often did. He tossed and turned on the straw mattress Magni had given him to no avail.

The pain in his ribs was gone now, thanks to the healing properties of the Apple of Idun he had eaten in Helheim. Though quite some time had passed since they escaped the underworld, the apple's healing magic continued to serve him, though its effects had diminished somewhat.

Part of him wished the apple's magic would expire already. Ever since eating it, he'd been anxious and full of energy, making it difficult to fall asleep. When was the last time he truly rested? He couldn't recall. Maybe in Svartalfheim when Mótsignir knocked him out. During the two months Sigurd spent mining ore, he hadn't slept a single night in his cell. His body had been teeming with too much energy for that.

Modi's snoring didn't help, either. The god of courage rumbled like a growling bear, the sound echoing through the cave like thunder, making Sinfjotli's ears ring.

He shut his eyes and tried to think of home, Hunaland, Baldur's ship, and his family in Valhalla... but no matter how hard he tried, his thoughts kept returning to the recent battle.

I only slew one troll, he reflected. *Sigurd slew four, Magni and Modi slew five, but I could only kill one.* It had been the largest and strongest member of the pack, but that did little to comfort him.

But it wasn't just wounded pride and the apple's energizing effects keeping him awake. Something else was bothering him. Sinfjotli rose from his straw mat and glanced at Sigurd. Even in sleep, his brother's body radiated heat beneath his fur blanket. The heat lapped Sinfjotli's face like a fiery tongue, even though he was several yards away from Sigurd. The snow around Sigurd's mat had melted, leaving behind sizzling rocks. The cave ceiling was damp and dripping, almost like light rain, and the air in the tunnel carried a metallic warmth. Not *warm*, but warmer than the raging blizzard outside.

Magni had claimed it felt like he'd thrust his hand into a vat of burning oil when he touched Sigurd's shoulder. Sinfjotli once had a similar experience. After the Trial of Svarblood, Sigurd's skin was burning hot like the surface of a furnace, branding Sinfjotli's palms with second-degree burns when he helped Sigurd to his feet. Those wounds had long since healed, but the phantom pains haunted him even now.

Every skinchanger developed new quirks after undergoing the Trial of Svarblood. Sinfjotli had learned that long ago from his mother, who had been tutored by a woods witch about how to help him and his father undergo the Trial. As a wolf, Sinfjotli was always quick to anger and willing to kill over the slightest insult. In his younger years, he used to fly into a blood rage whenever he smelled blood, but he had long since overcome this tick.

Other skinchangers might develop different quirks depending on the animal. Those who turned into mountain lions or other big cats became vain, sneaky, and cruel, always ready to turn on their comrades. Bears, however, were allegedly the worst. Those trials were gruesome, agonizing affairs. The skinchangers who passed the Trial of Svarblood and were reborn as bears would become stronger and fiercer but also lazy, temperamental, indolent, and gluttonous. They would rather spend their days stuffing their faces and drinking than fighting, hunting, or working, and come winter, they'd sleep nine hours out of every ten until the cold passed.

But what about a dragon? Sinfjotli stared at Sigurd and wondered how the Trial of Svarblood had changed his brother. Would his body always heat like a furnace whenever he entered a battle? Or was this the prelude to something worse?

"Can't sleep?" a voice asked.

Sinfjotli turned. Magni was sitting on the rim of the chariot, drinking a horn of mead.

"No," Sinfjotli admitted.

Magni rummaged through a nearby crate. He turned around with another drinking horn in his other hand and invited Sinfjotli to join him. Sinfjotli gladly filled the horn with mead from the nearby barrel and sat next to the god of strength on the edge of the chariot. He took a long swig and glanced at Modi, whose snores were still echoing throughout the cave.

"Why are you still awake?" Sinfjotli asked.

"Someone has to keep the barrier up," Magni replied.

Sinfjotli frowned. "What barrier?"

Magni gestured toward the entrance of the cave. "You can't see it, but Modi and I erected an ionic barrier to keep the wind and cold air from entering this cave. One of us has to remain awake to maintain it."

"I see," Sinfjotli muttered. No wonder the air felt metallic and made his hair stand on end.

"What about you?" Magni asked. "Why can't you sleep? Are you feeling alright? You're not in pain, are you? You took a nasty hit from that troll earlier."

"I'm fine, just bruised." His left side still felt somewhat sore. That pain would linger a while longer, he knew. But the feelings of inadequacy would remain for even longer.

Magni studied him as if he could clearly see the shame and indignation on his face. He took a deep swig from his horn and then patted Sinfjotli's shoulder so hard he spilled his drink. "You fought valiantly back there. No one would think less of you, least of all me. Never doubt that."

"If you say so." Sinfjotli groaned as he massaged his sore shoulder. If he wasn't in pain before, he was now. Magni's gentle love tap felt more like a solid punch. He wondered if the god of strength could not control his might. Sinfjotli wished Magni and Modi would show affection and encouragement in some other less physical way. He took a long sip of mead, which helped dull the pain.

"But the pain and frustration from our recent battle isn't the only reason you're awake, is it?" Magni said. "You're worried about Sigurd?"

"Yes," Sinfjotli said. He glanced at the horn Magni was holding in his right hand. "Are you feeling better now? Your hand got burned pretty badly when you..."

"It was nothing," Magni said. "Those burns healed hours ago."

"Oh, right," Sinfjotli muttered.

Magni was so friendly and down to earth that it was easy to forget he was an Aesir. Being the god of strength had its perks. Namely, he and Modi healed fast.

"It gave me quite a shock," Magni admitted as he took another swig of mead. "Sigurd's body keeps radiating heat. If we stayed here for a day, I reckon he could turn this whole cave into a sauna just by being here."

That wasn't an exaggeration. Sinfjotli could feel the air becoming hotter every second. Sigurd's body shimmered with heat, melting the snow and ice around him. He even smelled like smoke and fire. Lately, Sigurd's scent reminded Sinfjotli of the Huldra Brothers' forge and how it smelled when the dwarves were smelting a red-hot sword. His heartbeat was also unusually fast and loud. Sinfjotli could hear Sigurd's heart beating in his chest like a drum, even when they were far apart.

"Why is Sigurd's body radiating so much heat?" Sinfjotli asked. "Is this a side effect of the Trial of Svarblood?"

"I wouldn't call it a side effect." Magni frowned. "But there is definitely something amiss with Sigurd's body. When I touched his shoulder earlier, I sensed something powerful beneath all that heat. There was an angry presence within him, like a caged animal struggling to break out."

Sinfjotli could relate to that. When he first became a skinchanger, he often felt at war with himself. Sometimes, on long walks through the forest, he'd see a deer or elk, then salivate and feel a sudden urge to chase after them. Worse, he sometimes looked at humans the same way—like prey. The first time he'd killed several of Siggeir's warriors, he had to restrain himself from feasting on their bloody corpses. *Men are not food*, he'd tell himself. How often had he needed to remind himself of that on a battlefield?

Sometimes, at night, he'd hear the calls of other wolves and howl back, joining them on the hunt, ensuring they had a successful kill and partaking in the meal. Cavorting with wolves wasn't always bad, but it sometimes led to embarrassing moments. When he was fifteen, Sinfjotli spied a young she-wolf marking her territory in a forest clearing near his father's hideout. He smelled she was in heat and inexplicably felt his cock stir. It took every ounce of willpower he had to fight the urge to go to the she-wolf and court her as he would a human girl. *You are no longer human*, he told himself. *But you're no true beast, either. To mate with a beast would still be an abomination!*

Sinfjotli had clung to his humanity, actively suppressing the unnatural hunger and animalistic desire for years. His father also struggled, though he bore his cross in silence. He once described it as having two wolves fighting a battle within. One wolf was their original sense of self—human quirks and personality that carried over to their new bodies when they underwent the Trial. The other wolf was the beast—the instincts, the hunger, the primal urges inherited from the wolves they had become. He warned Sinfjotli that the two wolves were constantly battling for control, but so long as they continued to feed the good wolf and let the bad wolf starve, they would be alright.

But the bad wolf never went away. Sinfjotli had broken the hungry wolf within him long ago, but he could never truly tame it. Sometimes, the animal instincts completely overwhelmed his rational mind. The first time he'd met and battled Sigurd in Helheim, it happened. He'd let bloodlust and battle fever consume him when Sigurd slashed him with Gram. He'd turned into a wolf and continued fighting Sigurd even after he'd accepted they were brothers by blood. The thrill of combat had been intoxicating. Even as their bodies broke, as they were critically injured, he couldn't stop. If Baldur hadn't intervened, that duel would have ended in death.

But what cross will Sigurd have to bear? Sinfjotli was no expert on dragons, but he knew they were powerful. Far more powerful than wolves, mountain lions, or bears. How would the Trial of Svarblood change Sigurd in the long run?

"I shouldn't have let him undergo the Trial," Sinfjotli muttered. "I promised Father I wouldn't tell a soul about it. But I ended up breaking my word and helping my brother follow in our footsteps. I shall regret that until my dying day."

"Hmm... seems to me your regret seems questionable," Magni observed.

Sinfjotli stared reproachfully at him. "I broke a blood oath I made to my father never to tell a soul about the Trial of Svarblood! I watched my half-brother get eaten alive by a dragon, unsure whether the Trial would activate! What do you find questionable!"

"This." Magni tapped Kistfuskare's pauldron with a meaty finger. "You're wearing the armor and wielding the axe the dwarves forged because of your collective choices."

Confusion momentarily supplanted Sinfjotli's anger. "What are you getting at?"

Magni reflected for a moment. "Can you truly say you regret a decision while still benefiting from its consequences?"

Sinfjotli looked down at his drink, mulling it over. Then he gazed at his axe, and a realization dawned on him.

"Sigurd gave his life and body so I could have this armor and axe. If I hadn't accepted them, it would make his sacrifice meaningless, and we wouldn't be having this conversation here in Niflheim."

Magni shrugged. "I suppose it's a question for the philosophers. I wouldn't dwell on it. It's just the drunken ramblings of a god."

He leaned forward. "But Sigmund will understand. The Trial of Svarblood was the only way Sigurd could leave Svartalfheim *and* get the weapons and armor you needed. The Huldra Brothers had the right idea. The dwarves would have killed you both if Sigurd hadn't outwitted Ivaldi. Also, he wouldn't last long in Niflheim without his new physiology."

"You might be right." Sinfjotli sipped his mead. "But the price he paid was so steep. No one should have to endure the horrors Father and I did."

"Aye." Magni nodded. "The Trial of Svarblood is truly a reprehensible ritual—a hellish perversion of nature and the divine that should be buried and forgotten. Teaching humans how to become skinchangers will always be one of the frost giants' greatest sins."

Sinfjotli's eyes narrowed. "The frost giants taught it to humans?"

Magni nodded. "And we still curse them in Asgard for it. Eons ago, before man first thought to chronicle his deeds, a mighty giant crossed over to Midgard from Jotunheim. Back then, the barrier that separates Midgard from Jotunheim and the other realms wasn't as powerful as it is now. Powerful monsters and giants could exploit gaps and tears in it and cross over to your world. The Aesir would immediately send forces to dispatch or repel the invaders. But the giants would always wreak havoc and sow chaos before we dealt with them. They might destroy kingdoms, level mountains, or murder countless humans before my father, Týr, Odin, or Heimdall could dispatch them. But one invader was different. His name was Svarblood, and he was the first being to master the art of polymorphing. He could transform into any animal at will and stayed one step ahead of the Aesir by turning into a different animal and running away whenever they came close. He kept a low profile in Midgard and did not lay waste to villages or ravage the land as his predecessors had. Instead, he found a different way to sow chaos. He approached a tribe of humans and showed that he had the power to assume the form of any animal he wished. He offered to teach them how to get this power... but at a terrible price. They would have to let themselves be devoured by beasts and then seize control of their bodies. Many humans died in Svarblood's insidious trial. The few who passed and became skinchangers then experienced madness and bloodlust as their souls adjusted to their new bodies. They ravaged entire villages and slaughtered hundreds of animals. Eventually, Heimdall noticed the chaos and figured out how Svarblood always eluded his gaze. He, Loki, and Odin tracked down the shapeshifter and chased him back to Jotunheim with his tail between his legs. But the seeds of chaos he'd sown had already sprouted. The surviving skinchangers had taught other humans the insidious ritual so they could also attain the power of beasts. Most humans were horrified and shunned skinchangers, calling them abominations. But some craved the ability to assume the forms of beasts and willingly subjected themselves to the horrid Trial. Many died in vain. Those who survived were struck with madness and slaughtered fellow humans and other beasts at a dizzying rate. If left unchecked, the skinchangers would eventually drown Midgard in blood, exterminating themselves and all life."

Magni took another swig. "My grandfather put a stop to that. With the Vanirs' help, Odin cast a spell on all of humanity that made it nigh impossible for them to survive the Trial of Svarblood. Those who failed would have their very souls destroyed. The method worked, and most skinchangers died out. But the knowledge of the Trial persisted. Regrettably, Odin never eradicated the practice entirely. He's not someone that allows an asset to go to waste.

He saw the potential of skinchangers on the battlefield and wanted some of their ilk to fill the ranks of Valhalla. But he had no intention of loosening the restrictions of the Trial. He decided that only the worthy should be able to survive and become skinchangers."

"Is the Trial still practiced in Asgard?" Sinfjotli asked.

Magni arched an eyebrow. "What?"

"Many of the Aesir and Vanir can shapeshift. Everyone knows Loki is a shapeshifter. The legends say Freyja can turn into a falcon, and Baldur once told me that Odin shapeshifted into a snake to slip inside Mount Hnitbjörg. So did they all undergo—"

"No," Magni interrupted. "That savage ordeal only applies to humans. Gods and giants don't need to be devoured by beasts to become skinchangers. For us, shapeshifting is as easy as putting on an old, worn boot. The Vanir eventually figured out the secret to Svalbard's trick and taught the art of polymorphing to the Aesir as part of the peace treaty that ended the Aesir-Vanir War. Modi and I can polymorph, but we simply choose not to. We leave that subterfuge to our grandfather and Loki. We like our enemies to see us in our true forms and look them in the eye when we kill them."

Sinfjotli frowned. "But then, why do humans need to be devoured by beasts to become skinchangers?"

"Because that is precisely what Svarblood intended." Magni scowled. "Convincing humans to willingly let themselves be devoured by beasts and gamble their souls was Svarblood's greatest sin. I'm sure you're already aware, but only three in ten people ever survive the Trial. Those that fail don't just die. Their souls get destroyed. No afterlife. They simply cease to exist."

Sinfjotli was well aware of the risks. He touched the scars on his shoulder and shivered. Even after all these years, he could remember the white wolf's teeth sinking into his flesh, devouring his extremities and limbs piecemeal before tearing out his throat. At some point, he recalled praying for death.

He would have gladly welcomed oblivion just to put an end to the pain. "If the Trial of Svarblood is so draconian, why did Sigurd and I pass it?"

"Because you have the All-Father's blood in your veins. It's faint, perhaps four or five generations removed, but still there. Odin is a master of polymorphing, and it seems you, Sigurd, and Sigmund inherited his aptitude for it. Still, you should all count yourselves fortunate to have survived. I'm sure Freyja must have played a part in your survival."

Sinfjotli frowned. "What did the goddess of love have to do with my trial?"

Magni blinked. "You didn't know? She was the woods witch who taught your mother about the Trial of Svarblood and later oversaw your ordeal from afar. She was also the same woods witch with whom your mother swapped forms to trick and seduce your father. If not for that, you would never have been born. You owe Freyja far more than you can imagine."

Magni put his drinking horn to his lips and gulped. Soon it was empty, and he gave a thunderous burp. "Well, my horn's run dry." He rose to his full height. Sinfjotli could see how he was the god of strength. Magni's body was extraordinarily well-toned and muscled, and he was taller than Sigurd by a foot.

"Get some sleep," the god urged. "I'll start packing everything on the chariot. We'll leave when you wake up."

Sinfjotli wanted to help him, but as soon as Magni said "sleep," his body betrayed him. His eyes felt heavy and tired. His belly was full. He glanced around and suddenly felt nostalgic. The light crystal glowed like a campfire in the cave's center, and the crates were stacked like furniture. The cave reminded Sinfjotli of the hideout he'd lived in with his father as they trained. They spent many pleasant nights in Sigmund's cave when they weren't on the run or waging guerilla warfare against Siggeir's forces.

"Maybe a little sleep." Sinfjotli rose from the chariot, returned to his sleeping mat, and closed his eyes.

He woke up staring at the shadows dancing across the cave. His throat felt dry and raspy in the cold air. He sat up and saw that Sigurd was already awake and helping Magni store supplies in the chariot. Meanwhile, Modi was gathering the goats' bones and skins into a pile. With a wave of his war hammer, he revived the goats from the mound amid a flash of light.

"There's breakfast if you want any," Modi offered, nodding toward the wall. "We'll meet you outside." He seized the goats' reins and guided them outside. Magni lifted the entire chariot over his head and followed his brother.

Breakfast was a far cry compared to their last meal. Modi had made beef stew in a trencher hollowed out of a musty loaf and a mug of beer to wash it down. The bread was so stale and cold it might have chipped a man's teeth. In truth, Sinfjotli wasn't that hungry, but he needed to keep his strength up in Niflheim.

Between bites, his thoughts drifted to the goats. He felt terrible about eating Tanngrisnir and Tanngnjóstr, but their meat tasted *so* good.

When he finished his meal, Sinfjotli drained his mug and left the cave. Outside, he found Magni and Modi hitching Tanngrisnir and Tanngnjóstr to the chariot's yoke. Sigurd was standing on a prominently elevated ridge fifty feet above the cave, scanning the horizon with his snake eyes. When he saw Sinfjotli, he slid down the slope, and together they walked over to the chariot.

"Do we have our heading?" Modi asked as they climbed aboard.

"Aye," Sigurd said. "Mount Isa is still far away, but we're getting closer."

"Good." Magni nodded. "Let's not dally then." He lashed the reins, and the goats bolted into the darkness, leaving the cave behind. Sinfjotli wondered if it might become a home for frost trolls or other creatures that called this frozen realm home.

Soon, the topography became more rocky and uneven, and Sigurd reported they were near the mountain range he had spied earlier. As they rode over the rocky terrain, Magni turned to Sinfjotli and Sigurd. "You should both be on your guard from here on out. Those trolls were just the tip of the iceberg. There's no telling what else we might encounter on our journey to Mount Isa."

CHAPTER TWENTY-FOUR

A PEACE OFFERING

"**A**re you ready, Sigmund?" Baldur asked.

"Yes!" The small boy walking beside him nodded eagerly.

"Then hold on tight!" Baldur scooped the child in his arms, rushed forward, and jumped over the Bridge of Judgement. The fog and mist parted around him. He saw his ship moored in the river far, far below. The young boy in his arms squealed with joy as the wind rushed through their hair.

Seconds later, Baldur slammed into the *Hringhorni*'s deck with a thunderous THOOM. Baldur stepped out of the crater he'd created as the dust settled. Litr would probably scold him again for creating yet another hole in the *Hringhorni*'s deck. But that was fine. He was used to getting chewed out by the grumpy dwarf.

"That was fun!" Sigmund giggled. "Can we do it again?"

"Another time, perhaps." Baldur laughed as he set the child on the deck. Unlike his father, Sigurd, the young Sigmund enjoyed jumping off the Bridge of Judgement at terminal velocity. He reminded Baldur of his younger brother, Sigi. He certainly had proof of his lineage. In place of a pupil, his left eye had an image of an ouroboros, a serpent biting its tail. According to Gudrun, it was a hereditary trait that proved he was Sigurd's descendant. It was how Baldur located and identified Sigmund's spirit in the City of the Lost.

"So... will you take me to see my mother now?" The boy shivered. "It's awfully chilly here."

Chilly? Baldur thought. The *Hringhorni* wasn't *supposed* to be chilly. It was Hodr's job to keep the ship's atmosphere warmer than the rest of Helheim. Baldur looked around and noticed a few scattered snowflakes sprinkling the deck. No doubt his brother was slacking off somehow.

"Of course." Baldur nodded. "Let's not keep her waiting."

He started walking across the deck but stopped when he realized the lad wasn't following. Sigmund was still standing near the crater, staring wide-eyed at the burned masts towering above him. He looked intimidated and overwhelmed by the sheer length and size of the ship.

"Could... could I ride on your shoulders?" Sigmund asked innocently.

"Promise not to pull my hair?" Baldur asked.

"I promise!"

Baldur grinned. "Then hop on!"

The boy eagerly climbed up, and they started walking toward the ship's stern. As they journeyed south, passing by wandering spirits and shanty towns built by Litr, Baldur reflected on when he left to search for Gudrun and Signy's families in the City of the Lost a week ago. He had scoured the entire city three times, but so far, the only soul he'd found was Gudrun and Sigurd's young son Sigmund. Baldur had stumbled upon him while exploring the plaza where Sigurd and Sinfjotli had fought fiercely. Sigmund had wandered off the Path of the Dead and was alone until Baldur found him.

So where are the rest of them? Aurora, Hansel, Rekkr, Ragr, Svanhild, and the rest of Gudrun's children and her brothers? Where else could they be if they weren't in the City of the Lost?

Baldur shook his head. He could worry about that later. For now, he had to reunite this boy with his mother, Gudrun.

They reached the dining pavilion, where Baldur found his family going about their activities. He also discovered why the *Hringhorni* felt so chilly.

Hodr was wholly engrossed in a game of Tablut against Gudrun. She was surprisingly adept at the game, enough to make Hodr neglect his duties.

Meanwhile, Nanna sat at another table singing to Signy. She let the poor woman rest her head on her lap and lovingly caressed her hair as she sang. Nanna's euphonious voice had the power to soothe the fiercest rage. But Signy looked no different from when Baldur had left a week earlier. Her eyes were frantic, nervously searching for incoming threats or Helheim's emerald fog.

Baldur sighed. Gudrun had adjusted to her new, peaceful life on the ship. But Signy was having a much harder time. The trauma she had suffered from Helheim's brutal torment had left significant scars on her psyche. She wouldn't eat meat and had only recently started eating solid food again. She refused to use utensils, claiming they brought back horrific memories, and she spent most of her time staring at the emerald clouds and Hel's windswept palace in fear. Nanna's songs seemed to be the only thing capable of soothing her tortured spirit.

"I'm back!" Baldur announced enthusiastically as he placed Sigmund on the deck.

Gudrun looked up from her game, and the golden pieces fell out of her hand. Tears of joy streamed down her cheeks as she rushed forward and embraced her son.

"Thank you, Baldur!" Gudrun looked around expectedly, and her smile faltered. "You've done so much for me already, but I must ask where the rest of my family is?"

"I'm truly sorry, Gudrun. I can't find them. I've scoured the city countless times, but there are no traces of your daughter or your brothers."

"Oh no," Gudrun gasped. "Could they have become draugs? Or do you think they got sent to Niflheim instead?"

"I—I don't know. But I promise I'll continue searching until I..."

"There's no need," a shrill voice interjected. The air temperature plummeted enough to freeze Hodr's mead in his chalice, and the floorboards beneath their feet caked over in a layer of ice. Baldur turned to find Hel standing behind him.

The spirits in the dining pavilion jumped from their seats and fled in terror. High in the ship's rafters, Baldur's pet dragon, Twilight, roused himself and hissed angrily. Signy screamed, and Nanna and Hodr stepped in front of her as she cowered on the deck, clutching her body tightly. Gudrun clutched her son Sigmund against her chest.

"There's no need to waste your time searching, Baldur," Hel continued. "They're not here."

"What do you mean?" Gudrun demanded. "Where is my daughter, witch?"

She stood up, still holding Sigmund in her arms, and glared at Hel.

Hel lazily looked over at her. Most spirits would fearfully cower after making eye contact with the goddess of death. But Gudrun bravely stood her ground, trying to look as fearless as possible, even as her limbs trembled.

"I can see why Sigurd married you." Hel smiled. "You have courage, daughter of Gjuki. Your daughter Svanhild isn't here in Helheim. She never was."

"What?" Gudrun gasped.

"Svanhild has become a valkyrie," Hel explained. "Freyja was so fascinated with her that she sent her valkyries to rescue her before she got trampled to death by Jormunrekk's horses. She has spent the last two centuries in Fólkvangr serving as one of Freyja's... *wards.*"

She said that word like it could have several meanings, and they could pick which one.

Gudrun staggered backward. She set Sigmund down and stared skeptically at Hel. "You're lying! You must be. I saw her body after Jormunrekk returned it to me in a crimson cloak."

"You saw *a* body," Hel corrected sharply. "But it wasn't your daughter."

Gudrun's eyes widened as she realized Hel was telling the truth. "I—I don't understand. If what you're saying is true, then...?"

"...who was it that Jormunrekk's horses trampled to death that day?" Hel finished. The Queen of Helheim smiled. "It was his own daughter, Bodil."

"What?" Gudrun gasped. "Why? How could...?"

"It was thanks to the combined effort of Freyja and Frigga," Hel explained. "They had each taken a liking to your daughter for their own... different reasons. They were both outraged when Jormunrekk executed his own son out of jealousy when he learned he and Svanhild had become lovers. As the goddesses of love and family, they couldn't let that insidious act of filicide go unpunished. So they orchestrated a cruel trick to castigate him. Frigga cast a spell to make Jormunrekk's maiden daughter Bodil look like Svanhild. While Freyja safely spirited your daughter to Vanaheim, Jormunrekk's men seized Bodil and later trampled her to death at the gates of his castle. Her body was so mutilated afterward that no one realized who it was they had actually killed."

Gudrun turned pale as a wave of fear, guilt, and realization washed over her. "B-but if what you're saying is true... and Svanhild didn't die that day... then that means...?"

"You sent your three sons to their deaths for nothing since Svanhild didn't die," Hel confirmed.

Gudrun looked like she'd gotten shot by an arrow. She set Sigmund down and collapsed onto a nearby bench, her face awash with guilt and regret. She hugged herself tightly, both hands clutching her shoulders as her body shuddered. Tears flowed from her eyes, and she looked like she was about to throw up.

"If it's any consolation, your sons, Hamdir, Sorli, and Erp are in Fólkvangr, just like your daughter," Hel informed her. "Odin himself intervened and ensured their fight with Jormunrekk would be their last before escorting them all to Fólkvangr. Oh, and your brothers Gunnar and Hagen are there as well."

She sounded nettled as she mentioned that detail. "Although they betrayed Sigurd and orchestrated his death, the valkyries were sent to escort them to the afterlife. But Odin refused to let traitors and oath breakers like them into Valhalla, so they got sent to Fólkvangr instead."

The spirits around the ship whispered and murmured at that shocking revelation as Hel stepped closer to Gudrun. "That's almost unfair, isn't it? Sigurd and Sinfjotli are greater warriors than all of them put together, yet they got sent here to *my realm* while those worthless pieces of garbage got to go to Fólkvangr."

Hel continued walking toward Gudrun until Baldur stepped in her way.

"Why have you come, Hel?" he demanded. "Have you come to take their souls? I've already granted them sanctuary."

"No need to worry, my friend," Hel said. "Gudrun and Signy are of no interest to me, or any of their family members for that matter. I've only come to share a meal with you."

Baldur blinked, unsure if he'd heard her correctly. "Excuse me?"

"You never visit my palace, and you three always ignore my invitations to dine with me, so I decided to just come here instead. As the humans say, 'If the hermit won't come to the mountain, then bring the mountain to the hermit.' Look, I even brought my favorite plate."

Hel reached into her purple cloak and produced a ceramic plate. Baldur knew it was her favorite plate, Hunger, a magical item that never ran out of whatever food got placed upon it.

A wave of heat lapped Baldur's back as Nanna stepped forward. Her aura glowed so malignantly that Hel's icy footprints on the deck evaporated into mist.

"You think we would share a meal with you after *everything* you did?" she seethed.

"If you're referring to what happened at Gnipa Cave, on the Gjallerbru, here at the Bridge of Judgement, and that conversation Baldur and I had in my city afterward, that's all water under the bridge now," Hel said dismissively. "But I'm no fool. I figured you would be reluctant to dine with me, given everything that happened regarding Sigurd and Sinfjotli. So, I've come with several peace offerings."

Hel snapped her fingers, and dozens of spirits materialized around her. Their bodies solidified and took on corporeal forms. One was a little girl with blond pigtails and blue eyes. Another was a plump, bookish ten-year-old boy with curly blond hair. Nearby were two more boys with black hair and steely blue eyes who looked to be about twelve or thirteen. Standing beside them were nine tall men who looked a lot like Sinfjotli. Two more boys stood to their right, who looked somewhat like Gudrun. Last, there was a family of four with a muscular old man with sad blue eyes, long collar-length white hair that touched his shoulders, and a full white beard that touched his neck.

Signy shrieked joyfully, shouting that they were her nine brothers and her children, Rakr, Rekkr, Hansel, and Aurora. Gudrun also exclaimed that these were Ernak and Eitel, her sons fathered by her second husband, Atli.

Baldur turned to Hel. "What is the meaning of this?"

"It's one of my many peace offerings." Hel gestured to the family of four. "Sinfjotli asked you to track down his stepfather's former general Selkirk and his family and give them sanctuary on your ship. You also vowed to find all of Gudrun's children and reunite them with her. Well, I fulfilled both promises for you. I also brought Signy's brothers and children back and wiped their memories of everything Siggeir and my other draugs did to them."

That last detail wasn't a mere exaggeration. By her own admission, Hel never lied. However, she had a habit of manipulating her undead subordinates' memories. Anything that might challenge her servants' blind loyalty got erased until they were little more than obedient tools. It seemed she could also erase any traumatic memories, even from the most anguished victims.

Before Baldur could think to thank her, he heard Signy crumple to her knees on the deck. A series of expressions flashed across her face as she stared at her children's faces: shock, joy, remembrance, horror, fear, and heavy shame. Gudrun also had a similar reaction to seeing her other sons.

For a while, no one said anything. Then Aurora tentatively approached Signy. "M-Mother..." Aurora stammered.

"Are you sure?" Signy interrupted, her voice full of emotion. "Calling me, a sinful woman who demanded your death, your mother?"

"Mother..." Aurora started to tear up. But Baldur knew these were not tears of sorrow.

"Are you sure?" Signy asked again. "Calling someone like me, a worthless parent who treated her children as tools of her vengeance and wasn't able to do anything for you... a sinful woman like me, your mother?"

"Mother!" Aurora sobbed. Her voice was full of emotion. Her body trembled, and rivers of tears flowed down her face.

"Are you sure?" Signy reiterated, on the verge of tears. "After everything that happened, are you sure you still want to call me your mother?"

"Mother!" Aurora rushed forward.

"Aurora!" Signy threw her arms around Aurora. Mother and daughter continued crying in each other's arms as they embraced.

Baldur felt a tear roll down his cheek. Despite everything that had happened, both Signy and Aurora accepted each other.

"Oh, Mother, it's so scary here!" Aurora sobbed. She buried her face in her mother's shoulder. "I've been so afraid for so long!"

"I know, child." Signy shivered, obviously feeling phantom pains. "Believe me, I know. But we're together now. Everything's going to be alright."

"Alright?" Hansel repeated incredulously. The little boy trembled with anger. "You think we want to be here, woman?"

Signy looked up and stared in surprise at her son. "Hansel?"

"Don't you *dare* say my name!" Hansel turned his attention to his sister. "You're too forgiving, Aurora! Have you already forgotten? She ordered Sinfjotli to murder us that night in cold blood!"

"And she ordered Uncle Sigmund to murder Ragr and me simply because we weren't brave and we were the sons of Siggeir," Rekkr added.

"You think that's bad?" Eitel scoffed. "That's trivial compared to what our moth—to what *Gudrun* did to us!"

Eitel and his brother glared at Gudrun with looks of pure hatred. "One night, while we were playing during a feast, she slipped into our rooms, gathered us in her arms, and slit our throats! Then she hacked our bodies apart and tricked our father Atli into eating our flesh and drinking our blood to avenge her murdered brothers!"

"You vile witch!" Ernak seethed. "What is wrong with you? What kind of parent does that to their children!"

"She's not our parent," Eitel said. "I could never call someone as wicked as her my moth—"

Suddenly, Hel appeared behind them. Her foreboding presence was enough to cow them with mind-numbing fear. She kneeled and gently wrapped her long arms around the five boys. Their bodies tensed as if they had just been electrocuted.

"Now, now, children, this is supposed to be a joyful reunion." Hel smiled, though there was no warmth in her half-pristine and half-rotten teeth. "I understand it will be difficult to get over what happened. But you will all be here on this ship for a *very* long time. So I suggest you make peace with your mothers as soon as possible. It'll be *so* much more enjoyable."

She leaned closer and whispered in Ragr's ear, "And since I went through the trouble of making an exception and letting you stay on this ship, the least you can do is act pleasant and courteous while I'm here. Of course, if you don't wish to be here on the *Hringhorni*, you could return with me to my palace."

The boys all shivered, as if slabs of ice had replaced their spines.

"N-no, my lady," Ragr stammered. "T-that won't be n-necessary."

"So, you would rather be here then?" Hel asked.

"Y-yes... of c-course, my l-lady," Rekkr said.

"Good." Hel rose and stepped away, and all five boys collapsed to their knees. They scrambled away from Hel as fast as possible and hid behind Signy's and Gudrun's skirts. The fear they felt from Hel's veiled threat made them completely forget their animosity toward their mothers.

And with good reason. Baldur knew from experience just how terrifying Hel's palace of Eljudnir was. The horrors within the palace were not meant for mortal eyes. Seeing them would drive any human mad. It was also where some of the worst sinners in Helheim were subjected to unspeakable forms of torture. The mere thought of living there with Hel, even as honored guests, was enough to frighten these angry children into submission. It was better to live with the mothers who had orchestrated their deaths in cold blood than spend a minute in that terrifying palace.

But after a moment, the boys stiffened, remembering their anger. When Signy placed her hand reassuringly on Hansel's shoulder, he jerked away. He and the other boys scampered to the farthest table in the dining pavilion. Gudrun and Signy remained where they were, hands falling to their sides, faces shadowed with hurt.

"Is this some cruel scheme to torture these women without ever laying a finger on them?" Nanna demanded.

"Now, what gave you that idea, my dear?" Hel asked, sounding hurt. "I merely granted Signy's and Gudrun's greatest wish and helped Baldur fulfill his promise to Sinfjotli. I gave you what you wanted, nothing more. But sometimes, what someone wishes for isn't what they wanted."

She turned to Baldur. "Your intentions were pure and noble. But you failed to consider the children's perspectives. Did you think they would fly ecstatically into their mothers' arms after everything that happened? How naïve. Signy ordered her brother and their bastard son to murder her children. Gudrun killed her children with her own hands, carved up their bodies, and forced their father to consume their flesh and drink their blood. That isn't something a child can forgive."

"You're wrong, Hel," Baldur countered. "I always knew this was a possibility. Over the years, I've witnessed many unhappy reunions on this ship between old lovers, former enemies, and orphaned children and their estranged parents. I knew the children would be reluctant to forgive their mothers. But I decided it was still worth it. Even if the children feel bitter toward their mothers, I'll have kept my word as long as they're safe on this ship. Hopefully, they'll learn to let go of the past and move on."

Hel smiled. But this wasn't her usual sinister smile that could make any soul tremble in fear. It was a genuine smile full of admiration. "That's what I like about you, Baldur," she said. "You're always optimistic. You accept the bad while striving to find the good in others."

"Those are kind words. Thank you." Baldur glanced around the dining pavilion. All the children, except Aurora and Sigmund, huddled around a dining table, purposefully sitting as far away from their mothers as possible. Signy was having a tearful reunion with her nine brothers and introducing them to her daughter Aurora.

Nanna was preparing to escort Selkirk and his family to a new home farther down the deck near one of the giant masts. She came over to Baldur and glanced at Hel. "This is a kind gesture, but if you think…"

"Don't worry, there's more." Hel tapped the butt of her scythe against the deck, and her loyal servants, Ganglati and Ganglot, appeared behind her, holding several large crates.

It had been over a century since Baldur had seen them. Hel's manservant Ganglati was a ten-foot-tall, muscular man with pale white skin. He had long black hair that ran down his head and blank, white eyes. He looked dimwitted and slow-thinking, as if he was too lazy to think for himself.

Beside him was Hel's maidservant, Ganglot—a beautiful yet languid woman in her mid-twenties. Her voluptuous physique was offset by her absurdly long mane of unkempt purplish hair that reached down to her toes. She wore a sultry black dress that exposed much of her pale white skin, nearly as ghostly white as the right half of Hel's body. Her face bore an expression of extreme fatigue and apathy. Every few seconds, she'd inhale loudly, as if trying to suck in as much air as possible, the very act of breathing a chore.

For a while, neither servant moved. They stood as motionless as statues while still holding the heavy crates.

"Well?" Hel asked impatiently. "Go on then." She pointed toward Litr's workshop, and her servants started shuffling across the deck. They moved so slowly that they appeared to be standing still. But they made up for their indolence with their immense strength. Each servant carried a stack of three large crates, each weighing at least three tons, without breaking a sweat.

They stacked the crates before the smithy and returned to Hel's side as Litr rummaged through the containers. The dwarf pulled out some of the strangest materials Baldur had ever seen.

"Mist echoes from Niflheim," the dwarf mumbled, reading the labels. "Embers from Muspelheim? Frost giant sweat? Asgardian steel? Lumber from Vanaheim? What is all this?"

"My gift for you, Litr," Hel replied. "You always complain that you don't have enough tools or materials to make proper homes for the spirits on this ship. Well, I decided to rectify that. I arranged for Ivaldi and my great-great-grandfather Surtr to send you various tools and supplies."

Hel turned to Baldur. "This is only the first shipment. I promise to provide Litr with all the building materials he'll need to transform this ship into the paradise it deserves, making it a more comfortable place for all the spirits you've taken under your wing. I'll even provide you with draugirs to serve as your workers and builders."

"That won't be necessary," Litr said.

"Are you sure?" Hel said. "They're the best workers an architect could ask for. They don't need sustenance, never get tired sleep, and won't disobey orders. Well, my offer is still on the table. Just say the word, and I'll provide anything you need."

"I'll keep that in mind," Litr promised, though Baldur suspected he was just paying lip service. "But thank you, Hel. This is wonderful! I can't wait to get to work! I'll start by fixing those craters Baldur keeps making in the bow."

"I'm afraid you'll have to wait a little longer." Hel turned toward Baldur. "I have one last gift for you, my friend, that will appeal to everyone on this ship."

She snapped her fingers. At first, nothing happened, but then Baldur's pet dragon hissed in the rafters above. He glanced up and became wide-eyed. The clouds and mist above the ship swirled like water in a vortex. When the whirlpool stopped, images were being projected on the surface of the clouds.

In the vision, Baldur saw Sigurd and Sinfjotli, now wearing a redoubtable suit of armor and wielding an impressive axe, making their way through deep snow banks. Next to them were two familiar faces Baldur hadn't seen in years.

"Is that Magni and Modi?" he asked. "Why are my nephews traveling with them?"

"They met in Svartalfheim," Hel explained. "They told them they had to go to Niflheim on a suicidal quest to slay a giant, and they volunteered to accompany them. Those four are now inseparable."

Baldur looked back at the vision. "Is this a vision of the past?"

"No, it's happening right now," Hel said. "I enchanted the clouds above this ship to show you what Sigurd and Sinfjotli are doing. You'll be able to watch their journey as it unfolds. It'll provide everyone on this ship with a source of entertainment."

"You can do that? Truly?"

"My realm, my rules, Baldur. Now then, I've helped you fulfill your promise and reunited Signy and Gudrun with their families, provided Litr with the means to rebuild this ship into a paradise, and given you a way to watch Sigurd and Sinfjotli's journey. Surely that is enough of a peace offering for you to share a meal with me."

CHAPTER TWENTY-FIVE

KING OF THE CLOUDS

The thick haze obscured the summit of Mount Isa, making it impossible to see anything beyond that stormy veil. The air was heavy with moisture and swirling snowflakes, and the wind howled through the peaks, creating an eerie and bestial sound. Despite the foreboding conditions, there was a certain beauty in the way the clouds swirled around the mountain.

As they stared at the funnel cloud, pondering what awaited them inside, Sigurd reflected on their journey. They had spent an immense amount of time traveling across frozen valleys and traversing winding mountains. When they finally reached the mountain's base, they were all astounded by the sheer size. Even in the misty darkness, Sinfjotli, Magni, and Modi could discern just how enormous it was. The peak reached past the cloud cover, and its sheer bulk swallowed the horizon. Sigurd estimated it would take at least six months for a person to climb to the summit. But Magni promised the goats would make it in one-sixth that time.

Once they overcame the shock of the size of the mountain, they began climbing. Everyone stayed inside the chariot, letting the goats do all the work. Tanngrisnir and Tanngnjóstr scrambled up sheer cliffs with remarkable ease, too steep for any ordinary man to climb, and the heavy chariot in no way impeded their movements. As they climbed higher, the air became thinner, and the mist became so thick that Sigurd could barely see over fifty feet in front of him, even with Magni's light crystal illuminating their surroundings.

Sigurd estimated it took an entire week to climb to the top. When they arrived at the mountain's rim, they found a massive tornado swallowing the summit in a swirling cone of dark vapor. The funnel cloud was so dense that Sigurd couldn't peer through its veil, even with his superhuman vision.

"That doesn't look very welcoming," Sinfjotli remarked.

"There's something powerful in there," Magni observed. "I'm sensing an enormous amount of power and electricity."

"I sense it too," Sigurd admitted. Even without his telescopic vision, he could sense something dark and powerful at work within that storm that made the hairs on his arms and legs stand up.

"No turning back now," Modi declared. "Full speed ahead!" He whipped the reins, and Tanngrisnir and Tanngnjóstr charged straight into the tornado.

Sigurd felt like they had entered a different dimension as they passed through the funnel cloud. The chariot came to a halt within the eye of the raging tempest. The walls of the storm encircled the summit, churning around them in a murky black funnel.

A shiver ran down Sigurd's spine as he looked around. Everything felt unreal and warped. Goosebumps covered his arms, and his skin tingled with a strange cooling sensation. The air had a metallic scent, like the smell of oncoming rain. Mist hung in the air, and above them, thick tendrils of white clouds coiled and undulated in a way that made them seem alive.

Sigurd hopped off the chariot and almost collapsed face-first into a snowdrift. His movements had become sluggish. Unlike the thin air at the mountaintop, the air inside this tornado felt heavy, making him feel like he was walking through water. He cast a wary glance at the dark clouds. Bolts of electricity flashed between the tornado and the clouds above. He felt vulnerable, knowing he could be struck by lightning at any moment.

Sinfjotli stepped off the chariot, and as soon as Magni and Modi dismounted, Tanngrisnir and Tanngnjóstr turned and ran. The goats passed through the funnel cloud and vanished.

"There goes our ride," Sinfjotli murmured.

"Don't fret," Modi assured. "The goats will come back if we call them."

"We have more important things to worry about," Magni added. He studied the dark clouds and the mist. "There's electricity all over the place. *Something* is watching us."

Sigurd knew what he meant. There was a chill here that gave him a sense of unease. He couldn't zero in on it, but he could feel a vast presence in the air and mist around them, like water touching his skin. *Something* was definitely watching them. Sigurd couldn't sense what it was, but it was as if an unknown being was crawling across his body and was even present in the air he was breathing.

A searing blue-white lightning bolt crashed into the funnel cloud. The sudden flash left Sigurd near blind, and the ensuing thunderclap knocked him off his feet as the whole summit quaked beneath him. Blinking away the afterimages, he turned toward the swirling vortex. Electricity crackled through the dense churning mass.

"These clouds are so thick you could cut them with a sword," Sigurd thought aloud. On impulse, he drew Gram, deciding to put that old idiom to the test. Before anyone could stop him, he swiped his sword at the funnel cloud. The cloud parted effortlessly as he expected it would. But as he stepped back, a thick red fluid dripped from the severed mist.

Is that blood? Sigurd wondered.

"*Ouch! That hurt, damn it!*" a disembodied voice bellowed.

Sigurd blinked. He turned, but he couldn't locate the source of the voice. Sinfjotli shrugged as if saying, *It wasn't me.*

Suddenly, the tornado darkened. The mist thickened, and the wind picked up. Sigurd's skin tingled, and goosebumps sprang up over his arms. Magni and Modi stepped in front of the brothers.

"Electricity is building up all around us," Magni warned. "Brace yourselves!"

Tendrils of electricity burst from the funnel cloud and coalesced in the air above. Half a heartbeat later, a barrage of lightning bolts blasted the peak in a crashing BOOM.

The force sent them all flying out of the giant tornado, tumbling down the mountainside. When Sigurd stopped rolling, he opened his eyes and discovered they had landed on a massive mountain crest about a hundred feet below the peak.

Magni extended a hand and pulled Sigurd to his feet. He and Modi were completely unharmed. But since they were thunder gods, that wasn't surprising. Sinfjotli also looked unharmed, his armor having once again protected him.

Unfortunately, Sigurd hadn't been so lucky. Magni had tried to absorb the full blast, but Sigurd still took a stray bolt. He looked down at the blacked circle in the center of his smoking chest. His golden hauberk had done nothing to protect him. The lightning had gone straight through his body and blasted off his helmet, which now lay half-buried in a nearby snowdrift. His hair was scorched, his mouth tasted of ash, and his fingertips were black with soot.

"Are you alright?" Magni's voice sounded like an echo to Sigurd's ringing ears.

"I've been better." Sigurd coughed.

"You're lucky," Magni remarked, handing Sigurd his helmet. "That was enough lightning to kill twenty men."

"Indeed," the disembodied voice agreed. *"I'm impressed you all survived that!"*

The tornado swirling around the peak dissipated. The clouds above the mountain began churning like a hurricane as lightning cracked across the sky. The clouds darkened and unloaded a torrent of lightning, snow, and hail. A large funnel cloud emerged from the storm's center and snaked toward them. As it touched the mountain crest, the cloud condensed, reshaping itself into an enormous humanoid.

The giant stood about thirty feet tall, lean and muscular. His hair, beard, and kilt were made of wispy white clouds. His teakwood-colored skin contrasted with the pure gold of his eyes, radiating power like electrical sparks in a living storm cloud.

His most remarkable feature was his torso. His body was bisected right where his waist should have connected with the rest of his abdomen, and his torso hovered about a foot above his waist. If Sigurd concentrated, he could see electricity traveling between the giant's upper and lower body.

"A storm giant," Magni observed. "They're quite rare."

"My kin have your wretched father and grandfather to thank for our low numbers, Son of Thor!" the giant growled. "Some of your victims were my children! My name is Kári, the giant of the sky and storms, and I plan on bringing the full power of the sky upon you!"

As they eyed each other up, Sigurd noticed he could see clearly now. Niflheim was still as dark as ever. But the mist and cloud cover had dissipated after the storm giant showed up.

"I take it you were the reason the mist and cloud cover at the summit was so thick?" Sigurd deduced.

"That's right," Kári said. "I wasn't doing it consciously, mind you. I was having such a pleasant dream before you sliced me in half."

"I sliced you?" Sigurd asked.

Kári gestured at his split torso. "You're the reason my body is split in half right now. Curse that enchanted sword of yours! It'll take weeks for my body to return to normal!"

After a moment, Sigurd realized Kári was referring to when he sliced the funnel cloud with Gram minutes earlier. But it made little sense. Even if that tornado was Kári's body, why would such a perfunctory swipe cause so much damage?

"I'm going to make you all pay for splitting me in half and disturbing my slumber!" Kári reared his head back and fired a blast of white lightning from his mouth. The energy engulfed Magni, Modi, and Sinfjotli. But when the dust and smoke settled, Sigurd saw all three were unharmed.

"That tickled," Modi said, just to be mean.

"Did you forget that we're thunder gods, cretin?" Magni asked. "Lightning doesn't affect us."

"You think I don't know that?" Kári pointed at Sinfjotli. "I was aiming for the human over there. You two just got caught in it as well." Kári gave Sinfjotli a cursory inspection and arched an eyebrow. "Having said that, it appears the mortal is unharmed."

"Ivaldi and his sons forged this armor to adapt to any threat," Sinfjotli boasted while patting the Kistfuskare's breastplate. "It looks like that includes lightning."

"Tchah! How annoying." Kári turned toward Sigurd, looked askance at his singed hauberk, and smiled. "However, it looks like *his* armor offers no such protection."

Kári raised his hands, and tendrils of electricity erupted from his fingers, crackling and twisting in the air. The currents coiled together, merging and expanding into an enormous trident.

"I guess I'll start with you, creepy-eyed mortal." Kári hurled the lightning weapon at Sigurd. Before it struck, Magni stepped in. He grabbed the weapon with his bare hand and deflected the lightning. The trident zipped far away into the darkness and detonated somewhere at the base of the mountain, creating an explosion almost as large as Mount Isa.

"Ha, I haven't done that trick in ages." Magni laughed as he unsheathed his broadsword.

"It's been a while since we fought a storm giant," Modi agreed. He thrust out his hand, summoning his war hammer. "This should be interesting."

Kári scowled. "Don't assume I'm like the other storm giants you've faced. You and your father may command lightning, but I am the king of the clouds! I rule over the sky itself!"

"We'll see who the true ruler of the skies is." Magni glanced over his shoulder at Sigurd. "You and Sinfjotli better leave this to us for now. We'll soften him up for you."

That infuriated Kári. Scowling, he lifted his arms toward the sky and flexed his fingers. The clouds darkened as ten swirling funnel clouds formed and connected with the ground behind him, kicking up clouds of snow.

"You think me easy prey, Sons of Thor?" Kári seethed. "You and your father slaughtered thousands of my kith and kin. But here in Niflheim, I am all-powerful! You will pay dearly for trespassing in my kingdom!"

Kári extended his hands and pointed all ten fingers at the two gods. The swirling tornados undulated through the air like striking snakes as they smashed into Magni and Modi.

For a moment, the world vanished into pure white haze as snow and ice erupted from the funnel clouds, and Sigurd couldn't see a thing. Suddenly, his ears popped, and the clouds dispersed. From their stance, he inferred that Magni and Modi had swung their weapons with enough force to dispel the vortex.

"I really wish people would stop calling us that!" Magni said. He pointed his great sword toward the heavens as if trying to summon a lightning bolt.

But nothing happened. Magni frowned as he held his free hand toward the sky as if reaching out to grasp something. "What gives? I'm cut off from the sky?"

"Weren't you listening earlier?" Kári cackled. "I told you I am the king of the clouds. The skies of Niflheim are mine alone to command. You have no power here!"

Ten more tornados formed around Kári. They never touched the ground. Instead, they swirled, slithered, and undulated through the air like snakes around the storm giant. With a flick of his fingers, they all lashed out like real serpents scarring the ground and blasting the gods of strength and courage.

Sigurd's hair stood on end as the gale-force blast washed over him. He wanted to rush to help his two comrades but knew he and Sinfjotli would only get in the two gods' way.

Instead, he studied the storm giant's movements. Each tornado seemed linked to one of Kári's fingers. Whenever he flicked a finger, a tornado moved in whatever direction the appendage was pointing.

If I identify which tornados correspond to each finger, I can predict what direction we'll get attacked from based on which fingers he moves at any given time.

It was a sound strategy but ultimately unnecessary. Kári flicked his right index and middle fingers and left pinky and ring fingers. Four tornados slammed into Magni's and Modi's flanks. With a flick of his thumbs, two more crashed down on them from above. But before Kári could do anything else with the last four tornados, the billowing palls of snow dust and funnel clouds suddenly dispersed.

Magni and Modi were standing side by side. Electricity crackled around them, scarring the ground and turning the frigid air metallic.

"Don't you dare look down on us, *cretin*!" Magni warned. "We are the gods of strength and courage! Even cut off from the sky, our strength knows no bounds! Let's show him!"

"Right!" Modi nodded. He raised his war hammer while Magni held up his great sword.

"Landvinningur himins!" they shouted as they swung their weapons simultaneously. The gods' combined power created a powerful, explosive wave of force that dispelled the tornados and slammed into Kári.

"What the..." Kári exclaimed as he sailed backward. The storm giant slammed against the mountain behind him. The force of the blast pressing against him drove his body even deeper into the mountain, leaving behind a giant humanoid-shaped crater. The impact triggered a massive avalanche, sending one million cubic yards of snow shooting down Mount Isa in a roaring tidal wave of ice and debris. Kári vanished beneath the onslaught.

When the avalanche subsided, Sigurd took in the changed terrain. Magni and Modi's combined attack had literally reshaped the mountaintop. Entire sections had fractured, broken apart, and crashed down the slopes like tidal waves, smashing everything in their path. Thankfully, the jutting crest where they stood had spared them from the worst of it, forcing the avalanche to sweep past them instead of burying them alive.

"Holy shit!" Sinfjotli muttered.

"That was only a small taste of our strength," Modi said. "We were holding back for your sake. If we had gone all out, neither you nor the mountaintop would have withstood that."

"Thanks?" Sigurd said hesitantly. "And well done, both of you."

"It's far too early for congratulations," Magni warned.

As if on cue, Kári burst from the snow and ice. He staggered forward and then fell to his knees, panting. The gods' combined attack had taken a visible toll.

"Looks like Magni and Modi have got this in the bag," Sigurd thought aloud. "It shouldn't be long before... Hrrrk... Ggghkk... Arrrrrggghhhkkk..."

His lips continued moving, but no sound escaped his mouth. A moment later, Sigurd fell to his knees, suddenly unable to breathe. He gasped, but no air filled his lungs.

As he choked, Sigurd noticed Sinfjotli had also collapsed and was choking, and Magni and Modi were staggering on their feet.

"Oh, what's wrong?" Kári asked mockingly. "Did a mere storm giant literally take your breath away?"

"You..." Modi whispered as he and Magni dropped to their knees.

"I don't just control lightning and tornados," Kári boasted. "I can control and manipulate air itself. I can even remove all the oxygen from the area around me and asphyxiate my enemies if I choose to do so. It doesn't matter if lightning won't work on you. It doesn't matter if you both are the gods of strength and courage. Strength? Speed? Power? All these things are meaningless to me. Because even the mightiest warriors will fall to their knees if they can't breathe air!"

Kári wasn't wrong. The four of them seemed pathetically helpless as they lay suffocating. Sigurd's lungs felt on fire. His head was pounding like someone was striking it with a hammer. Under these circumstances, there was nothing he could do.

Sinfjotli staggered to one knee and hurled his axe at Kári. But Wolfsbane passed harmlessly through the storm giant's cloud body and embedded itself in a snowdrift on the mountain slope.

"Feeling desperate, puny mortal?" Kári snickered. "You should be. People always take the air they breathe for granted. On average, you humans can survive three weeks without food and three days without drinkable water. The average mortal can survive three hours without shelter in a harsh environment of extreme heat or cold before succumbing to the elements. But you can only survive *three minutes* without breathing. The air up here is almost nonexistent. But now it's all gone! And you're all helplessly lying there like a bunch of fish stranded on dry land."

Sigurd glared murderously at Kári and forced himself to stand on one knee. He had to move. Fight. Do something!

"By the way"—Kári grinned—"suffocation isn't the only thing you need to worry about."

Searing pain suddenly shot up Sigurd's left arm. For a moment, he thought he had gotten electrocuted again. But this felt much worse. He glanced down and noticed the wounds on his arm were burning, the blood boiling furiously like water in a heater. His eyeballs began boiling, too, and blood streamed out of his nose like a geyser dyeing the snowy ground beneath him red.

What's happening? Sigurd panicked as he clutched his bleeding nose. *Why is my blood boiling like this?*

"That's happening because you're inside a vacuum." Kári snickered, as if reading Sigurd's thoughts. "My initial lightning strike trounced you quite a bit earlier. It left many open wounds on your left arm, and now the blood in those wounds is boiling like water on a stove as it's exposed to this vacuum. Your blood will continue to boil, and you'll die from that long before you run out of air!"

Sigurd ground his teeth. The pain was maddening. He wanted to scream, but no sound escaped his lips.

"Also, under normal circumstances in this vacuum, we'd all be weightlessly floating around like snowflakes in the wind," Kári added. "But Niflheim's strong gravity keeps us firmly grounded. But that's alright. I quite enjoy watching you grovel on the ground like worms."

Kári watched them struggle in agony with venomous delight. But after a few moments, his smile faded. "I admit I'm impressed. Under these conditions, your blood should have dried up within twenty seconds. But you're still clinging to life. I suppose your body isn't normal." He glanced at Sinfjotli. "As for you, your armor must be acting like a pressurized suit, protecting you from the effects of this vacuum. I take back what I said earlier. Perhaps you *will* die from suffocation after all."

The storm giant's taunts enraged Sigurd. He wanted nothing more than to cut Kári to pieces. He tried to stand, but he immediately collapsed face-first into the snow. Numbness crept through his limbs, his heartbeat faltering in erratic bursts. Dizziness clouded his mind, lightheaded, as if his consciousness was slipping.

"There's no use struggling, warrior," Kári warned as he casually walked toward Sigurd. "In less than a minute, you'll pass out from lack of oxygen. After two minutes, your brain cells will start dying, and after three minutes, death becomes unavoidable. But don't worry. I won't let it escalate that far."

Kári loomed over Sigurd. He held out his left arm, and a javelin of searing blue-white electricity formed in his hand.

"I'll just kill you now while you're still conscious." Kári smiled. "I want to see the look in your eyes as your life fades away."

Sigurd could no longer move. All he could do was glare defiantly at the storm giant as he raised his javelin.

Suddenly, Kári's body tensed, as if he sensed danger. The storm giant leaped backward as a gray, bluish blur passed over Sigurd's body.

Sigurd looked up. Magni was standing over him, broadsword in his hands. Nearby, Modi was standing in front of Sinfjotli.

Sigurd was thunderstruck. Through sheer willpower, Magni and Modi had risen to their feet and almost caught Kári by surprise. Most people couldn't attack or even stand under these extreme conditions. But they were the Sons of Thor and the gods of strength and courage to boot. The rules of common sense didn't apply to them.

Sigurd inhaled sharply, greedily filling his lungs with the cold, mountainous air. Nearby, Sinfjotli gasped and panted.

As he gulped down the air like a fish breaking the surface, Sigurd wondered what had changed. Kári now stood several yards away, staring incredulously at Magni and Modi. Sigurd concluded that siphoning away all the air in the area must require an immense amount of concentration. Magni's sneak attack had momentarily made the storm giant lose focus, which was probably why they could breathe again.

Nearby, Sinfjotli staggered to one knee and stared in awe at their godly companions. "What gives?" he lisped out. "I thought you two were incapacitated."

"We were just playing possum and waiting for an opportunity to catch Kári off guard," Magni explained. "We're thunder gods and Aesir. We don't need to breathe air to function. We can even attend Aegir's parties under the sea with no need to surface for air. The only downside is that we can't speak under these circumstances."

"Is that so?" Kári noted. "You two don't need air? In that case, you won't mind if I just take it from you!"

Magni lurched, swinging his broadsword at Kári. But the storm giant easily avoided the attack and backed away. Kári thrust out his hand, creating a vacuum that sucked all the air from their lungs. Sigurd watched as Magni gasped, his breath torn through his mouth and into Kári's palm. He collapsed, clutching his throat. Modi soon followed. Even Aesir couldn't stand after having the air they needed to speak sucked from their lung.

"Lightning and asphyxiation may not work on *most* of you, but there are still plenty of ways for me to kill you!" Kári proclaimed. "Just like this."

He raised his hands above his head. Kári gathered all the fog and air around the mountain ridge above him and compressed it into a giant bubble visible to the naked eye. When the bubble was small enough to fit in his hands, he released the compressed air and sent it toward them.

"I warned you not to underestimate me." Kári smirked.

The air bubble decompressed and caused a massive air explosion. The air pressure in Sigurd's inner ear dropped so fast he blacked out.

CHAPTER TWENTY-SIX

WATER CYCLE

When Sigurd regained consciousness, he discovered he was lying on his back on the snowy mountain ridge. Bruises covered his face and body, and his muscles ached. But more importantly, he noticed he could breathe again.

Sigurd sat up. Sinfjotli lay on his back in a nearby snowdrift. Magni and Modi stood directly in front of them. Their shaggy fur outfits were torn to shreds. At the last second, they had stepped in front of Sigurd and his brother and received the full brunt of the explosion.

Kári was nowhere to be seen. Sigurd vaguely remembered the storm giant vanishing moments before the air explosion.

"*Koff*, we'll leave things in your hands for now." Modi coughed. His eyes rolled back into his head as he and Magni collapsed face-first on the ground. Kári suddenly materialized before the Aesir and nudged Magni's cheek with his big toe.

"Guess they're out for the count." Kári chuckled.

"Get away from them!" Sinfjotli hurled his axe at Kári, but it phased harmlessly through the giant's torso.

"Now it's your turn," Kári said. "I hope you won't be as conceited as they were."

"*You're* the arrogant one." Sigurd took a deep breath, exhaled, and grinned. "The fact I can breathe means you aren't siphoning all the air in the area. You are really underestimating us."

"The only reason I'm letting you breathe is that I want to hear you scream before I kill you!" Kári unstrapped the thirty-foot metal rod fastened to his back. He channeled electricity into it, turning the rod into a javelin-like weapon with energy flowing off each end in a fashion similar to flames.

"Now those two dimwits have been dealt with, I can relax and fight at my leisure." Kári tittered. "I hope you last longer than they did."

Sigurd wanted nothing more than to fight Kári. Unfortunately, his injuries had taken a heavy toll. He still hadn't fully recovered from the first lightning strike that had sent them tumbling from the summit. The air explosion had inflicted some grave damage, too. Sigurd's chest felt heavy, and some of his organs felt scrambled.

"I need a minute to rest," he announced. "Can you keep him busy until then?"

"Gladly." Sinfjotli nodded. He summoned Wolfsbane back to his hand and charged.

Kári let him approach. His javelin was leveled at the center of Sinfjotli's chest, energy flowing off the tip.

He's going to get impaled, Sigurd realized. He tried to warn Sinfjotli as he raised Wolfsbane above his head.

But before he could defend himself, Kári yelled, and lightning came crashing down from the sky, struck his spear like a lightning rod, and blasted Sinfjotli's chest. He sat down hard. His chest was smoking, and there was a burning smell in the air. But when the smoke settled, Sigurd saw Sinfjotli was completely fine. There wasn't a single scorch mark on the Kistfuskare's chest plate.

"Lightning doesn't affect me," Sinfjotli reminded him. "You can blast me all you like, but it won't do you any good! The Coffin Cheater will repel whatever you throw at me!"

"Why are you suddenly so conceited?" Kári scoffed. "You can't hurt me, either. That axe will never harm me, no matter how hard you throw it. It'll just pass through my body like smoke."

Sinfjotli growled. He chucked Wolfsbane right at Kári's face, but the axe phased harmlessly through his head.

Kári sighed. "This is a waste of time and energy. I used to enjoy toying with humans. Back in the day, my brother and I slaughtered thousands of humans before the Aesir strengthened the barrier around Midgard and kept us from entering. I had hoped killing you would be just as entertaining as it was back then. But this stalemate is as boring as a cloudless sky."

Kári glanced toward Sigurd. His eyes fell upon the smoldering scorch marks on his chest, and he smiled. "Maybe I'll play with you for a while, Snake Eyes."

"We're not finished yet!" Sinfjotli shouted.

"Yes, we are." Kári thrust out his left hand, and Sinfjotli suddenly levitated six feet off the ground.

"W-what the hell! What did you just do to me?"

"What's going on?" Sigurd demanded. "How are you suspended in midair like that?"

"I don't know!" Sinfjotli tried to touch his throat with his left hand, but some invisible force got in his way. "There's something weird on me. It has my arms and neck pinned down. It's like I'm being restrained by invisible inflatable shackles."

Sigurd narrowed his eyes. As he squinted, he noticed some strange inflated thing around Sinfjotli's neck, right wrist, and left bicep.

"Those aren't shackles," Sigurd said. "They're compressed air bubbles! You're being pinned in the air by air itself."

"It's a simple trick but an effective one." Kári boasted. "Now you and I can play with no distractions."

Kári opened his mouth wide, and his teeth glowed searing white.

Not good, Sigurd thought. He dove to the left as electricity erupted from Kári's mouth, scorching the ground where he'd been standing. The bright light and snow dust momentarily obscured his vision. He blinked several times and saw Kári approaching. Scrambling back, he barely avoided the giant's javelin as it cleaved the ground between his feet. He sprang upright. Kári didn't relent, swinging his javelin multiple times, forcing Sigurd to dodge.

Fighting a thirty-foot-tall foe wasn't easy. But Sigurd had faced enemies like this before. Size and strength equaled slowness, so he just had to be quicker, pace himself, avoid getting skewered or electrocuted, and wait for an opening.

The chance came swiftly. As Kári's spear stabbed forward, Sigurd rolled away and lunged. Gram bit into the giant's teak skin, and red blood trickled down his foot.

Kári bellowed. He pointed his left index finger at Sigurd and blasted him with electricity. By sheer luck, the attack missed as Sigurd scrambled away, rolled behind the giant, and struck again behind his knee.

That just enraged Kári. He jumped a hundred feet into the air and twirled his javelin above his head at an immense speed, causing a strong wind to sweep across the mountain ridge. Snow whipped in the air as a funnel cloud formed around Sigurd, turning everything white.

At first, Sigurd braced, thinking the cloud was supposed to sweep him off his feet and send him flying. But when he looked up and saw Kári grinning, he realized the tornado was just a distraction.

Above him, Kári sailed down, intending to skewer him with his javelin. Sigurd tried to evade the imminent danger, but the tornado kept him trapped with nowhere to go.

Suddenly, Sinfjotli burst through the swirling storm. He slammed into Sigurd, shoving him clear of the tornado just as Kári's javelin struck the ground, unleashing electricity in every direction. The winds sent them hurtling across the mountain ridge, teetering on the edge, dangerously close to sending them both tumbling down the mountainside.

"Thanks for the assist," Sigurd muttered as he and Sinfjotli rose to their feet. "How did you break out of Kári's restraints?"

"I summoned Wolfsbane and used it to pop the air bubbles," Sinfjotli explained. "It took a little effort since I couldn't move my right hand freely, but it did the job."

"You made it just in time, then," Sigurd said as the tornado subsided. Kári was staring daggers at them both. His gaze seemed to turn the surrounding air metallic, but Sigurd ignored it and stared intently at Kári's bleeding leg.

"What is it, fool?" Kári growled. "Are you surprised you actually cut me?"

"Not really." Sigurd pointed toward Kári's bisected torso. "When you first appeared, you claimed I split you in half when I sliced the funnel cloud on the summit. You may be powerful, but you're not invulnerable."

"If I were you, I wouldn't let two lucky slices give you the wrong idea," Kári warned. "The wounds you just dealt will be the last time you'll *ever* touch me."

"I've fought annoying guys like you before who said the same thing." Sigurd scoffed. "Are you sure you want those to be your last words?"

That got the giant good and angry. Kári yelled, and a blast of lightning came down from the sky, hit his spear like a lightning rod, and channeled toward Sigurd. He wouldn't have survived if Sinfjotli hadn't leaped in front of him and taken the brunt of the blast. The impact knocked him onto his back, but he scrambled to his feet. His chest plate was glowing slightly, but otherwise, he looked unfazed.

"Thanks for that, brother," Sigurd said as he rushed toward Kári.

Kári let him approach, grinning with anticipation. Sigurd faked a strike at the last second and rolled between the storm giant's legs. He stood and thrust with all his might at the giant's right thigh.

But somehow, Gram missed his leg and struck empty air.

How could I have missed? Sigurd's aim had been perfect, and he'd performed that thrust countless times, yet Gram had missed Kári's leg by six inches. Had the storm giant dodged somehow? Sigurd hadn't seen him move a muscle.

Sigurd didn't have time to dwell on it as Kári turned around and swung his javelin in a sweeping motion, forcing Sigurd to duck.

I have to try again to find out. Sigurd kept dodging Kári's thrusts and electrical blasts and waited for an opening. Eventually, Kári raised his javelin above his head for an overhead strike, leaving himself open; Sigurd rushed in. This time, he performed a backward slash aimed at Kári's kneecap. But the sword again missed Kári's body and swung at empty air.

It happened again? He's not dodging and isn't using any illusions, yet somehow, I can't hit him!

Was something making him miss? Sigurd didn't have time to dwell on it as Kári thrust his javelin down at him. Sigurd side stepped out of danger and then rushed forward. This time, he performed a simple thrust aimed at Kári's right foot. He wasn't even trying to inflict any significant damage. He needed to figure out what was going on. Time seemed to slow down as Sigurd focused intently on the tip of his blade.

This time, Sigurd saw it happen. When Gram got within striking distance of Kári's foot, the sword inexplicably veered to the side, and the point dug into the snow beside the giant's big toe.

"Something wrong?" Kári mocked. "Your aim appears to be off." He raised his javelin toward the heavens. Sigurd's hair stood on end, and he instinctively backed away as a lightning bolt struck the ground where he'd been standing.

"What the hell, Sigurd?" Sinfjotli complained. "Why is your aim so awful?"

"It's not!" Sigurd snapped. "Kári is redirecting my sword before it reaches him."

"You sure about that?" Kári grinned. "Maybe your aim really is awful."

"Cut the crap, Kári!" Sigurd snarled. "How are you doing this?"

"How many times must I repeat myself?" Kári sighed. "I told you I am the king of the clouds. I can control air and even distort the atmosphere."

"You're distorting the atmosphere?" Sinfjotli repeated.

"That's right. I can compress and distort the surrounding air. You might think of it as bending space. Every attack that comes near me will twist and wind right past my body. Neither of you can hit me!"

"Is that a fact now?" Sigurd laughed.

Kári narrowed his eyes. "You find that amusing?"

"You distorted the atmosphere around you to redirect my sword out of fear. How could I not be amused by that?"

"Of course, I avoided it, you simple-minded fool!" Kári fumed. "Who would willingly let a bee sting them?"

Sigurd and Kári charged toward each other. The storm giant lunged, javelin tip flashing, but Sigurd sidestepped just in time. Dropping low, he slid between Kári's legs, then sprang to his feet. He pivoted and rushed toward his opponent's legs, intent on hitting him from behind.

Kári glanced over his shoulder at him and laughed. "That's not going to—"

Something phased through Kári's neck. Sigurd glanced up in time to see Wolfsbane spinning wildly above his head. He figured Sinfjotli must have thrown it while Kári was distracted. But sadly, the axe had passed harmlessly through the storm giant's throat. Half a heartbeat later, it froze midair before reversing course and spinning back toward Sinfjotli. Kári looked away as the axe zipped by him. Sigurd saw his chance. He lunged and instinctively thrust Gram at Kári's left leg.

This time, the sword embedded itself deep in the giant's calf, and Kári let out a yelp.

"You little ant!" Kári turned and swept his javelin along the ground, tearing a gaping gash in the mountain ridge. Sigurd barely avoided the attack, diving aside and scrambling to Sinfjotli's side.

Sigurd glanced down at the blood splattered across Gram's tip and the blood dripping from Kári's leg.

I hit him, he thought. *I actually hit him!* But Kári claimed he could distort the space around him. So why had the attack connected?

As Sigurd mulled over that question, he glanced at Sinfjotli's axe, and his eyes widened.

Kári looked away, Sigurd recalled. Kári had been distracted by the axe spinning by him. At that moment, he stopped distorting the surrounding atmosphere.

Something similar had happened earlier. When Magni had caught Kári by surprise, the storm giant lost focus, causing the air vacuum to dissipate. Kári's powers must require immense concentration. If he got distracted, the ability would cease.

But Sigurd suspected Kári had another weakness. He could only distort the space around his line of sight.

An idea formed.

"Sinfjotli," Sigurd whispered.

"Yeah?"

"Watch my back and be ready. There's something I want to confirm."

"Are you two done discussing your fight strategy?" Kári asked impatiently. "Whatever you're planning won't work. But at the very least, please try to make it entertaining this time."

"Oh, it'll be entertaining," Sigurd promised. "But not for you."

He rushed forward. Kári moved to intercept. But at the last moment, Sinfjotli hurled his axe straight at the giant's face. The axe phased harmlessly through his head, a decoy. But the sudden attack startled Kári and made him lose focus. Sigurd lunged low, landing a good, clean hit on the giant's groin. Kári let out a strangled noise and fell to his knees, clutching his crotch.

"Who's laughing now, huh?" Sigurd mocked.

Kári bellowed. He grabbed his javelin and swung mindlessly behind him. The weapon's point slashed toward Sigurd like a scythe. Sigurd raised Gram, planning to slice the javelin in half at the shaft.

Gram can cut through anything, Sigurd remembered. *I can't say I've ever cut lightning before. This will be a first!*

He should have known it was a terrible idea. The warning signs were all there. Static energy built in the air. The hair on his arms stood on end. A tingling sensation ran through his entire body, a primal alarm telling him to stop. But by then, it was already too late to stop. Gram met the javelin.

A flash—white light.

A roar—deafening.

A shock—like the wrath of the gods themselves.

Millions of volts of electricity raced up Sigurd's arm.

"Hnnrgh!" He dropped Gram, crashing to his knees. He couldn't see properly; he couldn't even breathe properly for a few moments. The pain was everywhere. Third-degree burns covered his right hand and arm, while the fingers and palm on his left hand were blackened from where the energy had channeled out of him. His muscles seized, locking his limbs in violent tremors as if he were having a seizure.

"Didn't think that one through, did you?" Kári mocked. "Did you honestly think a mere human like you could touch a bolt of lightning with a metal weapon and *not* suffer repercussions?"

Kári raised his javelin and thrust it right at Sigurd's head. But before it could connect, Sinfjotli stepped forward and parried the attack with his axe. Electricity raced across the axe and into Sinfjotli's arm, but he was unaffected by it.

251

With a powerful shove, Sinfjotli deflected the attack, then swung low, aiming for Kári's left leg. Wolfsbane once again passed harmlessly through the giant's cloud body. Kári stepped back and swung his javelin like a scythe. Sinfjotli dodged, but Kári anticipated that. He shifted his grip, flipped the weapon, and drove the opposite end straight into Sinfjotli's chest. Sinfjotli tried to block, but the blow was too fast and powerful. The impact discharged massive amounts of electricity, sending him tumbling backward. Wolfsbane flew out of his hand, spun wildly through the air, and nearly grazed Sigurd's right shoulder as it zipped past him.

Sinfjotli landed hard on his back, his armored torso smoldering. The snow around him melted, turning to slush. Kári's javelin had struck with enough power to level mountains. But it did not faze Sinfjotli. He soon sat up.

"That tickled," Sinfjotli sneered.

"Your boasting is as unseemly as it is redundant," Kári warned in an unamused tone. "Nothing has changed. Your brother has a weapon that can harm me but can't fight me without electrocuting himself. You can counter my electricity but lack a weapon capable of hurting me. You're both stuck at an impasse."

"There's a simple solution to that," Sigurd countered. "Sinfjotli, catch!"

He snatched Gram off the ground and tossed it at Sinfjotli. In hindsight, he should have been more careful. Gram was one of the few weapons that could damage the Kistfuskare, and it could have easily lopped off Sinfjotli's left hand as it spun through the air. Thankfully, Sinfjotli turned around and caught it without issue.

Then he ran.

Before Kári could react, Sinfjotli slashed the storm giant's right leg. Kári grimaced, then retaliated, swinging his javelin like a club. Sinfjotli summoned Wolfsbane back to his right hand and blocked the strike. Blue flickers of electricity shot up his arm, raced off his shoulder, and scarred the surrounding snow, but Sinfjotli stood his ground. With Wolfsbane holding back Kári's javelin, he thrust Gram at the giant's left foot.

Sigurd, struggling to rise, found the strength to stand and watched the two sparring. Kári was on the defensive now. He swung his javelin in a wide arc, but Sinfjotli caught the tip with his axe head. He raised his left arm overhead and sliced Kári's javelin in half with Gram. With a snap like a blast of thunder, the weapon exploded.

A shockwave ripped through the battlefield.

Heat—hotter than dragonfire. Light—blinding, golden. The force—a crushing wave that swept Sigurd off his feet and squeezed the breath out of him.

When his ears stopped ringing and his vision cleared, Sigurd discovered he was standing on one knee near the slope of the mountain ridge. Kári stood higher up, near the slope of the mountaintop, staggering and confused. He clutched only half of the splintered remains of his weapon. The other half lay jutting out from the snow twenty feet away. The sheer force of the javelin's destruction had blasted a perfectly cone-shaped pit—thirty feet deep—and triggered an avalanche that sent half the ridge tumbling down the mountain.

Sinfjotli was still standing in the same spot, completely unfazed. Not a step lost. Not a scratch gained. Kári staggered back; Sinfjotli rushed in for the kill. But just as Gram arced toward Kári, the giant thrust out his left hand. A sudden blast of wind—furious, howling—slammed into Sinfjotli, sending him flying.

He struck the ground twice before skidding to a stop right next to Sigurd. He rose to his feet but suddenly gasped and his knees buckled. He dropped Gram and Wolfsbane and doubled over, clutching his throat.

A moment later, Sigurd collapsed to his knees, too, unable to breathe. His skin and wounds started boiling again. He knew this feeling. Kári had created another vacuum that was siphoning all the air from the mountain ridge.

"Nice try," Kári said. "But that was your last trick."

As Sigurd and Sinfjotli writhed on the ground, gasping for air like drowning men, Kári picked up the other half of his javelin and strolled toward them.

Sigurd tried to stand, but his legs were like lead. He crumpled face-first into the snow and ice. The cold enveloped him, whispered to him. *Relax. Let go. Surrender.* It took every ounce of willpower to stay conscious.

A massive foot appeared beside Sigurd's face. With a casual flick of his toes, the storm giant flipped Sigurd onto his back. Sigurd's eyes cracked open, staring up at the figure towering over him. Both halves of Kári's broken javelin hovered above him. The giant tensed his arms, and electricity channeled throughout each piece until both halves of the spear looked like long, curved fangs.

"This is about all the time I'll allow myself to play with you, humans," Kári announced. "Time to pay for all the wounds you dealt—with interest. As you mortals say, 'Sow the wind, reap the whirlwind!'"

He thrust the lightning daggers down at Sigurd's chest. Time stretched, seemed to slow. The tips of the javelins inched closer. He wanted to move; his body refused to obey. Was this it? He wondered what he would die from first. Asphyxiation? His blood boiling? Or would it be impalement by Kári's weapons?

It turned out it wouldn't be any of them. At the last second, a humanoid shape appeared above him and grabbed Kári's daggers. As Sigurd wondered what had happened, air coursed through his windpipe again. His lungs expanded, oxygen cycled through his brain, and his murky vision started returning to normal.

"Sorry we took too long," a familiar voice said.

A muscular man with blond hair was standing over him.

"M-Magni?" he croaked weakly between ragged breaths.

Sure enough, the god of strength was standing over him. He held the shafts of Kári's broken javelin in each hand. Pure tendrils of energy from the weapons undulated around his hands like snakes. But that only amused Magni as he snapped each shaft in half like twigs.

Kári staggered backward and dropped the broken pieces of his javelin. "No! How...?"

Before he could say anything else, Modi vaulted over Magni and swung his war hammer, slamming it into Kári's face. The storm giant sailed through the air and crashed into the mountainside, making the entire mountain tremble. High above, the impact dislodged a massive sheet of snow, triggering an avalanche that roared down the slopes, burying Kári under tons of ice and debris.

When the dust and tremors settled, Magni offered a hand and helped Sigurd stand. Modi did the same for Sinfjotli.

"You're both okay?" Sigurd rasped, still struggling to regain his breath.

Magni smirked. "You didn't think that explosion would be enough to take us out of the fight, did you?"

"I'm glad... you're alright." Sinfjotli wheezed. "But how are we able to—"

An enormous blast of lightning struck Mount Isa. Snow evaporated into steam, and chunks of ice shattered as Kári burst from the snow.

"NO!" he raged. "How the fuck are you two conscious after taking the full brunt of that air explosion?"

"We were just playing possum again," Modi corrected. "We needed some time to figure out a way to counter your ability to siphon away our air."

"Horse shit! You're bluffing!" Kári clenched his fist, creating another vacuum high above them that began sucking away all the air in the area.

"Didn't I just say that wouldn't work?" Modi asked in a nettled tone. He and Magni clasped their hands together. Tendrils of electricity erupted from their bodies and channeled into the snowy ground and the surrounding mist. The snow and fog evaporated into a watery vapor. The Sons of Thor continued channeling their energy, and after a moment, Sigurd felt warm air pass through his nostrils.

"I admit, aerokinesis isn't our forte," Modi confessed. "We cannot freely control or manipulate air as you can, Kári. However, we're both experts at the water cycle."

"Water cycle?" Kári repeated. "What in the blazes are you talking about?"

"Our air supply right now is limited, so I'll be brief," Magni forewarned. "All water follows a natural cycle of evaporation, condensation, precipitation, and collection. When heated, water evaporates into water vapor, condenses to form clouds, and then precipitates back to earth as rain and snow. The rain or snow then runs off into streams or rivers and collects into lakes or the ocean. Before long, the cycle repeats itself. As storm gods, we can manipulate that cycle, and by adding an extra step, we can generate breathable air."

"What?" Kári gawked. "How?"

"If you still don't get it, let me put it in simpler terms." Modi gestured toward the icy ground. "We're standing on a mountain of snow and ice enveloped by thick fog. In a sense, we have an endless supply of water. All we have to do is evaporate the snow and ice around us into vapor and then use our powers to transmute it into breathable air."

"Understand now?" Magni asked. "You can take away as much air as you want. We'll just generate more."

Kári clenched his fist. The vacuum above them absorbed the air even faster, but Magni and Modi matched him, generating more.

"Modi, take over for a minute," Magni requested. "There's something I've got to do."

Modi nodded and channeled even more electricity than before. Magni relaxed his body and turned to Sigurd and Sinfjotli. He placed a hand on Sigurd's shoulder. A jolt of electricity traveled down Sigurd's spine and ran throughout his body. His body tingled and trembled, but after a moment, he felt perfectly fine. He examined his hand. It was now covered in a dim yellow aura. The third-degree burns he'd suffered earlier began healing. Every hair on his arm stood straight like trees as his fingers and hand jittered. A numbness settled over him, but beneath it pulsed a deep, invigorating power.

"What did you just do?" Sigurd demanded.

"I gave you a boost," Magni replied. "Sinfjotli, hand me your axe for a moment."

Sinfjotli thrust out his hand, recalled Wolfsbane, and handed it over. Magni channeled electricity into the axe. Lightning wrapped around the blade, crackling at an unnatural frequency. When he returned it, the axe looked sharper than before, its edge vibrating at an almost imperceptible speed.

"I imbued your weapons and bodies with a spark of my power," Magni explained. "Now your axe will harm Kári, Sinfjotli. And, Sigurd, you can strike him without being electrocuted."

"Thanks?" Sigurd said hesitantly.

"Don't mention it." Magni clasped his hands together and resumed generating more air for them.

"We'll let you take charge for now," Modi said. He glanced up at the vacuum above them. "Kári is still absorbing all the surrounding air with that vacuum. So we'll keep generating air for you and provide additional support."

"Sounds good to me." Sigurd picked up Gram and pointed it at Kári. "Let's continue where we left off."

CHAPTER TWENTY-SEVEN

HAILSTORM

N ow that Sigurd and Sinfjotli could fight Kári without reservation, the battle turned in their favor.

As Sigurd moved to attack, Kári generated a sword of electricity in his right hand to block the strike. As Sinfjotli moved in to attack from the other side, Kári created a second blade in his other hand and parried Wolfsbane. He then used both energy swords simultaneously against them.

The three remained locked in a fierce duel for almost two minutes. Steel clashed against lightning, neither side gaining ground until Sigurd and Sinfjotli struck simultaneously. Kári tried to block both. One sword deflected Wolfsbane, but Gram sliced right through the other, cleaving the energy before slashing across Kári's chest.

The storm giant backed away, his electric swords flickering before fading completely. From the look on his face, Sigurd could tell that Kári was feeling helpless and vulnerable, like a cornered animal. His body started turning into wispy white clouds, presumably to retreat.

"Not happening!" Modi shouted. An arc of electricity erupted from his body. It sailed over Sigurd's head and zapped Kári's cloud body mid-shift, forcing him back into a corporeal form and sending him crashing to one knee.

Sinfjotli didn't hesitate. Wolfsbane slashed, carving a devastating gash across Kári's chest.

Kári staggered away, gaze darting to his wounds—a sizeable X-shaped slash on his torso, tiny tendrils of electricity crackling around the gash, pulsing like blood welling from a wound.

"You all are pissing me off!" Kári seethed. "You keep slashing and stabbing me. Allow me to return the favor!"

Kári clapped. Sigurd's eardrums popped as the storm giant amassed his energy. Kári reared his head back and spewed a plume of black clouds from his mouth. They merged with the thick clouds high above them. The sky darkened, turning the color of ink, and rumbled.

Sigurd braced for a lightning bolt. But nothing like that happened. As he stared at the sky and pondered what Kári was planning, something tapped his left shoulder. He turned just in time to see an ice pellet bounce off Sinfjotli's armor.

Is that hail? Sigurd wondered.

Sure enough, hail began to fall in unrelenting sheets. At first, they were as harmless as ordinary raindrops. But as the hailstorm raged on, Sigurd noticed a change. The hailstones grew—even larger and longer and sharper! After about thirty seconds, they had transformed. The hail pellets were now shaped like arrows—ice-forged projectiles plummeting from the sky. Sigurd raised Gram above his head and batted away every frozen arrow that came his way.

The ice arrows continued falling. Trying to fend them off was like trying to evaporate each raindrop as they fell from the sky. Usually, that would be impossible, but not for Sigurd. During his years of training, his mother had him walk through a thunderstorm without getting wet by batting every single raindrop before it could touch him. This situation was quite similar. Sigurd continued deflecting every single ice arrow with Gram, ensuring that none touched him as he slowly inched his way toward Kári.

That is until the storm giant used a dirty trick. A warm tingle ran through his legs. Half a heartbeat later, a massive blast of electricity enveloped his body.

"Uoooh!" Sigurd groaned. Time seemed to slow down at that moment, giving him just enough time to realize what had happened.

Kári had stomped his foot, sending a ground current surging through the mountain. The electricity traveled up Sigurd's legs, straight through his body, and blasted Gram out of his hands. Sigurd didn't even have time to think, "Oh shit!" before the arrows fell upon him. Several struck his back and shoulders, and another struck his helmet, forcing him to his knees. The arrows continued to fall, forcing Sigurd to face-plant into the snowy ground.

And still the arrows kept coming. His golden hauberk, armor, and helmet held strong, protecting him from being pierced or impaled. But that didn't stop the pain. Each impact felt like a war hammer had hit him. Every strike stole the strength from his limbs, keeping him from fully picking himself off the ground. The most he could do was lift his head. From the corner of his eye, he saw Sinfjotli. His brother had also been brought to his knees by the arrows' sheer number and blunt force.

"How do you like my Hail Arrows?" Kári cackled. "Each one is as hard as carbon steel and sharp enough to pierce through flesh and rock alike!"

He wasn't bluffing. From the corner of his eye, Sigurd noticed a massive glacier, about two hundred feet from the mountain ridge, crack and splinter from the constant storm of arrows. The deafening downpour of ice arrows drowned out the booming sound of the shattering glacier. Shards of ice flew up as the arrows pummeled the ground, only to be struck by other Hail Arrows and breaking into smaller fragments that whirled into the storm's vacuum. The air became thick with swirling ice and snow, making it difficult to see.

Kári turned his attention to Sinfjotli. Then he looked past him and belched out laughing. "I see that your armor affords you some protection, mortal. But it looks like your friends weren't so lucky!"

Sigurd followed Kári's gaze and saw that Magni and Modi had dozens of arrow shafts jutting from their bodies.

"Magni! Modi!" he screamed, horrified. The Sons of Thor were drenched in blood and covered in enough arrow shafts to resemble porcupines. But they continued to stand like sentinels, even as the arrows continued piercing their flesh.

"Why aren't you dodging?" Sigurd demanded. "Why are you just standing there? Use your powers to...?"

Sigurd's words faltered as realization struck. He was *talking*! He was still breathing, even though the air vacuum high above them was still sucking up all the air in the area. That's why Magni and Modi weren't dodging this attack. They were generating air for him and Sinfjotli to breathe even as razor-sharp arrows impaled their bodies.

"What were you fools thinking traveling through Niflheim wearing nothing but those leather garbs?" Kári mocked as an arrow tore through Magni's leather jerkin. "Did you think *courage* was all you needed to survive in Niflheim? You're both crazy. No, I take that back. You're just plain stupid! If you had worn armor, you might have been able to protect yourselves from this onslaught."

Magni and Modi didn't respond to the giant's provocations. They clenched their teeth as a dozen ice arrows impaled their shoulders, back, and even the nape of their necks. But they persevered and continued generating breathable air for Sigurd and Sinfjotli.

"No witty retort?" Kári observed. "I suppose it's taking all your concentration to generate this air. Fine by me. Stand there in silence and get skewered to death!"

The arrows started falling in even more unrelenting waves. The gods of strength and courage fell to their knees after getting pierced by about a hundred more shafts.

"No!" Sinfjotli roared. "I won't let it end like this!"

Through sheer willpower, Sinfjotli pushed himself off the ground onto his hands and knees and then transformed into a ten-foot-tall wolf. The

Coffin Cheater also transformed with him. Sigurd watched the armor morph, expand, and change shape to adapt to Sinfjotli's changing body until he was staring at an enormous wolf covered in jet-black armor.

The Hail Arrows kept falling like sheets of rain as Sinfjotli rushed over to Magni and Modi and stood over them like a wolf protecting its cubs. The ice arrows shattered harmlessly against the Kistfuskare's metal plating as Sinfjotli shielded Magni and Modi from the hailstorm.

"An armored wolf?" Kári tittered. "Now there's something you don't see every day. Using your sheer bulk as an umbrella to shield them from the arrows—clever. But you're too late. I doubt they have the strength to keep generating air for you in that bloody state."

"Don't underestimate us!" Magni warned. He and Modi tensed, and electricity radiated throughout their bodies. The energy incinerated the icy arrows protruding from their bodies, tearing apart what remained of their shirts.

Magni momentarily stopped generating air and summoned his great sword to his hand. He hurled it, sending it spinning like a boomerang, forcing Kári to dodge. The blade struck the mountain behind him, triggering another avalanche. A massive portion of Mount Isa's summit broke apart and raced down the slopes.

As Kári turned, distracted by the cascading destruction, Sigurd saw an opportunity to strike. He snatched Gram and, through force of will alone, forced himself to stand, pushing through the hailstorm. With a final surge of strength, he closed the distance. Kári barely had time to react. Sigurd's blade flashed through the air, severing the giant's left leg in a decisive strike.

The hailstorm weakened as Kári collapsed to the ground, writhing in pain. The Hail Arrows lost their shape and turned into large pellets no larger than a clenched fist.

"You little bastard!" Kári raged, his eyes blazing in fury. "Why aren't you a human pincushion right now? My hailstorm is powerful enough to wipe out an entire army!"

"Ha, any army that would fall to something like that must surely have a king or general too stingy to give them proper equipment and armor."

"What!" Kári's eyes widened as he grasped the full import of Sigurd's words. "Impossible! Those Hail Arrows were as sharp and hard as carbon steel. That golden armor you're wearing shouldn't have been able to do anything!"

"That's where you're wrong," Sigurd countered. "My armor can't stop a lightning bolt. But it's more than enough to protect me from those arrows. After all, it's ten times harder than steel!"

"Is that so?" Kári growled as he stood up. To Sigurd's shock, Kári's severed left leg moved and propped up beneath him as if it were still attached to his body.

What the hell? He can still move and stand on that leg even though it's no longer connected to his body! Sigurd glanced at Kári's bisected torso and then realized that the notion wasn't too farfetched. After all, Kári's cloud body wasn't normal. Unlike living creatures, clouds could split apart or merge and maintain their general shape as they traveled across the sky.

Chopping up Kári's limbs was as effective as slicing off a cloud fragment. No matter what they did, the storm giant's limbs would still maintain their shape and function.

"You just said your armor can't stop a lightning strike? Well, in that case..."

Kári thrust his right hand toward the heavens. High above them, the clouds darkened and rumbled. Lightning cracked across the sky as a massive funnel cloud formed and connected with Kári's hand. The tornado crackled with tendrils of electricity, which coalesced and formed into an enormous lightning spear.

Alarms blared in Sigurd's head. Every strand of hair on his body stood up, drawn toward the weapon's energy. Unlike the metal javelin he'd wielded earlier, the spear Kári held was pure electricity. Exponentially more powerful than any lightning bolt Kári had unleashed before.

"This spear is my strongest," Kári proclaimed. "It'll burn you to ash with over two hundred million volts of electricity!"

"I see. That's very scary indeed." Sigurd took a deep breath, glanced at the sky, and smiled. "By the way, it seems you've yet to notice." He pointed toward the thick cloud cover above them. "That hailstorm you summoned has stopped, and the air vacuum you created earlier has also vanished. Which means..."

At that moment, Modi leaped over Sigurd's head and buried his war hammer into Kári's chest.

"...Magni and Modi are now free to act as they please." Sigurd finished.

Kári staggered backward and coughed up what looked like blood. He looked up and glared at Sigurd with eyes full of hate and malice.

"Damn you!" The giant rushed past Modi and tried impaling Sigurd with his spear. But Magni appeared before him and parried the thrust with his great sword. The sound of their weapons clashing was like a blast of thunder, and it sent tendrils of electricity flying in every direction.

As he held the storm giant at bay, Magni glanced over his shoulder and smiled proudly. "Great job rattling him. Modi and I will take it from here."

Sinfjotli appeared next to Sigurd, and together, they watched as Magni and Modi beat the tar out of Kári. If he was calmer, the storm giant could've created another vacuum to cripple them and force Magni and Modi back on the defensive. But fortunately, Kári had lost all sense of composure. He lashed out wildly, swinging his spear in every direction, desperate to land a blow. But all his attacks fell short.

As they fought, Modi dashed behind Kári and struck the back of the giant's right kneecap with his war hammer, forcing the storm giant to his knees. As

Magni rushed forward for the kill, Kári thrust his spear at him. But Magni sidestepped the attack and then swung his great sword down on the shaft, severing it in half.

The spear exploded, sending heat and energy everywhere.

CHAPTER TWENTY-EIGHT

THE FROZEN GOD

W hen the ringing in his ears stopped, Sigurd opened his eyes and looked around.

Kári lay battered and beaten at the bottom of a crater, a cone-shaped pit plunging forty feet deep. Magni and Modi loomed over the rim, holding their weapons at the ready in case the storm giant tried to get back up.

Sigurd stared in awe. When Magni shattered Kári's spear, the resulting explosion decimated the mountaintop, sending half the ridge they stood on tumbling down the slopes. Tendrils of electricity had sparked everywhere, vaporizing most snow layers.

He should have been caught in the blast—but Sinfjotli had acted quickly. The giant armored wolf had stepped between him and the explosion, shielding him from the blast.

After assuring Sinfjotli he was alright, Sigurd and his brother, still in wolf form, joined Magni and Modi at the crater's edge.

Sigurd studied their faces as they loomed over their beaten foe. He had expected the Sons of Thor to celebrate this glorious victory. Instead, they looked utterly disappointed.

"That's it?" Magni exclaimed. "We traveled through Niflheim for *this*! The frost trolls were more of a challenge than this waste of air!"

"This was... mildly amusing at best," Sigurd agreed.

Kári had been a formidable opponent, but Sigurd sincerely doubted the storm giant was one of the most powerful giants in all the Nine Realms. Heck, the dead giants Hel had summoned back in Helheim had been more of a challenge. Then again, this had been a four-on-one battle. Kári had been fighting against two thunder gods and two skinchangers. That would be tough, even for a mighty storm giant like Kári.

"Uncle Heimdall must be going senile," Modi grumbled. "He promised we'd encounter 'the most powerful frost giant in the Nine Realms atop Mount Isa.' Instead, we found a mere storm giant. We've already slain dozens of them before, and our father has killed hundreds of them in the past. How are we supposed to step out of his shadow with this?"

Isn't surviving the journey through Niflheim and reaching the top of this mountain already an accomplishment? Sigurd wondered.

"Fr... Frost... giant?" Kári coughed. "You came... all this way looking for...?" He smiled and laughed maniacally.

"What's so damn funny?" Magni demanded.

"You fool!" Kári cackled. "I'm not the giant you seek. You must be after my father's head. But Fornjót the Destroyer is beyond you fools!"

"Fornjót the Destroyer?" Sinfjotli repeated. The armored wolf curled his lips into a toothy smile. "I like the sound of that name."

"It is an interesting moniker." Modi grinned. "Tell us where we can find this 'Destroyer,' and I'll grant you a quick death."

"Isn't it obvious?" Kári chuckled. "You're standing on him!"

A massive blast of wind bombarded them as they tried to grasp his words. The wind turned the entire world white as it picked up snow from the ground. The frigid cold air felt like billions of tiny razors against their skin as it blasted them from every direction. As Sigurd and his comrades covered their faces for protection, Kári's body dissipated into clouds and blew away with the wind.

"Damn, he got away!" Magni cursed once the wind subsided.

"I don't sense him," Modi grumbled as he scanned the thick clouds above them. "But the slippery bastard is here somewhere. Now, where..."

"Guys," Sinfjotli interrupted nervously. "W-what is that?"

Sigurd turned toward the mountain, and his mind screeched to a halt. The wind Kári had summoned to escape had stripped away an entire layer of snow from the mountaintop, revealing a giant blue eyelid encased beneath a wall of solid ice. Its skin was the color of permafrost, and its ice-covered eyelashes were as long as trees.

Before Sigurd could fully comprehend what he was looking at, the wall of ice cracked. Then shattered. The eyelid snapped open, revealing a vast deep blue eye that burned with an unnatural cold. The eyeball glanced around and then looked down at them.

The ground rumbled and quaked like a bucking horse, throwing everyone off their feet. A deep, resonant crack echoed from high above. Sigurd looked up just in time to see the summit—where they'd first encountered Kári—breaking apart. Massive slabs of ice and rock splintered away, unleashing tons of snow and ice that sped down the mountain slope.

"The entire mountain is shaking!" Sigurd panicked.

"No! It's falling apart!" Sinfjotli corrected.

"You're both wrong," Modi muttered as he helped Sigurd to his feet. "It's waking up!"

Sigurd looked at him and then back at the giant blue eye. But before his mind could fully grasp the implication of those words, the mountain crest they were standing on broke apart, sending hundreds of chunks of rock, ice, and the four of them plunging down the mountain.

"Brace yourselves!" Magni hollered as they were swept up by the avalanche.

But this was no ordinary avalanche. Usually, snow and ice slide diagonally down a mountain slope. But this was different. Instead of tumbling at an angle, it felt more like they were falling straight down and bouncing off the ground like a stone kicked down a rocky hill. From the brief glimpses Sigurd could catch as they tumbled, it looked like the mountain was expanding. The summit kept rising higher above the dense cloud cover with each second.

They could worry about the implications of that later. For now, they had to survive this avalanche.

As they were swept away like twigs in a raging river, Sinfjotli scooped up Sigurd in his mouth. Magni and Modi grabbed his haunches and hoisted themselves onto the armored wolf's back. In his wolf form, Sinfjotli's sheer size and strength allowed him to withstand the waves of snow and trudge through the avalanche without being buried alive.

But not for long. The entire mountain was tearing apart, the powerful avalanches shooting down the slopes in unyielding waves of destruction. If they didn't escape now, they'd be buried alive beneath thousands of tons of snow and ice.

Amidst the chaos, Magni seized Sigurd's arm, pulled him free from Sinfjotli's mouth, and sat him onto the base of the wolf's neck. Sigurd spotted a small mountain crest about a hundred yards away that was withstanding the avalanche. He guided Sinfjotli toward it. The armored wolf pushed forward, powerful limbs churning through torrents of snow, fighting against the current. Step by step, he forced his way through the speeding snow until he reached the crest.

As soon as they were on stable ground, Magni and Modi hopped off Sinfjotli's back. Modi wrapped an arm around Sigurd while Magni lifted the armored wolf off the ground with a single arm. The gods of strength and courage then leaped hundreds of feet into the air with enough force to shatter the icy mountain crest they'd used to propel themselves. A tidal wave of snow rushing down the mountain immediately swept away the ice and rock fragments.

They soared through the air for almost a full minute before landing on a mountaintop five miles from Mount Isa. Magni and Modi landed with enough force to leave two massive craters in the rocky surface.

As soon as Modi set him on the ground, Sigurd's knees buckled beneath him, and he doubled over on the snowy crater, gasping for air. Sinfjotli's legs also gave out, and the giant armored wolf collapsed on his belly, sides heaving with labored breaths.

"That was too close!" Sigurd panted. "We barely escaped that avalanche!"

"It's far from over," Magni announced grimly, looking back at the mountain. "That was just the beginning."

Sigurd stood up, wiped away the dog saliva still smearing his face before it turned to ice, and turned to look where Magni pointed.

What he saw would haunt him for a long time. Mount Isa was crumbling apart, its slopes collapsing in an unstoppable torrent of snow and ice like a raging river. A pillar of icy particles shot skyward, touching the clouds. From this distance, it also looked as if the colossal mountain was rising, as if something long buried beneath all that snow and ice was awakening, pushing to the surface.

No! Sigurd realized. *Not something. Someone!*

An enormous cloud of snow and ice crystals engulfed the air, and they could see nothing for a while. Then, as the veil of frost began to settle, Sigurd saw what had been entombed: a colossal giant seated upon a gigantic throne of ice.

The titan's skin was thick and blue-gray skin, his glowing blue eyes radiating an eerie light. His muscular frame was well-defined, and his bulging veins were visible beneath his frozen skin if Sigurd looked closely. Bare-chested, he wore only a large, shaggy black loincloth covering his waist and buttocks. His long, wispy white hair reached his shoulder blades, and a long mustache and chest-length beard framed his formidable face. Icicles encrusted his hair and facial hair, catching the light like frozen stars whenever he moved. On his head, jagged icy horns sprouted, jutting out like points on a crown.

But more than anything, the giant was enormous! As Sigurd leaned back to gaze at the giant's full size, he realized they'd made a grievous misassumption when they arrived in Niflheim. There had never been a frost giant waiting for them at the top of Mount Isa. The frost giant was the mountain itself!

"T-that must be Fornjót the Destroyer," Sigurd whispered.

"No doubt about that," Magni agreed. "This is definitely the frost giant Uncle Heimdall promised we'd find."

Sigurd glanced at the layers of snow and ice still burying the giant's lower body. Thousands of tons of snow and ice still clung to his shoulders and neck. If Sigurd were to guess, the giant must have been sleeping beneath millions of tons of snow and ice for millennia.

How long has this giant been sleeping on that throne for the snow and ice to pile on top of his body so thickly? Sigurd didn't have long to dwell on that thought as Fornjót finished digging his way out of the mountain. Thousands of tons of snow and ice rolled off his shoulders and the rest of his body, creating enormous mountains of snow around his feet as he stood up. The throne of ice cracked and shattered into rubble as large chunks of ice crashed against it.

Fornjót was so tall that his elbows touched the clouds. As he stood there, his breath parted the overcast clouds around him enough for Sigurd to glimpse his face. Fornjót raised his arms above his head and opened his mouth. Sigurd braced himself for an incoming attack, but to his surprise, the giant just yawned. His breath turned to hail as the air left his lungs.

"I've never seen a giant this huge!" Magni exclaimed. "He's even bigger than the frost giant King Thrym and Utgard Loki combined! He might even be bigger than Surtr!"

The giant stretched his limbs and moaned as if trying to remember how to move his joints. After a few more tense minutes, Fornjót stopped stretching and glanced down as if finally noticing them.

"Are you the ones who dared to wake me from my slumber?" Fornjót's booming voice sounded deep and slow, and it took a while for his voice to reach them because of how big he was.

No one responded. Everyone's ears were still ringing from the giant's deafening voice. Fornjót frowned, and Sigurd worried he was angry that they weren't responding to his inquiry. But when the giant squinted and leaned closer to the ground, Sigurd realized Fornjót was having trouble seeing them clearly.

"You seem like maggots to me." Fornjót frowned. "Bah! It's too dark to tell. Let me remedy that."

He raised his arms outward and clapped. The sound was as loud as a volcanic eruption. The shockwave parted the dense cloud cover above and created an enormous rift in the sky. For the first time in perhaps eons, sunlight shone through Niflheim's cloud cover, illuminating the snowy mountainous landscape around them.

As they basked in the warm rays of light for the first time in months, Sigurd realized something. "It stopped snowing!"

"That's impossible," Magni objected. "Niflheim's blizzards are supposed to be endless. Even our father isn't powerful enough to end these blizzards."

"And yet there's not a single snowflake raining down on us," Sigurd pointed out. "The wind has also stopped, even though it's been blowing incessantly since we came here. The blizzards and wind subsided as soon as Fornjót clapped his hands. Does that mean... he can manipulate Niflheim's weather? Is he truly that powerful?"

"There, that's better." Fornjót sighed as his eyes adjusted to the rays of light shining on his face. "Now, let me have a good look at you."

His voice was not at all the eardrum-splitting rumble it had been moments ago. However, it still shook Sigurd's and Sinfjotli's skulls like an eerie dirge echoing directly into their heads, penetrating their guts and bones. It took a hefty amount of concentration and willpower to avoid falling to their knees as Fornjót leaned down and studied them intently. As he came closer, Sigurd realized just how massive this giant was. His eyes were as large as the stars. The four of them were like tiny fleas compared to this towering giant.

"Just as I thought," Fornjót grumbled. "*Maggots*! So you were the ones standing on my nose?"

The full import of that question took several moments to be fully realized by Sigurd's already strained mind. When it did, icy terror gripped his heart.

"Are you kidding me!" Sigurd gasped. "That mountain ridge we fought Kári on was this giant's nose? Is he truly that big?"

Fornjót straightened his back and sighed. "I find it hard to believe you are the ones who awoke me."

"Actually, that responsibility lies with me," a voice said.

"Who said that?" Fornjót scanned the misty valleys and frozen landscape around him, trying to locate the source.

"I did, Father." The voice replied, louder than before.

"Look up there, on his left shoulder!" Sigurd pointed. "It's Kári!"

Their most recent foe stood leisurely on Fornjót's left shoulder, looking down at them with crossed arms. Fornjót turned his head and looked down at the storm giant.

"Kári?" Fornjót blinked. "Is that you, my son?"

"Indeed." Kári nodded. "It's been a couple of eons since we last saw one another."

Fornjót's eyes widened. "I've been asleep that long?" He shook his head in disbelief, which caused icicles the size of trees to dislodge from his hair and beard and rain down like meteorites. "It doesn't matter. Why have you woken me this early? The sun and moon haven't been devoured, which means Ragnarök isn't upon us yet."

"Oh, it's simple." The crazed storm giant extended a finger at the four of them. "Those 'maggots' down there claimed they were on some foolish quest to slay you. So, I thought I'd wake you to show them just how hopelessly outmatched they are."

"Slay me?" Fornjót repeated. "Slay *ME*!" He burst out laughing. His laughter was louder than any blast of thunder Sigurd had heard. It reverberated throughout the valley, shattering glaciers, triggering avalanches, and causing the ground to quake.

"You're quite arrogant for a bunch of maggots!" Fornjót chuckled.

"Don't underestimate us," Modi warned. "Our father Thor and grandfather Odin have killed thousands of you frost giants before."

"Frost giants? Bah!" Fornjót bellowed indignantly. "Don't be so foolish as to lump me in with that race of weaklings! I am as far beyond the frost giants as they are beyond you mortals!"

"Is that so?" Magni asked. "Care to test that claim?"

Magni and Modi pointed their weapons toward the sky. The clouds rumbled, and a second later, a massive lightning bolt blasted Fornjót in the chest.

Sigurd cheered. But when the clouds of dust cleared, his smile died. Fornjót wasn't even fazed. Magni and Modi had blasted him with enough lightning to split a mountain in half, but there were no signs of damage or duress anywhere on the giant's body. Fornjót hadn't even moved an inch. He just stood there, glowering at them.

As Sigurd and his companions gaped, Kári turned to his father. "I think I'll take my leave for now and let you have some fun with them, Father." His body faded into clouds and disappeared in a wave of lightning.

At that moment, the temperature plummeted. The clouds above darkened, the rift in the sky closed, and the rays of sunlight vanished. It started snowing again, but the weather felt noticeably different. Niflheim wasn't as dark as before. But the icy wind and the mix of ice and rain seemed actively hostile. Somehow, it felt even colder than before.

"So maggots, you ventured into Niflheim to slay me?" Fornjót asked derisively. "Your resolve is admirable. But your lack of strength bores me. It makes me want to *YAWN*!"

As he spoke, Fornjót opened his mouth wide and bellowed a swirling blizzard from his mouth.

Thinking fast, Magni whistled, summoning Tanngrisnir and Tanngnjóstr. Sinfjotli turned back into his human form, and they all jumped into the chariot and sped away from the raging blizzard cloud.

The goats zipped across the landscape and retreated to the summit of a gigantic mountain ten miles away. When Sigurd looked back, he saw that the raging blizzard had frozen everything it touched. The entire landscape had been frozen over and buried beneath ten feet of solid ice. They would all be frozen statues right now if not for Magni and Modi.

They stepped off the chariot, and the goats bolted away. As they gazed in awe at the cataclysmic aftermath of Fornjót's breath attack, the mountain quaked beneath their feet as the massive giant leisurely walked toward them.

"He's slow, but his stride is huge," Sigurd noted. "He'll catch up to us in no time!"

Within a few steps, he traversed the entire ten-mile distance and loomed over them. Fornjót was even more intimidating up close. The mountain they were standing on barely reached his kneecaps.

"I'm impressed you survived that and scurried away," Fornjót said. "Then again, maggots often get lucky during storms. I wonder if you'll be so lucky a second time."

Fornjót reared back his head and opened his mouth wide. But as he inhaled deeply, Magni and Modi raised their weapons toward the heavens, and a bolt of lightning blasted the inside of Fornjót's mouth and the back of the giant's throat. Fornjót staggered backward, coughing. But he didn't fall.

"I take back what I said about Uncle Heimdall." Magni smiled hungrily. "This monster is everything I'd hoped for and more!"

Sigurd glanced nervously at Magni's and Modi's eyes. Their eyes reminded him of a hungry predator about to pounce on juicy prey it had been stalking for days. Sigurd glanced back at Fornjót's sheer bulk and pondered just what kind of battle was about to unfold. He wondered if he and Sinfjotli could even do anything.

"Getting cold feet, Sigurd?" Modi asked, as if reading his thoughts.

"No," Sigurd lied. "I'm just wondering what kind of strategy we should employ."

"Do you two want to take point and soften him up like we did with Kári?" Sinfjotli asked.

"No," Magni decided. "We should all fight him together."

Sigurd stared blankly at him. *Fight Fornjót together? How would they even manage that?*

"I'll be blunt," Modi said. "Fornjót isn't an enemy that Magni and I can beat alone. We held nothing back in those last two attacks, but neither had any effect."

Fornjót kept coughing from their recent sneak attack, but he wasn't in any genuine pain. He sounded more annoyed and frustrated than injured. He looked and sounded more like a man experiencing aspiration after a foreign object had entered his windpipe.

"If we're going to beat this monster, we must all work together in a group offensive," Magni warned. "Distractions, sneak attacks, decoys. To battle him, we'll need to use all those fighting strategies and more."

"That goes without saying," Sigurd said. "But is there anything Sinfjotli and I can *do* against him?"

Modi studied him with an inscrutable look. He walked over, pulled his middle finger back with his thumb, and flicked Sigurd's forehead with enough force to send him flying across the mountaintop and crashing into a large glacier.

"What the hell was that about?" Sigurd demanded as he pulled himself from the ice.

"I should ask you that same question!" Modi retorted. "Where is this self-doubt coming from? What are you so scared of after coming this far? Are you intimidated by his size? Who cares if Fornjót is massive? That didn't hold you back when you fought all those undead Jötnar in Helheim."

Sigurd faltered as he reminisced about the grueling battle on the Gjallerbru. Brynhild defeated most of the undead giants on her own, but he had also taken down a few, even though they were sixty times larger than him. But he still needed Brynhild's help to pull it off.

"But why'd you hit me?" Sigurd complained as he rubbed his swollen forehead. "It feels like you nearly took my head off."

"The fact your head is still attached to your shoulders after getting flicked by *a god* shows how durable your body has become," Modi retorted. "It also proves you have what it takes to survive this battle."

Modi was about to say more, but at that moment, the ground quaked as Fornjót finished coughing and walked back to the mountain they were standing on.

"Listen, Sigurd, anyone who fights with half-hearted resolve is guaranteed to lose a battle," Modi warned. "There isn't any shame in being afraid. The disgrace comes from letting fear master you. When you toss fear aside, there is no limit to what you can accomplish. Even if your opponent is stronger and you have no reason to live, never forget that you can still fight!"

"And remember that you're not alone," Magni added. "You have your brother, me, and Magni fighting by your side! Fornjót is powerful, but a pack of wolves can kill a bear if they all work as a coordinated team. It doesn't matter how insignificant our attacks might be. If we all work together, then we *will* succeed!"

Their words touched Sigurd and filled his heart with courage. He smiled, unsheathed Gram, and glanced up at their titanic foe.

"That was inconvenient." Fornjót sighed. "Feels like I swallowed a fly." The giant grinned. "But you maggots have piqued my interest. If you are all really Odin's descendants, I hope you'll put up a decent fight."

Fornjót stomped the ground with his foot. The land quaked and rumbled as a giant icy edifice erupted from the earth. It was so tall that Sigurd had to lean back to see the top. When he noticed the enormous arrow-shaped tip at the top, he realized it was a colossal spear made of solid ice. Fornjót grabbed the spear, broke off the base from the ground, and hoisted it over his head.

"Kári claimed you maggots came here to kill me," he said. "You're quite arrogant for a bunch of weaklings. Let's see if you're up for the task."

Fornjót thrust his spear at them, and their epic battle began in earnest.

CHAPTER TWENTY-NINE

THE DESTROYER

"**B**race yourselves!" Magni shouted as Fornjót swung his spear. The giant ice spear swept across the landscape like a giant scythe through a wheatfield, sheering the tops off many mountains as it approached them.

Modi hefted his war hammer and swung at the incoming spear. The force of the blow shattered the spearhead and sent chunks of ice flying in every direction.

Sigurd cheered his comrade, but Fornjót was unimpressed.

"That's a nifty toy you got there, maggot. Mind if I try it?"

Fornjót waved his hand over the jagged end of his broken spear. There was a flash of blue-gray light, and when it faded, Sigurd saw Fornjót was now holding a massive war hammer. It looked identical to Modi's, albeit on a much larger scale.

Fornjót can create gigantic weapons made of ice and reshape them at his leisure, Sigurd realized. *His control over ice and cold is absolute!*

"We're going to jump!" Magni warned as Fornjót raised the massive war hammer over his head. The god of strength wrapped an arm beneath Sigurd's shoulder. Modi holstered his hammer and grabbed Sinfjotli. They leaped thousands of feet into the air as Fornjót's giant hammer raced toward them. The colossal hammer flattened the mountain they'd been standing on, creating a massive mile-wide canyon where it once stood.

Thankfully, Fornjót wouldn't be doing that a second time. The frost giant had swung his war hammer with so much force the impact shattered the hammerhead and shaft.

"You won't find any refuge in the air!" Fornjót warned as they sailed over his head.

A shadow rippled over Sigurd's face. He glanced up. A giant chunk of ice one thousand feet in diameter was speeding toward them.

"I know you can't fly, so up there, you're as good as trapped!" Fornjót declared.

"Modi, take Sigurd!" Magni shouted. "I'll deal with this!" He hurled Sigurd like a rag doll at Modi and summoned his great sword to his hand as he sped toward the incoming meteorite. With a single swing, Magni cleaved the giant chunk of hail in half.

As the fragments rained down from the sky, Modi landed hard on an enormous ice sheet, the impact sending a jolt through Sigurd's bones. Magni soon appeared beside him, setting Sigurd and Sinfjotli down. But no sooner had their feet touched the ground than Sigurd sensed danger drawing near. The earth trembled beneath their feet, and large crevasses formed on the ice shelf.

"You'll find even less refuge on the ground!" Fornjót warned.

"Jump!" Modi exclaimed. He grabbed Sinfjotli while Magni grabbed Sigurd and leaped into the air again.

Half a heartbeat later, dozens of razor-sharp icy spikes burst from the ground. The stalagmites continued chasing them until they were over six hundred feet in the air. The four hurtled through the air, landing on another ice sheet several miles away. As they regained their footing and looked back, Sigurd's breath caught. What had once been a flat ice shelf was now a forest of towering mountain-sized stalagmites, their razor-sharp tips glinting like frozen spears.

The air turned frigid again, and a shadow enveloped them. Sigurd looked up. Hundreds of razor-sharp icicles were raining down on them. Magni and Modi channeled their power to destroy most of them with tendrils of electricity, but a few slipped by. Sigurd and Sinfjotli moved swiftly, slicing apart the strays.

When the last ice shard fell, a deep chill ran up Sigurd's legs, a freezing numbness seeping into his bones. Then the ground trembled—a slow, thunderous quake. He lifted his gaze just as Fornjót approached and loomed over them.

"No more jumping around, little fleas!" He smiled.

Sigurd reached out for Magni so they could jump away, but his feet wouldn't budge. He glanced down and discovered why. The surrounding ground had entirely frozen over, burying their feet and everything below their kneecaps beneath two feet of solid ice.

"We let our guard down!" Sigurd growled. "We were so focused on Fornjót and those giant icicles that we didn't realize our feet had frozen over."

Sigurd watched helplessly as Fornjót created a giant ice sword and hefted it over his head. Before he could swing it, Modi raised his hammer over his head.

"This might sting," he warned before hammering the ice. Cracks formed, and electricity channeled through the hammerhead into the ice encasing them. The energy raced up Sigurd's legs and exited through the fingertips of his left hand, making him feel numb and short of breath. After a moment, the entire ice sheet crumbled apart.

Magni and Modi didn't dawdle. They grabbed Sigurd and Sinfjotli and jumped away just as Fornjót brought his ice sword down on the mountain, slicing it in half.

"You won't escape!" Fornjót bellowed as he twisted his body around and swung the giant ice sword while they were still in the air.

Magni and Modi both swung their weapons at the giant blade, and the resulting shockwave devastated the landscape below them. Several mountaintops crumbled to rubble, and a large crack opened in the ground.

Eventually, the ice sword succumbed to the combined strength of Magni and Modi's attack and shattered.

Magni and Modi then reached out, grabbed Sigurd and Sinfjotli, and landed on another mountaintop.

"Something's wrong," Sigurd announced after Magni let go of him. "That ice sword resembled Gram. Earlier, Fornjót made a war hammer that looked much like Modi's and then a great sword resembling Magni's."

"He's mimicking the forms of our weapons and then using them against us," Sinfjotli inferred.

"He's toying with us and showing off," Magni growled. "Typical. Frost giants can't resist proving their strength against the Aesir. He's flaunting how much stronger he is."

A shadow enveloped them as Fornjót loomed over them again, holding the broken hilt, all that was left of his mighty ice sword. He examined the fractured weapon and chuckled. "I can see the appeal of using these weapons. You maggots have made some interesting toys over the years. But it seems they're too brittle. Or maybe I'm just too strong? No matter."

He tossed aside the broken sword. The ice weapon soared through the air and crashed into an enormous mountain. Sigurd saw the sword hilt jutting up from the mountaintop when the billowing snow and ice clouds settled. From this distance, it looked like a sword lodged in stone.

Fornjót held up his huge hands and wiggled his fingers. "I'd rather crush you with my bare hands. I need nothing else."

Sigurd tried to calm himself and assess the situation. Fornjót was unlike any opponent he had ever faced, but he had to have some weakness they could exploit.

He got himself under control with a series of well-drilled breaths, steeled his nerves, and calmly reflected on the course of their battle. Fornjót was strong enough to contend with the gods of strength and courage. No, his strength likely surpassed theirs. His power was leagues beyond theirs, and he had the complete topographical advantage here in Niflheim. He could summon storms, transmute the air around him into icy projectiles, and manipulate the wintry landscape beneath their feet.

Their only tactical advantage was Fornjót's immense size. The frost giant's mammoth size and girth made his attacks cumbersome and easy to telegraph. But they weren't easy to dodge. Fornjót could flatten an entire mountain into dust just by stepping on it, and he could cover a distance of over three miles with a single swing of his arm. Regardless of how far away they jumped, Fornjót could close the distance with a few simple steps.

From the moment he laid eyes on Fornjót, Sigurd knew the frost giant was far more powerful than they could ever be. But he never imagined the towering giant would be *this* much more powerful. Sigurd felt like an ant staring into the sky above him. Fornjót was in a class of his own, far above any level mortal men could fathom. Even though they were fighting alongside two gods against Fornjót, it felt like they were nothing more than leaves being whipped about by a raging hurricane.

"Hey, Sigurd, don't you think it's time you and Sinfjotli joined in?" Modi huffed.

"Pardon?" Sigurd muttered.

"Slaying Fornjót is *your* task," Magni reminded. "We don't mind helping and sharing in the glory. But so far, Modi and I have been doing all the work while you two have been standing on the sidelines. It is high past time you and Sinfjotli contributed."

Sigurd grimaced. "I want to fight, but is there anything we *can* do? We're like pebbles fighting a mountain."

"Do I need to flick your forehead again?" Modi threatened. "I told you not to think such useless thoughts! It doesn't matter how insignificant your attacks may be. Even raindrops can wear away mountains if you give them long enough!"

"But Sigurd and I can't jump and dodge the way you can," Sinfjotli pointed out. "We'd never be able to hit any of his vital areas."

"Then focus on an area you *can* hit," Modi advised. "Fornjót is big, but his anatomy is just like any other Aesir or human, albeit on a much greater scale. He shares all the same pressure points and vulnerable spots we do."

Focus on an area you can hit, Sigurd reflected as he studied Fornjót.

His first instinct was to attack Fornjót's throat, but he realized that wasn't viable. The frost giant's long, ice-covered beard completely covered his throat and upper chest. Moreover, his long hair also completely covered the back of his neck. His beard and hair were covered in huge chunks of ice and were essentially giant shields protecting the most vulnerable areas of his body.

Sigurd knew that was the case because the same was true for his own hair. His hair and facial hair had grown out during their journey through Niflheim. No blade, save for Gram, could cut a single strand. At first, he considered it an annoying side effect of becoming a skinchanger. But he soon realized it was a blessing in disguise. The back of the neck was every creature's greatest blind spot, the throat and windpipe their most vulnerable area. But by letting his hair and beard grow, he had created a natural defense, much like a lion's mane shielding its vital points. Thus, he knew attacking Fornjót's neck wasn't viable.

Worse, without Magni's and Modi's help, it was unlikely he and Sinfjotli could even reach Fornjót's neck or damage the giant's face and chest. At best, he and Sinfjotli might inflict some damage on the giant's feet and reduce his mobility. In that case, the obvious target would be...

"His Achilles tendons," Sigurd said. "We should attack his Achilles tendons and ankles. If we force him to his knees, it'll be easier to hurt him."

Modi nodded with approval. "Magni and I will distract him, giving you two a chance to approach."

"Hey, maggots," Fornjót called out. "Is this the extent of your power? It's far from enough to satisfy me. All you've done is dodge and jump around like frogs. You haven't even landed a single attack on me. Can't you make this more thrilling?"

Magni and Modi bared their teeth.

"As far as battles go, this is just sad." Fornjót huffed. "I feel as though I'm just squashing bugs."

"You want to see power, monster?" Modi shouted.

"You two might want to avert your eyes," Magni warned. He and Modi raised their weapons, chanted in an incomprehensible language, and then clashed their weapons against each other. A booming sound like a mountain splitting in half echoed as the great sword and war hammer struck against each other. Sigurd had barely enough time to squint his eyes shut as a massive burst of light erupted from the two weapons.

"ARGH!" Fornjót bellowed.

"My eyes!" Sigurd wailed as he collapsed to his knees. Suddenly, a muscular arm wrapped around his waist. The next thing he knew, Sigurd lost contact with the ground and soared through the air.

"I warned you to look away," Magni chided, his voice like a distant echo amidst the ringing in Sigurd's ears.

Sigurd rubbed his throbbing eyes until the sunspots faded. Once his vision returned, he discovered Magni had picked him up along with Sinfjotli, jumped, and they were now soaring toward Fornjót. The frost giant was currently crouched on one knee, rubbing his eyes.

Modi didn't give him a chance to recover. The god of courage leaped toward him and slammed his war hammer into Fornjót's temple with enough force to knock the frost giant face-first into the ground.

It did little, however. Fornjót recovered, stood up, and resumed his battle with the god of courage.

Meanwhile, Magni springboarded off a mountaintop and stealthily approached Fornjót from a different direction. He got Sigurd and Sinfjotli as close as possible to Fornjót's feet without drawing attention to himself, deposited them on a large ice shelf, then rejoined his brother in battling the frost giant.

Sigurd and Sinfjotli started their approach but encountered a problem. The snow was too deep, rising up to their chests. To remedy this, Sinfjotli shifted into his wolf form and let Sigurd climb onto his back so they could trek through the deep snow.

Sigurd and Sinfjotli slowly approached Fornjót's left foot. The giant, engrossed in his battle with the gods of strength and courage, heeded them no more than he would a clew of worms in the mud.

Modi was right, Sigurd thought as they got close. Fornjót's anatomy was like a human's, but on a larger scale. Sigurd could see every facet of the giant's foot: his long, shaggy white hair, wrinkles, and even the bulging blue veins and bones beneath his skin.

Of course, the only area that mattered was his tendons. Sever those, and the mighty giant would collapse like a felled tree.

However, given their enormous difference in size, Fornjót's Achilles tendons were still located more than a hundred feet above their heads.

They changed tactics. They ran along Fornjót's foot, striking everywhere they could reach. Perched on Sinfjotli's back, Sigurd thrust Gram into the right side of his foot, opening a long, thin gash from heel to big toe. Sinfjotli, for his part, clawed, bit, and tore chunks of flesh from the giant's foot.

However, the wounds were all superficial. Fornjót didn't even look down, making Sigurd wonder if the giant could feel the cuts.

Thus, they changed tactics and attacked the giant's left heel, hacking for a full minute. Their efforts finally reached bone—but even then the damage to the heel bone failed to accomplish much.

"It's no use." Sinfjotli huffed. "His skin is just too damn thick!"

"We could use their help now," Sigurd muttered, glancing at the gods fighting above them. "How are we supposed to reach the tendon?"

"We could use the topography to our advantage," Sinfjotli suggested. "If we get on a high hill, we might reach the tendon the next time he takes a step."

"That's—"

Sigurd never finished his train of thought because, at that moment, the battle between the gods and the frost giant escalated.

Magni had leaped a thousand feet into the air toward Fornjót's head. The giant reared his left arm back and punched the god. His meaty fist collided with Magni as the god swung his sword.

The resulting clash from their blows was so fierce that the shockwave devastated the surrounding landscape. When it subsided, Sigurd saw that neither of them had moved. Fornjót's strength could rival even the god of strength.

But the clash served as a helpful distraction. With Fornjót's attention on Magni, Modi bypassed the giant's defenses and landed a blow on his throat with his war hammer, catching the giant off guard. The hit was strong enough to send the giant staggering backward. But as he stumbled, he threatened to crush Sigurd and Sinfjotli beneath his enormous right foot.

Sinfjotli, still in his wolf form, raced forward with Sigurd on his back, desperate to escape the shadow of the danger zone. Given Fornjót's sheer size, their best hope was to race into the space between his toes. But as the darkness encompassed them, Sigurd, against all reason, decided he'd had enough.

He glanced up and drew Gram. They were directly beneath the shadow of Fornjót's ring toe. As Sinfjotli sprinted right, Sigurd leaped off the wolf's back. He prayed to Magni, Týr, Odin, Thor, and all the gods of battle as he channeled every ounce of his strength and swung.

Gram passed through the giant's flesh like a knife through warm butter. A torrent of blood erupted from the wound, blinding Sigurd, then he went flying, carried away by the blast wave as Fornjót's foot slammed into the earth.

When he came to, Sigurd found himself submerged in darkness and cold. Suddenly, a ray of light emerged as two paws broke the surface above him. Sinfjotli reached down, gently seized Sigurd with his paw, and dragged him out of the snowdrift.

Sigurd wiped the warm blood from his eyes and looked around. The air was thick with the overwhelming scent of iron and the surrounding snow was dyed dark red. He turned to see a giant severed toe lying a hundred feet away from them. The shockwave had sent them both flying away. But amazingly, Sigurd had sliced off Fornjót's right pinky toe.

Sigurd burst out laughing. "I did it! I actually hurt him! In some small way, I touched that unreachable height!"

Unfortunately, his triumph turned to ash. Losing his toe merely annoyed Fornjót and got his attention. The giant looked down at them and sneered. "What are you celebrating for?" Fornjót seethed. "You're nothing but insects that had the nerve to bite my foot. And you deserve to be crushed like pests!"

Fornjót raised his right leg and tried to stomp on them. But at that moment, Magni appeared beside them amid a lightning bolt, raised his hands over his head, and grabbed the giant's foot. The surrounding ground shattered and cracked, but the god of strength was steadfast.

"Get ready!" Magni warned. "We're going to knock him flat on his back."

"That's insane!" Sinfjotli exclaimed. "You can't possibly topple someone that big and heavy with brute strength!"

"You think so, huh?" Magni said indignantly. "You're just a mortal, Sinfjotli. You know nothing about *true* strength!"

The muscles in Magni's arms swelled as he used his might to push upward. With that, Magni pushed Fornjót's leg high into the air, throwing the giant off balance.

Modi appeared in the air behind the giant's left leg and slammed his war hammer against the back of Fornjót's kneecap. The two powerful attacks forced Fornjót off his feet and sent the giant flying backward onto a mountain range about two miles away from their current position. Two mountains flattened beneath his weight, and the impact sent an enormous cloud of snow dust and ice crystals into the air.

"Get ready," Modi warned as he landed next to Sigurd. Half a heartbeat later, the shockwave hit them.

This epic battle was unlike anything Sigurd had ever seen. The landscape changed with every clash, and the sheer scale of their cataclysmic battle was mindboggling. Entire mountains had been flattened or smashed to rubble. Giant crevices the size of canyons had opened in the ground. Sometimes, the sky split open whenever Fornjót clashed against Magni and Modi, allowing glimpses of sunlight to appear in the sky.

I can see why Fornjót is called The Destroyer, Sigurd reflected. *If we were fighting in Midgard, he could easily lay waste to entire nations and completely redraw the maps with little effort.*

"Get ready," Magni warned. "He's coming!"

Sigurd turned and watched as Fornjót emerged from the giant cloud of dust.

"How absurd!" Fornjót scoffed. "It's laughable that mere insects could topple me."

Fornjót stomped his foot against the ground. The landscape trembled and quaked. But this wasn't like an earthquake. Sigurd sensed something dangerous was about to happen from the unique feel of these tremors.

Magni sensed it as well. "Brother, jump!" he warned.

"Got it." Modi nodded. He grabbed Sinfjotli while Magni wrapped his arm around Sigurd's waist. They then leaped hundreds of feet into the air.

As they soared through the air, Sigurd glanced down. The once-flat ground had transformed into a jagged battlefield, dozens of icy spikes, each the size of mountains, jutting violently from the earth.

Fornjót has the topographical advantage. He can reshape Niflheim's atmosphere and terrain to suit his needs. Sigurd looked back at Fornjót and smiled. This monster was unlike anything he and Sinfjotli had ever faced.

But as Sigurd stared in awe at the mighty frost giant, he noticed something peculiar. Fornjót still had five toes on his right foot.

What the hell? Sigurd thought. *Why does he still have five toes? I know I cut one off. Did he somehow reattach it when we weren't looking?*

Before he could dwell on it further, Magni and Modi landed on a mountaintop and deposited Sigurd and his brother on solid ground. As soon as Sigurd was back on his feet, he glanced back to where they had been moments ago and saw the amputated toe still lying amidst the giant ice spikes.

He didn't reattach it, Sigurd realized. *So why does Fornjót have another toe where there should only be a stump? Did he magically regrow another toe somehow?*

As the giant casually approached them, Sigurd studied Fornjót's right foot and ankle. There was no trace of the wounds that he and Sinfjotli had inflicted—not a scar, not a mark. His blue, sinewy flesh looked completely untouched. And even though Modi's recent attack should have shattered his kneecap, Fornjót could still walk on his left leg.

Sigurd paused, an idea forming in his head. "Hey, Magni!"

"Yes?" Magni replied.

"I need your help," Sigurd said. "I want you to throw me at him."

"What? Why?" Magni demanded.

"I have an idea," Sigurd explained. "It took everything I had to cut off that single toe. But if I combine Gram's sharpness with your added strength, I should be able to inflict a serious wound across his body."

Magni looked skeptically at his brother.

Modi shrugged. "It's worth a shot."

Magni opened his mouth, but before he could speak, Fornjót called out. "You fleas are certainly good at jumping and running away. But is this all the Aesir are capable of these days?"

Magni and Modi took offense to that.

"You want to see genuine power?" Magni scowled. He held his great sword behind him while Modi raised his war hammer.

"Landvinningur himins!" they shouted as they swung their weapons simultaneously. The combined power of the gods of strength and courage created a powerful, explosive wave of force that slammed into Fornjót.

"What the...!" Fornjót bellowed as the force pushed him backward. For a moment, he teetered, then his feet lost contact with the ground, and he flew backward. He flattened two mountains beneath his sheer bulk as he crash-landed and skidded across the terrain, sending a gigantic cloud of ice and debris into the air.

"Amazing!" Sigurd exclaimed. "Well done, you two!"

"That won't keep him down for long," Modi warned. "But I have another idea. Sinfjotli, stick with me. There's something I want to try."

"In that case, I'll take Sigurd with me," Magni volunteered. "We'll get as close as we can without drawing attention."

Sigurd didn't even have time to voice his opinion as Magni wrapped an arm around his waist, leaped from the mountaintop, and headed toward the billowing cloud of dust.

The cloud helped mask their approach as they leaped from mountaintop to mountaintop. Fornjót didn't see them coming or get in position behind his left foot as he stood up and shook the dust from his body. His eyes were trained on Modi and Sinfjotli, now soaring several hundred feet above his head.

Sinfjotli had transformed back into a human, and Sigurd watched as he reared his arm and hurled Wolfsbane. The axe spun wildly through the air and embedded itself in Fornjót's right eye. However, Fornjót didn't even seem to feel it.

"That didn't do a thing!" Sigurd complained. "He didn't even blink!"

"Oh, he'll feel it!" Magni promised. He pointed at Modi, who was channeling his energy into his hammer. "Remember how I imbued Wolfsbane with a piece of my power? Well, that spark is still active. It'll act like a lightning rod, summoning Modi's lightning to it!"

As if on cue, Modi raised his war hammer toward the heavens, and a bolt of lightning shot down from the sky toward him. It then veered right at Fornjót's face and blasted him, catching the giant off guard.

"ARGH!" Fornjót bellowed, clutching his eye. He picked up a nearby mountain in his left hand and flung it at Modi and Sinfjotli like a snowball. Because Fornjót was partly blinded, his aim was off, and it barely missed them by a hundred feet. Modi and Sinfjotli landed on another mountaintop and then jumped again. Fornjót bellowed angrily as he tried to swat them out of the sky.

"That certainly got his attention." Sigurd chuckled. He turned to Magni, but his mirth faded when he saw the dour expression on the god of strength's face. "Is something wrong?"

"Modi's attack should have been more powerful." Magni frowned. "He can split a mountain in half with that much lightning, but it didn't even damage Fornjót's eye."

Magni held his hand to the sky as if to summon a lightning bolt, but nothing happened. "Something is wrong. It almost feels like something is pushing against my will, wresting the sky from my control."

"It's probably Kári," Sigurd said. The storm giant had vanished earlier when the battle began. But he hadn't left Niflheim. He was still in the clouds somewhere, watching the fight unfold and finding some way to hinder their efforts. But that was irrelevant to Sigurd's plan. Fornjót's attention was on Modi and Sinfjotli. The time to act was now!

"Go on then," Sigurd urged. "Toss me!"

"Are you sure about this?" Magni asked as he grabbed Sigurd and lifted him over his head. "This may not work out how you imagine. I can't guarantee your safety. Have you thought about how you will land yet?"

"I'll be fine," Sigurd insisted. "Just hurry."

"Don't say I didn't warn you." Magni sighed. He twisted his body and then threw Sigurd high over his head.

Sigurd felt like his skin was peeling off his face as he sailed through the icy air. The wind stung his exposed skin like daggers, forcing him to squint his eyes shut. Still, Sigurd fought through the pain, intent on his task.

As he sailed through the air alongside Fornjót's left leg, Sigurd drew Gram and stabbed deep into Fornjót's flesh. The blade was so sharp that it sliced through effortlessly, allowing Sigurd to maintain momentum as he rocketed through the air and carved through the giant's brawny flesh, inflicting a long-jagged gash. Fornjót noticed the pain and looked over his left shoulder just as Sigurd reached his waist and back, presenting an even better target. He continued his airborne assault, dragging Gram upward in a brutal arc across Fornjót's back. As he neared the giant's head, he adjusted his swing and lopped off Fornjót's left ear. Fornjót roared, clutching the side of his head. Sigurd sailed over his head.

Sigurd kept flying another five hundred feet before gravity caught up with him, dragging him into a rapid descent. As he fell, he twisted his body midair to get a better look at Fornjót. His attack had inflicted a long-jagged rent running from Fornjót's left thigh to his left shoulder. It wasn't a severe wound. Given his size, it was probably only a mere paper cut.

But it served its purpose. Sigurd watched as the long gash he inflicted closed shut.

It's as I suspected. Fornjót has a healing factor. He can regenerate from any wounds we inflict.

This complicated matters. Fornjót was already a force of cataclysmic destruction. But if he could also heal from any injuries they inflicted, then that made him practically invincible. How could they hope to defeat an enemy who could recover from any wound they...?

Sigurd paused. He glanced down at the cursed sword hanging from his right hip. He recalled his intense battle against Heidrek the Troublemaker and how the old king boasted that any wound Tyrfing inflicts never heals. Sigurd wondered what would happen if he used the sword against Fornjót. Would it prevent the giant from healing?

Sigurd decided to test that theory. But as he reached for Tyrfing with his left hand, he hesitated as he remembered Heidrek's final warning.

It must kill a man every time it's drawn. If you value your brother's life, never draw this sword unless an unprecedented threat appears.

Sigurd faltered. Tyrfing *might* prevent Fornjót from healing. But the price... Sigurd looked down at Sinfjotli, who stood beside Magni and Modi hundreds of feet below. Once he drew Tyrfing, the sword would compel him to kill his brother since Sinfjotli was the only other human in Niflheim. That was precisely why Sigurd had refused to draw it since their battle on the Gjallerbru.

Before he could debate with himself further, Fornjót bellowed in rage and turned to face him. Sigurd was now at the giant's eye level as he fell to the earth. Fornjót's deep blue eyes burned with raw hatred, his massive hand still clutching the bleeding stump where his left ear had once been.

"Damn insect!" Fornjót reeled his right arm back to punch Sigurd.

Alarms went off in Sigurd's head. He was free-falling, completely exposed. There was no way he could dodge that punch. The sky crackled above him, and the air tasted metallic. Magni and Modi were probably trying to summon lightning to save him, but he knew they wouldn't be in time.

No other choice. I'll have to use Tyrfing and pray that Magni and Modi stop me before I hurt Sinfjotli.

Sigurd braced for the incoming punch, his fingers tightening around the hilt of Tyrfing. But before he could draw the cursed sword, there was a flash of white light followed by a crashing boom.

Jolting, excruciating pain raced through Sigurd as he vaguely realized he had been struck by lightning. Electricity reverberated throughout his body, paralyzing his limbs. Amidst the searing pain, chilly hands pressed against his shoulders and neck. From the corner of his eye, Sigurd saw the color of his attacker's skin: teakwood.

"Did you forget about me?" Kári whispered in his ear.

"You!" Sigurd gurgled.

"Hurl insults at me while you still have time," Kári goaded. "Rage against the wind all you like. But it won't change anything! As long as you're under the open sky, you're my prey!"

Before Sigurd could think to muster what little strength he had left and swipe Gram behind him in a backward slash, Kári pointed a finger forward at Fornjót's incoming fist and said, "This is for that savage beating you and your friends gave me earlier."

Kári's body turned into clouds and fluttered away with the wind. With his body still paralyzed by lightning and falling midair, Sigurd couldn't move out of the way in time, and Fornjót's fist slammed into him.

CHAPTER THIRTY

REQUIEM OF THE WIND

Sinfjotli watched in horror as Fornjót punched Sigurd. Time seemed to slow down at that moment. The blow was so powerful it shattered Sigurd's armor and knocked off his helmet. Gram flew from Sigurd's hand and landed in a deep snowbank near Sinfjotli.

Sigurd flew into the bottom of a vast canyon a mile away. Part of Sinfjotli vaguely remembered that the canyon had been created earlier when Fornjót slammed that gigantic ice war hammer against the ground.

"Sigurd!" Sinfjotli shrieked. He retrieved Gram from the snowdrift and sprinted toward the canyon. But Fornjót arrived before he did, making it in just three steps. The primordial giant stood over the canyon's rim with a disappointed expression, while Sinfjotli was barely a quarter of the way there.

"He lasted far longer than he should have for a mortal," Fornjót grumbled while rubbing the gash on his back and the stump of his left ear. "Still, he wounded me several times. I'll give him a burial as a sign of respect."

Fornjót ripped off the top of nearby mountain and pressed it into the canyon, filling it and burying Sigurd under thousands of tons of snow, rock, and ice. He then bellowed out a blizzard from his mouth, and a sheet of ice over nine feet thick formed on top of the snow.

Sinfjotli stopped running and fell to his knees. That was it. Sigurd was done for. Even if that punch hadn't killed him, there was no way he could survive being buried beneath all that snow and ice. Even if he hadn't been squashed flat beneath all the ice, he would soon be dead from asphyxiation.

Magni and Modi appeared next to Sinfjotli and gaped in shock. Suddenly, Kári rematerialized above the newly formed sheet of ice and began stomping his foot against it.

"Ha, serves you right!" Kári laughed. "Enjoy your icy tomb!"

That snapped Sinfjotli out of his shock and despair and filled him with rage. He summoned Wolfsbane to his right hand while still brandishing Gram in his left.

"Kári, you rotten bastard," Sinfjotli snarled. "Sigurd could have avoided that attack if you hadn't blasted him from behind! You dirty coward!"

"You crossed a line!" Magni seethed. "No honor means no mercy!"

"Especially for cravens like you!" Modi added darkly.

"I'm just an opportunist." Kári turned around to face them. Electricity crackled throughout his body as another lightning spear appeared in his hand. "There are no rules in war. Only a fool would give up a chance at victory because of a code of honor. The whole point of a battle is to win at all costs. Things like honor, chivalry, and principles are meaningless and serve no other purpose than to lead to your demise. Anyhow, that's one pest down and just three more to go."

Sinfjotli's face contorted with rage, his muscles bulging as he gripped Gram and his axe, one in each hand. Behind him, Magni and Modi's bodies crackled with electricity, their bodies radiating pure, unrestrained fury. But before anyone could act, a shadow enveloped them. Fornjót appeared behind Kári. The frost giant raised his fist high above his head. Magni and Modi raised their weapons, preparing to counter the incoming punch.

But Fornjót wasn't aiming at them.

With a bone-crushing force, the giant slammed his fist right on Kári's head! The storm giant vanished beneath the frost giant's titanic hand. His energy spear detonated, but the explosion was muffled beneath the giant's meaty hand. When Fornjót pulled back his arm, Sinfjotli saw Kári lying face down at the bottom of a massive crater over a hundred feet wide.

Magni's and Modi's power and fury subsided, and Sinfjotli's jaw dropped. They all stared at the crater, unsure how to process what they had just witnessed.

"Wh-what," Sinfjotli stuttered. "Why did he...?"

Fornjót reached into the crater and picked up his son's body between his thumb and index finger, much like a child picking up a tiny ant.

He lifted his son to eye level. "Kári, why did you interfere?" His voice was ice and thunder, his glacial-blue eyes burning with indignation. "Who the hell do you think you are, brazenly coming back here and blindsiding him like that? I was about to smash him to dust with my fist before you zapped him. What gives you the right? Who gave you permission to interfere in *my* fight? Answer me!"

"I... I'm sorry, I was trying to help." Kári coughed. "His back was wide open, so I thought..."

"Help?" Fornjót interrupted. "*Help?* You thought *I* needed **HELP?**" Fornjót pinched Kári's body between his massive fingers, causing the storm giant to wail.

"Father, please!" Kári pleaded, shuddering. "I'm sorry! Just... aieeee... please don't do this!"

"You forgot what I taught you and your siblings long ago," Fornjót seethed, ignoring his son's desperate pleas for mercy. "No matter what happens, you never interfere in someone else's fight! Especially mine!"

Fornjót reared his head back and inhaled.

"FATHER, NO!" Kári screamed.

His plea was ignored. Fornjót exhaled a blizzard. The winds bellowing from his mouth were so cold that Kári's cloud body calcified into an icy statue. Fornjót then crushed the frozen storm giant in the palm of his hand.

"I hope my other children didn't turn out as arrogant, gutless, and stupid as he did." Fornjót opened his hand, and pieces of Kári's shattered body rained to the ground.

Sinfjotli's mind was in disarray. "H-he killed his own son?" He gasped.

Behind him, Magni and Modi bellowed. Tendrils of electricity erupted from their bodies, scarring the surrounding ground.

"What are you two maggots getting so worked up about?" Fornjót asked wearily. "Kári brought that fate on himself for having the temerity to interfere in my battle. You planned to kill him yourselves, right? You ought to thank me for saving you the trouble. It's one less enemy for you to fight."

"You monster!" Magni roared. "How could you murder your son in cold blood?"

He and Modi leaped hundreds of feet into the air, their weapons crackling with energy.

"I am the lord of all creatures of frost," Fornjót replied. "I can do what I please."

The giant extended his hands, and the Sons of Thor vanished inside his titanic fists before they could react. Fornjót spun around and hurled each of them at two distant peaks several miles away. They slammed into the mountainsides with an earth-shaking BOOM. When the billowing dust clouds cleared, Sinfjotli saw Magni and Modi encased in the center of two massive craters on each mountainside.

Fornjót scratched his icy beard and smiled. "How about I give you two a proper burial as well?" He picked up two nearby mountains, one in each hand, and hurled them at Magni and Modi. The mountains sailed through the air and collided with the peaks where Magni and Modi had crashed. The impact was catastrophic—rock and ice shattered, avalanches roared, and within seconds, the mountains cracked apart and the Sons of Thor were buried beneath millions of tons of snow and ice.

"Magni! Modi!" Sinfjotli wailed.

He started sprinting toward the mountains of crushed snow and ice but stopped dead in his tracks. A giant shadow swallowed him. He looked up. Fornjót was looming over him with a look of utter disappointment plastered across his face.

"That was... mildly amusing at best." Fornjót sighed. "I expected more from Odin's grandsons. But now it's your turn, maggot."

Fornjót raised his foot. Reacting on instinct, Sinfjotli threw his axe up at one of the giant's toes. But Fornjót didn't even notice it. Sinfjotli gripped Gram, brandishing the legendary blade, but it was just a show of bravado. All he could do was stare up helplessly as the giant foot slammed on top of him.

CHAPTER THIRTY-ONE

SON OF YMIR

Sinfjotli opened his eyes, lying face down at the bottom of a massive crater. Amazingly, he hadn't died. Although Fornjót had stomped on him with enough force to flatten the ground for an entire mile, the Kistfuskare had protected him.

Sinfjotli pushed himself upright, testing his limbs. No scratches. No broken bones. Even with the giant's weight pressing against his back and driving him deeper into the ground, Ivaldi's magical armor had protected him just like it was designed to.

As Sinfjotli retrieved Gram and got his bearings, he thanked Ivaldi and his sons for designing such a formidable suit of armor.

Fornjót had already turned his back on Sinfjotli and was walking to a mountain covered in deep craters and scars from the battle. With a mere wave of his hand, an enormous formation burst from the ground. It was a throne made entirely of ice, with cushions and armrests made from piles of deep snow. Fornjót sat down and crossed his legs, absently scratching at his icy beard, sending icicles the size of buildings raining down.

"How deplorable!" Fornjót scoffed. "These so-called gods are weak. I got excited when I learned they were Thor's brats. I thought they'd be able to leave me a scar that wouldn't fade or scare me enough to give me a chill. But it seems they were just as weak as an ant. And they're too soft. Getting agitated and emotional because I executed Kári? What kind of warrior takes pity on his enemy? Bah! The Aesir are *nothing* like they were in the old days."

Fornjót glanced up at the sky. He waved his hand, and Niflheim's thick atmosphere cracked open just enough to provide a glimpse of the World Tree. He stared at the giant ash tree and all the distant realms nestled amongst its branches, lost in deep thought.

"Back in the old days, the Aesir were just a tribe of murderous thugs," Fornjót reminisced aloud. "The very concepts of 'justice' and 'camaraderie' meant nothing to them. They were brutal warriors who used whatever means necessary to defeat their enemies. The lives of others, even their subordinates, humans, family members, and children, carried no more weight to them than a melted snowflake. That detachment and callous nature were precisely why they were a force to be feared. But now... it seems things have changed. They have gotten soft over the years. They've grown too attached to the humans they created, and instead of sacrificing and exploiting others to achieve their goals, they hesitate and try to shoulder the burden alone. How utterly disappointing!"

Fornjót waved his hand, and the rift in the sky closed. He leaned back on his ice throne and stared blankly into space, an idea clearly forming in his head.

"I planned to amass my strength and power here in Niflheim to prepare for Ragnarök. But there's no reason to wait if the Aesir have become this weak. I might as well march on Asgard and raze it right now."

"You're getting ahead of yourself!" Sinfjotli called out defiantly. "We aren't finished here! As long as one warrior stands against you, you'll never be able to claim victory!"

Fornjót glanced down. "Tch, one maggot survived. I suppose some insects are harder to crush than others. Huh? Aren't you the one I just stomped on? How are you still...? Oh, I see. It's because of that armor you're wearing. It prevented you from becoming a bloody stain on the ice."

Fornjót leaned forward and scrutinized Sinfjotli. "I must say, that is an impressive suit of armor. It has been made from primordial ice and fire, and many protective spells are woven into the metal plates. The metal is unlike anything I've seen. Did Surtr, by any chance, forge that armor for you?"

"The dwarves of Svartalfheim forged it," Sinfjotli said.

"Dwarves! You mean those tiny shrimps the Aesir created from the maggots feasting on my father's flesh?" Fornjót belched out laughing. "Maggots forging armor for other maggots! What an amusing thought! Bwa ha, ha, ha, ha, ha!"

The frost giant soon regained his composure. "As absurd as it sounds, you're probably telling the truth. After all, Surtr is too busy forging his flaming sword to do anything else."

"My armor isn't the only thing the dwarves forged for me!" Sinfjotli thrust out his right hand. His axe dislodged itself from Fornjót's toe and returned to his hand. Sinfjotli stepped forward and assumed a defiant combat stance, brandishing Gram and Wolfsbane.

"Just what do you expect to accomplish with those puny weapons?" Fornjót asked. "Why did you even bother getting back up in the first place? You've seen it with your own eyes. You can't defeat me. Whether you fight me with that axe and sword, as a wolf, or alongside gods, the result will remain the same. You *cannot* win."

As he spoke, the clouds of Niflheim swirled and drew closer to him, wrapping around his injuries like bandages. Sinfjotli watched in amazement as all of Fornjót's injuries healed.

"No fucking way." Sinfjotli gasped as he watched Fornjót's ear regenerate. "You... what *are* you, Fornjót?"

"What am I?" Fornjót smiled. "Such a broad question. I suppose you could say that I am to the frost giants what the Aesir are to you mortals. I am the snow and wind howling throughout the realm, the living embodiment of winter. I am a primordial! I am a son of Ymir!"

"Ymir? You mean the progenitor of all life whom Odin and his brothers killed and fashioned into Midgard? But I thought all of Ymir's children drowned after Odin stabbed him except for his grandson Bergelmir and his wife."

"And that is a crime the giants will never forgive!" Fornjót snarled. "My brethren and I were old long before Odin and his brothers were an itch in Bor's ball sack, yet those three *traitors* arbitrarily decided *they* should be the ones who ought to shape creation. They slew my father and murdered countless numbers of my brethren as collateral damage. The giants will never forgive the Aesir for the genocide perpetrated against them!"

Fornjót scowled. The air thickened, turning icy and dense. The chilly air prickled Sinfjotli's lungs, making each breath a struggle. His bones ached under the creeping cold. But after a moment, Fornjót calmed down and regained his composure.

"But not all of Ymir's eldest children drowned in that deluge. A few of us survived. I was resting here in Niflheim then, so I was spared the great flood's wrath. My nephew Bergelmir and his wife rode out the deluge in a boat and found refuge in the land you now call Jotunheim, where they founded the long line of giants you call Jötnar or frost giants. And there was one more giant who survived the great flood in Muspelheim. Or rather, I suppose it's more accurate to say that he was *born* because of it. Bah... I'm getting off-topic. Not all primordial giants perished when our father got murdered. We few survivors swore an eternal oath of vengeance against Odin and his entire line."

Fornjót gazed up at the sky, his expression darkening. He waved, and the clouds parted again, allowing sunlight to pierce the gloom. The giant squinted, his icy blue eyes narrowing as he peered, not just at the sky but beyond, as if staring up at the canopy of Yggdrasil.

"Kári woke me up too early. I planned to remain asleep here in Niflheim, gathering my strength to prepare for Ragnarök. But I've changed my mind. If *this* is all that Odin's descendants can do, then I have nothing to fear and no reason to wait. I'll climb up the World Tree and lay waste to Asgard. Surtr and the other giants can join me if they want. But I doubt anything will be left of Asgard by the time they arrive."

Fornjót's boasting was no mere bravado. He had complete command of the weather. He could hurl mountains like snowballs, create blizzards, manipulate the ground beneath his feet, and use the cold to heal his injuries. Fornjót was a force of nature in a weight class of his own. Giants, Aesir, and mortals were nothing compared to him.

Fornjót seemed to sense Sinfjotli's trepidation. "Now you've seen the scale of my power, I'll ask again. Why are you still holding those weapons? Do you still intend to fight me after everything I've told you? How foolish and arrogant."

He pointed toward the ice-filled canyon he'd punched Sigurd into and then at the mounds of ice he had buried Magni and Modi under. "You saw what I did to your brother and the so-called gods of strength and courage. What makes you think a tiny maggot like you stands any chance against me alone?"

"I'm not fighting you because I can see myself winning this battle," Sinfjotli admitted. "The only reason I continue to fight is that I *have* to win!"

Fornjót arched an eyebrow. "You have already experienced the vast difference in our powers, yet you actually think you can defeat me? Most beings want to preserve their lives. I can't comprehend this."

"You think I'd give up just because you're more powerful than me? I knew you were stronger than us from the moment I saw you. Honestly, I'm uncertain if you *can* be killed. But that doesn't matter. The stakes are just too high for me to back down."

Sinfjotli closed his eyes and recalled his fateful meeting with the Norns at Wyrd's Well. A shiver ran up his spine as he remembered their warning. "If I die, Hel will torture me into subservience and force me to kill my family at Ragnarök. The only way to prevent that horrible future is to keep moving forward and complete all the tasks we are given. The Aesir have tasked us with killing you, and I'm determined to see this through to the very end. I refuse to give up and die! Even if it's just me left, I will beat you, Fornjót!"

"I grow tired of this tedious nonsense." Fornjót sighed. "In the end, while you have your resolve, determination, and all that drivel, it isn't enough to compensate for your weakness. It certainly isn't enough to entertain me. This is about all the time I'll allow myself to converse with the insignificant worm that is a mere human. I'll wrap this up and march on Asgard."

Fornjót rose from his ice throne. Sinfjotli tried to retreat and put some distance between them, but his legs wouldn't move. He looked down and discovered that his feet and calves were encased beneath a thick ice sheet that had spread from Fornjót's toes.

Sinfjotli swung his axe and thrust Gram at the packed ice, frantically chipping away at his frosty prison. The Coffin Cheater automatically began heating like a furnace as it adjusted to and attempted to melt the icy trap. Given enough time, he could free his limbs through sheer brute force. But for now, Sinfjotli could do little but watch as the titanic frost giant towered over him.

"Normally, I'd refrain from exerting my power to dispatch a mere *insect*. I'd prefer to crush you with my bare hand or beneath my feet. Unfortunately, that isn't a viable option because of your magic armor's remarkable durability. But I have a solution that will resolve both of our dilemmas. Since you're so reluctant to die, I won't kill you. Instead, I'll freeze you in a solid block of ice seven hundred layers thick under pressure so great you won't be able to move a finger."

Fornjót reared his head back and inhaled deeply just as the Coffin Cheater finished melting the ice around Sinfjotli's legs. Sinfjotli pulled his feet free and brandished his weapons. But it was just for show. He couldn't block this breath attack or even avoid it. Worse, Sinfjotli's body was approaching its limit. He had already transformed into a wolf twice during the last few hours. His body could only endure one more transformation before it gave out. But even if he transformed into a wolf and somehow evaded Fornjót's breath attack, what good would it do? Magni and Modi had been no match for this giant. What chance did Sinfjotli have alone?

"Forgive us, Father," Sinfjotli despaired. "We failed." He closed his eyes and prepared for the inevitable. As he waited, he heard a loud hissing noise in the distance. Half a heartbeat later, a blast of cold air knocked him to the ground.

I can still move? Sinfjotli's eyes snapped open. Fornjót stood motionless, towering above him. The giant had stopped his breath attack at the last possible moment, but he had still exhaled enough air to knock Sinfjotli off his feet.

Fornjót didn't seem to notice Sinfjotli scramble to his feet. His attention was fixated on something in the distance. Sinfjotli followed Fornjót's gaze, and his breath caught. The piles of snow and ice scattered across the area were steaming, rapidly melting into slush. Then the slush started boiling!

Wait, isn't that the canyon where Sigurd got buried?

Suddenly, a giant scaly arm burst from the slushy ground, sending a spray of steaming water and ice into the air. The earth trembled as the rest of the creature clawed its way free, then a pair of enormous golden wings unfurled from its back.

Sinfjotli's jaw dropped. Emerging from the frozen wasteland was a glittering golden dragon—easily the most beautiful thing Sinfjotli had seen since entering Niflheim. Gleaming gold scales covered its body, shimmering like beaten gold in the faint sunlight, even here in the darkness of Niflheim. Each of its four powerful legs was adorned with five ten-foot-long talons. Its head and neck boasted long spikes, horns, and a cascade of platinum hair running down its spine. Tufts of red fur covered the back of its kneecaps, elbows, and the tip of its tail. But its most remarkable feature, beyond its beauty, beyond its splendor, was its gargantuan size. The magnificent beast was around a tenth of Fornjót's size!

"Is that Sigurd?" Sinfjotli wondered aloud. He wasn't entirely sure. This golden dragon was at least ten to twenty times larger than the one that had devoured his brother in Svartalfheim. But there was no mistaking its idiosyncratic golden slit eyes or the distinctive, ugly scar on its chest that looked identical to the one on Sigurd's sternum.

"No doubt about it," Sinfjotli mumbled. "This is definitely Sigurd."

Fornjót took a single step toward the dragon, almost stepping on Sinfjotli as he called out, "Who are you, creature?"

The glorious golden dragon spread its wings, reared back its head in a battle stance, and replied with a heaven-piercing roar. The violent tremors tore through the air and petrified Sinfjotli's every organ with instinctive terror. Sinfjotli had never heard anything more beautiful and viscerally terrifying in his entire life. It sounded like a mix between a song and a scream.

"It appears you can't understand what I'm saying," Fornjót observed, unimpressed. "Regardless, you are much more qualified to face me than this puny maggot."

Fornjót inhaled deeply, sucking all the air in the area into his lungs, and bellowed a swirling beam of frost from his mouth. The raging blizzard froze everything it encountered as it raced toward the enormous golden beast.

In response, the dragon reared its head back and unleashed a gigantic golden fireball as bright as the sun. The opposing forces collided and violently canceled each other out. The force of the shockwave was so powerful that it swept Sinfjotli off his feet and sent him flying hundreds of feet into the air. He crash-landed on a mountain of snow and ice two miles away from where he had been standing moments earlier.

Sinfjotli picked himself off the ground and watched as the cloud of steam faded away in the distance.

"Impossible!" Fornjót exclaimed. "Fire cannot burn in Niflheim! No magic in all the Nine Realms can create a blaze here!"

The dragon didn't seem too concerned by that fact. It spread its wings and lunged at Fornjót. It raked his face with its claws, leaving four long, jagged rents. Fornjót staggered backward and tripped over his icy throne. The towering seat shattered beneath the giant's weight, sending a massive cloud of snow, ice, and dust into the air.

Fornjót emerged from the dust cloud with a twisted, hungry smile. "I don't know how you got here, beast, but I suppose I can live with never knowing. Those puny gods I fought before bored me. Maybe now I'll have a decent challenge!"

The dragon answered with a roar that shook the world. Fornjót bellowed back at him as the two titans rushed toward each other. Sinfjotli staggered to his feet and watched in awe as the primordial giant and golden dragon clashed.

CHAPTER THIRTY-TWO

FRIENDLY FIRE

The titanic battle between the frost giant and the golden dragon was unlike anything Sinfjotli had ever witnessed. The golden dragon was a blur of motion, evading Fornjót's punches, dodging his ice breaths, darting beneath the giant's grasping hands, and blasting him with golden flames. Whenever Fornjót lunged, the dragon would twist away at the last moment, swooping beneath the giant's legs or under his arms, then veering back to strike. It raked its claws down the giant's back, opening a long-jagged wound before flying away. Fornjót could do little to counter these hit-and-run attacks. His gigantic size and sheer bulk, once an advantage, now made him too slow to match Sigurd's speed.

As Sinfjotli watched, awestruck, the mountain of snow and ice he was standing on suddenly rumbled beneath his feet. He looked down in time to see a muscular hand burst through the surface several yards away.

"Whoa, what the hell!" Sinfjotli backed away. A second beefy arm burst through the snow, followed by a familiar face, pulling himself to the surface.

"Damn! My head hurts!" Magni grumbled as he finished pulling himself out of the ice. Purple and black bruises covered his face and chest, while blood gushed and trickled down his face from a deep gash on his forehead. Otherwise, he looked alright. Half a heartbeat later, Modi appeared beside his brother amid a bolt of lightning. He looked just as injured as his brother but still had the strength to stand.

"Magni! Modi!" Sinfjotli laughed. "You're okay!"

"Of course," Modi groaned, trying to sound valiant. "It takes more than that to kill us!"

"It *was* enough to knock us unconscious," Magni conceded while rubbing his bleeding forehead. "Having an entire mountain collapse on top of you will do that. It feels like my skull is cracked. Geez, this is probably how Father felt after he got the chunk of that stone giant's skull lodged in his forehead!"

"Will you be alright," Sinfjotli asked. "Can you still fight?"

"My brain is beating against the walls of my skull like a drum." Magni groaned, still rubbing his throbbing, bleeding head. "But we'll manage. Putting our splitting headaches aside, what happened while we were unconscious? Where's Sigurd?"

Sinfjotli pointed at the dragon sweeping over Fornjót's head.

Magni and Modi glanced at the intense battle raging in the distance, and their eyes widened.

"He transformed into a dragon already?" Magni gasped. "I didn't think he'd know how to do it right away."

"I don't think he transformed consciously," Modi said. "His mind probably sensed it was in danger and subconsciously transformed to protect himself when Fornjót buried him under all that snow and—"

He never finished that train of thought. At that moment, Sigurd and Fornjót clashed with their elemental breath attacks. The dragon spat out a golden fireball while Fornjót unleashed a raging blizzard. The opposing elemental forces collided, triggering a massive explosion that sent snow clouds racing throughout the landscape and into the sky. The shockwave even reached the mountain the three of them stood on and blasted them with winds that were both blisteringly hot and freezing cold.

"What should we do?" Sinfjotli asked once the shockwave and winds subsided.

"This battle is too intense," Modi replied, shaking the snow from his hair and beard. "Let's just hang back here and watch."

Magni and Sinfjotli concurred. And with that, they watched in silence and awe as Sigurd and Fornjót continued tearing each other apart.

Sigurd had retaken to the air and was soaring circles around Fornjót. The giant tried swatting Sigurd to the ground. But Sigurd easily dodged. He swooped down at Fornjót's face and blasted him straight in the eyeball with a golden fireball. Fornjót collapsed to the ground, clutching his burning right eye socket.

"Well done, Sigurd!" Magni cheered.

"Atta-boy, Sigurd," shouted Modi.

Magni and Modi's cheers were as loud as a blast of thunder. As their booming voices echoed throughout Niflheim, the dragon turned toward them, and its golden eyes dilated. The dragon beat its wings and soared.

"What's he doing now?" Magni asked as the dragon flew closer, with no signs of slowing down.

At the last moment, Sinfjotli noticed the scales on Sigurd's belly and throat glowing orange and realized what was about to happen. Sinfjotli had only seconds to warn Magni and Modi to flee before a column of golden flame erupted from the dragon's mouth.

Magni and Modi vanished amidst two bolts of lightning as Sigurd incinerated the mountaintop in a strafing run. Sinfjotli had no means of escape and got fully engulfed by the flames. Thankfully, the Coffin Cheater protected him from the fire, just as Ivaldi promised it would. But the heat was unbearably hot, and blisters erupted across Sinfjotli's skin.

When Sinfjotli opened his eyes, he discovered he was standing in the center of a sea of flame. The entire mountaintop was burning. But the fires soon subsided, possibly because of the extreme winds and the lack of combustible material.

A shadow rippled across Sinfjotli's face. He glanced up to find Sigurd hovering above him. The enormous golden dragon beat its wings furiously, creating a hot wind that irritated Sinfjotli's throat. The dragon glared at him and hissed with flames dancing across its teeth.

"What the fuck, Sigurd?" Sinfjotli exclaimed. "We're on your side!"

"I don't think he knows that," Modi remarked as he and Magni reappeared beside Sinfjotli amidst two lightning bolts. "Frankly, I don't think he's even capable of distinguishing friend from foe right now. Look at his eyes! He's in a state of blind rage, completely devoid of rational thought! His mind is just a vortex of fury now. He's attacking everything and everyone indiscriminately."

Sinfjotli stared into the dragon's golden eyes and felt a chill that had nothing to do with Niflheim's cold. Modi was right. Those golden snake eyes were unmistakably Sigurd's—but there wasn't a single trace of his brother in them. He saw only the feral, unthinking glare of a bloodthirsty predator. No consciousness. No trace of humanity. No familial recognition. The dragon's gaze was a window into pure, unbridled rage.

Sinfjotli, Magni, Modi, and the dragon eyed each other, tension thick in the frozen air. No one moved. Then, Sigurd—or rather, the beast he had become—arched his head, coiling like a drawn archer's bow. But before he could do anything, the ground quaked. In the distance, Fornjót stirred. The mighty frost giant bellowed, shaking the heavens, demanding that the dragon return and face him.

A giant chunk of ice hurtled over their heads, crashing into a valley several miles away. Sigurd lost interest in the three of them. With a powerful beat of his wings, he soared away, full attention on the colossal giant.

As the golden dragon flew, Sinfjotli thought about the blind rage he'd seen in the dragon's eyes. He's seen it before. Not in battle. Not in any enemy. He'd seen that look before in his nightmares.

This must be the side effects of the Trial of Svarblood! Sinfjotli realized. When a skinchanger who underwent the Trial of Svarblood transforms for the first few times, they often lose control of their beast form and could become a danger to both enemies and allies. The first time Sinfjotli and his father turned into wolves, Sigmund attacked Sinfjotli in a blood rage and nearly killed him. Sigurd was experiencing his first transformation. The fury, the overwhelming instinct to destroy—this was exactly what was supposed to accompany that first transformation.

"What should we do?" Sinfjotli asked.

"For now, let's just hang back and watch how this plays out," Modi advised. "Stepping into the middle of this battle would be like throwing raw meat in front of a beast. Get in their way, and we'll literally get chewed up. So let them fight."

CHAPTER THIRTY-THREE

THE HEART

Sinfjotli, Magni, and Modi watched quietly as the two titanic beasts clashed in the distance.

The air was thick with the scent of charred earth as Tanngrisnir and Tanngnjóstr bleated triumphantly, hauling Thor's chariot up the jagged slopes of a mountain.

Sinfjotli exhaled sharply, his breath visible in the frigid air, tore his armored fingers from the railing, and stumbled off the chariot.

But as he recomposed himself, the sight of the destructive path Fornjót carved in his pursuit of Sigurd stole the air from his lungs. What had once been a pristine vista of snowy mountains and ice shelves had been reduced to a cratered, cracked wasteland.

The golden dragon unknowingly guided Fornjót away from the mountains Magni and Modi had been buried under and far to the west of Mount Isa's ruins. They'd clashed every step of the journey, each blow leaving a new wound in the earth. They covered so much ground that Magni and Modi ran out of peaks to jump across, forcing them to summon their father's goats to catch up.

The trail of destruction guided them to the crest of a vast valley, nestled within a monstrous mountain chain that stretched northward like the frozen ribs of a forgotten beast. Sigurd had called this range "The Spines" during their journey to Mount Isa—a jagged backbone of stone stretching further than even Sigurd's eyes could see.

But even these ancient peaks had been no match for the giant's fury. Fornjót had plowed through two of them like a stampeding bull as he chased the dragon into the valley, leaving an enormous gap in the mountain range.

Magni and Modi smacked the goats' behinds, urging them to flee. But Sinfjotli hardly noticed the goats flee east. His gaze remained fixed on the distant clash in the vale where his brother battled the primordial.

Fornjót tried punching and then grabbing Sigurd. But the dragon easily dodged his fists in midair. But the dragon easily dodged his fists in midair. The giant tried to backhand Sigurd, but the dragon spread its wings and flew off. Fornjót bellowed a blizzard at Sigurd, who flew up and vanished into a bank of clouds. Despite his shiny golden appearance, Niflheim's thick atmosphere cloaked him like a chameleon blending with its surroundings. Fornjót's head turned side to side, scanning the sky, searching for any trace of his elusive enemy. Sigurd appeared from behind, bursting from the clouds. He grabbed the back of Fornjót's head and slammed him face-first into the ground. But he didn't stop there. Without losing momentum, the dragon dragged Fornjót across the land, grinding his face through rock and ice and carving a deep trench into the earth. With a final heave, Sigurd slammed Fornjót into the base of a mountain.

"Amazing!" Sinfjotli shouted. "Sigurd may not be as big as Fornjót, but he can still match his strength! And he's nimble in the air. Fornjót can't even touch him."

He may have spoken too soon. As Fornjót lay face down, seemingly beaten, the frost giant reached out, scooping up a massive handful of snow and ice. Without looking, he flung it behind him.

Chunks of rock and ice whizzed past Sigurd, distracting him—just long enough for Fornjót to strike.

In an instant, the giant's massive hand clamped around Sigurd, catching him in midair. Fornjót stood up and turned. Sinfjotli's breath hitched. The giant's nose and upper lip were gone, ground away by fiction when Sigurd had dragged him across the icy plains. Parts of his brain protruded through his forehead. His right eye had been burned to jelly when Sigurd blasted him square in the face earlier. But his left eye was still intact, seething with unfiltered hate.

"Curse you, you miserable worm!" Fornjót gurgled. "You'll pay for that!"

Fornjót squeezed Sigurd. The dragon roared as the pressure increased. Then, it reared its head back and inhaled deeply. Sinfjotli braced, expecting a massive fireball. Instead, the beast spewed out a billowing cloud of purple gas that burned Fornjót's skin and turned the surrounding snowflakes into a sickly green color.

Fornjót immediately released Sigurd and backed away. He glanced down at his right arm—blackened, necrotic patches were already spreading, veins rupturing as the wounds began to bleed profusely. Fornjót gritted his teeth, reached up, and ripped his own arm off at the shoulder. With a grunt, he tossed it at Sigurd. It missed, crash-landing on the mountaintop near the gap in the mountain range.

"Nice try, beast," Fornjót snarled. "But you won't kill me with just..." He trailed off. His eyes widened at the enormous poison cloud billowing around him. Then he looked back at the golden dragon hovering hundreds of feet above. Sigurd's chest was glowing, and his long serpentine neck was bent back, preparing to release. Panic washed over Fornjót's bloodied face as he realized what was about to happen.

The dragon unleashed a torrent of flames that ignited the poisonous cloud and engulfed Fornjót in an enormous explosion.

Sinfjotli clapped his hands over his ears, but it did little to muffle the deafening detonation. The explosion was so intense that several nearby glaciers shattered like glass, and it was bright enough to briefly turn the darkness of Niflheim into day. The blaze vaporized the mountain Sigurd had slammed Fornjót into earlier, along with several mounds of rock and ice within the blast radius. Sinfjotli winced, feeling the inferno's heat on his face—like a blast from an oven.

When the firestorm finally subsided, all that remained was a sixty-thousand-foot cloud of smoke, dust, and steam where Fornjót had once stood. High above, about thirty thousand feet above the ground, the golden dragon hovered, its wings stretched wide as it circled the billowing cloud of destruction. The dragon reared its head back and roared.

"Incredible!" Sinfjotli laughed. "I've never seen anything like that before! Have you?"

"Unfortunately, we have," Magni replied.

Sinfjotli glanced at his comrades, expecting triumphant grins, but his own smile faded. Neither of them was smiling. Magni's and Modi's expressions were grim, eyes full of concern, not victory. They stared at the lingering explosion and then glanced at the severed limb resting on the mountain a mile away. The frost giant's detached arm had begun to dissolve. The sizzling flesh deteriorated, and where it withered, the surrounding snow turned a sickly green.

Magni and Modi turned their attention back to Sigurd, who was still circling the cloud of dust and smoke.

"Modi, does Sigurd... does that creature remind you of *him*?" Magni asked.

"Yeah." Modi nodded. "There's only one dragon that can spew both poisonous gas and fire."

"What are you talking about?" Sinfjotli demanded. "I don't understand what you're implying here."

"Think back to when Sigurd underwent the Trial of Svarblood," Magni instructed. "Now ask yourself: Does the dragon fighting Fornjót look different from the one that devoured your brother?"

Sinfjotli looked at the golden dragon soaring around the enormous cloud of smoke, dust, and snow. "Well, now that you mention it, this dragon looks slightly different from Old One Horn. It's much bigger and is supposed to be missing one of its horns. Also, its front legs look more like humanoid arms. If it reared up on its hind legs, I reckon it would almost look human."

"You'd be right," Magni agreed. "*That* dragon looked more humanoid in appearance than any other. His scales might be a different color now, but there is no way I wouldn't recognize that distinct size, shape, and fighting style."

"What are you insinuating?" Sinfjotli demanded. "Talk sense, man."

"That dragon isn't Old One Horn," Modi said. "The creature fighting Fornjót the Destroyer is what Fafnir the Dragon looked like before Sigurd slew him."

Sinfjotli stared dumbly at Modi as his mind slowly grasped the full implications of that statement.

"T-that's absurd!" Sinfjotli said. "Those who pass the Trial of Svarblood take over the body of the creature that consumes them. Sigurd is supposed to look like Old One Horn."

"You're forgetting an important detail," Modi said. "To initiate the Trial of Svarblood, a candidate must first consume the heart of the same type of animal they wish to be reborn as. Once they drink the potion, the heart they consumed becomes the new vessel for their soul and temporarily allows them to cheat death. If they pass the Trial, the heart takes over the animal's body, allowing them to be reborn as a skinchanger. But the heart also determines how the candidate will look after the Trial ends. For instance, Sinfjotli, your father once told us that the wolf that devoured you had a snow-white coat. But whenever you transform, your fur is jet black. That's because the heart you consumed long ago belonged to a wolf with a jet-black coat."

Sinfjotli blinked. He had never really thought about it before. But Modi's account would explain why his fur was jet black.

"Sometimes physical traits of the heart's original owner carry over to the skinchanger's new body," Modi said. "That's why most skinchangers don't always resemble the animal that consumed them. The differences are usually too minuscule to notice. But not in Sigurd's case."

"What do you mean?" Sinfjotli asked.

"The heart that Sigurd consumed to initiate the Trial belonged to Fafnir the Dragon," Magni said. "And it looks like Sigurd inherited much more than Fafnir's appearance. He's also inherited the monster's power and techniques."

"But that—" Sinfjotli began.

"Sinfjotli, the dragon fighting Fornjót is undeniably Fafnir," Modi said. "That cloud of poisonous gas and the massive explosion he caused proves it. Fafnir was the only dragon in the realms capable of breathing fire *and* poisonous gas. When he was alive, Fafnir breathed noxious gas into the land around his lair so no one would go near him or his treasure. Mere skin contact with the gas could kill almost any average person. You can see with your own eyes what happens when it breaks through the skin and enters the body. As a result, the land around Gnitaheath was naught but a barren wasteland. Whenever Fafnir bestirred himself from his pile of treasure to drink water from a nearby stream or hunt for food, he would always blow a cloud of poison into his path, ensuring he could not be ambushed. If anyone got too close, he'd ignite the poisonous gas, incinerating the trespassers in a fiery explosion. It was a dirty but very effective tactic, and Sigurd used the same attack on Fornjót."

Sinfjotli was still skeptical, but the evidence was overwhelming. The dragon that had devoured Sigurd and the one fighting Fornjót were as different as night and day. Old One Horn had been a hoary old beast, powerful but lazy. This one was bigger, fiercer, and full of fiery rage.

"I still don't understand," Sinfjotli muttered. "Even if he *looks* like Fafnir, Sigurd shouldn't be able to breathe poison like the original dragon did. How could he have inherited that ability as well?"

"I can't say for certain." Modi shrugged. "But I have a theory. People often say that the heart is where the soul lives. Perhaps consuming Fafnir's heart allowed a fragment of the dragon's soul to live on within Sigurd. It has remained dormant all these years. But during the Trial, it resurfaced and caused Sigurd to take on this form, which allowed him to inherit all the abilities that Fafnir once possessed."

That explanation made sense, at least in theory. Sigurd's trial had been unique. No human had ever attempted to become a dragon or undergone the Trial of Svarblood under the same conditions. Usually, a candidate devoured an animal's heart right before being devoured themselves. But Sigurd had consumed Fafnir's heart *years* ago. Moreover, he had eaten the heart of a fully sentient dragon who had used to be a dwarf, which could have also somehow impacted the Trial's outcome.

Sinfjotli paused as he suddenly remembered something Sigurd told him. "Could it be...?"

"What is it?" Magni asked.

"Sigurd told me that during his Trial, he woke up in the cavern of Gnitaheath and fought Fafnir the Dragon in a savage battle. He assumed Fafnir was supposed to represent Old One Horn's soul. But what if that wasn't the case? What if that was actually the real Fafnir he was facing?"

"It's certainly a possibility," Modi admitted. "Fafnir's ultimate fate was a mystery even to us. Years ago, our sister, Thrúd, got sent to Midgard the day Sigurd slew Fafnir and Regin to ensure their souls were banished to Helheim before they could become vengeful draugirs. She reported she sent Regin to Helheim without issue. But she couldn't find any trace of Fafnir's soul. Odin and our parents assumed Fafnir willingly moved on to Helheim and thought nothing of it. But Thrúd wasn't convinced that was the case. She was certain a spirit as malevolent and greedy as Fafnir, who'd spent his life greedily guarding his treasure, wouldn't move on to the underworld without a fight and would try to linger in Midgard. Now, we might have proof that wasn't the case after all."

Sinfjotli's eyes widened. "But that means..."

"Sigurd's greatest enemy has lived within him all this time," Modi finished. "And now Sigurd has literally turned into his greatest enemy."

As Sinfjotli contemplated the grim implications of that statement, he looked up at the golden dragon as it soared overhead. There were so many questions and possibilities jumping through his mind. He consciously tried to cast most of them aside until only one crucial question lingered.

"Do you think that Sigurd... or Fafnir has a chance at winning?" Sinfjotli asked.

"Hard to say." Magni shrugged. "Fafnir was one of the mightiest dragons who ever lived. But we are dealing with a primordial frost giant here. He might stand a chance to..."

"How absurd!" Fornjót roared. The entire landscape trembled and quaked at the sound of his voice. Sinfjotli, Magni, and Modi turned and watched as a giant tornado funneled down from the sky and enveloped the cloud of smoke and dust. A minute later, Fornjót emerged from the thick funnel cloud, and Sinfjotli's mind came to an abrupt halt, and his jaw dropped. Fornjót's face had completely healed. Even his eyes, nose, and lips, which Sigurd had scraped to bloody bits, had somehow regenerated, and his right arm, which was still enveloped in mist and fog, was slowly regenerating itself!

Even more alarming, Fornjót had somehow gotten even larger! The giant looked twice as big as he had minutes ago.

"It's absurd that a bunch of maggots and a flying lizard have the *temerity* to think they could kill me!" Fornjót bellowed indignantly.

The tornado and cloud of dust subsided as Fornjót's right arm finished regenerating. Visible veins covered his forearm, and it looked stronger than before. He clapped, and the skies of Niflheim darkened. Sinfjotli looked up, and his eyes widened. His heart began racing like a caged bird inside his chest. As he gaped in shock and despair, his axe and Gram slipped from his trembling hands as colossal ice meteorites rained down from the sky.

CHAPTER THIRTY-FOUR

HEAVENWARD HALBERD

S infjotli had always been fond of rainstorms. In his youth, he would sometimes stand outside the cave where he and his father hid from Siggeir's relentless bounty hunters. With his arms outstretched, he would tilt his face to the sky, letting the rain kiss his skin.

"Cherish that feeling," his father had told him. "Rain is grace. It is the sky descending to the earth. Without rain, there would be no life."

But there was no life in the colossal chunks of hail falling from the frosted heavens now. Only death rained down from the skies of Niflheim.

The chunks of ice dropping from the clouds were easily over two hundred fifty feet in diameter. Every time one struck the ground, it flattened the land and sent towering plumes of dust and debris into the air. Sometimes, a glacial meteor would crash dangerously close to the mountain Sinfjotli was standing on, and the resulting shockwave would knock him off his feet.

As the meteorites plummeted from the heavens, fearsome gales roared, howling like a cacophony of mad beasts. Each time a meteorite struck land, it created a rumbling sonic boom that made Sinfjotli's ears ring. He could barely hear himself think. He felt minuscule, vulnerable, and defenseless in the face of such apocalyptic devastation.

This is like what Kári did earlier, Sinfjotli reflected. *But it's exponentially more powerful and on a much broader scale!*

Earlier, Kári had boasted that his ice arrows were powerful enough to wipe out an entire army. But Fornjót's ice storm was powerful enough to wipe a whole continent off the map! Sinfjotli could do very little except watch as the colossal ice meteorites rained down destruction across The Spines and the landscape beyond. He was caught in the blast radius, even at this distance. He would have had no chance of surviving this on his own.

Thankfully, he wasn't alone. He had the gods of strength and courage to support him. Magni and Modi leaped into the air and destroyed any meteorites that threatened to crush them with their weapons and power. Meanwhile, Sinfjotli remained on the mountaintop, wielding Gram and Wolfsbane, slicing apart the smaller fragments the Sons of Thor failed to vaporize.

Their actions were efficient but not subtle. Thunder boomed whenever Magni and Modi channeled lightning to vaporize the incoming ice meteorites. The whistling and whizzing meteorites helped mask some of the sound but the brilliant, obnoxiously bright light show would be visible for miles as they summoned lightning and channeled electricity.

If Fornjót noticed, he didn't care. His attention was fixated entirely on Sigurd.

Amidst the chaos, Sinfjotli noticed the golden dragon flying around and dodging the meteorites as they rained down from the sky. Sigurd was moving nimbly through the air, but speed alone wouldn't be enough to save him. His sheer bulk made him an easy target for the falling meteorites.

If he had been calmer, Sigurd could have retreated to a safe distance and forced Fornjót to chase after him. Alas, rage and bloodlust still consumed the dragon. Even as the beast dodged the meteorites, it seemed more intent on resuming its battle with Fornjót. It kept one eye firmly trained on the frost giant, waiting for an opportunity to strike. If it got hit by even one of these massive meteorites, that would be the end.

But Sinfjotli didn't have time to worry about the dragon. He had to keep himself safe. Shards of ice rained down in every direction and pattered off Sinfjotli's armor as he glanced around at the unfolding destruction. This hailstorm of death was obliterating the entire landscape. Mountains were being flattened, their towering peaks shattered to dust. Each time a hailstone crashed to the ground, it gouged out craters miles in diameter, reshaping the frozen peaks into an apocalyptic ruin. Even the mountain they stood on was taking a beating despite their efforts to destroy the meteorites.

How long is this rain of destruction going to last? Sinfjotli wondered. *This has lasted much longer than Kári's hail storm did, and Fornjót shows no signs of stopping.*

Sinfjotli had no time to dwell on it. A shadow appeared over him as another colossal meteorite fell from the sky. This one was large enough to flatten the mountain he was standing on and everything within seven leagues. Magni and Modi leaped high into the air to intercept it. Modi slammed it with his war hammer, shattering it to pieces. Magni followed up, using his great sword to hack and slash those fragments into smaller pieces.

As Sinfjotli avoided the falling fragments they had failed to destroy, he heard a roar and noticed Sigurd charging toward Fornjót. As the dragon dashed between the falling meteorites and flew closer to the giant, Fornjót gnashed his teeth. He channeled his power further, summoning a fresh barrage of meteorites from the sky.

This time, they were smaller but far more numerous—a concentrated blizzard of death. Sigurd was fast, but even his speed had limits. Several struck his back and left wing, causing him to plummet to the earth and crash into a large ravine. Meteorites pounded the glittering beast, battering his body and burying him under tons of ice.

"No! Sigurd!" Sinfjotli cried.

"Pay attention!" Modi warned. The god of strength appeared in front of Sinfjotli just in time. He swung his war hammer up at a giant sixty-ton chunk of ice that was seconds from flattening them both. The meteorite exploded into thousands of shards of ice that scattered in every direction.

Sinfjotli apologized for getting distracted and looked back at the gorge where Sigurd had fallen. The ravine was now packed with the shattered remains of dozens of ice meteorites, but there was no trace of the golden dragon or sign that it was trying to dig its way to freedom.

"I don't think Sigurd can endure this," Sinfjotli said. "We should go help him."

"Forget about your brother for now," Magni advised as he landed next to Sinfjotli. "Sigurd is still too dangerous to approach in his current state of mind. If we try to rescue him, he'll just attack us. He'll have to endure the pain for now."

"More importantly, look at Fornjót." Modi pointed. "He hasn't moved a muscle since he started this hailstorm of death, and he hasn't said a word either, even though he's quite boisterous, vainglorious, and condescending. I'm guessing it's because this attack requires immense concentration. He's entirely focused on controlling this storm, which means he's wide open right now."

"Is he, though?" Sinfjotli asked skeptically. "There are still all these falling meteorites to contend with. I doubt we can get near him during this mayhem."

"Those won't be an issue," Magni promised. "Now that Kári's dead, our connection to the sky has been restored. We can use our full might against him."

He clapped, and Sinfjotli's eardrums popped as the god of strength channeled his energy. Modi did the same.

"Sinfjotli, cover for us so we can amass enough power to end this chaos," Modi requested.

Protecting the gods of strength and courage from the falling meteorites while they amassed their energy was a tall order. Thankfully, it was doable.

Fornjót had shrunk the blast radius of the hailstorm, focusing his assault on Sigurd with more concentrated attacks. As a result, the meteorites raining down from the sky were now much smaller and easier to destroy, and since their mountain was positioned near the outskirts of the blast radius, the three of them weren't being bombarded as heavily as before.

But that didn't mean they were safe.

The few meteorites still threatening them were massive—between thirty and forty feet in diameter, large enough to flatten their mountaintop. As one such meteorite fell from the sky, Sinfjotli hurled his axe at it and split it in half. However, the two halves of the meteorite still threatened to crush them all. Now two separate forces of destruction. Sinfjotli summoned Wolfsbane back to his hand, then launched himself in the air. With his axe in one hand and Gram in the other, he twisted midair and diced the descending ice, hacking the two halves into tiny bits.

Every muscle in Sinfjotli's body screamed in pain as he landed back on the icy ground. His legs buckled, and he botched the landing, nearly falling flat on his face. His arms felt like lead, his weapons like heavy anchors, their weight dragging at his exhausted limbs. It took every ounce of strength he had to slice apart these meteorites. He couldn't keep this up forever.

Thankfully, he didn't need to. As shards of the shattered ice rained down around him, bouncing off his armor, Sinfjotli noticed static energy filling the air. A strange physical tingling sensation spread throughout his body, especially in his hands and feet. The air suddenly tasted metallic, and dizziness washed over him.

It was time.

Sinfjotli stepped back, his breath shallow, as Magni and Modi raised their hands, and tendrils of lightning erupted from their fingers. They continued channeling electricity until the energy coalesced into eighteen enormous javelin-like weapons hovering around their bodies. The mountain trembled beneath their feet. The air glowed, Sinfjotli's ears popped, and every hair on his body stood on end.

Magni and Modi reared their arms back and hurled the enormous javelins. The massive streams of lightning traveled through the air like pure streams of unstoppable power. Every meteorite in their path was vaporized as the javelins surged forward, slammed against Fornjót's chest, and detonated.

The ensuing blast lit up the dark world of Niflheim, turning night into day. The titanic explosion sent Fornjót hurtling through the air. He bounced several times against the ground, tumbling head over heels before slamming into the mountains bordering the other side of the valley. Many peaks crumbled beneath his weight, sending a massive cloud of dust, snow, and debris five thousand feet into the air. The burst of explosive energy was so powerful that it blew Sinfjotli off his feet even though he was far away from the explosion. He would have been sent flying for miles if Modi hadn't grabbed his leg and pulled him back.

Modi set Sinfjotli down on the icy ground as the explosion settled down. Sinfjotli gaped in awe at the devastation they had caused. The energy javelins had carved long grooves across the snowy earth as they zipped through the air. The deep mile-long furrows in the permafrost reminded Sinfjotli of rows of plowed soil in a farmer's field. The explosion had also sent tendrils of electricity in every direction, which had scarred the earth and burned everything within the blast's epicenter.

Incredible! Sinfjotli thought. *So this is the power of the Aesir.*

"Just be thankful our father wasn't the one who unleashed that attack," Modi said, as if reading Sinfjotli's thoughts. "Otherwise, you would have been dead from being this close to the blast, even with the Kistfuskare protecting you."

Sinfjotli had no reason to doubt their words, given the cataclysmic destruction they had just caused. The Sons of Thor had ravaged the landscape almost as much as Fornjót had. Before the hailstorm, the mountain they were standing on was part of a vast range stretching over two thousand miles long. In the aftermath of Fornjót's devastating ice storm and Magni and Modi's destructive attack, this battered mountain was the only peak that remained relatively intact within a one-hundred-mile radius. The rest were peppered with enormous craters or had been outright flattened into dust by meteorites and lightning.

Sinfjotli glanced up at the sky and noticed that the hailstorm had stopped.

Is it over? Sinfjotli wondered, hopefully. *Did we get him?*

Suddenly, the ground quaked. In the distance, the giant cloud of dust and debris began swirling around like a massive tornado. A colossal foot emerged from the funnel and stomped on the ground, causing giant fissures to spread throughout the already battered landscape.

"So you pests are still alive?" Fornjót growled as he emerged from the cloud.

Sinfjotli gaped in shock as the mighty frost giant advanced toward them. He definitely wasn't imagining it this time! Somehow, Fornjót had grown even larger than before! Thick, tattoo-like patterns now covered his arms and legs. Fornjót had also gained a huge horned helmet with curved crescent-shaped black horns jutting from the helmet's forehead. Aside from a smoking crater in the center of his chest, Fornjót looked utterly unfazed by Magni and Modi's destructive attack.

"Very good, you three," Fornjót seethed. "By all means, keep annoying me. It will only make your deaths that much more satisfying!"

The giant clenched his fists, and the temperature plummeted. The air became as thick as congealed blood. Sinfjotli's nose started bleeding, and his throat and lungs ached with every breath. When layers of ice started forming on their flesh, Magni and Modi channeled electricity throughout their body to counteract it. The Coffin Cheater burned as hot as a furnace as it adjusted to the drastic change in temperature.

"You maggots just had to spoil my fun!" Fornjót said. "I was having a blast crushing that flying lizard before you brazenly interrupted me. I can't *stand* it when vexing pests meddle in my battles!"

The air suddenly became so frigid that the wound on Magni's forehead stopped bleeding—his blood freezing solid. He and Modi continued channeling electricity throughout their body, desperately trying to counteract the drastic temperature change and prevent themselves from freezing.

With their panic rising, Magni and Modi pointed their weapons toward the heavens. They channeled electricity into the sky. The clouds roared in response. A storm of lightning bolts fired down, turning the ground as black as Svartalfheim's desert as their power increased, but Fornjót just ignored them and kept walking toward them.

"Brace yourself, Sinfjotli!" Magni warned as he and Modi stood side by side and swung their weapons simultaneously, shouting, "Landvinningur himins!"

Their combined attack generated an explosive wave of air that absolutely devastated everything in its path. It slammed into Fornjót, and the resulting explosion dwarfed Mount Isa.

Unfortunately, the attack barely fazed Fornjót. The frost giant staggered backward and fell to one knee, but didn't topple. He planted his hand into the frozen ground for balance. Then he stood up and continued approaching.

The air became colder with every step Fornjót took. Sinfjotli couldn't move. It felt like layers of ice had formed between his elbows, kneecaps, and armpits. Magni and Modi couldn't do anything, either. They were now channeling electricity inward, using their own power through their bodies to counteract the drastic drop in temperature. If they stopped, they would turn into frozen statues.

Fornjót reared his head back and inhaled deeply, preparing to belch out another blizzard—a merciless blast that would encase them all in ice. But before he could, a giant scaly arm grabbed Fornjót's face and slammed his head against the ground.

The tremors knocked everyone off their feet, the shockwaves rattling Sinfjotli's bones as he scrambled for balance. When the dust cleared, his eyes widened. High above Fornjót, the golden dragon hovered. Sigurd had dug himself out of the rubble. But he hadn't emerged from the hailstorm unscathed. One of its wings jutted at an awkward angle, the sharp ridges of bone visible beneath torn membranes. Smoke curled from fresh wounds along its back and neck, blood dripping in slow streams as it lurched through the air, struggling to stay aloft.

Fornjót got back on his feet and angrily tried to swat Sigurd out of the sky. The dragon barely avoided the attack, then roared as the two monsters resumed tearing each other apart.

But the tide of the battle had shifted; it was abundantly clear that Fornjót now had the upper hand. The relentless hailstorm had taken a visible toll on Sigurd's body, his fireballs not as large or as powerful as earlier, now only narrowly avoiding the giant's attacks.

Meanwhile, Fornjót showed no signs of fatigue or weakness despite Sigurd, Magni, and Modi's earlier onslaughts. In fact, he seemed to be even stronger than before!

Fornjót reared his right arm back and threw a punch at Sigurd forcing the dragon into a dive under the giant's fist. Fornjót had anticipated this maneuver and slammed his left fist into Sigurd before the dragon could react.

The blow sent the dragon soaring into the ground with a loud boom. When it emerged roaring from the ensuing dust cloud and took to the air again, Sinfjotli could tell that the punch and impact had broken some bones by how its body shuddered, its wingbeats erratic and uncoordinated. But the golden dragon forced itself to keep fighting through sheer rage and bloodlust.

"Sigurd can't keep fighting like this," Sinfjotli announced. "And Fornjót is showing no signs of stopping."

"You're right," Modi agreed. "I don't think our father or grandfather ever struggled this much against a frost giant."

"This is insane," Magni complained. "We've thrown everything we've got at him, and he keeps getting back up! How is he this powerful? Is there no limit to his strength?"

Sinfjotli frowned. *Strength?* The word strongly resonated with him. He thought about the frost trolls they had faced recently. After they slew them, Magni mentioned that creatures of frost draw their strength from cold weather.

Suddenly, Sinfjotli remembered something Fornjót had casually mentioned: *I planned to amass my strength and power here in Niflheim to prepare for Ragnarök. But there's no reason to wait if the Aesir have become this weak.*

"Of course!" Sinfjotli exclaimed. "Magni, you said earlier that creatures of frost are at their strongest in the cold. We're standing in the coldest realm, and Fornjót is the strongest creature of them all. He's been drawing his strength from Niflheim's eternal frost and using the extreme cold to regenerate his injuries and empower himself."

"But that's impossible," Magni objected. "Frost giants are tough sons of bitches, but not a single one of them should be able to regenerate their body parts just from being exposed to cold weather. It shouldn't even be possible for a frost giant to have that type of ability."

"True, but Fornjót isn't like most frost giants, is he?" Sinfjotli pointed out. "He's old and primordial. He claimed to be a son of Ymir, and after everything I've seen, I believe he's telling the truth. He's more like a force of nature than a monster. Common sense rules don't apply to him so long as he remains exposed to this extreme cold."

"Even if we know the secret of his strength, it won't change anything," Modi pointed out. "He's invincible as long as he's standing in Niflheim."

"If that's true, then all we have to do is knock him unconscious, drag him out of Niflheim, and force him to fight us in a different realm," Sinfjotli proposed. "That way, he won't be able to regenerate."

"That won't work," Magni said, shaking his head. "Even if we could incapacitate him, Niflheim is twenty times larger than Midgard. Fornjót would recover from his injuries and wake up before we could drag him out of the realm."

"Then maybe we could trick him into leaving," Sinfjotli said. "I once heard that giants can't resist proving their strength against the Aesir. Maybe we could goad him into leaving Niflheim of his own volition and force him to fight us on equal footing."

"Frankly, I think that option got thrown out the window when we began this fight," Modi countered. "And with how this battle has progressed, I think we're well beyond the point of deception or even having a civil conversation with that *thing*."

"Damn it all!" Sinfjotli cursed. If they couldn't force or deceive Fornjót into leaving Niflheim, how else could they defeat this monster in this realm?

Sinfjotli paused. *'Monster in this realm?'* Where had he heard that phrase before? He thought about everything he knew about Niflheim. Modi previously warned them that a monster dwelt beneath the root of the World Tree in Niflheim. Even the gods of strength and courage had been terrified by the thought of interacting with Nidhogg. They had opted to fall thousands of feet through Niflheim's thick atmosphere rather than risk a confrontation with the fearsome creature. Could *it* stand a chance against Fornjót?

It has to, Sinfjotli thought. The Norns once told him that the monster that gnaws at the root of Yggdrasil is destined to be the only living creature to survive Ragnarök. If anyone could best Fornjót, it would be a creature that had destiny on its side.

"You're right, Modi," Sinfjotli conceded. "*We* might be unable to kill Fornjót while he's at full strength here in Niflheim. But another monster in this realm might."

Modi's eyes became as wide as plates. "Great bleeding fuck, lad, you can't possibly mean..."

"I know it's a desperate and suicidal plan," Sinfjotli said. "But it's all we have left to try."

"And just how are you planning to get Fornjót to the root of Yggdrasil?" Magni gestured to the dark clouds above them. "Without Sigurd to guide us through this darkness, we don't even know where it is right now!"

"That shouldn't be an issue," Sinfjotli assured, "because *Sigurd* will be the one to take Fornjót there."

Modi knit his eyebrows together. "What? How?"

"I have a plan," Sinfjotli assured. "But for it to work, I need you to toss me onto Sigurd's back."

"Have you gone mad," Magni exclaimed. "Did you forget that he'll attack anyone in his current state? You saw how he attacked us before!"

"That's a risk I'm willing to take," Sinfjotli replied. "If things take a turn for the worst, the Coffin Cheater will protect me from whatever Sigurd does."

"But..." Magni protested.

"Look at him!" Sinfjotli pointed at the dragon. "My brother is fighting with everything he has and is not sane! He's already taken critical injuries. He won't be able to keep this up for much longer. I refuse to stand idly by while my brother stakes his life battling Fornjót."

Magni and Modi looked back at the titanic fight between the primordial frost giant and the ferocious dragon. They saw how much Sigurd was struggling. They looked back at Sinfjotli and nodded.

"Alright." Modi sighed. "What's the plan?"

CHAPTER THIRTY-FIVE

A DESPERATE MESSAGE

"Ugh, this is such a terrible plan," Magni grumbled. The god brought two fingers to his mouth and whistled. The sharp, shrill sound cut through the tumult of Sigurd's and Fornjót's battle like a knife through butter. The goats Tanngrisnir and Tanngnjóstr appeared moments later and galloped over to them. Sinfjotli hopped onto the chariot and started rummaging through the supplies.

"Are you sure about this?" Modi asked. "It's not too late to back out."

"Do you have a better idea?" Sinfjotli challenged as he rummaged through several crates.

"Well... no," Modi admitted.

"Then just have faith in me." Sinfjotli grabbed a cord of rope from a crate and hopped off the chariot. He tied the rope around his waist, using it as a makeshift sheathe to holster Gram.

"I'm ready," Sinfjotli announced.

Magni grabbed Sinfjotli and lifted him off the ground, holding him over his head like a spear. He adjusted his grip as he looked up at Sigurd.

The battle had shifted several miles east of The Spines. The dragon was now soaring thousands of feet above the ground instinctively recognizing that Fornjót was now too dangerous and powerful to engage in close-quarters combat. Thus, the beast opted to stay well out of the giant's range and pelted

Fornjót with fireballs while the giant responded by hurling mounds of ice and enormous ice spears at it.

"This may not work out how you envisioned," Magni warned. "I can throw you in his general direction, but Sigurd might fly away before you reach him. It's also possible that you could get caught in the crossfire of one of their attacks or that Sigurd will attack you the moment he sees you."

"And there's no guarantee Magni and I can catch you afterward," Modi added. "If you fall from that height..."

"It wouldn't be the first time I've had a painful landing," Sinfjotli muttered, thinking back to when Baldur hurled him and Sigurd across the Gjallerbru while he held off Hel's undead army. That crash landing had left them both paralyzed and on the brink of death. But things were different this time. "The Coffin Cheater will protect me from the worst. It allowed me to survive crashing into the ground after jumping off the root of Yggdrasil. So just throw me as fast as you can."

Magni heaved a heavy sigh. "Don't say we didn't warn you."

They watched and waited for an opportunity. After Sigurd and Fornjót unleashed breath attacks that canceled each other out, Magni saw his chance. He reared his arm back and hurled Sinfjotli like a javelin, launching him into the sky.

As Sinfjotli rocketed through the air, he thought about how eternally grateful he was to Ivaldi and his sons for forging this suit of armor. He was moving so fast through the frosty air that he would have lost his face to frostbite if he wasn't wearing the Coffin Cheater. As it was, he could barely see anything through the blinding snowflakes and the cloud of steam created by Sigurd and Fornjót's attacks. He prayed Sigurd hadn't moved.

Eventually, he saw a winged shadow through the cloud of dust. Half a heartbeat later, Sinfjotli slammed into Sigurd's right flank with enough force to jostle the dragon midair. The world turned upside down as Sinfjotli spun through the air before landing on something hard and warm. When the ground shifted beneath him, Sinfjotli realized he had landed on Sigurd's hindquarters. Then he realized he was sliding off the dragon. Alarmed, he flipped onto his stomach and tried to grab hold of something. But at that moment, Sigurd flapped his wings, and the sudden motion bucked Sinfjotli off before he could secure a foothold.

Time seemed to slow down as Sinfjotli plummeted toward the earth. Thinking quickly, he summoned Wolfsbane to his right hand and swung it at the dragon's nearby tail. The axe burrowed deep enough into the dragon's scaly tail to stop Sinfjotli's descent and gave him an anchor to hold on to.

Unfortunately, that also got Sigurd's attention. The dragon hissed angrily as Sinfjotli climbed onto the tail. He grabbed onto one spike lining the dragon's tail and held on for dear life as the beast shook and shuddered, trying to buck him off. It twisted its body and swung its tail back and forth, but Sinfjotli held on.

Suddenly, the dragon tensed. Sinfjotli heard a crackling or popping noise approaching. The dragon flapped its wings and soared higher as a sixty-thousand-ton mountain sailed past them. Sinfjotli watched Fornjót's projectile soar toward a distant valley and crash, sending a cloud of dust and debris miles into the air.

As Fornjót angrily demanded Sigurd come down and face him, the dragon lost interest in Sinfjotli and resumed its titanic battle with the giant.

Sinfjotli saw his chance. He purposely left Wolfsbane embedded in Sigurd's tail as he climbed up toward its back. Reaching the base of the spine, he found enough footholds to stand up on his hands and knees.

He immediately felt how hard the golden scales were and the immense heat radiating from the dragon's body. Even though he was wearing the Coffin Cheater, a suit of armor designed to protect him from extreme heat and cold, he felt as if he was pressing his hands and knees against the walls of a burning furnace. Sinfjotli ignored the slight pain and clambered along the dragon's back. He took his time grasping the hard scales and the many spikes jutting from the dragon's spine for handholds. He needed to be vigilant. Every time Sigurd flapped his leathery wings, the resulting air current threatened to hurl him off. But Sinfjotli took his time and pressed onward.

Eventually, Sinfjotli reached the base of Sigurd's neck and encountered another dilemma. There weren't many footholds to work with, and the dragon was moving too much for him to safely cross.

Suddenly, heat surged beneath Sinfjotli's hands as Sigurd reared its head back and prepared to unleash another fireball at Fornjót.

Ah, screw it! Sinfjotli stood up and bolted across Sigurd's bent neck as the dragon belched a torrent of flame toward the earth. He reached the dragon's head and grabbed one of its biggest horns before he lost his footing and held on for dear life.

"Sigurd!" Sinfjotli called out.

The dragon didn't respond. Sinfjotli could see no discernible ears on its head, and he doubted it could hear him over this shrieking wind and Fornjót's raging bellows.

I'll have to get his attention. Sinfjotli drew Gram from his makeshift sheath and pricked the sword into a small soft spot he found between the scales on the back of the dragon's head.

It wasn't a severe injury. The tip of the sword barely pierced through the dragon's scales. But it definitely got Sigurd's attention. The dragon roared, and its head snapped back, nearly throwing Sinfjotli off. Gripping an enormous horn, he tried to keep his hold, but he lost his grip when Sigurd suddenly lunged forward, and he tumbled down the reptilian head.

He came to a stop right at the tip of the dragon's snout where its nostrils were. Two enormous, angry golden eyes locked on him. Sinfjotli stood; the dragon glared, nostrils flaring as smoke billowed beside his feet.

This is how I die. My brother will kill me while he's in a blind rage. Sinfjotli closed his eyes and waited for the inevitable. But nothing happened. A moment passed. Then another. He opened his eyes. The dragon's gaze had changed. The fury was still there, but its golden eyes weren't just filled with rage. Its slit eyes had dilated, and beneath the storm of aggression, there was the slightest of glints of concentration. It seemed to be staring at something. Sinfjotli followed its gaze and realized it was staring at Gram, which was still in his hand.

Does he recognize it? Sinfjotli wondered. Gram was Sigurd's trusty sword. His brother knew this blade better than the back of his hand.

Sinfjotli held the sword aloft and dangled it in front of him. The dragon's eyes followed the movement, tracking it as he waved the blade to the left and right.

Sinfjotli didn't know what to make of this. Had Sigurd subconsciously recognized the sword? Or was the dragon just staring in awe at the weapon that had harmed it? Regardless, he had the beast's attention.

"Listen, Sigurd, you must take Fornjót to where the root of the World Tree connects with the ground," Sinfjotli instructed. "It's the only way to defeat him. We'll help weaken him so you can carry him off somehow. Got it?"

The dragon didn't react. Sinfjotli wondered if Sigurd could even understand him. Suddenly, the dragon's pupils contracted, and it roared. The dragon veered its head to the left and then swung its head to the right in a sudden motion that sent Sinfjotli hurtling to the earth.

Time seemed to slow down as he plummeted. The dragon became smaller and smaller. The wind roared in his ears as he fell into darkness.

What incredible power, Sinfjotli thought. *I can't regain my stance or even turn my head because the wind pressure is too intense!*

Suddenly, Sinfjotli wasn't falling. He was rising! Something slammed into him from below with enough force to cancel out his terminal velocity and send him speeding in the opposite direction. He felt sinewy arms wrap around his waist and looked up. Modi had leaped into the air and caught him as he fell.

Together, they soared through the air and then landed on a mountaintop in The Spines that had been cratered by one of Fornjót's meteorites. Modi placed Sinfjotli beside the giant meteorite protruding from the mountaintop, and then they both gazed up at Sigurd.

Did it work? Sinfjotli wondered. *Did he even understand what I said?*

The earth quaked as Fornjót picked up another mountain and hurled it at the dragon. Sigurd easily avoided the enormous projectile.

"I'm tired of this cat-and-mouse game," Fornjót bellowed. "Come down here and face me now, beast!"

The dragon roared. It flapped its wings and disappeared into a bank of clouds.

"That trick won't work on me a second time," Fornjót warned. "If you don't come down here willingly, I'll just force you out of the sky!"

Fornjót raised his arms. Sinfjotli realized Fornjót was planning to create another hailstorm to force Sigurd back to the ground, and he warned Modi to stop him. But as Fornjót clapped, Sigurd suddenly appeared before the giant and blasted him right in the eyes with a golden fireball. Fornjót stumbled backward, bellowed in pain, and blindly tried to swat Sigurd out of the sky. But the dragon had already flown away. Then, as sudden as a thunderbolt, Sigurd appeared behind the giant and dove straight at Fornjót's head. The dragon raked the giant's neck with its claws and ripped off his right ear with its teeth before flying away.

Modi and Sinfjotli watched in awe as the dragon continued engaging in more hit-and-run attacks. Sigurd's attacks had become more precise, coordinated, and surgical. He systematically targeted the giant's weak spots and other vital areas necessary for movement and dismantling Fornjót piecemeal. It was reminiscent of how Sigurd usually fought when battling tough opponents, albeit much sloppier.

However, Sinfjotli knew this wouldn't be enough. Fornjót was healing at an even faster rate than before. It took less than three minutes for his eyes, neck, and ear to fully regenerate.

As Sinfjotli and Modi watched the battle enter a new phase, a bolt of lightning struck the mountaintop, and Magni appeared next to them.

"Looks like your gamble paid off." Magni applauded. He patted Sinfjotli's back. "I had my doubts, lad, but it seems you got through to him somehow."

"We're not finished," Sinfjotli reminded. He pointed Gram at Fornjót. "Let's move on to the next phase of the plan and reinforce Sigurd. We must weaken Fornjót as much as possible."

CHAPTER THIRTY-SIX

A FINAL PUSH

After formulating a strategy, Sinfjotli, Magni, and Modi watched and waited from a safe distance as Sigurd and Fornjót continued their epic struggle on the frosty plains northeast of The Spines' ruined mountaintops. Sinfjotli couldn't help but admire the destructive results of their battle. Their clash had sent violent shockwaves in every direction. It had entirely cleared the landscape of the deep snow cover, revealing a vast thick ice sheet.

Eventually, Sigurd flew up and disappeared into a bank of clouds. Fornjót scanned the skies intently, looking for any trace of the golden dragon.

"Now's our chance!" Magni announced. He wrapped his arm around Sinfjotli's waist and leaped. They shot up, soaring hundreds of feet. Sinfjotli gripped Gram tightly as the ground fell away beneath them.

"Are you ready, Sinfjotli?" Magni asked as they sailed two hundred feet over Fornjót's head.

"Yes," Sinfjotli replied. "Now throw me with all your strength, Magni!"

"Ha, you wouldn't survive it if I did!" Magni laughed. He reared his arm back and hurled Sinfjotli right at Fornjót.

As Sinfjotli rocketed toward the giant, he straightened out his body, arms extended over his head as if diving into the water. Gram was in his hands, and the blade whistled slightly as it cut through the air.

Fornjót must have heard the noise because he turned and saw Sinfjotli rocketing toward him.

"You!" he muttered.

"Too late," Sinfjotli shouted. He held Gram above his head and used it like a spear, perforating Fornjót's left shoulder. For a second, everything became red as he passed through the flesh and muscle, the blade carving a path. His vision cleared when he emerged through the other side. As he sailed through the air, he glanced over his shoulder, taking in the massive wound he had inflicted.

He didn't have time to celebrate. Sinfjotli looked ahead—he was speeding toward the ground. If he hit at this velocity, he might burrow so deep underground that no one would ever find his body.

Thankfully, Modi appeared and caught him just as planned. The impact knocked the wind from Sinfjotli's lungs as he slammed into the god of courage. The icy ground cracked beneath Modi's feet, and an enormous crater formed around him. But the worst had passed.

Modi gingerly set Sinfjotli on the ground. As he tried to recover his breath, he looked up at the damage. Fornjót now had a five-foot wide hole in his left shoulder that was wide enough for a person to pass through.

A wound of that magnitude would usually be life-threatening. But Fornjót was so massive that it probably just irked him.

Still, the attack served its intended purpose. Sinfjotli had specifically damaged the ligaments in Fornjót's shoulder blade, which disabled the limb's mobility. Fornjót's left arm now dangled limply from his side.

"Damn insect!" Fornjót growled.

"Now's your chance, Magni!" Modi called.

Lightning crackled in the sky above. Fornjót glanced up and saw Magni hurtling toward him from his left flank. Electricity crackled around his greatsword, empowering and elongating the blade's reach.

Fornjót's eyes widened as he realized Sinfjotli's attack had been a distraction. He tried to stop the god of strength from getting closer, but the gaping wound rendered his arm useless, leaving him unable to defend his head.

With a thunderous war cry, Magni slashed his broadsword diagonally, the blade cleaving through Fornjót's face. A large portion of the frost giant's head sheared away—one of the curved horns from his helmet split off, tumbling alongside the jagged remnants of his skull as Magni descended toward the earth.

Fornjót hollered, his agonized roar shaking the frozen expanse. He had turned his neck to the right at the last moment, mitigating some of the damage. But everything to the left of his jaw and eye socket was gone, leaving jagged bone and raw, exposed brain matter along the left side of his head.

But the worst injury was yet to come. Modi raised his war hammer toward the heavens and summoned a massive bolt of lightning that blasted Fornjót's exposed brain.

Sinfjotli covered his ears as Fornjót bellowed. His roar was so loud that it triggered avalanches in The Spines and shattered an entire ice sheet into pieces. The giant staggered backward, crushing several mounds of ice beneath his feet as he grasped his smoking head with his right hand.

But amazingly, Fornjót didn't fall. Even after losing a portion of his head and having his exposed brain blasted by lightning, the mighty frost giant remained on his feet!

"Are you kidding me!" Magni complained as he landed next to Modi. "We sliced off a portion of his head, damaged his brain, and he's still standing upright! What a damn monster!"

Fornjót was a monster—there was no other word for him. He had reshaped the battlefield at will, shrugged off attacks that should have been fatal, and endured wounds no living being should have survived. Even with half his head cleaved away, he still stood. Still fought.

A loud shriek pierced the air. Sinfjotli looked up as the golden dragon emerged from the clouds. Sigurd, either drawn in by the scent of blood or sensing weakness in his opponent, dove upon Fornjót from the giant's now blinded left side.

Sinfjotli cheered, thinking this was the end. That this was the opportunity Sigurd had been waiting for. He just had to blindside Fornjót, incapacitate the frost giant, and then drag him away to the root of Yggdrasil.

Unfortunately, Sigurd had been too noisy in his approach. As the golden dragon dove at Fornjót's head, it made the mistake of unleashing another piercing shriek that could be heard a dozen miles away. Sensing danger, Fornjót turned and blindly swung his left arm up at the dragon in a sweeping motion. Sinfjotli had only seconds to realize that Fornjót's left arm had already healed from the crippling wound. The blow sent Sigurd careening into a cratered peak in The Spines about a mile away. The impact triggered an avalanche that buried Sigurd under tons of snow and ice.

Sinfjotli's heart skipped a beat as Sigurd vanished beneath crushing layers of snow and ice. After a few tense moments, Sigurd emerged. Sinfjotli sighed, but his relief soon turned to ash. The dragon was in immense pain. Sigurd tried to take flight three times, only succeeding on the third attempt. Even then, his movements were unsteady, his wings faltering. He lurched through the air, at times swooping low and springboarding off a mountaintop or hill to gain the momentum necessary to remain aloft.

"Sigurd's strength is waning," Magni observed. "He's taken too much damage. He won't be able to keep this up much longer. If he takes another hit like that, he's finished."

Sinfjotli looked back at Fornjót, who still clutched his wounded head but showed no signs of stopping. Sinfjotli noticed a layer of ice forming over the giant's head wound, resembling a scab. Fornjót was regenerating the parts of his brain and head that Magni had destroyed. If his head regenerated as his right arm had earlier, Fornjót would become even more powerful after healing.

"Fornjót isn't anywhere weak enough!" Sinfjotli warned. "We need to create another opening for Sigurd and weaken that damn giant as much as possible."

"Alright." Magni nodded. "I've got another idea. Modi, distract him and buy me some time."

"Got it."

Magni brought two fingers to his mouth and whistled, summoning their goat chariot. He hopped inside and sped away.

Meanwhile, Modi hefted his war hammer.

"You better step back, Sinfjotli," Modi warned as he swung the war hammer against the ice sheet beneath their feet. The ground cracked, and an enormous jagged circle formed. Modi holstered his weapon and grabbed hold of the ice. The muscles in his arms swelled as he used his wrenched a massive chunk free, hoisting it over his head. The iceberg was several hundred times his size and easily weighed over fifteen million tons.

"This is for throwing that mountain at me earlier!" Modi shouted as he hurled the iceberg at Fornjót.

It was an impressive display of strength. But the iceberg proved to be about as harmless as a snowball. The mountain of ice slammed against Fornjót's bare chest and shattered into thousands of pieces.

Fornjót glowered and began marching toward their position.

"Insects, insects, insects!" Fornjót shouted. "You little bugs cannot kill me no matter how hard you may try. How many times must I say that before you believe me? Compared to me, Aesir, Vanir, humans, elves, dwarves, giants, and beasts are all inferior. To me, you are all nothing but ants!"

"You're right about one thing," Modi remarked. "We are tiny compared to you. We're too small for you to notice, even when we're literally beneath your feet."

Fornjót narrowed his good eye. "What are you talking a... argh!"

Fornjót suddenly toppled forward. The ice sheet cracked beneath his massive weight, sending a cloud of snow and ice in every direction.

"What!" Fornjót roared, pushing himself off the ground. The giant peered over his shoulder, gaze narrowing as the cloud of dust around his legs settled. Sinfjotli spotted Magni standing next to Fornjót's mangled left foot. The god of strength had moved in stealthily, approaching from the giant's now blinded left side. It seemed Magni had grabbed hold of Fornjót's left foot and then flexed the muscles in his arms, using brute force to topple him. That alone caused Fornjót to veer and skitter deeply into the ground.

But Magni hadn't stopped there. He had also used his godly strength to twist Fornjót's left foot to the side, breaking the giant's ankle and several other bones.

"My foot! How dare you!" Fornjót roared.

"Nice work, brother!" Modi applauded. "Now it's my turn!" He leaped hundreds of feet into the air and brought his war hammer down on the back of Fornjót's head. The force of the blow drove the giant face-first into the ground. The earth shuddered from the impact, and a massive crater formed beneath Fornjót's bloody head. The ensuing cloud of dust and debris lifted Sinfjotli off his feet and sent him flying dozens of yards.

But the Sons of Thor weren't finished yet. Modi landed on the ground next to the giant's right ear, while Magni touched down on the left side of his head. They each grabbed part of the giant's head and dragged Fornjót face-first across the icy ground. For over a mile, they hauled Fornjót, leaving behind a gory trail of blood before slamming the mighty frost giant against the base of a delipidated mountain in The Spines, which promptly collapsed and buried Fornjót's head and upper body beneath thousands of tons of snow and ice.

It was a devastating, brutal attack, but all it did was enrage Fornjót. As the dust settled, the giant's fists burst through the piles of snow and ice, nearly snaring Magni and Modi in their grasp. The Sons of Thor leaped two hundred feet into the air, but Fornjót was ready. Still partially buried, he raised both clenched fists high and slammed them against the ground. The earth heaved and cracked, and Sinfjotli realized what was about to happen. Before he could shout a warning, dozens of serrated ice spikes erupted from the ground. One speared Modi's left side before he could react.

"Modi!" Sinfjotli screamed.

The god of courage plummeted to the ice sheet and crash-landed about a hundred feet from Sinfjotli. The impact sent shards of ice in every direction. Sinfjotli ignored the shrapnel as it shattered against the Coffin Cheater and rushed to help his fallen comrade.

Modi lay bloodied at the bottom of a thirty-foot-deep crater, his ribs exposed through the gaping hole, and pieces of skin hung loosely from his back like torn rags.

As Sinfjotli gawked at the ghastly state of Modi's injury, Magni appeared next to him in a lightning bolt. He leaped into the crater, wrapped an arm around Modi's waist, and carried him out as if he weighed nothing.

"Thanks, Magni," Modi groaned as Magni helped him stand. He held out his hand, summoning his trusty war hammer. The weapon's weight almost knocked him to the ground when it returned to him, and he leaned on it like a crutch.

"Can you fight?" Magni asked.

"I'll manage," Modi groaned. He coughed up a mist of blood and fell to his knees, still clutching his left side. "Don't worry, I'm fine."

"The hell you are!" Sinfjotli countered. "That attack ran you through! Your internal organs are still mangled."

"Just forget about it!" Modi insisted. "Now is not the time to get distracted."

He pointed toward Fornjót. They watched as the frost giant pulled himself out of the snow and rubble and rose to one knee. When he turned around to face them, Sinfjotli almost retched at the hideous sight of his face. Fornjót's nose, lips, front teeth, and the tip of his tongue were gone, and parts of his brain were exposed through his sheered-off face. Most of his face had been destroyed from the friction he'd suffered as Magni and Modi dragged him across the icy plains. Only his right eye remained intact, and it was full of hate.

"Unforgivable!" Fornjót roared. "You impudent ants will—"

Before he could finish, a flash of gold streaked across the battlefield as Sigurd slammed full force into Fornjót's back, sending the giant sprawling face-first into the ground. The dragon grabbed the back of Fornjót's head, lifted him effortlessly, and slammed his face against rock. The earth shuddered from the impact, and a massive crater formed beneath Fornjót's head. Thunder echoed as Sigurd repeatedly slammed Fornjót's face against the ground again and again. The giant's head exploded in a shower of blood, each impact scattering chunks of bone and flesh in every direction.

When Fornjót stopped moving, the dragon reared its head back and roared triumphantly. Sinfjotli brandished Gram. He couldn't lower his guard yet. Most beings would be dead after having half their skull sliced off, their face destroyed by friction, and then taking such a brutal beating from Sigurd. But they were fighting Fornjót, a being who defied all logic. The frost giant was probably just unconscious.

But Sinfjotli's greater concern was Sigurd's disposition. The dragon's attacks had become more coordinated and concise, but there was still no telling what he might do next. And Sinfjotli still didn't know if Sigurd understood the instructions he had conveyed earlier or if the beast was capable of rational thought. He worried Sigurd might squander this opportunity they had given him and continue attacking Fornjót. Or worse, he might attack them instead.

But for once, it seemed like the Norns were smiling in their favor. Sigurd hopped onto Fornjót's back, claws sinking deep into the giant's flesh like meat hooks. The dragon spread its wings and with a mighty beat, took off with its prize in its clutches.

Sinfjotli didn't think it was possible, but somehow Sigurd lifted Fornjót off the ground and flew higher.

"What the hell?" Sinfjotli muttered. "He could barely fly a few minutes ago. Where did all this strength and energy come from?"

"Look at his forehead," Magni said, pointing. Between Sigurd's horns was a glowing red symbol, visible even from this distance.

"That's the Uruz rune," Magni explained. "While you two distracted Fornjót, I got a hold of Sigurd and drew that symbol on his forehead. He almost burned and eviscerated me several times, but it's done the job. He now has the strength and energy to see this through."

"But won't that rune also triple the pain from Sigurd's injuries after it wears off?" Modi pointed out.

"Aye." Magni nodded sadly. "But as long as Sigurd pulls this off, it'll be worth it."

Sinfjotli should have been more worried by that. But he was too awed by the spectacle taking place above him. Despite being much smaller than Fornjót, somehow, the golden dragon carried the giant higher into the sky like a golden eagle with a goat in its talons.

Magni was right, Sinfjotli thought. *I know nothing about true strength.* He watched as the golden dragon soared higher and higher with its prize and disappeared into Niflheim's thick atmosphere.

"It's all on you now, Sigurd," Sinfjotli muttered. "Make it count."

***

Sinfjotli, Magni, and Modi would not see what happened next. But one god would bear witness to the chaos. Far away in Asgard, Heimdall stood vigil on his watchtower. He had been watching the titanic battle in Niflheim unfold.

The thick atmosphere could not assuage his piercing gaze. His keen senses allowed him to see and hear every detail in the icy realm, even from such a great distance.

He watched as Sigurd flew higher and higher, dragging Fornjót with him. Even in its battered and bloody state, the dragon carried the frozen giant into Niflheim's stratosphere.

Heimdall marveled at the dragon's strength and determination. Though the frost giant was incomprehensibly heavy, Sigurd fought through fatigue and pain, ascending ever higher into the upper reaches of the atmosphere.

But as the dragon breached Niflheim's thermosphere, the lack of oxygen and his grievous injuries finally took their toll. The dragon plummeted like a falling star, its prize still in its clutches. With the last of its strength, Sigurd angled their descent and maneuvered himself and the giant, adjusting its fall trajectory.

They fell from so high that Fornjót's body glowed hot from atmospheric reentry, making it look like a comet crashing down to the earth. Both giant and dragon reached the troposphere and crashed into the root of Yggdrasil, triggering an earthquake so massive that it caused the entire World Tree to shake.

CHAPTER THIRTY-SEVEN

A TRIAL OF LOVE AND HONOR

"What am I going to do with you, Brynhild?" Odin sighed.

The All-Father sat on his large golden throne. His ravens, Huginn and Muninn, perched on his shoulders, while his pet wolves, Geri and Freki, sat near his feet. The golden throne was on a large iron dais with high and narrow steps.

Brynhild looked around at the other assembled gods, meeting their faces individually. Each god had their own massive and unique throne, collectively arranged in an inverted U-shape with Odin's head throne, Hliðskjálf, in the center and taller than the rest. Next to Odin sat a beautiful woman with golden hair braided over one shoulder. She wore Asgardian armor over her turquoise dress. It was Odin's wife and queen, Frigga.

Next to her sat her stepson, the god of thunder, Thor. His eyes sparked with energy, and his trusty hammer hummed with power as it hung from his belt, the Megingjörð. The metal gloves, Járngreipr, covered his meaty hands. His wife, the beautiful lady Sif, sat next to him. Her long golden hair flowed loosely over her shoulders.

Next to her sat a gaunt-looking man on a chrome-and-leather throne—Týr, the god of war. Beside him was Baldur and Nanna's son Forseti, the god of justice, seated on his father's former throne.

Hermod and Vidar, the messenger god and the god of vengeance, respectively, sat near the end.

There were fewer gods seated on the other side of the room. On Odin's left sat Brynhild's former master, Freyja, the goddess of love and war. Her throne wasn't as big as the Hliðskjálf but was just as big as Queen Frigga's, partly because she was considered Odin's equal. Her father, Njörd, the god of the sea, sat nearby on a throne made of driftwood.

Bragi, the god of poetry, was the next god. Beside him sat his wife, Idun, the goddess of youth and fertility.

Three of the fifteen thrones were unoccupied. Freyja's twin brother, Freyr, had abstained from the meeting, which wasn't surprising. He seldom left his sovereign realm of Alfheim. His throne, made of gold and situated between Freyja and Njörd, was as stunning and graceful as his sister's.

The empty throne between Njörd and Bragi belonged to Lord Heimdall. He never neglected his duties to watch over the realms from his watchtower, but Brynhild knew he was listening to the trial unfold thanks to his superhuman hearing. The last vacant throne next to Idun once belonged to Nanna, but it had remained unoccupied since her tragic death.

The giant thrones overlooked Valhalla, the Hall of Heroes. Countless Einherjar occupied the hundreds of seats and tables covering the floor between the gods' thrones. The hall had five hundred and forty doors. Some had been left open, allowing sunlight to spill across the floor. The rafters high above were made from spears, and the ceiling was thatched with polished golden shields that reflected light from the braziers.

Brynhild's legs trembled beneath her. She wasn't usually timid, but having the eyes of the gods and every denizen in Valhalla glued upon her was daunting. Facing Hel's entire army of undead warriors seemed like child's play compared to the unease she felt now. Even seeing her former master Freyja and some of her sister valkyries seated at a nearby table couldn't give her succor.

"The last time you disobeyed me and muddied my plans was when you allowed King Agnarr to triumph in the battle against Hjalmgunnar, the King of the Goths," Odin recalled. "I punished your insubordination by making you mortal, cursing you so that you could never harm a living creature, and leaving you in a deep slumber on Hindarfjall until a man without fear awakened you. When that fearless man came along, you fell in love with him but later conspired to murder him."

"My memories of Sigurd were erased after he drank Grimhild's potion," Brynhild tried to explain. "I was—"

"Your motivations are irrelevant." Odin cut her off. "Sigurd wasn't supposed to die such a dishonorable death. But because you schemed to have him murdered, he got sent to Helheim. He must now travel the realms with his brother and complete many impossible tasks before Hel relinquishes her claim to their souls. This could have been avoided if you hadn't meddled with our plans a second time."

"But she saved their lives on the Gjallerbru," his wife, Frigga, pointed out. "They would have surely perished if not for her."

"True," Odin conceded, stroking his beard. "And because of that, I'm in a quandary of what to do with her."

"With all due respect, All-Father, my fate is not for you to decide," Brynhild announced brazenly.

Odin stared crossly at her. "I am the Lord of Asgard, Protector of the Nine Realms, and Master of Fate."

"Are you?" Brynhild tittered. "How many of your plans have gone awry? More than you care to admit, I wager."

Odin glowered at her with his one good eye, and Brynhild coldly returned the stare. They continued staring daggers at each other until one of the Einherjar rose from his seat and cleared his throat.

"If it pleases you, All-Father, may I give my opinion on this matter?"

"By all means, Sigmund, speak," Odin said. "I'm curious to hear your opinion on the matter, considering her pivotal role in your son's death."

Brynhild's eyes widened as she turned to face this grizzled warrior. She had heard rumors about Sigmund through his son Sigurd and several other sources. But he was unlike anything she expected. Sigmund was a stocky bull of a man. He was at least six feet seven inches tall, broad-shouldered, and mighty in appearance. He was one of the older-looking denizens of Valhalla. His long hair and beard were gray, but Sigmund still had a muscular physique and a stomach as flat as oak.

Sigmund examined her with piercing steel-blue eyes. "My son loves her deeply. If you're giving my sons a second chance, why not give her one too?"

Odin looked at the other warriors seated around Sigmund's table. "What about you, Helgi and Hámundr? I'd like to hear your opinions on the matter."

Two warriors rose. Their similar features marked them as brothers. The elder brother, Helgi, wore a suit of sea-green armor. He was a clean-shaving, fair-skinned man with spiky, waist-length brown hair with shoulder-length bangs framing the sides of his face and covering most of his left eye. Beside him sat a gorgeous valkyrie with golden metallic wings, who nodded encouragingly at Brynhild.

The other warrior wasn't nearly as impressive. Hámundr was shorter and had a leaner build than his brother. He was handsome, but he wasn't as comely as Helgi. No valkyrie would ever lose their heart to him. Still, he more than earned his place in Valhalla. Brynhild vaguely recalled Sigurd once telling her about his half-brother's final deeds. After Sigmund fell in battle, Hámundr and his sister-in-law Sigrún mustered what remained of the Volsung army in a valiant last stand to defend Völsung City. They bravely defended the city Sigmund had built for months until they eventually died in a final blood charge. Hámundr, Sigrún, and all the men who served under them had earned their place in Valhalla and Fólkvangr.

"As someone who also fell in love with a valkyrie, I know how tumultuous it can be," Helgi began. He glanced nervously at his wife. "But if our roles were reversed... if I was in Sigurd's position, and Sigrún was in Brynhild's, then I would do everything I could to reunite with her. I would also forgive her for killing me. I know Sigurd has already forgiven her."

"I agree," Hámundr said. "It's clear Sigurd loves and cherishes Brynhild dearly. If we execute her... I'm certain it would take the heart out of our brother."

Several Einherjar started murmuring at their tables. Some agreed with what Helgi and Hámundr were saying. Others didn't. But soon, a stern voice cut through the whispers.

"You lads are too soft!" All heads turned as a powerfully built man rose from the Volsungs' table. His steel-blue eyes cut through the room. Jet-black hair streaked with silver framed a square-cut beard, neatly kept but betraying no softness.

A hush fell. Braziers crackled, and several Einherjar whispered in each other's ears. Brynhild heard someone whisper the man's name: Rerir the Stern.

Brynhild had no personal history with him. But she had heard stories about Sigi's infamous son. Rerir had a flinty reputation; a hard man, people said, stern and unforgiving, humorless, and cold with an unbreakable code of honor and a zealous sense of duty and justice that governed his actions. He hated treachery more than anything else. He had proved as much when he brutally executed his uncles for killing his father, subjecting them to unspeakable horrors.

Rerir looked askance at her, his eyes stern and unforgiving. Brynhild's hand trembled. Though she was a valkyrie who had lived for millennia, she felt herself shrink in Rerir's presence. She knew she would get no support from him.

"She might have saved them in Helheim," Rerir acknowledged, "but a good deed does not wash out the bad. Regardless of her actions and her mutual affection for Sigurd, the fact remains that she betrayed him and conspired to have him murdered. She must be punished somehow."

"Rerir speaks true," the god Vidar concurred.

"Nonsense!" Everyone turned as another large man rose from Rerir's table. This man was almost eight feet tall with a long, thin black mustache that spiked upward, a narrow and trim beard, a prominent cleft chin, and long black hair reaching his waist. He also had a large spear strapped to his back.

He looked a lot like Rerir and Sigmund. Brynhild heard several Einherjar whisper his name in hushed tones: "Völsung."

So this is Sigurd's grandfather, Brynhild thought, *the one the Volsung bloodline is named after.*

"You're being far too stern, Father," Völsung argued. "Sigmund and my grandsons are right. Brynhild should be shown leniency. She fought her way into Helheim just to reunite with Sigurd, and she helped them slay over a million draugirs! That act of bravery alone deserves admiration and recognition."

Many Einherjar concurred with Völsung. But some didn't. They stamped their feet, shook their fists, and yelled that she deserved to be punished. Warriors began shoving one another. Someone flung a plate at Brynhild's head. It hit Rerir in the chest when she ducked, making him fulminate. Helgi and Hámundr drew their weapons, and Sigrún summoned her wings and vowed to cut down anyone who pointed a blade at her fellow valkyrie.

For a moment, it seemed to Brynhild as if she were standing atop a small rock in the middle of a stormy sea. Shouts of "Mercy!" and "Punishment!" surged back and forth. Some warriors brandished their weapons, and it seemed like a savage battle would break out on her behalf in the Hall of Heroes.

"Cease this infernal discord... I DEMAND SILENCE!" Odin roared, his booming voice echoing around the chamber like a blast of thunder.

All talking died down. Valhalla was now silent except for the crackle of the hearths. The Einherjar sheathed their weapons and took their seats. Everyone's eyes were trained on Brynhild and Odin—all the gods and past heroes. Then Týr cleared his throat and rose from his throne.

"Rerir makes a valid point, as do Völsung, Sigmund, and his sons," Týr surmised. "Brynhild should be punished and rewarded fairly. Wouldn't you agree, Father?"

Everyone's eyes shifted to Odin as he leaned back on his throne. He ran his hand through his long beard, mulling over the various points the Volsungs and the Aesir had discussed.

"Freyja, didn't this woman used to be your servant?" Odin asked. "Brynhild is yours to deal with however you see fit. I wash my hands of her."

"Of course, Odin." Freyja nodded. She looked back at Brynhild with a calm but very stern look. "Don't think for a second that you'll get off lightly, my dear. I have several grueling tasks in mind for you."

Brynhild looked down and bowed. "I accept whatever tasks you may give me, my lady."

Not everyone agreed with this decision. Some hot-blooded denizens of Valhalla drew their weapons, shouting that Brynhild deserved a harsher punishment. Others rose, hollering in her defense. It seemed like a battle was about to be waged in Valhalla in her name when suddenly, the ground shook. Dozens of stained-glass windows lining the walls of Valhalla shattered while several other glass panes glass fell and exploded into tiny shards. A large marble bust of Odin toppled from its pedestal, crashing to the ground.

Plates of food and mugs of mead fell from tables and spread across the floor as the denizens of Valhalla were tossed from their seats as if bucked by a horse. Brynhild stumbled backward amid the seismic shock, knocking over a table. The table splintered in half, bringing goblets of mead, platters of fruit, slices of freshly carved ham, a broth of crab and monkfish, and a large bowl of crushed ice and oysters showering down upon her.

Brynhild rose from the wreckage and wiped the traces of broth from her eyes. Her armor was splattered with mead stains and ham, and her wings were covered with grease, broth, and oysters. She spread her wings and took to the air to overlook the chaos.

The earthquake showed no signs of subsiding and was actually growing stronger. Braziers were overturned, plates and silverware slid off the tables, and marble and gold statues crumbled to pieces amid the violent tremors. The shaking was so intense that several gods almost fell off their thrones.

"What's going on?" Thor demanded as he rose unsteadily from his throne. "Are we being attacked?"

"It feels like all of Asgard is being ripped apart," Sif observed.

"It's not just Asgard that's experiencing these tremors," Odin announced from his throne. "The other eight realms are being similarly affected. The entire World Tree is shaking!"

"Why is this happening?" Frigga demanded.

Amidst the chaos, Brynhild heard distinctive croaking. She glanced at the bone-white wooden doors as two ravens dashed through the entrance of Valhalla and perched on Odin's shoulders. Odin cocked his head to the side, listening as his ravens Huginn and Muninn croaked frantically at him, their voices sounding almost human.

"I've just received word from Heimdall," Odin announced. "He says something catastrophic happened to the root of the World Tree in Niflheim. He also reports that Sigurd, Sinfjotli, Magni, and Modi have been fighting a primordial frost giant there."

"Magni and Modi," Thor exclaimed. "Why the fuck are my sons in Niflheim?"

As Thor waited for an explanation, one of his servants, Thjálfi, leaned over to his sister and whispered, "I hope Tanngrisnir and Tanngnjóstr are alright."

"What did you just say, Thjálfi?" Thor demanded. He rose from his throne and made his way to the table. "Why are you worried about my goats?"

"Oh, you didn't know?" Thjálfi blinked innocently. "Lords Magni and Modi took your goats and chariot with them when they went to Svartalfheim to receive their weapons from the dwarves. They told me you permitted them to use your chariot."

"WHAT!" Thor roared.

Thjálfi's sister, Röskva, shook her head and sighed. "You just had to open your big mouth, brother."

A hush fell over Valhalla, making the Hall of Heroes eerily silent amidst the violent tremors. The air crackled and smelled of ozone. Brynhild's ears popped, and a moment later, Thor's entire body erupted with power, and lightning crackled from his eyes.

"Those **IDIOTS**!" Thor bellowed as he brandished Mjolnir. Tendrils of hissing electricity erupted from the mighty giant-slaying hammer, making the feathers on Brynhild's wings tingle and stand up on end.

"I should have known those two numbskulls were behind something this chaotic!" Thor roared. "And they had the audacity to steal *MY* chariot! Unforgivable! I'm going to wring their scrawny necks for this!"

"Calm yourself, my son," Odin cautioned. "Magni and Modi have fought valiantly against the frost giant, but they are not the ones who caused these tremors. The responsibility lies entirely with Sigurd."

Thor's power and anger subsided. He dropped Mjolnir and stared blankly at Odin, utterly shocked by what he had just heard. Then, everyone in Valhalla began mumbling in surprise.

"Sigurd," Sigmund whispered. "My youngest son... caused all this?"

CHAPTER THIRTY-EIGHT

THE FEAST OF THE DEAD

Sharing a meal with the goddess of death wasn't as unsettling as one might imagine. Despite her unnerving appearance and foreboding presence, Hel was a very well-mannered, polite, and courteous guest.

It had been over a century since Baldur and his family had supped with Hel, and he had forgotten her composed demeanor. Though her visage remained as eerie as ever, Hel ate with quiet discipline, never complaining about the food. Her refined table manners were one of the few lessons that Baldur's mother, Frigga, imprinted on Hel during her time in Asgard.

It wasn't enough to assuage the spirits' trepidation, however. The souls Baldur had gathered in the dining pavilion had come to the feast more out of loyalty to him than a desire to dine with the Queen of Helheim. Many stared apprehensively at Hel and the two intimidating servants standing behind her. Ganglati and Ganglot looked like they were about to fall asleep on their feet as they awaited Hel's next command.

Thankfully, the food was good enough to lift everyone's spirits. Tonight, Nanna had prepared suckling pig, perfect roasted fat-stuffed quails with a savory filling, a large baked pike, buttered mushrooms, many salads, and other small delicacies. For dessert, she served pies, pastries, and all the ale they could drink. The spirits eagerly helped themselves to the feast and passed many succulent dishes between the tables. The mouthwatering food and fragrance filled the air with many scents, ironically creating a warm and inviting atmosphere in this cold hell.

Hel seldom left her seat despite having a voracious appetite. Her plate, Hunger, was a magical item that functioned much like a cornucopia. It always stayed supplied with whatever food was placed upon it, so Hel never had to leave the table for more food or ask for seconds. At the start of the feast, she sampled everything Nanna had prepared and then continued eating everything on her plate over twenty times in a row.

Baldur leaned back on his throne, satisfied that this uneasy feast was progressing relatively well. Nanna sat to his right, and Hel sat between him and Hodr on a unique chair her servants had brought from her palace. Signy and Gudrun sat on either end of the table. Hel had insisted they sit at the head table as honored guests, but Nanna had kept them as far from Hel as possible. Gudrun's son, Sigmund, sat beside her, and Signy's daughter, Aurora, sat beside her mother on the other end of the table.

The rest of their children had been seated at a distant table next to Selkirk and his family. It had only been a few hours since Hel had delivered them to the ship, and the boys still harbored intense resentment toward their mothers. Nanna had seated them far away from their mothers to avoid an incident, though still close enough to be treated as honored guests.

Signy's brothers sat at a nearby table, draining an entire barrel of ale. Some were in a drinking competition with Litr to see who could out-drink the dwarf. Unsurprisingly, they were losing one by one. Litr could out-drink anyone on the ship.

Baldur stared at the overcast sky. Earlier, Hel had enchanted the clouds above the ship to depict Sigurd's and Sinfjotli's journey as it unfolded, giving everyone something interesting to watch to pass the time. But she had temporarily suspended the spell to have a proper civilized feast with no "distractions." He wished he could see what Sigurd and Sinfjotli were doing right now. He wondered why they were traveling with Magni and Modi.

Hel stopped eating after an hour. Baldur estimated she had consumed over one hundred and forty-four thousand calories but hadn't gained a single pound. She still looked as slim as ever in her ragged purple dress.

Hel leaned back in her chair and smiled. "That was a fabulous feast, Nanna. Mortals should start worshiping you as the goddess of cooking."

"You flatter me," Nanna said cooly.

Hel didn't seem to notice as she turned to Baldur. "And thank you for bringing everyone together. You're a fabulous host."

"Thank you," Baldur managed.

Hel's eyes narrowed. "You seem troubled, my friend."

"Not troubled. I'm just... perplexed." Baldur gestured to Signy's and Gudrun's children and then to the many crates piled outside Litr's forge. "You returned Gudrun's and Signy's children and brothers, gave Litr a never-ending supply of materials, and enchanted the clouds to entertain us. You went out of your way to make amends with me so that I would share a meal with you. But I cannot fathom why."

Hel's smile faded. For a moment, she looked genuinely hurt. "Do you really have to ask? It's because I consider you my closest friend."

She took a long sip from her drinking horn and leaned back in her chair. "Back in Asgard, you were one of the few people who treated me and my brothers kindly. Unlike Odin, Týr, and Heimdall, you never had ulterior motives. You saw past our appearance and alleged reputations and treated us with genuine kindness. You comforted me when Thor hurled my little brother, Jörmungandr, into the ocean, and you were one of the few Aesir who objected to the decision to bind Fenrir. You even wept when Odin thrust that sword into his mouth. Your compassion touched me, so I've always strived to make your time here in Helheim as comfortable as possible."

"How exactly?" Hodr asked.

"For starters, I was the one who arranged for this ship to be brought to Helheim," Hel replied. "Have I never mentioned that before? I expected you would all get sick of staying in my palace, and I gave you your own place to live. I offered to let you take the city above us as your kingdom even though you opted to remain on this ship. Later, I agreed to let you become a co-ruler of Helheim and receive all the righteous spirits to give you something to pass the time."

"Honestly, even I was saddened when you died, Baldur. I obviously can't let you leave Helheim, but I'll still do everything I can to ensure you're comfortable here."

Baldur was speechless. He had long suspected there was good in Hel, but he never realized she could be so magnanimous. He glanced around the ship and at the many spirits crowded around it. This was possible because he had treated her with kindness and compassion. Anyone who claimed that "no good deed goes unpunished" had never been on Hel's good side.

Baldur wiped a tear from his eye and smiled. "Thank you... my friend."

"Um... excuse me?" a faint voice called.

Everyone in the dining pavilion turned to the end of the high table as Gudrun nervously stood up. "Your Highness..." she began.

"Spare me the honorific titles, darling," Hel interrupted.

"Oh... alright." Gudrun swallowed, steeling her nerves. "I was wondering if you could tell us any news about my husband."

"Your husband?" Hel laughed. "You no longer have any right to call him that, Gudrun. You may not have been formally divorced, but Sigurd no longer harbors any affection for you."

Gudrun scowled. "You're lying!"

"I never lie, dear," Hel assured. "Why should I? Lies are too kind. Truth is often the most harmful thing of all."

"But I *know* Sigurd," Gudrun insisted. "He would never..."

"If you don't believe me, then see for yourself." Hel snapped her fingers. High above, the overcast sky swirled as images appeared in the clouds. Baldur saw Sigurd and Sinfjotli traveling across giant twisting tree roots. But something was wrong. They weren't wearing the same outfits they were in the previous vision Hel had shown them, and there wasn't any trace of snow or ice.

"What's going on?" Baldur questioned. "Aren't they in Niflheim right now?"

"This isn't the present," Hel explained. "What you're seeing happened some time ago, right after they escaped Helheim and parted ways with Brynhild."

"I see." Baldur remained silent and watched Sigurd and Sinfjotli walk across the twisting ash-white roots.

"Do you still love her?" Sinfjotli asked spontaneously.

"Love who?" Sigurd questioned.

"Gudrun," Sinfjotli clarified. "I'm just wondering how you feel now that you learned the truth."

"I'd be lying if I said I didn't harbor feelings for her. But these sentiments can't compare to how I feel about Brynhild. My love for Gudrun is like foliage in a forest. Time will change it just as winter changes the trees. But my love for Brynhild will never fade. It is like the bedrock that the entire forest is planted over."

"So you don't despise Gudrun for tricking you into marrying her, thus making you an oath breaker?" Sinfjotli pressed.

Sigurd looked down at the Andvaranaut and twisted the golden ring on his finger.

"I don't hate her. But I don't think I'll ever be able to forgive her, either. Any love I once had for the Gjukungs died once I learned how they betrayed me."

Sigurd continued speaking, but Hel snapped her fingers, and the vision faded before they could hear the rest of the conversation. Gudrun fell back into her chair as if she had been shot by an arrow. She looked utterly devastated.

Nanna left her seat to comfort her. But as she was halfway across the table, someone called out to Hel in a gruff voice.

Everyone's eyes turned toward Litr as he left Signy's brothers at their table and approached the dais.

"There's something I'd like to know," Litr began. "Sigurd was wearing a magic belt, and Sinfjotli was wearing a magic suit of armor and holding an axe in the vision you showed when you arrived. That was the work of Ivaldi's sons and the Huldra Brothers. I'd recognize the craftsmanship anywhere. How did they get their hands on it? What happened between that vision of Niflheim and the one you just showed us?"

"And while we're on that topic, why are Magni and Modi with them in Niflheim?" Baldur added. "It's been bothering me this whole time."

"Oh, it's quite a tale," Hel assured. "After they escaped Helheim, Sigurd and Sinfjotli journeyed across the roots of Yggdrasil to Niflheim. The brave fools plunged headlong into the icy realm and nearly froze to death. But the Norns saved them and brought them to their cave before they perished. Sigurd drank from the Well of Destiny, and afterward, Sleipnir appeared and took them to Svartalfheim."

"And then the dwarves forged those magical items?" Hodr inferred.

"Hardly." Hel snorted. "They captured the two of them and put Sigurd on trial for murdering Fafnir and Regin." Hel raised a hand. "I know, Litr! 'Fafnir and Regin were disgraces in the eyes of every dwarf,' you are thinking. 'There is no way he'd go that far for his disowned grandsons.' But we all know how much of a stickler Ivaldi is for the ancient laws. Sigurd had murdered his kin and needed to be punished for it. The dwarves imprisoned Sinfjotli and forced Sigurd to work like a slave in their mines for almost two months. But eventually, Sigurd enlisted the help of the Huldra Brothers and found a clever way to outwit Ivaldi."

"How?" Hodr asked.

"He underwent the Trial of Svarblood," Hel answered.

"He did *what*?" Signy screamed.

"The Trial of what now?" Gudrun frowned.

"He became a skinchanger after being eaten alive by a dragon," Hel explained.

Gudrun went pale. Her grief and sorrow subsided and were replaced by fear and horror.

"Why would he *do* such a thing to himself?" Nanna demanded.

Hel shrugged. "I couldn't say. Sigurd told Ivaldi it was to atone for killing Regin, but I don't buy it. I imagine he had ulterior reasons that are known only to him. Regardless, he survived the Trial and cheated death."

Nanna arched an eyebrow. "You sound pleased."

"I am thrilled," Hel said. "I am overjoyed that he passed the Trial and survived. If he had failed, his soul would have been destroyed, and there wouldn't be an afterlife, meaning I couldn't torment him for eternity."

Nanna shot Hel a fierce look.

"Ah... forgive me, Nanna, I forgot how much it irks you when I discuss my work at the dinner table. Anyhow, after the Trial, the dwarves forged the armor and magic items they needed. They then met Magni and Modi, who took them to Niflheim on Thor's stolen chariot. They are currently fighting against my ancestor, Fornjót the Destroyer."

Fornjót the Destroyer? That was a name Baldur hadn't heard in many years. He was an ancient frost giant supposedly on par with Surtr. A wave of concern washed over him. Even Magni and Modi weren't strong enough to stand up to a foe like that.

"How are they faring?" Baldur asked.

"Quite well, actually," Hel said. "Their battle is quite a sight to behold. I will allow you to see it all unfold after I leave this ship. It has been unlike anything I have ever seen in recent years! Even more remarkably, Sigurd transformed into a dragon and is now fighting Fornjót on equal footing."

"What else is happening?" Hodr asked eagerly.

"I won't spoil the surprise," Hel promised. "I'll allow you to see it for yourselves... or in your case, Hodr, have someone else describe it for you. Anyhow, I think I'll take my leave now."

She rose from her seat and snapped her fingers. Ganglati and Ganglot picked up the chair and her magic plate and followed Hel across the deck. But before she could leave the dining pavilion, little Sigmund stood on his chair and called out to her. "Miss Hel, what are you planning to do to my daddy and uncle?" he asked innocently.

Hel paused, turned around, and smiled. This wasn't the warm, friendly smile she had given Baldur earlier; it was much more sinister.

"I am *so* glad you asked, Sigmund," Hel said gleefully. "I won't go into all the gory details since I know how much it bothers Nanna. So I'll show you instead."

Hel snapped her fingers. An emerald fog rolled on deck from the River Gjöll. As the mist dissipated, Baldur noticed something had appeared on deck next to Hel.

The humanoid creature was unlike anything Baldur had seen in Helheim before. Its power and aura were equal to, if not greater than, a draug's, yet the creature looked different from any draug Baldur had seen. Most draugs were between ten and thirty feet tall and could take on various shapes and physiques. But this creature was only around six feet tall and looked very human. It had a very scrawny body and wore a white jacket, black belt, white pants, black socks, and white boots with a longsword hanging from its side. Its light blond hair was styled to one side, with the tips fanning out from his face. The upper half of its face was covered by a tall white mask with three small horns, which seemed to make its eye sockets look hollow.

Three distinctive features stood out about this creature. First, its abdomen was covered in hundreds of stitches, giving the impression that someone had severed the being in half and then reattached its torso to its waist. Second, a sword was fastened to its belt, which Baldur recognized as an elfish blade.

Third, the creature had a bizarre aura. No matter how he studied it, Baldur couldn't sense any emotions or hostility emanating from it. It just felt... vacant and devoid of any feeling.

"What *is* that creature?" Nanna demanded.

"Guttorm!"

All eyes turned to Gudrun as she rose from her seat and stared in horror and disbelief at the creature standing beside Hel.

Baldur stared back and forth between her and the creature. He recalled Guttorm was the name of her youngest brother, who had murdered Sigurd and their son. But this creature didn't resemble Gudrun, especially with the mask.

"Are you sure that... *thing* is your brother?" Nanna asked skeptically.

"Yes." Gudrun nodded. "I'd recognize that sword anywhere." She pointed at the sheathed blade hanging from the creature's waist. "That's Mimung. Sigurd gifted Guttorm that sword on his sixteenth birthday. It's the same sword he used... that fateful night."

As a small wave of despair washed over Gudrun, Hel smiled and turned to the creature. "Guttorm?"

"Ahh?" he responded in drooling syllables.

"Why don't you remove your mask for your sister," Hel suggested. "It's been years since you've seen each other."

Guttorm grabbed his mask and lifted it off his head. Everyone gasped at the hideous sight of his rotting face. His skin was sickly gray and covered in stitches. But it was his eyes that disgusted everyone. They were slit, the pupils were an orangey-red hue, and the sclerae were glassy white. There was something unnerving about those eyes. After a moment, Baldur realized what it was. Guttorm's eyes vaguely reminded him of Sigurd's snake eyes!

Gudrun gulped as she walked away from the high table and stepped off the dais. Her face was awash with emotion as she nervously approached the creature.

"Guttorm?" she called. "Guttorm it's me, Gudrun."

The creature turned toward her. Guttorm looked right at Gudrun, but he didn't *see* her. He didn't see her at all. There wasn't a trace of familial recognition or emotion in his eyes.

"Guttorm, say something!" Gudrun pleaded.

"You're wasting your breath, dear," Hel informed. "He can't talk. I tortured him without mercy until your brother's ego imploded. He no longer has a sense of self. He is now nothing more than a mindless weapon of mass destruction bound to obey my every command."

Gudrun staggered back, her face expressing a flurry of emotions: shock, horror, sadness, disgust, and anger.

"You vile witch!" Gudrun exclaimed. "How could you do this?"

"That's an odd reaction," Hel noted. "Why are you getting so upset? Do you feel pity for your brother? Isn't he the man who murdered your husband and son out of spite and arguably sent your life into a cycle of misery and sin? Don't you feel somewhat satisfied seeing the punishment he's been given?"

Gudrun faltered and bit her lip. She looked back at Guttorm, and another wave of emotions washed over her face.

"Even if I felt satisfied, that doesn't make this right. You took my brother and turned him into this... this thing on a whim!"

"You're mistaken," Hel informed her. "Guttorm *asked* for this."

"What!" Gudrun staggered backward, almost tripping over the steps of the dais. Whispers and murmurs erupted throughout the dining pavilion.

Baldur studied the doltish creature who was now aimlessly looking around the ship. He knew Hel never lied, but he suspected there was more to this story. Who in their right mind would ask to be reduced to this mindless, wretched state?

"W-why on earth would he ask for *this*?" Gudrun demanded.

"You can thank Gunnar and Hagen for that. Your brothers brainwashed Guttorm thoroughly. His hatred and envy of Sigurd persisted even after he died." Hel gestured to the stitching on his abdomen and waist. "Guttorm couldn't stomach the fact that Sigurd had sliced him in half with his last breath or that his body was unceremoniously tossed into a ditch and left to rot amongst putrid sheep carcasses while Sigurd received a grand heroic funeral. Honestly, I didn't give him much thought when I first judged his soul in my palace. I sent him to Niflheim to receive the usual punishment reserved for traitors and murderers and thought nothing of it. But after Sigurd and Sinfjotli escaped Helheim, I recalled his soul back to Helheim on a whim. When I informed Guttorm that Sigurd had escaped Helheim, it broke him. His envy and hatred exploded like an erupting volcano. Guttorm ranted about how unfair it was. He'd endured unspeakable horrors in the Valley of Corpses while Sigurd had escaped the underworld. He cursed Sigurd's name. Guttorm condemned the Aesir for abandoning him and cursed the Norns for weaving him such a pitiful, unremarkable life.

"He then begged me to make him strong and to purge him of all his weaknesses and shortcomings. He beseeched me to give him powerful eyes like Sigurd's, implored me to make him Sigurd's equal in battle, and above all else, he asked me to make him a powerful warrior everyone would fear. I granted his wish, but at a hefty price. I stripped Guttorm of his ego, memory, ability to speak, and all other forms of rationality. A mere tool does not need such things. They would only get in the way. He is now a pure, unthinking, living weapon of mass destruction bound to obey my every command."

"You...!" Gudrun seethed.

"You should be proud of your little brother," Hel insisted. "He's become a capable warrior. He slaughtered over ten thousand draugirs as a penultimate test. For his final test, I had him fight against your second husband, King Atli, whom I had recently turned into a draug. They fought for an entire week before I ordered them to stop after I grew bored. Guttorm couldn't kill Atli or dispatch him the way a valkyrie might. Nevertheless, he mercilessly dominated the fight through sheer brutality. I lost count of how many times Atli begged for mercy. He yielded over a dozen times, but Guttorm didn't relent. He ruthlessly sliced apart his opponent's body no less than two hundred and seventeen times. When it was over, I stripped Atli of his rank and power, banished his soul to the Valley of Corpses, and allowed Guttorm to replace him as a draug."

Hel glanced at the mindless humanoid creature and smiled. "I consider this... thing a prototype of what I intend to turn Sigurd and Sinfjotli into. Of course, I'll have to add many extra steps in their case. They have become exceptionally powerful since they left my realm. Turning them into the perfect living weapons will be *quite* a challenge."

Gudrun scowled and opened her mouth. But before she could speak, Baldur's pet dragon rose from the rafters and roared. Everyone glanced up as Twilight spread his wings and took to the air.

As Twilight soared over the ship, Baldur suddenly felt a cold, sticky liquid splash onto his right hand. He looked down at his drinking horn. The ale sloshed angrily in the horn and spilled over the rim even though he wasn't moving his hand.

A moment later, a tsunami of chaos swept over them as Helheim was struck by a massive earthquake. Spirits screamed in terror as the giant ship rocked violently in the River Gjöll. Silverware and platters of food rolled off the long tables and shattered against the deck. Glaciers and enormous chunks of ice rained down from the Bridge of Judgement above them, creating massive monster waves that rocked the *Hringhorni*. Several skyscrapers in the City of the Lost collapsed, sending clouds of dust and rock into the air. Far to the north, Baldur heard Garm howl in rage and confusion. Even the sky was affected by the chaos. The thick emerald clouds were split in half as if someone had sliced them with a sword.

Baldur and his family got to work restoring order on the ship. Hel stood still in the center of the dining pavilion near Guttorm and her two servants as the chaos unfolded around them. She smiled and stretched her arms toward the heavens.

"Yes! This is the power Sigurd has gained: the power to make the mighty World Tree tremble."

Baldur stopped what he was doing and stared blankly at Hel. "Sigurd did this?"

Hel nodded, then gazed up at the sky and waved her hand. The illusion in the clouds returned, depicting a golden dragon and an enormous frost giant lying amidst towering mountains of humanoid bodies.

"I eagerly await the day you fail, Sigurd. I have *so* many ideas for what I intend to do to you and your brother. You'll get subjected to all the suffering in this world until your egos shatter and then rebuild you in my image. But until that time comes, continue struggling. It'll make my inevitable victory so much more satisfying."

CHAPTER THIRTY-NINE

HEL'S SWORN ENEMIES

Sinfjotli would never forget the moment Sigurd crashed into the World Tree. Through dark clouds, Sinfjotli sensed something from above him, approaching with unfathomable speed. Looking up, he saw a mass of light in the distance that looked like a gigantic heated rock through the gloom. But Sinfjotli knew what it was.

The falling giant and dragon slashed through the northern sky like a comet and struck the root of Yggdrasil. The ground vibrated beneath their feet like a flag rippling in the wind as a thunderous roar echoed around them. The massive shockwave flattened everything it touched as it sped toward them.

Sensing the encroaching danger, Sinfjotli turned into a wolf for the third and final time. He didn't flee, knowing it was futile. Instead, he stood over Magni and Modi and used his body and armor to shield them from the incoming chaos.

Everything turned dark as the shockwave hurled him into a churning mass of snow and ice. The freezing debris swept over him and pressed down like he had been immersed in concrete. The pressure was so great he couldn't move his paw. He couldn't see or hear anything, either, but still, he held firm, intent on protecting his comrades—he could breathe. That could only mean that Magni and Modi were still alive and transmuting the surrounding snow into breathable air.

A minute later, he noticed a flicker of light shining through the snow beneath him and realized it was Magni's light crystal.

"You two okay?" Sinfjotli called out, his mouth being the only part of his body he could move.

"I've been better," a faint voice replied. From the sounds of pain, Sinfjotli figured it must have been Modi.

"Hang on; I'll get us out of here," Magni echoed.

Sinfjotli sensed energy building up beneath his abdomen where his comrades were. A loud crashing sound came from above, and Sinfjotli was suddenly enveloped by a flash of light.

When he opened his eyes, Sinfjotli discovered himself over Magni and Modi at the bottom of an enormous sizzling crater. Magni had used his power to call down a gigantic lightning bolt from the sky. The column of lightning did not affect the two gods and Sinfjotli, thanks to his armor, but it vaporized all the snow and ice, freeing them from their icy tomb.

Now that they could move freely, they scaled the crater, climbing to the surface. When they reached the crater's rim, Sinfjotli turned back into a human. As he finished shifting, the clouds of snow and dirt thrown up by the shockwave began falling back to earth. The dust slowly settled, revealing a changed landscape.

The titanic battle with Fornjót had already reshaped and altered the Niflheim's landscape. But the devastation before them now made all that earlier destruction seem like child's play. Niflheim's cloud cover has been completely blown away by the blast. The ground itself had been ripped open by massive fissures, wide enough to rival the canyons of Midgard. The violent tremors that shook the earth had been so intense that the surviving mountains in The Spines all the ice spikes that Fornjót had erected had been utterly uprooted, leaving nothing but a barren wasteland in their wake.

As Sinfjotli's eyes drank in the cataclysmic destruction, he noticed the eerie and surreal silence that had descended on the realm. There was no howling wind or roaring avalanches. Niflheim was dead quiet. Sinfjotli had never heard anything so silent before.

He sat on the ground and gazed up at the bisected sky. The dim sun and stars were barely visible through the thick, parted clouds. But it was so beautiful.

This is such a strange feeling, Sinfjotli reflected. There were no flowers, grass, or fauna on this desolate plain. He had just fought the most titanic and widespread battle of his life and was surrounded by apocalyptic destruction. So why did Sinfjotli feel so integrated and at peace with nature?

"Holy shit," Magni muttered, shaking his head. "You two are just as strong and dangerous as Grandfather promised."

"Odin *anticipated* something like this would happen because of us?" Sinfjotli asked.

"That's right." Modi nodded. "Long ago, our grandfather told us: 'Somewhere in Midgard, there's this family descended from your uncle Sigi that carries the name "Volsung." Someday, they shall be Hel's sworn enemies.' I didn't believe a word of it then. But after seeing you two in action and how you fight, I think there may be some credibility to that claim."

Sinfjotli wasn't sure how to feel about that. It was flattering being touted as 'Hel's sworn enemies,' but it also reminded him of the gravity of this journey and what would happen if they failed to reach Valhalla. Helheim wouldn't be merciful toward its queen's enemies.

Sinfjotli shook his head. He could worry about the implications of Modi's claim later. For now, they had to focus on finding Sigurd.

"At least we know his location." Sinfjotli stood and pointed north, where an enormous shadow extended across the northern horizon. Even from this distance, Sinfjotli could easily discern that it was the root of Yggdrasil because of its sheer size and the many tertiary roots sprouting from it.

As he stared at the tree root, several objects fell from the sky. Sinfjotli looked up and saw dozens of snowflakes.

"It's snowing again," Sinfjotli muttered. Ever since he'd woken up, Fornjót had forced the eternal blizzards of Niflheim to cease so he could see better. But snowflakes were raining down again, and the thick mist was returning.

"If it's snowing again, does that mean something happened to Fornjót?" Sinfjotli asked. "Is he dead?"

Magni reached toward the heavens, and a moment later, a white bolt of lightning zapped his fist.

"Not quite," Magni reported. "Something powerful still holds the heavens in its thrall. Fornjót's alive, but he's becoming weaker by the second. His control over the sky is slipping. It's like torrents of water breaking through a crumbling dam."

"That's not the case, brother." Modi raised his arm toward the heavens. "Fornjót's control of the sky is intermittently increasing and decreasing. It's like he's getting stronger and then weaker all at once."

"You lost me," Sinfjotli said.

"To continue with my 'cracks in the dam' analogy, one moment the cracks seal themselves shut, then they open even larger than before, and then shut again." Magni furrowed his bleeding brow. "Just what the hell is going on?"

"Not sure, but we should hurry," Modi suggested. "There's no time to lose."

Magni whistled, summoning the goat chariot. They hopped on and started racing north to where the root of Yggdrasil connected with the earth.

As they followed the root north, Sinfjotli looked around at all the devastation the earthquake caused. Niflheim was a complete mess. Mountains had been uprooted and smashed to rubble. Giant fissures the size of canyons had emerged in the ground, and the thick atmosphere above them was distorted, allowing daylight to shine through.

"Such devastation," Magni muttered. "I can't believe he actually damaged Yggdrasil's root."

"The Guardians of Yggdrasil will be furious." Modi grimaced. "I hope we never see them."

Sinfjotli furrowed his brow. "Wait, you mean this happened because Sigurd hit the root of the World Tree? I don't see how that alone would cause all this devastation."

"That's because you don't understand or appreciate just how important Yggdrasil is," Modi said. "The Nine Realms could not exist or maintain their forms without the World Tree anchoring everything in place. Nobody knows when or how the tree came to be. But our grandfather claims the tree was old even when Ymir was still suckling on Auðumbla's udders. Each of the Nine Realms exists among the tree's branches and roots, with the tree itself existing in Utgard, the realm between realms. Its roots extend into the underworld and the two primordial realms, the trunk passes through Midgard, and its branches extend high into the heavens. The tree maintains the stability of the Nine Realms and also nourishes and provides sustenance to all life. For example, the root here in Niflheim collects and detoxifies the water from the Well of Destiny and the other eleven rivers. Then, it transports it to other realms where it becomes the source of all valleys and rivers."

"You lost me again," Sinfjotli warned.

"We're trying to explain that the tree's very existence supports all creation," Magni clarified. "Subsequently, there are serious repercussions to damaging it." He gestured to all the rubble and devastation.

"This destruction happens more often than you might think," Modi added. "There are many creatures that affect the World Tree's health. One of Asgard's duties is to keep the most dangerous parasites in check and minimize the damage they inflict upon the World Tree."

Modi paused. "However, there is one creature in particular that we simply cannot contain or stop. The most terrifying, powerful, and destructive creature lives in the Nine Realms."

He gulped and took a deep breath. "Nidhogg, the dragon of the apocalypse. When that... *thing* isn't busy feasting on corpses, it gnaws the root here in Niflheim. Every time Nidhogg bites the root, it triggers a terrible calamity somewhere in the realms."

"According to Grandfather, when Nidhogg gnaws through the root, Ragnarök will begin in earnest," Magni added. "The devastation and tremors we just experienced are *nothing* compared to what will happen at Ragnarök once that monster finishes gnawing."

Sinfjotli looked around at the devastated landscape and the tattered clouds above them. All this cataclysmic destruction occurred because Sigurd had slammed Fornjót into Yggdrasil's root. Yet, according to the Sons of Thor, this was nothing compared to what would one day unfold at Ragnarök. It was hard to envision. But it demonstrated how dangerous Nidhogg was and how much peril Sigurd was in.

He frowned as he mulled over everything Magni and Modi had told him, realizing something was awry. "Hang on. You mentioned that Nidhogg feasts on corpses. How is that possible? It sounds like it's filled with millions of corpses, but I thought only the strongest lifeforms could survive in Niflheim. How could so many bodies be piled together in one place with just one creature scavenging them?"

"You'll understand when we arrive," Modi promised grimly.

They refused to say anything else on the matter and continued driving Tanngrisnir and Tanngnjóstr in silence. Sinfjotli looked around at the devastation the earthquake had caused. It was likely Sigurd had landed in the middle of Nidhogg's lair and was now at the horrid creature's mercy.

He tried not to think about that. He tried to distract himself somehow. Sinfjotli glanced at Modi. The god of courage clutched his bleeding side as he whipped the reins.

"You should take it easy," Sinfjotli warned. "That wound—"

"It's nothing," Modi interrupted. "We should be more worried about Sigurd."

"He's right," Magni said. "I imagine the Uruz rune has worn off and taken its toll by now."

Sinfjotli's eyes widened. "That's right! You claimed the healing rune has a substantial cost, right?"

"I wouldn't call it a healing rune," Magni scoffed. "The Uruz rune represents resurrection and endurance. Think of it like taking a shot of energy to the heart. It'll revitalize someone who's completely exhausted, allow them to keep fighting, and increase their strength, allowing them to achieve unattainable heights. But it *doesn't* heal their wounds. The rune draws out all of someone's strength down to the last inch of their life. It also exerts an unfathomable strain on their body, although they remain numb to it while the brand remains active. But once it wears off, their body will suffer an ungodly backlash as all the damage they suffered before returns hundreds of times worse!"

Sinfjotli gulped. Sigurd had been electrocuted several times by Kári, punched into a canyon by Fornjót, and bombarded by countless meteorites during Fornjót's hailstorm of death. The dragon couldn't fly properly after getting swatted by the frost giant. Magni had claimed that one more hit from Fornjót would kill him. If those wounds got exponentially worse, Sigurd's body would break apart into a pile of flesh and broken bones. Could he even survive...?

"Don't dwell on it!" Modi snapped as if reading his thoughts. "Let's just hope Fornjót is finally dead and we make it in time."

He and Magni whipped the reins, and Tanngrisnir and Tanngnjóstr bolted even faster.

Sigurd, please be alright, Sinfjotli prayed. *Don't die on us!*

Chapter Forty

Beyond the Threshold of Agony

Darkness veiled Sigurd's vision. His head throbbed fiercely. Distantly, he could hear the wind echoing and a deep, bone-rattling noise filling the area. Something putrid drifted up his nostrils, making him want to gag, and there was a vague sensation of something cold landing across his body.

Above all else, there was pain. Every blurry shred of light his eyes could discern when he tried opening them sent sharp needles lacing through his brain. Slowly, the scattered threads of his consciousness sluggishly wove together, oozing like molasses. But as his consciousness slowly returned, the pain intensified.

When he finally opened his eyes fully, the first thing Sigurd saw was a humanoid corpse staring down at him with glassy-white eyes like pearls. The cadaver was in a horribly grotesque condition. Its entrails fell out a festering wound on its abdomen and dangled over Sigurd's head like black vines. The corpse had a hole in its head big enough for Sigurd to see its brains. The body was so emaciated and decayed Sigurd couldn't tell if it had been a man or woman. But he was certain it had once been human.

Sigurd felt like his muscles and bones had melted as he could not summon any strength at all. His head throbbed fiercely. Every noise was like a hammer blow to his skull. Even the simple act of breathing was a struggle.

He tried his best to survey his surroundings. Many other human corpses were lying naked and stacked on top of one another, with green and rotted flesh sloughing off their bones. Sigurd gradually realized he was lying on a massive pile of humanoid corpses. As he gagged from the putrid smell of puss, rancid meat, and decay, Sigurd noticed that his own body stank of sweat, sulfur, and blood.

When Sigurd got over the horror of his macabre surroundings, he continued looking around. He was lying on the slope of a mountain composed entirely of corpses. Hundreds of other mountains of stacked corpses towered in the distance. Some mountains were over two miles in height. It appeared he was lying in the center of a uniquely shaped crater on the mountain slope, but he couldn't tell what the shape looked like while lying on his back.

Above him was a giant ash-white tree root extending upward into the sky. It had to be part of Yggdrasil's root that he had traveled on with Sinfjotli, Magni, and Modi earlier. But it looked severely damaged. Many of the large tertiary roots had snapped in half, and deep puncture marks riddled the bark as if something with long sharp teeth had repeatedly bitten into it.

Niflheim's thick fog had dispersed, and the heavens above had split open. Sigurd could clearly see the sun through the gap in the clouds, but it was too far away to give off any warmth.

He tried to sit up to get a better look, but his body didn't respond to his brain's commands. His whole body was paralyzed. Half a heartbeat later, his entire body exploded in unfathomable pain.

It felt like every bone in his body was broken. A sharp pain erupted from his sides with every ragged breath. He could feel his body literally falling apart from the inside. His muscles tore and ruptured, and the bones beneath them broke apart amidst the spasms. Sigurd wanted to scream out, but his mouth wouldn't open. His jaw was probably broken. Frankly, it was a miracle he could breathe in this crippled state while being racked by ungodly pain.

The worst part was that Sigurd couldn't escape into blissful unconsciousness. The searing pain raced throughout his body like volts of electricity, keeping him wide awake and heightening all his senses, forcing him to live through each nightmarishly painful moment.

He could still move his eyes. As wave after wave of unfathomable pain washed over him, Sigurd used his superhuman vision to peer as far away as he could. About a mile away, he saw Fornjót the Destroyer lying face down near the base of one mountain of corpses. Fornjót's body was twisted and bloody. There were deep puncture wounds to his shoulders and back, as if a ferocious beast had sunk its claws deep into his flesh. From what Sigurd could infer, the giant had fallen face-first into the valley from an extremely high altitude and left a massive, bloody, human-shaped indentation in the gorge.

Sigurd had no clue how he or Fornjót had arrived at such a ghastly place. The last thing he remembered was being electrocuted by Kári and then getting punched by Fornjót. Did that punch send him crash-landing into this putrid place? If so, why was Fornjót here as well, and lying broken on the ground? Had Magni and Modi somehow incapacitated the giant and sent him flying? Thankfully, it looked like the primordial giant was finally dead.

Suddenly, the mountain beneath him rumbled. In the distance, steam began emitting from the giant's body as it lifted its arms off the ground.

Are you kidding me? Sigurd thought. *What does it take to kill this monster?*

Fornjót lifted his head and torso off the ground, leaning on his arms. When the giant looked up, Sigurd nearly gagged at the hideous state of his face. Fornjót's nose, lips, front teeth, and the tip of his tongue were gone, and parts of his brain were exposed. Based on the injuries, Sigurd inferred that most of his face had been destroyed through some form of friction. Only his right eye remained intact, and it was full of hate.

Fornjót started crawling toward Sigurd. The fall and impact broke his back and paralyzed his lower body, making him rely solely on his arms to move. However, it looked like his body was repairing itself. Sigurd watched in horror and disgust as Fornjót's left eye, forehead, nose, teeth, and entire face regenerated.

By the time Fornjót reached the mountain that Sigurd was lying helplessly on, the giant's body had healed enough for him to stand up on his knees. The giant towered over Sigurd and the mountain of corpses with a murderous look in his eyes. He raised his right hand high above his head in a clenched fist.

"I very nearly died just now, you bastard." Fornjót laughed weakly. "But this is the end. We're still in Niflheim, so all the damage you inflicted upon me will soon heal. But as a show of respect for putting up such a remarkable fight, I'll finish you here and..."

He never finished his threat, nor did he have time to scream. Something serpent-like and large enough to bloat out the sky shot out from beneath the root of the Yggdrasil and closed its jaws around the mighty frost giant's head. Sigurd heard Fornjót's muffled, terrified screams as the giant desperately clawed his hands against the fields of corpses as the mysterious creature dragged its prey away beneath the root.

At that point, the pain from Sigurd's injuries completely overwhelmed him. His eyes rolled into the back of his head, and he slipped back into blissful unconsciousness.

CHAPTER FORTY-ONE

THE VALLEY OF CORPSES

"Here we are," Modi announced grimly. "Welcome to the Valley of Corpses."

They stood on the edge of a steep cliff overlooking a deep canyon filled with billions of corpses. The root of the World Tree branched down from the sky and burrowed deep into the center of this putrid gorge. Mountains of corpses towered around it in randomly sized mounds.

"There are so many!" Sinfjotli gagged. Physiologically, Sinfjotli was a wolf, and his sense of smell was a hundred times stronger than a human's. But right now, he wished that wasn't the case as the nauseating odor of billions of mounds of decaying flesh mixed with the cold, musty air of the canyon filled his nostrils. He had smelled the rancid stench of the corpses long before they arrived at the valley, but now that they were up close, it took every ounce of willpower to keep himself from vomiting.

Sinfjotli tried to distract himself from the putrid stench by studying his surroundings. The canyon stretched so far that he doubted even Sigurd could see the other side with his telescopic vision. In the center of the canyon was the root of Yggdrasil. One end of the tree root burrowed deep into the center of the canyon, while the other extended up into the clouds of Niflheim.

A sizeable green river flowed through the canyon somewhere below the shadow of the titanic tree root. Glaciers filled with frozen corpses hugged the sides of the river, occasionally breaking apart. Icebergs floated eerily across its glowing green waters. If Sinfjotli squinted, he could see swords and other weapons flowing beneath the water's surface.

Sinfjotli gulped as memories of Hel's undead army flashed through his mind. He thought about the massive undead army Garm had summoned from the shores of Náströnd. Sinfjotli glanced at the billions of corpses strewn about the canyon and wondered what would happen if they all sprang to life and attacked them.

"Don't worry, these are just corpses," Modi said as if reading his mind.

"*Actual* corpses," Magni stressed. "These won't try to attack you. They can't move."

Sinfjotli stared at the god of strength. His words didn't sound very reassuring, but they reminded Sinfjotli he wasn't alone. Even if these corpses could spring to life, Sinfjotli had nothing to fear. Last time, he and Sigurd had fought Hel's undead army with the aid of a valkyrie. He had been practically naked throughout that long battle and had to keep using the draugirs' weapons. But now he had a suit of magical armor and the gods of strength and courage at his back. Those corpses would pose no threat to him. Sinfjotli took a deep breath and resumed scanning the valley.

He noticed odd markings on the canyon walls. The canyon reminded him of a gigantic crater from a meteorite. But as Sinfjotli studied the circular walls, he realized a meteorite couldn't have created this vast depression. The walls were sheer, smooth, and straight. It looked like someone had magically ripped out a massive chunk of the land and left this enormous smooth crater behind.

That jostled Sinfjotli's memory. "Baldur once mentioned Helheim and Niflheim were a single realm before Hel split it in half," he recalled aloud. "Could this be...?"

"Yes." Modi nodded. "This place is where Hel split Niflheim in half and fashioned her own separate realm from the pieces she took."

"Subsequently, because they were once one realm, Niflheim and Helheim are connected in a manner that transcends space," Modi added.

"Is that why there are so many corpses here?" Sinfjotli asked.

"Aye." Magni nodded grimly. "When someone perishes in a dishonorable death, their souls are sent to Helheim. Meanwhile, their bodies are cast down here to the Valley of Corpses. Their weapons are also cast into the Slidr, the green river running through the valley. When Nidhogg gets bored of gnawing at the root of Yggdrasil, he takes breaks to feast upon the mountains of corpses."

The dragon must never go hungry then, Sinfjotli thought. *There are billions of corpses here.*

As he gazed at the towering mountains of corpses, Sinfjotli felt overwhelmed and worried. He anticipated they'd need to locate Sigurd amidst some valley or mountain range. He hadn't expected to find this massive canyon of the dead when they arrived at the root of Yggdrasil. It presented quite an interesting problem.

"We shouldn't linger here longer than necessary," Magni urged. "Let's grab Sigurd and skedaddle before that monster finds us."

"We'll have to locate him first," Modi reminded him. "So, what's your plan, Sinfjotli? How are we supposed to find Sigurd? It'll be like searching for a diamond in an ice storm."

It wouldn't be easy, but thankfully, Sinfjotli had already prepared for this kind of situation. Without saying a word, he held out his right hand and scanned the valley. After a few moments, Wolfsbane boomeranged into his hand.

"He's over there." Sinfjotli pointed northeast toward the tallest mountain of corpses from where the axe had come.

"Then let's get moving," Modi said as he seized the reins of the chariot.

Unfortunately, Tanngrisnir and Tanngnjóstr refused to go on. The mighty goats had ridden through the darkness of Niflheim and bravely assisted them during their fight against Fornjót. But they outright refused to enter the rotten vale. Sinfjotli could tell from the fearful look in their eyes that they sensed danger. That wasn't a good sign. It was yet another reminder of the terrible ravenous beast that called this rotten valley its home.

Magni and Modi decided to reach the mountain on foot. They gathered some supplies from the chariot and sent Tanngrisnir and Tanngnjóstr away. Once they were gone, Magni wrapped an arm around Sinfjotli's waist while Modi carried their supplies. He and Modi then leaped from the cliff into the canyon. They then hopped across the mountains of corpses like frogs across lily pads, covering great distances with every jump.

This valley was already the stuff of nightmares. But Sinfjotli soon found another reason to fear this morbid place. As they made their way northeast toward the root of Yggdrasil, they landed at the summit of a mountain of corpses. As Magni and Modi scanned the valley and debated where they'd jump next, Sinfjotli made the mistake of looking down at the bodies beneath their feet. He had noticed that every corpse in this valley was missing its finger and toenails, almost like someone had deliberately removed them. As he studied the putrid fingers and toes, he noticed the eyes of some of the more recent corpses move and glance up at them.

"By the gods!" Sinfjotli exclaimed.

"Yes?" Magni and Modi both responded, leaving Sinfjotli confused until he recalled they were both Aesir.

"Those corpses looked at me!" Sinfjotli screamed. "Their eyeballs moved and looked *right* at us!"

Magni and Modi glanced down and grimaced. They hurriedly jumped to the next mountain.

"What the fuck is going on?" Sinfjotli demanded as they sailed through the air. "You said this is a valley of *corpses*. But some of these bodies are still alive!"

"Not exactly," Modi replied as they springboarded from another mountaintop. "Normally, this place is just a dumping ground for the bodies of the dishonorable dead. But this place is also used by Hel for a special punishment reserved for those guilty of adultery, murder, treason, and oath-breaking. The souls found guilty of those crimes are banished to this valley, where they remain trapped inside their own corpses, unable to move as Nidhogg feasts upon them. The entire time, they remain conscious of everything."

"That's horrible!" Sinfjotli grimaced. He gazed around and wondered if his mother had been here at some point. She had committed many wicked deeds that would justify being sent here. Had she been trapped inside her own body, waiting for Nidhogg to devour her?

"Don't dwell on it," Magni warned, as if reading Sinfjotli's mind. "Time is of the essence right now. We need to find your brother quickly."

They continued moving and finally reached the tallest mountain in the valley, which was fifteen thousand feet tall. Standing on the summit, they noticed a massive humanoid-shaped indentation around the mountain's base. They deduced this was most likely where Fornjót had crash-landed. Judging from the handprints and drag marks in the mounds of crushed corpses, it looked like Fornjót had crawled toward this mountain but suddenly got dragged away by something.

As Sinfjotli studied the drag marks, he noticed something glimmering on a ridge about two hundred feet below the summit. He peered down the slope and glimpsed golden armor amongst the corpses.

"He's down there!" Sinfjotli scrambled down the slopes of dead bodies while Magni and Modi followed. They reached the spot and found Sigurd sprawled in the center of an enormous fleshy crater. From the distinct shape of the depression, Sigurd had crash-landed into the mountain as a dragon and then shapeshifted back into a human.

Sinfjotli was relieved that his brother was still in one piece and hadn't been buried alive beneath an avalanche of dead bodies. But his joy turned into appalling horror when he saw the extent of Sigurd's injuries.

Sigurd's body lay twisted and mangled, his golden armor severely damaged in several places from Fornjót's earlier blow. His bruised skin had taken on a pale, bluish hue, and in several places, bones jutted grotesquely through torn flesh. Though his chest still rose and fell, each breath was ragged and weak. He was barely clinging to life.

Magni and Modi kneeled and gently lifted Sigurd's body out of the crater. They quickly crafted some makeshift splits from the materials they had brought from the chariot and fastened them to Sigurd's limbs while ensuring his head remained facing up.

"He's got at least thirty broken bones, including a fractured jaw and several broken ribs," Magni reported. "He might have a punctured lung and several other internal injuries. And because of the Uruz's side effects, he's probably in more pain than we can imagine. He's in dire need of healing."

"Then let's hurry and head back to the goats," Sinfjotli suggested.

"We can't leave." Modi shook his head. "Sigurd's body is too fragile right now. He wouldn't be able to handle the stress as we jump across all these mountains of corpses. We'll have to heal him here."

"Can you heal him?" Sinfjotli asked skeptically. "I mean, is it even possible?"

"*I* can't, but hopefully, this will." Magni reached into his pocket, pulled out a large golden apple, and handed it to Sinfjotli. He felt a familiar tingle as he ran his fingers over the fruit.

"Feed this to Sigurd," Magni instructed. "It's an Apple of Idun we brought from Asgard."

"You had this with you the entire time?" Sinfjotli exploded in outrage. "You kept devouring poor Tanngrisnir and Tanngnjóstr when you could have just eaten this to satiate your ravenous hunger?"

"We were saving it in case of emergency," Magni explained. "In hindsight, it was the right call. Sigurd needs it more than any of us right now."

Sinfjotli gnashed his teeth but didn't argue further, knowing that time was of the essence. Since Sigurd was unconscious and barely able to move his mouth, Sinfjotli used his axe to dice the apple into tiny thin slices small enough to swallow and carefully fed each piece to his brother. After ingesting a few pieces, color returned to Sigurd's skin, and his breathing strengthened. His eyes opened and blinked furiously before focusing on Sinfjotli's face.

"Bro... ther?" Sigurd croaked weakly.

"I'm here, Sigurd," Sinfjotli assured.

Sigurd peered around and realized that his arms, legs, and neck were tied in splints, preventing him from moving. His eyes darted around, taking in his surroundings. Shock and horror washed over his face as he beheld all the corpses strewn around them.

"W-where?" Sigurd lisped weakly.

"It's complicated," Sinfjotli said. "Don't talk. You're critically injured. You need to eat this. It'll heal you."

Sigurd blinked in surprise. His eyes narrowed as he noticed the golden apple slices in Sinfjotli's hand. The gleam of the fruit's skin told him everything he needed to know. Sigurd cracked his mouth open with great difficulty, making it easier for Sinfjotli to place each piece in his mouth.

When Sigurd had finished, he leaned his head back and took a deep, laborious breath.

"Will he be alright?" Sinfjotli asked.

"For now." Magni nodded. "The apple will function as a pain killer as it heals his wounds. But it'll take quite some time to recover, given the extent of his injuries."

"Rn," Sigurd lisped suddenly.

"What?" Sinfjotli asked.

"Rn. Hs **hre**," Sigurd croaked a little louder.

"What's he muttering?" Modi asked.

"I think he said, 'Run. He's here,'" Sinfjotli guessed.

Magni stood up and scanned the putrid landscape. "What happened to the frost giant? I don't see Fornjót anywhere."

"… ate… him," Sigurd lisped out.

Modi's eyes widened. "Are you saying you devoured him?"

Sigurd stared at him with a confused look. He shook his head slightly.

"The… dragon… under… the… tree… root," he croaked.

They turned toward the root of Yggdrasil. The colossal root burrowed into the center of the valley, casting a long, dark shadow as it extended upward into the sky. Hundreds of secondary and tertiary roots branched out from the primary root and burrowed deep into the corpse valley. They looked like long, bony fingers reaching out to grasp the corpses. They reminded Sinfjotli of branches in a bird's nest.

Sinfjotli noticed movement beneath the root, and he glanced at the shifting shadow. His heart skipped a beat, and his blood ran cold as he beheld the gargantuan monster nesting beneath the tree root.

Sinfjotli thought he would never see a more enormous creature than Fornjót the Destroyer. He was dead wrong. The creature lying beneath the root of Yggdrasil was big enough to make Fornjót look like a child and Sigurd's dragon form seem like a hatchling. His scales were jet black, making it difficult to see him beneath the shadow of the tree root. But there was no camouflaging his enormous bulk. His serpentine body was long enough to coil around the tree root if he desired, and his crocodilian jaws were big enough to envelop half of the root of Yggdrasil in his gaping mouth. He had giant bat-like wings furled at his sides, and piercing twisted horns erupted from his head. He also had enormous reptilian yellow eyes that resembled Sigurd's, but his pupils were far more malevolent and unnerving. The massive claws on his arm-like forelegs, which could scar Yggdrasil's root, sank deep into the Fornjót's flesh.

Fornjót's head had vanished into the darkness of Nidhogg's gullet, yet the frost giant still lived—his limbs flailing, struggling in vain. If he listened closely, Sinfjotli could hear Fornjót's muffled screams from within the dragon's throat. Niflheim had healed all the damage he, Sigurd, Magni, and Modi had inflicted. But Fornjót's impressive healing factor couldn't save him now he was in the jaws of Nidhogg. It was merely prolonging his agony.

Sinfjotli, Magni, and Modi watched in horror as Nidhogg cruelly swung the giant's body back and forth like a rag doll. Sometimes, the dragon would tear off the giant's limbs and wait until its body finished regenerating. Eventually, the dragon grew bored of playing with its food and chomped its enormous jaws down on Fornjót's neck, killing the mighty frost giant. As the giant's body went limp, Nidhogg began devouring its prey. Although thousands of serrated teeth lined his mouth, Nidhogg didn't bother chewing or ripping the giant into smaller pieces. Instead, he swallowed Fornjót's body whole, like a snake when it eats large prey. Sinfjotli watched as all traces of Fornjót the Destroyer vanished.

The word *terrified* did not even begin to describe how they all felt as they watched the macabre sight unfold before them. Fornjót had been the largest and most powerful foe they had ever faced, yet Nidhogg had effortlessly devoured him.

Unfortunately, their nightmare wasn't over. Nidhogg poked his snout from beneath Yggdrasil's root. The dragon sniffed the air and flicked his forked tongue. "I smell warm living blood," the dragon hissed. "Odin's blood!"

The full import of that statement took several moments to be fully realized by Sinfjotli's already strained mind. When it did, icy terror gripped his heart.

"Oh shit," Sinfjotli whispered. "He's coming for us now! I really didn't think this plan through!"

They might have eliminated Fornjót the Destroyer, but now they faced an even worse threat—one they had absolutely no chance of defeating.

CHAPTER FORTY-TWO

PLEASE DON'T EAT THE MESSENGERS!

Nidhogg emerged from the shadow of the colossal root and scanned the Valley of Corpses, twisting his long serpentine neck through the mountains of corpses like a snake.

Thinking fast, Sinfjotli, Magni, and Modi tried playing dead and hiding in plain sight amongst the other corpses that surrounded them. To help camouflage himself, Sinfjotli ordered the Coffin Cheater to take on the appearance of a corpse. This desperate strategy kept Nidhogg from finding them right away, but it only delayed the inevitable.

"Is there anything we can do?" Sinfjotli whispered as they crouched amongst the corpses.

"Against him?" Magni asked nervously. "Nothing. There's not a single damn thing we could do to hurt that *thing*. Even our father with Mjolnir in hand, or Freyr with his magic sword, or our grandfather with Gungnir could do little else but annoy it. That dragon is prophesied to be the only living creature guaranteed to survive the destruction of Ragnarök. What would we be able to do to hurt a creature that powerful?"

The fear in Magni's voice was palpable. That even the god of courage feared Nidhogg was a testament to how dangerous the dragon was. All they could do was continue camouflaging themselves amongst the corpses as the dragon scanned the valley, searching for them.

"It's pointless to hide from me because I can smell your blood!" Nidhogg warned. Judging from the stench of the dragon's putrid breath and booming voice, Sinfjotli figured they had only a few moments before the dragon found them.

Sigurd stirred next to him and coughed weakly. "Bro... ther?" he lisped.

"Hold still Sigurd," Sinfjotli warned. "If that *thing* finds us, we're dead."

"Li... listen!" Sigurd struggled to say more—his jaw hadn't completely healed yet, and he struggled to form complete words. Sinfjotli pressed his ear to his brother's mouth and listened intently. The only word Sinfjotli could make out was "messenger."

Before Sinfjotli could process what that meant, they were suddenly blanketed by a gigantic shadow.

"Ah! There you are!" Nidhogg swiped his claw at the base of the mountain of corpses, triggering an avalanche of dead bodies that exposed their hiding spot and sent them all tumbling down the slopes. When the avalanche of corpses stopped, Sinfjotli nervously looked up and found the dragon of the apocalypse looming over him.

Nidhogg was even more terrifying up close. His colossal maw was filled with thousands of rows of serrated teeth like a shark's mouth. Sinfjotli could see dozens of corpses and severed limbs lodged between the dragon's teeth like plaque, and his eyes burned like molten fire.

There was no point in running. Nidhogg could swallow the entire mountain of corpses they were standing on if he wanted to. His crocodilian-shaped head was just that absurdly big. Sinfjotli wondered what would happen if he died here. Would he and Sigurd get sent back to Helheim to be tormented? Or would they remain trapped inside this dragon's stomach for all time?

Nidhogg loomed in closer and sniffed the air. When he exhaled, Sinfjotli nearly vomited from the fetid stench that overwhelmed his nose. Nidhogg's breath was the most putrid, sickening odor Sinfjotli had ever smelled, and the dragon's scorching breath was hot enough to blister Magni's and Modi's skin.

"I see," Nidhogg observed, flicking his forked tongue. "Thor's sons and two of Odin's descendants stand before me. Perfect! Your warm blood will remove the chilly aftertaste that frost giant left in my mouth. It's been so long since I tasted the warm blood of the living!"

Nidhogg reared back. His long serpentine neck bent like an archer's bow. A mighty shadow enveloped the ridge they were standing on as Nidhogg unhinged his jaw and opened his mouth impossibly wide.

Terror gripped Sinfjotli's heart. The dragon was going to envelop the entire hill they were standing on in his massive jaws, and there was nothing they could do to stop it!

...Or was there? Sinfjotli still didn't know what Sigurd was trying to relay earlier. But one word Sigurd kept repeating gave him a flicker of hope: "Messenger." It was worth a shot.

As Nidhogg lunged toward them, Sinfjotli screamed, "Nidhogg, please stop! We're not food or sacrifices! We're messengers!"

Nidhogg stopped at the last moment. He closed his jaw and stared at them.

"Messengers?" Nidhogg repeated.

"Th-that's right!" Magni exclaimed. "We come bearing a message from Gullinkambi!"

Sinfjotli didn't know who or what Magni was talking about. But Nidhogg did. The dragon narrowed his eyes at the mention of the name Gullinkambi. He leaned closer to better inspect the two gods and mortals. His snout hovered about twenty feet above their heads.

In the smoldering pits of Nidhogg's eyes, Sinfjotli saw his reflection. His armor still looked like a withered and emaciated corpse. He noticed how small he looked, how frail and scared compared to the mighty beast before him. He prayed Nidhogg didn't catch on to whatever this ruse was.

"Why didn't Ratatoskr deliver this message himself?" Nidhogg asked suspiciously. "The squirrel is normally the one to deliver messages up and down the World Tree. He takes great joy in it, too."

"Um... he... sent us ahead," Modi stammered. "It's a long, arduous journey traveling up and down the World Tree. He needed a break. So, he tasked these two warriors with coming in his stead. My brother and I offered to help escort them here and helped them brave all the perils of Niflheim."

"Very well," Nidhogg said, slinking back beneath his lair under the tree root. "Let's hear this message. What does the eagle have to say to me this time?"

"Of course." Sinfjotli nodded. "Just a moment, please." He turned to Magni and Modi.

"Alright, what is he talking about?" Sinfjotli whispered. "I think Sigurd wanted me to tell Nidhogg that we're messengers. But what is all this about a squirrel and an eagle?"

"He's referring to Ratatoskr," Magni explained. "He's the messenger squirrel that acts as an intermediary between Nidhogg and Gullinkambi, the golden eagle that perches atop the branches of Yggdrasil and creates the warm summer winds that blow through Asgard and Midgard. Ratatoskr runs up and down the World Tree delivering messages and insults between the two."

"Okay..." Sinfjotli managed. He glanced back at Nidhogg. "So, what happens when he realizes we're not actually messengers?"

"He won't," Modi promised. "Look, Ratatoskr usually makes up more than half the insults he delivers. Whatever you can think of, Nidhogg will probably just believe it. If you play your cards right, he might send us away to deliver his own insult to the eagle. Now hurry and say something, *anything* before that *thing* eats us!"

"But why do *I* have to be the one who insults him?" Sinfjotli complained.

"Nidhogg will get suspicious if *we* pretend to speak on Ratatoskr's behalf," Modi explained. "Think about it. Wouldn't the gods of strength and courage acting as a substitute for a messenger squirrel arouse suspicion? He'd probably think it's beneath us?"

"Well?" Nidhogg hissed. "I'm waiting."

"Apologies." Sinfjotli bowed. "It's been a long journey here, and we're all very weary. The message. Right, well... um... the eagle... he says... that your breath reeks with the stench of millions of rotting corpses."

Nidhogg wasn't impressed. "Am I supposed to be insulted by that fact? Of course, my breath smells like that. Look around. I've spent *eons* feasting upon the corpses of the dishonorable dead. Is that truly all Gullinkambi has to say?"

"*That's* the best insult you can come up with!" Magni rebuked quietly. "His breath stinks!"

"Look, I've never been the best at flyting or coming up with clever insults," Sinfjotli admitted. "I'm the type of warrior who'd prefer to fight his opponents and bash in their heads rather than waste time trading clever insults. Besides, the stench of his breath is so sickening that I can barely think clearly."

"You daft fool!" Modi chastised in hushed whispers. "Think of something else before you get us killed!"

"Never mind." Nidhogg sighed. "I hoped you had something clever to report. But I suppose that eagle's brain is emptier of insults than Odin's left eye socket. I'll eat you now to warm the chilly aftertaste that frost giant left in my mouth."

"Wait, there's more!" Sinfjotli shouted. He desperately tried to come up with an insult. He needed a slight capable of wounding the pride of an ancient and powerful creature like Nidhogg. As he contemplated what to say, Sinfjotli stared at the giant tree root Nidhogg had been gnawing. The ashen root was covered in deep puncture marks and old scars but still looked relatively healthy. Sinfjotli remembered the Norns once told him and Sigurd they must keep watering the World Tree root daily to remedy the damage Nidhogg inflicts upon it.

Suddenly, an idea popped into his head. "The eagle... he also said... that... you're a weak and pathetic worm!" Sinfjotli shouted the last part with fiery determination.

"What was that?" Nidhogg bellowed. Black gouts of flame hissed between his teeth. The corpses stuck in between his teeth ignited, making his scaly lips look like they were on fire.

"The eagle thinks you're weak and pathetic," Sinfjotli repeated confidently. "He told us: 'Nidhogg is pathetically weak. Look at him! It's taking him an eternity to gnaw through a single tree root. Remind him of what a pathetic worm he is.' That's what the eagle has to say to you!"

Nidhogg roared, slamming his tail against the mountains of corpses and the root of the World Tree. He unfurled his bat-like wings, dislodging corpses that had spent years accumulating on his body like barnacles on a whale. He spewed black flames everywhere, igniting the corpses that rained down across the valley, making them look like burning, rotting, fleshy snowflakes were falling from the sky.

Nidhogg's tantrum paused as the dragon reared its head toward the sky. Something had caught its attention.

"RATATOSKR!" Nidhogg roared in rage and fury. The sound stabbed at everyone's minds like a flaming sword.

"*I'm right here!*" a cheerful voice answered. Suddenly, a gigantic red squirrel emerged from the clouds, climbing down the root of the World Tree.

"Sorry for the late arrival. I was just coming to tell you that the eagle—"

"I ALREADY KNOW WHAT GULLINKAMBI SAID!" Nidhogg bellowed. "Now take these 'messengers' with you to the top of the Yggdrasil and deliver *my* message to the eagle. Tell him: 'Come Ragnarök, I will *rip* him to shreds and feast upon his blasted charred carcass. THEN WE'LL SEE WHICH ONE OF US IS TRULY WEAK!' NOW GO!"

For a moment, Ratatoskr looked confused. But after seeing Magni, Modi, Sinfjotli, and the injured Sigurd on the mountain slope, the squirrel smiled, or at least he appeared to.

"You got it!" Ratatoskr chuckled. He leaped from the root of the World Tree into the valley and hopped across the mountains of corpses to their location. When Ratatoskr reached them, Sinfjotli realized he was much bigger than he appeared from a distance. He was nowhere near as big as Fornjót or Nidhogg, but the four of them were still like tiny fleas compared to him.

"Hop on," Ratatoskr urged. "I'll give you guys a lift to the top of Yggdrasil. You'll have the best view from the best tour guide in all the Nine Realms!"

Sinfjotli saw no reason to refuse the offer. Magni picked up Sigurd, and everyone climbed onto the squirrel's back.

Once they were all secure, Ratatoskr hopped across the mountains of corpses, leaped onto the root of the World Tree, and scurried up. Nidhogg watched them climb up the tree for a while with baleful eyes before he resumed gnawing the root of the World Tree in frustration.

CHAPTER FORTY-THREE

THE MISCHIEVOUS MESSENGER SQUIRREL

T ears of joy streamed down Sigurd's cheeks as warm sunlight touched his face for the first time in months. He wanted to burst into a joyful song. His brain felt like it could break from all the jubilation as the warm rays washed over him.

The giant squirrel Ratatoskr had just emerged from Niflheim's icy atmosphere, carrying them into the light. The sun, moon, and stars hovered high above them near the canopy of Yggdrasil, basking them in their radiant glow.

Far in the distance, he could see Helheim and even fiery Muspelheim connected to the roots of Yggdrasil. Further up the trunk, Sigurd's superhuman sight traced the outlines of Midgard, Svartalfheim, and the enormous realm of Jotunheim. The realms were far away but still close enough that he could discern details.

Sigurd relished the warm feeling. No longer would he have to endure the darkness and frigid conditions of Niflheim. He was finally leaving that frozen hell behind.

He sat up and basked in the light. The Apple of Idun Sinfjotli had fed him in the Valley of Corpses was doing its job. Sigurd's body had continued healing as Ratatoskr climbed through Niflheim's icy atmosphere. He was still critically injured, but his body had healed enough for him to sit up and speak, albeit with difficulty.

"I swear on the bones of my ancestors that I will never take the sun's warmth for granted again," Sinfjotli vowed. He ordered the Kistfuskare to unravel its helmet from his head so he could feel the sun's rays. Tears of joy continued to stream down his face. Then his eyes widened as horror and realization washed over him.

"What's wrong?" Sigurd asked weakly.

"We left Tanngrisnir and Tanngnjóstr behind!" Sinfjotli exclaimed. "They're still down there in Niflheim. We need to—"

"Calm down." Magni brought his fingers to his mouth and whistled. The sound was louder and sharper than a blast of lightning.

Sigurd soon heard a distant rumbling sound amidst the ringing in his ears. He looked back in time to see the mighty Tanngrisnir and Tanngnjóstr breach through Niflheim's atmosphere and appear next to Ratatoskr.

Seeing the three creatures standing side by side was an amusing sight. Tanngrisnir and Tanngnjóstr were as large as bison, and the chariot they pulled was half the size of a longship. But Ratatoskr dwarfed them. The giant squirrel was easily a hundred times larger than them, making them look like tiny fleas. It felt unnatural seeing a squirrel that was bigger than two goats.

"What now?" Sigurd asked. "Should we get off and let them take us the rest of the way?"

Magni looked up at the World Tree and pursed his lips. Sigurd noticed a trace of fear in his eyes as he stared at the canopy.

"Nah," Magni said. "We'll let Tanngrisnir and Tanngnjóstr head back to Asgard ahead of us. They've been through enough on our account."

Magni and Modi jumped off Ratatoskr and approached the goats. They fed them a couple of oats and whispered something in their ear. Then, they spent a moment ensuring that all their supplies were secure in the chariot. After that, Magni and Modi jumped back onto Ratatoskr's back. Tanngrisnir and Tanngnjóstr reared on their hind legs and bolted straight up the trunk of Yggdrasil, dragging the chariot with them. Sigurd watched until they vanished from sight.

"Why'd you send them away?" Sinfjotli asked.

"You made a good point earlier in the Valley of Corpses, Sinfjotli," Modi explained as he wrapped himself in a glowing cloak he'd retrieved from the chariot before he and Magni leaned back on Ratatoskr's fur with their hands holding the back of their heads. "You pointed out how we kept eating them to conserve our strength. We figured they deserved a break. We'll just hitch a ride on Ratatoskr and take the scenic route instead."

Sigurd saw through the lie at once. "You just want to delay returning to Asgard because you fear Thor's wrath, right? You're afraid Thor will kill you both when you set foot in the realm for stealing his chariot, and you're sending the goats back to your father, hoping it will soften the blow and give his rage time to cool. Am I mistaken?"

Magni and Modi sheepishly looked away. Sigurd could tell he'd hit the nail on the head. But he didn't mind. He concurred with this decision. He leaned back and relished the feeling of Ratatoskr's soft fur, as warm and comfy as sheepskin and it smelled of hazelnut and oak. It felt much more comfortable than that cramped, rickety chariot.

They had all been through so much in Niflheim. They had spent months traveling through total darkness, survived an attack by hungry frost trolls, and fought a storm giant and later a primordial frost giant. Sigurd had been struck by lightning several times, had the air sucked out of his lungs, and nearly died after getting punched by Fornjót.

After everything they had endured, it felt right to enjoy some well-deserved rest. They'd earned this respite.

"Even if Father murders us, I look forward to seeing Asgard again." Modi sighed. "I've had enough of cold, windy darkness."

Sigurd's eyes widened. "We're headed... to Asgard?"

"Aye." Magni nodded. "Your wounds need further treatment. Even with the Apple of Idun and our power, healing you completely is beyond us. We'll have to take you to Uncle Heimdall's watchtower for further treatment."

Ratatoskr turned his head and looked over his shoulder at them. "I don't mind giving you a ride to the top of the World Tree. But you'll have to reach Asgard on your own. I'm on a tight schedule delivering messages between Nidhogg and Gullinkambi. I don't want the dragon to get angrier than he already is. But I could probably convince that vainglorious eagle to fly you to Asgard."

"Sounds good to me," Modi said.

"And me," Magni added.

"No complaints here," Sinfjotli agreed.

"Fine by me," Sigurd concurred.

"Alright," Ratatoskr said. "If everyone's settled, I'll get moving. Better hold on tight."

With that, Ratatoskr began the long journey to the top of Yggdrasil in earnest. They clung to the fur on his back. Ratatoskr consciously kept his tail raised upward as a precaution to prevent any of them from tumbling off. That wouldn't be an issue since the tail was as large as an island. Still, Magni kept one arm wrapped around Sigurd, securing him as he and his brother searched for a safe and comfortable spot. They settled near the base of the squirrel's fluffy tail, where they could sit back and relax without fear of slipping.

"It'll take nine days to reach the top of the World Tree," Ratatoskr announced. "You best get comfy."

"You can count on that." Magni laughed. "I could sleep for an entire year after everything we endured on this adventure."

Sigurd managed a weak smile. Bards and poets would waste gallons of ink and mountains of parchment writing tales of this exploit if they ever heard the story.

Sigurd reclined on Ratatoskr's tail, gazing up at the six realms hovering above him on the World Tree. From this distance, the realms appeared as detailed and expansive as the moon on a clear night in Midgard. Sigurd could see facets of the realms in picturesque detail. He could observe the continents and oceans of Midgard, examine the dark plains of Svartalfheim, and marvel at the diverse landscapes of Jotunheim, from its jungles and forests to its plains, mountains, and oceans.

As Sigurd stared, Modi sat up and proudly clapped Sinfjotli's shoulder. "You've got some balls, lad! I never imagined anyone was brave enough to insult Nidhogg so brazenly! And I'm the bloody god of courage! I'll ensure they tell stories of this adventure in Asgard for years!"

"I have to ask," Ratatoskr interjected, "what did you say to Nidhogg? I've been delivering messages between him and Gullinkambi for eons, but I've never seen him get this angry."

"I told him the eagle thinks he's a weak and pathetic worm," Sinfjotli recounted. "And I mocked him for taking so long just to gnaw through a single tree root!"

Ratatoskr stopped climbing up the trunk of Yggdrasil. The squirrel looked over his shoulder and stared at Sinfjotli. "Bor's breath, you're a bold one!" The squirrel laughed. "This changes everything. Looks like I'll have to come up with darker insults from here on out."

Sigurd cocked his head to the side as he gazed up at the squirrel. He remembered hearing an old wives' tale about a squirrel that served as a messenger for a dragon and an eagle. Ever since Magni and Modi told them about the fearsome dragon Nidhogg, who dwelled beneath the root of Yggdrasil, Sigurd suspected it might be the same creature from the tale. That's why he had instructed Sinfjotli to tell the dragon they were messengers. It was a desperate gambit, but it paid off in the end.

As Ratatoskr resumed climbing the tree, Sigurd noticed Sinfjotli was staring into space. "What's on your mind, brother?"

Sinfjotli glanced at him before gazing up at the squirrel's head. "Ratatoskr, I'm curious about how the exchange of insults between the eagle and Nidhogg began. Also, why do you act as a mediator between them?"

"I started doing it at Odin's request," Ratatoskr answered.

Sigurd blinked. "Odin orchestrated this?" He turned to Magni and Modi. "Did you two know?"

Magni shook his head. "Grandfather's always been very tightlipped about his schemes." He looked up at Ratatoskr's head. "I'm guessing All-Father didn't disclose why he wanted you to do this and kept his reasons to himself."

"No, he made his intentions clear to me from the start," Ratatoskr corrected. "It's because he's afraid. Nidhogg is one of the most powerful living creatures. Odin fears him almost as much as Fenrir, and for good reason. Even if all the realms united against him, it's unlikely they'd triumph. The dragon is just *that* powerful. He's able to gnaw on one of the roots of existence. Whenever he damages Yggdrasil's root, it triggers a calamity somewhere in the realms. When he finishes gnawing through the root, it will cause tremors so great that it will uproot mountains and set loose the gods' chained foes. It will be one of the many catalysts that trigger Ragnarök.

"Odin accepted long ago that he can never prevent Ragnarök," Ratatoskr continued, "but he can delay it. Since he can't outright kill Nidhogg or prevent him from gnawing on the root, Odin resorted to subtly distracting him to curtail his chaos. First, he arranged for all the corpses of the dishonorable dead to be sent to Niflheim as an offering, hoping to divert Nidhogg's hunger. When that proved insufficient, he asked me to deliver messages between him and Gullinkambi. Both creatures live at opposite ends of the World Tree, and it can take weeks before they get a response from the other. Odin figured that would keep Nidhogg occupied.

"However, I wasn't content with delivering mundane messages like 'How's the weather?' or 'How's your day going?' So, I came up with a wiser and more entertaining solution. Instead of acting as the intermediary between two distant correspondents, I started a flyting contest between the two, and it has worked tremendously!"

"How so?" Sinfjotli asked.

"Flyting isn't easy," Ratatoskr explained. "Singers, poets, and writers can spend days or even weeks trying to come up with the best insult. That's especially true for dragons and giant eagles. While Nidhogg remains preoccupied racking his brain trying to come up with the perfect insult for Gullinkambi, he's not gnawing on the root of Yggdrasil. That gives the Norns ample time to heal the damaged tree root from within their cave."

Sigurd leaned back against the squirrel's tail and reflected on the bizarre arrangement. It was an unusual, complex, but admittedly creative way to delay Ragnarök. But thankfully, it had saved their lives. They would have assuredly gotten killed if Nidhogg hadn't believed they were messengers.

Suddenly, the World Tree began shaking. The four of them crawled to the edge of Ratatoskr's tail and looked down at Niflheim far below them. Sigurd peered through the gathering clouds and announced that Nidhogg was still gnawing on the root, and he looked pissed.

Sigurd noticed Sinfjotli looked uneasy. "What's wrong, brother?"

"I was thinking about what Nidhogg told Ratatoskr to tell Gullinkambi. You saw the fierce look in his eyes. That wasn't a threat. It was a promise. Did... did I inadvertently doom Gullinkambi to perish at Ragnarök?"

"I wouldn't dwell on it too much," Ratatoskr advised. "Odin claims Nidhogg is destined to partake in the ultimate battle at Ragnarök. If the All-Father were here, he'd probably tell you everything has worked out for the better. If Nidhogg is now intent on battling Gullinkambi, then he won't bother battling the Aesir at Ragnarök. And that will shift the course of the battle in the gods' favor. But you're right about one thing. The feud between Nidhogg and Gullinkambi will take a darker turn now."

"You don't sound too upset," Sigurd noted.

"Oh, on the contrary, I'm excited!" Ratatoskr exclaimed. "This opens so many possibilities. The insults between them have gotten quite stale and mundane lately. I had to 'improve' upon their tedious slurs. But now... now things will become interesting! I can already envision all the menacing, juicy threats I'll deliver!"

"But what about the root of Yggdrasil?" Sinfjotli pressed. "Will it be alright? Nidhogg seemed pretty intent on devouring it after I mocked him. I—I haven't hastened Ragnarök, have I?"

"Don't get hung up on it," Ragnarök advised. "Like you brazenly pointed out, it's taking Nidhogg an eternity to gnaw through that giant root. He won't get any closer soon. If the Norns are to be trusted, he won't be able to gnaw through the root completely until after Fimbulwinter when Sköll and Hati catch the sun and moon. He certainly won't forget that bare-faced insult. But he'll get over his anger once he and Gullinkambi resume trading insults again. I could probably help ease the tension by adding my own touches here and there. But there's no use in worrying about something like that. You should all just sit back and enjoy the ride."

For a while, nobody said anything. They rested in silence on Ratatoskr's cushy, furry tail as the squirrel continued climbing the trunk of the World Tree.

"Are you feeling any better?" Sinfjotli asked.

"No." Sigurd huffed. "I can talk, but that's about it. I can barely move; it hurts to breathe, and I feel nauseous. Frankly, I can't even think of the right adjective to accurately describe the pain I'm feeling."

"Your insides are definitely mangled," Magni agreed. "The apple should fix your organs, but I expect you'll be pissing blood for a bit."

"It's not just my kidneys that are shot." Sigurd wheezed, taking a cautious breath. "My fingers, forearms, ankles, thighs, back, and intestines; I don't think there is a single intact organ or bone inside me... At least that's how I feel."

"Your heart, brain, eyes, ears, and mouth still work," Modi reminded him. "And your lungs too... or at least one of them. That's all you need under the circumstances. Just kick back and bask in the radiance of the World Tree as the apple heals you from within. We've more than earned this reprieve after that herculean battle."

"I just remembered," Sinfjotli muttered. He reached to his waist and pulled Gram from the makeshift scabbard he'd attached it to. "You can have this back now. Holding it might help your fingers remember their strength."

"You can have this back as well," Magni announced as he handed Sigurd his magic helmet, Tarnhelm. "I recovered this after Fornjót punched you."

They laid the helmet beside him and gently pressed the sword into his hand. Sigurd's fingers closed weakly around the hilt of his trusty weapon. Holding it felt comforting, but the helmet brought back many terrible memories as he stared at it. It reminded him of those final moments before Fornjót's fist slammed into him, then waking up in the Valley of Corpses.

"How did... you find my broken body?" Sigurd croaked out. "There were... billions of corpses... in that valley."

"It's all thanks to Wolfsbane," Sinfjotli announced as he proudly showed off his axe. "Getting you to take Fornjót to Yggdrasil's root was a desperate plan. But if it succeeded, I figured we'd need some way to track you down afterward. So, I purposefully left my axe embedded in your tail before scrambling up your back. I planned to call it back to my hand afterward to give us a general idea of your direction. Turns out, it wasn't hard to figure out where you landed. That impact wasn't subtle. But the axe still came in handy when we came across those mountains of corpses. Wolfsbane had already been dislodged from your tail by the impact. But recalling it still helped us narrow down your general location."

"I see." Sigurd sighed. "It's... good that you found me. That place was... the stuff of nightmares."

"I'm just glad you could understand the plan." Sinfjotli smiled.

Sigurd frowned. "What plan?"

"Don't you remember?" Sinfjotli asked. "While you were fighting Fornjót as a dragon, Magni threw me into you. I looked you straight in the eyes and told you to carry Fornjót to the root of Yggdrasil. I guess you added a few extra steps along the way."

"I... I don't remember," Sigurd confessed. "I barely remember... anything after Fornjót punched me."

Sinfjotli's eyes widened. "Wait, you mean to say that you really were unconscious the entire time? Your body was operating solely on primal instinct?"

"Not exactly." Sigurd frowned. "How do I explain this? I was vaguely aware of what was happening but had no thoughts or feelings. I was just watching from a distant darkness. It felt like a dream in which I was floating beneath a frozen lake, looking up at the surface. I could see the events of the real world unfolding on the water's surface, but I couldn't think, speak, or act. I had no control over my body and couldn't feel any pain. It felt like I was battling something inside a dream... except someone else was doing the fighting. I remember seeing your face on the water's surface, and I thought I could hear a voice. But I don't know if it was yours. It sounded garbled, like someone attempting to speak underwater. But I think... I understand what the voice was trying to convey. Perhaps through sheer willpower and instinct, I subconsciously made my body do what you instructed."

"Sigurd, there's something else you need to know," Magni cautioned. "You looked exactly like Fafnir while you were in your dragon form. You even used the same abilities and attacks."

As Magni described his dragon form, Sigurd opened and closed his mouth several times. Then he leaned back as another wave of pain washed over him, jabbing pains throughout his entire body. But the worst was in his chest. The scar on his sternum was blazing hot. Whenever he took a breath, the pain sharpened as if a white-hot knife was stabbing him in the heart and lungs.

No, not a knife. Knives couldn't inflict pain like this. It felt more like his organs were being gnawed on by teeth belonging to a ghost.

Fafnir, Sigurd thought. *I ate his heart and bathed in his blood, but he still haunts me. He lashes out at me from beyond the grave. From the heart of whatever hell I sent him to, he sinks his teeth into my chest and twists.*

Or maybe Fafnir wasn't in Helheim? Perhaps he was much closer than Sigurd realized.

"Magni, Modi, is it..." Sigurd faltered. "Is it possible that some small part of Fafnir lived on within me after I ate his heart? And is living with me even as we speak?"

They each shrugged. "I still can't say for certain," Modi admitted. "But if it is the case, it would explain so many things."

"Like why Sigurd didn't go on a murderous rampage after passing the Trial of Svarblood and slaughter all the dwarves?" Sinfjotli asked.

Magni nodded. "If a second soul already accustomed to being a dragon passed the Trial alongside Sigurd, it could have allowed Sigurd's mind and soul to acclimate to his new body and keep all the rage and murderous impulses in check. But when Sigurd got punched and buried alive by Fornjót, that presence seized its chance and took the reins."

"It's a valid theory," Modi conceded. "It's also possible that Sigurd merely inherited many of Fafnir's memories and instincts and was using them subconsciously. That could explain how he knew how to unleash Fafnir's poisonous breath." He shrugged. "But we can neither validate nor dispute either theory because no mortal ever underwent the Trial of Svarblood under the same circumstances as Sigurd."

Magni gently tapped Sigurd's shoulder. "Sorry we can't give you a more solid answer than that."

"It's fine," Sigurd lied, looking away nervously as he contemplated the grim implications of everything they'd told him.

The body of my greatest foe has become my future. Sigurd placed a hand over the scar on his chest, recalling something Fafnir told him during the Trial of Svarblood: *Maybe I'm actually here. Perhaps eating my heart all those years ago allowed a part of my essence to live on within you.*

Sigurd glanced down his bandaged chest, picturing the ugly scar that lay beneath it. *Fafnir,* he wondered. *Do you still live within me, even now? If so, whose side are you on?*

The only answer he received was silence.

END

EPILOGUE

"Another round for the Calamitous Valkyrie!" Helgi Hundingbane called.

A serving girl rushed over with eight mugs of ale on a platter. Brynhild and the nearby Einherjar snatched the cups before the poor servant set them on the table and ordered her to get more.

As the exhausted servant dashed back to the kitchen, Brynhild, Völsung, Rerir, Sigi, Sigmund, Hámundr, Hjordis, and their companions shoved to their feet from the wooden benches. A few drunkenly tripped over them, spilling ale on themselves and bringing everyone to laughter.

It fell to Rerir to lead the toast. "To the gods who lead us into battle against the invaders!"

Everyone clanked their mugs together and drank. The ale was so thick you could cut it with a sword. It burned Brynhild's throat like oil as she chugged. But she didn't stop until her mug was empty and grabbed another fresh cup from a passing servant.

"To the brave warriors of Valhalla, who fought, died, and fought again until the threat was vanquished," Hámundr toasted next.

They drank again.

Völsung pointed his cup toward Brynhild. "To the Calamitous Valkyrie, who slew more enemies than even my grandfather!"

"Mind your tongue, boy," Rerir snapped, but still drank, as did everyone else. He seemed more vexed that his father, Sigi, was being looked down on than the toast.

That made Brynhild smile as she chugged the mead. Alcohol and battle had the power to turn bitter foes into comrades. Less than a week ago, Rerir and many other Einherjar shouted maledictions at Brynhild and called for her execution. Now, they drank in her honor.

Sigmund raised his mug. "To my sons, who allowed us to have our greatest scrap in years!"

Few drank to that cheer except Sigmund, Völsung, and Sigi. Not even Brynhild dared take a sip.

Thankfully, Hjordis saved the party's mood by raising her mug. "To Brynhild, who slew more foes than anyone at this table, and is why we won!"

Everyone drank to that toast except Brynhild. Though flattering, Hjordis's toast felt like an over-exaggeration.

When Yggdrasil trembled and shook Asgard to its core, rifts in reality opened as the stability of the Nine Realms became compromised, allowing many creatures from other realms to show up. Panicked marauders from Midgard, draugirs from Helheim, blind creatures from Niflheim, and Jötnar from Jotunheim all appeared within Asgard's borders. Most were confused and angry. Some enterprising individuals saw this as an opportunity and ravaged the realm while Asgard's defenses were compromised.

Fortunately, they didn't have time to damage the city or realm because of Asgard's overwhelmingly swift response, which Brynhild was partly responsible for. Most of the Aesir, Vanir, valkyries, and Einherjar had assembled in Valhalla to attend Brynhild's kangaroo trial before the chaos began. This gave them a miraculous and decisive home-field advantage, allowing everyone to march out of the Hall of Heroes as a single cohesive army and ferociously obliterate the invaders before they got near the capital city.

The combined might of all Asgard's forces eliminated the inter-realm invaders in less than a day. By the gods, it was a glorious victory! Gods, valkyries, and legendary heroes all fought as one against overwhelming odds. Such a glorious battle had never happened before and likely would never happen again until Ragnarök.

Brynhild dispatched countless foes… admittedly far more than the Volsungs. That much was true. But Heimdall was the true king of the hill at the end of that blood-drenched day. The Watchman of the Gods slew more foes than any valkyrie or god. Brynhild shivered as she recalled him wielding Hofund at the invaders, killing at least five foes with every swing.

He wasn't the only Aesir who spilled rivers of blood. Brynhild's ears still rung from the thunderous crashes Mjolnir made whenever Thor swung his hammer, smashing foes to bloody smears. The creeks near the battlefield still ran red from the corpses Freyja, Týr, and Vidar had slain.

Miraculously, not a single Asgardian perished. Hundreds of Einherjar from Midgard did, but because they were fighting in Asgard, the valiant dead revived and returned from Valhalla faster than their enemies could kill them.

Sadly, Asgard's spectacular victory was the only bright light amid the chaos sweeping the realms.

Brynhild's mirth faded as she stared at the frothy ale in her mug. Asgard was the first realm to be restored to order. But the other eight realms weren't so lucky. They still awaited word from Heimdall to assess the damage, but the outlook was bleak based on everything they'd endured here in Asgard.

Regardless, it felt right to celebrate such a glorious victory. And no one knew how to party better than Valhalla's residents.

The Volsungs and heroes who distinguished themselves the most were permitted this feast by Odin's decree. The rest of the Einherjar were in the city of Gladsheim, helping with repairs or clearing the fields beyond of corpses.

Everyone drank and devoured everything on the table like wildfire, forcing the servants to dash toward the other side of Valhalla for more provisions.

In the corner of Valhalla, opposite the gods' thrones, was the Aesir's kitchen, where the chef god Andhrímnir was hard at work. He was roasting Sæhrímnir, a giant boar the size of a mammoth, on a colossal spit and slicing chunks of meat into his magic bronze cauldron, Eldhrímnir. Both the boar and cauldron were enchanted. Sæhrímnir's flesh regenerated as fast as Andhrímnir could slice it off, giving the chef a never-ending supply of meat that his cauldron cooked instantly.

As Brynhild sucked the meat off a rib, she watched and listened with her keen ears as two breathless servants complained to Andhrímnir. Although they weren't looking at her, Brynhild could tell they spoke of her and listened.

"...like a raging wildfire!" one servant complained. "They eat through the dishes before we even set them on the table!"

"That means they brought an appetite," Andhrímnir said as he ripped a huge chunk of flesh from the boar and plopped the whole thing in his giant pot. The Aesir wiped the sweat from his brow and smiled. "It's proof they fought for their pride and others."

The other servant stole a glance at Brynhild and sneered. "But for us to serve *her*? It's—"

"An honor," Andhrímnir interrupted as he stirred his cauldron. "It doesn't matter if someone's a saint or criminal, rich or poor, or Aesir or mortal. I'll feed them all the same."

He said more, but Brynhild missed it as Sigmund called for another toast. Everyone shuffled to their feet and raised their mugs. But a foreboding presence washed over them before anyone said anything.

Brynhild suddenly felt like a boulder was pressing down on her shoulders. The pressure was so intense she dropped her mug and tripped over the bench. She had the grace to twist her body around and land on her forearms and knees.

Inches from her face were a pair of immaculately chiseled legs. Looking up, she found her former mistress, Freyja, looming over her.

"Your Majesty." Brynhild scrambled to her feet and kneeled. Everyone else except Sigi bent at the knee and paid her homage. The founder of the Volsungs sat on his bench, casually sipping his mead.

Does he have a death wish? Brynhild wondered. *Freyja has obliterated people for less disrespect. Why won't he at least take a knee?*

Then she remembered Sigi was called the Maverick Aesir. He may be Einherjar now, but once upon a time, he was an Aesir and thus Freyja's peer.

"Auntie Freyja, always lovely to see you." Sigi picked up another mug and offered it.

The goddess of love and war didn't accept the cup. She eyed it as if it were filled with writhing maggots, then studied each of the Volsungs as they stood up.

Sigi shrugged. "More for us then." He handed the mug to his grandson, Völsung, then snatched a meaty rib and gnawed at it like a dog. "So, what brings you to my table, Freyja?"

"Business." Freyja turned to Brynhild and frowned. "Asgard is in ruins, yet you're here celebrating?"

Her tone was gentle but still felt like a shot to Brynhild's heart. She bowed her head. "I'm..."

"There's nothing to apologize for." Sigi tossed aside the rib and stood. "This party is for her. She fought as well as anyone else at this table. Better even. Without her trial, we wouldn't have been assembled when the Great Cataclysm struck and had an overwhelming advantage. Brynhild earned this victory feast."

His words were as bold as brass, and he brazenly stared Freyja dead in the eyes as if daring her to object. That sent shivers down Brynhild's spine. The goddess of love and war had killed men for lesser insults.

But Freyja didn't seem to care this time.

"You're not wrong," she conceded. "But the feast is over for her, at least. Brynhild and I have much to discuss."

Sigi looked at Brynhild for a while, then nodded. "So be it. But come back any time, dear." He tapped Rerir's head with his greasy fingers. "Despite my son's reservations, you'll always be welcome at my table."

Rerir's face turned dark red as he swatted Sigi's hand aside, bringing everyone at the table to laughter. Even Freyja cracked a smile. Brynhild finished her drink, left her seat, and followed her master out of Valhalla through one of the hall's ninety-nine gilded doors. They passed beneath the red-gold boughs of Glasir, the Aesir's sacred tree, and overlooked the city below.

Even in its dilapidated state, Asgard's capital city took Brynhild's breath away. The city was divided into nine towering tiers, each encircled by one-hundred-foot-high walls and teeming with alleys, narrow passageways, houses, and palaces—each level could function as a miniature city. At the summit stood Valhalla, the Hall of Heroes, and Valaskialf, Odin's imposing palace. Just below was Fensalir, Queen Frigga's palace. Freyja's palace, Sessrumnir, had once occupied the third level but had transferred to Vanaheim centuries ago. Njörd's palace, Noatun, rested on the fourth, while the fifth was home to Bilskirnir, Thor and Sif's formidable palace containing five hundred and forty rooms, the largest of the realm. The lower four tiers sported smaller but impressive palaces and houses of varying heights. Buildings shone like gold and silver stars with their thatched roofs and smooth marble colonnades. The colorful and flourishing plants adorning each meadow and window were also impressive.

Water flowed through the city's tiered canals. Except instead of flowing down, the water flowed upward, blatantly defying gravity. It was a brilliant blend of magic and architecture that Aesir picked up from Alfheim's elves.

However, many of the aqueducts were cracked, and palaces, homes, and other gorgeous buildings were damaged in the earthquake. Below, Brynhild could see many gods and Einherjar busy reconstructing their glorious city. She spotted Thor carrying ten-ton marble columns over his shoulder like a bundle of sticks. Idun was summoning roots and vines to shift through the rubble, stabilizing structures teetering on collapse. On the eighth teer, Týr and Bragi were helping Einherjar carry supplies.

Freyja frowned. "Why are you smiling?"

Brynhild blinked. "Pardon?"

"You had a perpetual scowl plastered across your face since your trial, but you've had a big fat grin for some time now."

Brynhild touched her face and realized her master was right. She hadn't even noticed it or that her facial muscles were aching from smirking.

"Are you pleased seeing this devastation?" Freyja shook her head. "I taught you better than that. I know you resent Odin, but don't extend that grudge toward all—"

"That's not it! It's just..." Brynhild considered for a moment. "I'm still bitter about being summoned away from Sigurd's side and spending months traveling up Yggdrasil just to endure a kangaroo court staged by a crabby Odin, but I'm more overjoyed to be by your side once more."

Freyja's gaze softened somewhat. "It's been a long while since you were in my service. Unfortunately, you won't remain by my side for long. There is much to do, and I wasn't paying lip service in Valhalla when I promised I'd give you arduous tasks."

Brynhild's smile melted faster than frost under a scorching summer sun. She sighed, composed herself, and then stared attentively at her master. "What is the state of the realms now?"

"Bleak," Freyja admitted as they resumed walking. "Niflheim is more of a ruined wasteland than before. Asgard and Vanaheim weathered many earthquakes. But the invasions are the real thorns in our sides."

Brynhild arched an eyebrow. "There are other invasions across the realms?"

Freyja nodded. "The damage sustained to Yggdrasil's root during the battle in Niflheim destabilized all the Nine Realms' borders, allowing many nasty foes and invasive species to cross over. We dealt with the bedlam in Asgard, but chaos still grips the other realms. Some enterprising Jotun sorcerers capitalized on the chaos and crossed the rifts into Alfheim. My brother and the elves are busy eradicating the intruders. Legions of ogres and species native to Jotunheim have entered Svartalfheim, but Ivaldi and his people aren't perturbed. I imagine he'd have the balls to call this a blessing. They'll remain underground and wait for the invaders to starve and burn in the deserts and swamps or let them cut themselves to pieces at Niðavellir's gates before they harvest their corpses for materials. However, Midgard is one unholy mess right now. The tremors caused Jörmungandr to stir, allowing countless ogres and invasive species from Svartalfheim, Vanaheim, and Jotunheim to cross over. The Aesir and Vanir will have our hands full dealing with this chaos once we stabilize Asgard's and Vanaheim's borders."

"What of Helheim and Muspelheim?" Brynhild inquired.

Freyja grimaced. "Those realms closest to the tremors were the most affected. Helheim, caught in the epicenter, tore open with spatial rifts. Though its borders have stabilized, the damage is done. Countless draugirs, damned souls, and dozens of draugs escaped through the portals and crossed over to Midgard and the other realms. With their invasion, many restless spirits in Midgard have arisen from their barrows and are wreaking havoc. Hel's not lifting a finger to help, so the valkyries will be stretched thin dealing with the mess. As for Muspelheim... well, not even Heimdall knows *half* of what occurs in the Surtr's realm. No fire giants have crossed over, but the tremors triggered massive volcanic explosions, some of which sent volcanic debris crashing into Midgard. Bizarre things are happening at the crash sites. Heimdall claims strange life forms are emerging from the flaming debris that are completely unknown to us. Knowing Odin, he'll advocate that we study them instead of eradicating them."

Brynhild heaved a sigh as she took in all the chaos. "I imagine dealing with these invaders will be part of my penance?"

"Eventually," Freyja confirmed. "But I have another task in mind for you for now. I must remain in Asgard to deal with the reconstruction efforts and await Magni's and Modi's return. Odin plans to call a folkmoot in Valhalla when Thor's boys arrive. All the gods, except my brother Freyr, Heimdall, Sol, and Mani, will attend."

Brynhild blinked. The realms were in chaos, yet the All-Father planned to have all the gods assemble for a briefing?

She sneered. "The self-proclaimed 'Protector of the Realms' seems to care more about hearing his grandsons' report about the Battle of Niflheim than doing his job."

Freyja shrugged. "You're not wrong. But you should keep those insolent thoughts to yourself. You know better than anyone else what happens when someone rubs the All-Father the wrong way."

Freyja nodded toward Glasir, where a snow-white raven was perched amid the tree's red-gold leaves.

One of Odin's ravens, Brynhild knew at once. The All-Father may only have one eye, but he had a million eyes and ears spread across the realms through his flock.

The raven stared at Brynhild as if daring her to say something treasonous. Freyja tsked and flicked her finger, unleashing a gentle but mighty wind spell that shook leaves from the tree and sent the raven flying in a panic.

Freyja's feathery cloak glowed as she transformed into a falcon. "Let's fly somewhere more private. There's someone I want you to meet."

Brynhild summoned her valkyrie wings and flew after her master. They flew down to Njörd's palace on the sixth level of Gladsheim. The god of the sea's palace was vast and beautiful, with expansive courtyards, gardens, and columned green and blue marble pavilions. The gardens were sculpted with glowing sea plants and coral that usually couldn't survive outside the sea. But with the god's power, it was possible. The other nearby buildings were made of gleaming marble. Glowing fish, eels, and sharks darted in and out of the windows and swam through the air.

"It seems like a waste of magic to sustain marine life this far from the sea," Brynhild noted as she landed.

"Father gets homesick easily," Freyja said as she shapeshifted back into her humanoid form. "He wanted to bring an entire sea with him when he, my brother, and I were traded as hostages during the Aesir-Vanir War. But Odin talked him out of it. This is the closest he could get to bringing the sea here."

As a glowing shark floated past Brynhild, she remembered when Sigurd took her from Hindarfjall to the sea.

Freyja frowned and scrutinized Brynhild with her dazzling, sharp eyes. "You're scowling again. Are you still bitter about being called away from Sigurd's side?"

Brynhild lowered her eyes. "I'd be lying if I said I wasn't. I spent an entire lifetime chipping away at Odin's curse and struggling to enter Helheim. Once I did, I had to fight for every inch of ground through the underworld to reunite with Sigurd and keep fighting the undead with everything I had. When we were finally reunited after all that time and struggling, you and Odin summoned me to Asgard, making me spend months flying up Yggdrasil only to endure a mummer's farce of a trial."

She squeezed her hands until blood trickled between her knuckles. "Even worse, Sigurd got captured by dwarves and underwent the horrid Trial of Svarblood! And now, according to Heimdall's report, he lingers near the brink of death following their ordeal in Niflheim. If I'd been there, I could have—"

"Perhaps that's precisely why Odin summoned you back to Asgard," Freyja interrupted.

Brynhild blinked. "Odin told you that?"

Freyja snorted. "Odin never discloses his plans, not even to dear Frigga. His motives have and may always remain an eternal mystery. But I wager he deliberately ordered you two separated so there would be nothing to prevent Sigurd from becoming stronger."

"*Stronger?*" Brynhild seethed. "How could you say that? You know how much pain he suffered. How he still suffers. Yet you defend All-Fa...?"

"Brynhild," Freyja rebuked calmly yet icily. "Get a hold of yourself. You're causing a scene."

Brynhild's gaze darted around the surroundings, and she realized that the residents of Asgard were staring at them. Some appeared worried, trying to understand what was happening, while others seemed curious, as if enjoying the entertainment. However, most of them looked at her with contempt, making her feel embarrassed and angry at the same time. Her rage toward Odin and all the pain he'd caused her still overwhelmed her mind, but she clenched her jaw, took a deep breath, and bowed her head low, apologizing for her insubordination.

As the seconds ticked by without a reply, Brynhild glanced and saw Freyja studying her with an unreadable look.

"You have a right to feel angry being summoned away from your beloved and all the pain he's suffered." Freyja's supple fingers moved to her bosom and fiddled with her glittering necklace. "I understand that rage all too well. I'd give anything to be reunited with Od. I'd move the stars themselves if I could see him just once more."

Brynhild cracked a smile, which earned her a sharp stare and a frown from Freyja.

"Why are you grinning?" her queen demanded.

Brynhild stood straight and held her hands up. "I was just reminded of something. I used to say the same thing when I was transferred to Odin's services. After every battle, I'd look up at the stars and wish to return to your side. Despite everything, I'm overjoyed to be by your side again."

"Not for much longer. While I help restore order here, you will head to Vanaheim with a certain valkyrie. You'll further her training in between helping with the reconstruction efforts in my home realm."

Brynhild arched an eyebrow. "Is she a recruit?"

Freyja cracked an immaculate smile and shook her head. "This girl has been under my wing for many years. She shows promise, but her training remains... incomplete. I believe you can push her to bring out her full potential."

Brynhild narrowed her eyes. "I'll gladly fulfill any task you give, but... why me?"

"Because you and this valkyrie share a connection," Freyja answered cryptically. "Speaking of which, here she is."

A shadow passed overhead. Another valkyrie swooped down, landed before Freyja, and kneeled dutifully.

She was a dainty-looking thing. Her wings' middle and greater coverts were bright purple feathers, while the remaining feathers were all silver, making her wings resemble honey warts. Her dark brown hair was braided at the back with two strands at the front that flowed loosely beneath her helmet, which was fashioned in the visage of a serpent. She wore an unusual visor beneath her helmet that reminded Brynhild of special glasses the dwarves sometimes made that allowed archers to strike targets with pinpoint accuracy. But this fledgling didn't have a bow or any other weapon, which piqued Brynhild's interest.

"You summoned me, Mistress?" the valkyrie said, her head still bowed low.

Freyja nodded. "Stand and remove that helmet. I'd like you to meet your new mentor."

The valkyrie stood and tensed when she beheld Brynhild. Based on her hunched shoulders, rigid posture, and the piercing glare emanating from beneath the visor as she removed her helmet, Brynhild sensed the valkyrie seethed with bitterness. Whoever she was, they shared an icy history.

Brynhild sighed, thinking this new mentorship would begin on a wonderful start. However, that thought came to a screeching halt as the girl removed her visor and glared at Brynhild with piercing eyes.

Brynhild's eyes widened. "What the...!"

This valkyrie's gold slit eyes resembled a serpent's as it prepared to strike a mouse. Brynhild vaguely realized this girl wore the visor so her icy gaze wouldn't trouble others. But that wasn't why her sinister eyes were so shocking to Brynhild. They looked identical to Sigurd's snake eyes.

As Brynhild racked her brain, pondering how this was possible, a distant memory from her loathed marriage to Gunnar flashed through her mind. Sigurd wasn't the only mortal with piercing snake eyes. There was another who inherited it from him.

Brynhild's tongue somehow voiced the name her mind could not think. "S-Svanhild?"

The girl narrowed her eyes and glowered at Brynhild, similar to how Sigurd looked when irritated. "It's been a long time, *Auntie* Brynhild." She whispered out of courtesy, barely attempting to mask her animosity.

Brynhild's eyes widened further. Sigurd's children from his illegitimate marriage used to call her that. She took another look at the girl, just to be sure. This was, without a doubt, Sigurd's daughter.

Freyja cleared her throat as a thousand questions flashed through Brynhild's mind, snapping her back to reality. "You two will spend much time together. I suggest you clear up the iciness and head to Vanaheim. You have much to do."

Did you know? Reader reviews are very important to an indie author's success.

They validate our work and help others find our stories. If you enjoyed The Frozen God, please leave a review filled with stars.

Click the link or scan the QR code below:

D on't forget your free gifts! Click here to tell me where to send them or scan the QR Code:

***

Continue the journey on the following pages with sample chapters of *Seasons of Havoc*, the next book in this series, compliments of yours truly.

SAMPLE CHAPTER I:
Sun and Moon

Mani's knuckles were as white as the moon as he gripped Hrimfaxi's reins and urged him onward. The shining steed pulled the moon chariot at an even faster pace, making the god's free-flowing hair and silver robes ripple like flags.

<You can't run forever!> Hati howled behind him.

The god of the moon was sick of hearing the Celestial Wolf's incessant promises of doom. Mani whistled, rousing his companions, Bil and Hjuki, from their sleep.

"Hand me my bow, then take the reins," he ordered.

Bil nodded as she seized the reins. Her brother, Hjuki, snatched the silver bow and quiver from the supplies in the chariot and handed them to Mani. Notching an arrow, the god of the moon turned to face the creature of his doom.

Hati hadn't aged a day since the chase began. The black wolf looked just as zealous as when he and Sköll began chasing Mani and his sister Sol across the heavens. Old scars and fresh arrow wounds covered his black fur, emitting streaks of blue light that followed him like a comet's tail as he raced through the heavens after his prey.

Mani channeled his power into the arrow and fired, unleashing a blue torrent of raw power that struck Hati right between the eyes. The Celestial Wolf growled, but it was more out of annoyance than pain.

"Why do you and Lady Sol keep doing this, Master?" Bil asked. "Shooting Hati and Sköll won't stop them."

"It makes us feel better," Mani replied, firing another shot.

The arrow sailed down Hati's gullet and exploded inside him. The Celestial Wolf coughed up light, smoke, and blood, but kept running.

Fenrir's brood was relentless. Sköll and Hati never ceased chasing Mani or Sol since the day the Aesir set them loose. These beasts couldn't be reasoned with and never stopped to eat or sleep. They'd doggedly pursued the Mani and his sister across the heavens around Midgard every day and night.

We brought that on ourselves, Mani thought as he stole a glance at Hjuki. *We refused to move across the heavens because of what happened to these two, which forced the All-Father to unleash Fenrir's sons upon us.*

As Mani holstered his bow and took the reins from Bil, he glanced down at Midgard and wept. Some fellow Vanir often called Mani the "Melancholic God" on account of how often he and Sol cried about humanity's plights. What happened to Bil and Hjuki had been so horrific Mani and his sister refused to move the sun and moon across the heavens until they'd been revived. But they'd asked too much, and in the end, Odin strong-armed them into resuming their duties under threat of death by the Celestial Wolves.

But what Midgard was currently enduring was exponentially worse. When the Yggdrasil trembled, it leveled entire cities and mountain ranges. Worse, the stability of the realms had been disrupted, allowing creatures from the other realms to cross over.

From the telepathic message he'd received from his father, Mundilfari, all the realms had plunged into a great cataclysm. Forces from Jotunheim invaded Alfheim and waged a bloody war against the elves. Invasive species were overrunning Vanaheim's ecosystems, wreaking more havoc than the terrible monster that had plagued his fellow Vanir for generations. Svartalfheim was also dealing with its fair share of inter-realm invaders, though they were faring better than others.

But Midgard experienced the worst impact. The realm below Mani was the shining jewel of the Nine Realms. And now, that jewel was being ravaged by creatures from Vanaheim and Svartalfheim, frost giants from Jotunheim, strange fire-like entities from Muspelheim, and even undead from Helheim. Everywhere Mani looked, people suffered.

Mani wished he could do something. Before he and Sol took up the mantle of dragging the sun and moon chariots, they spent every breath helping humanity and the elves of Alfheim. In the past, he and Sol would stop shining down on the world in protest until the chaos was resolved. But the Celestial Wolves prevented them from doing that.

If I let Hati nab me, it'll trigger Ragnarök early, Mani thought. *That's the last thing we need right now.*

Hrimfaxi whinnied. Mani whipped the reins harder, thinking Hati had gained on them. But he realized something else was amiss when a shadow enveloped him and the chariot.

Mani's eyes widened as he beheld a massive ash-white tree branch covered in leaves plummeting toward them.

Even Yggdrasil's branches aren't safe from this cataclysm, Mani thought as Bil and Hjuki screamed.

"That branch will flatten us!" Hjuki panicked.

"Not just us," Mani intoned. "If a branch that size strikes Midgard, it'll wipe out all life in the realm."

"What can we do?" Bil shrieked.

"This." Mani whipped Hrimfaxi's reins, changed course, and raced toward the incoming branch.

He waited until the chariot was directly below the branch before bringing Hrimfaxi to a halt, releasing the reins, and snatching his bow from Hjuki.

Mani retrieved an arrow from his quiver and clutched it until his knuckles were as white as snow, channeling as much power into the projectile as he could before notching and firing it.

The arrow was no bigger than his forearm. But when it struck the branch, it exploded in a circular blast of silver and blue light that obliterated the branch, vaporizing the bark and leaving a swirling cloud of debris that shimmered like the stars.

Midgard wasn't out of danger yet. The branch had been the size of a continent. Mani's arrow had blasted it into smaller but equally dangerous pieces. Any of them could cause catastrophic damage if they reached the realm.

But Mani couldn't concern himself with that right now. He'd veered off course and stopped the chariot, giving Hati a perfect chance to pounce on him. He needed to deal with the wolf now or lose everything.

Notching another arrow, Mani channeled as much power as he could before turning, preparing to unleash everything he had on his dreaded...

Mani's eyes widened. "What the...?!"

Hati was gone. The Celestial Wolf should have been making a bee-line for him amid the hail of debris. But the black wolf had vanished. Mani scanned the falling twigs and leaves, thinking Hati was masking his approach by hiding amongst them. But he could sense no trace of the wolf that had chased him endlessly.

Hjuki appeared beside Mani, gawking at the empty void. "Where did...? How...? When...? Why?"

Mani had no answer. He was so stunned that he forgot all about the branches falling toward Midgard until a voice shrieked, "Brother, pay attention!"

A dozen golden arrows zipped past him, vaporizing the falling branches in fiery orange-yellow explosions.

Still stupefied by Hati's disappearance, Mani slowly turned his head at the approaching golden chariot.

It had been years since he had been this near Sol. Their paths across the heavens often prevented them from approaching each other.

Mani drank in the beauty of his twin sister's radiant features as she stood with her golden bow still vibrating in her hands. She looked so regal in her golden armor, with a spiky circular crown adorning her head. Her long, golden locks glowed with power and occasionally burst into flame. Her pupilless, glowing eyes cast rays of golden light everywhere she glanced.

Beside his sister stood her daughter, Sunna, holding Skinfaxi's reins and urging the fiery golden horse forward. Mani's niece had grown comely since the last time he'd seen her. Soon, she'd be just as beautiful as her mother. Maybe prettier than his daughter, Aradia.

Mani glanced at the trail of golden light the sun chariot left in its wake as Sunna parked it beside Mani's moon chariot. He expected to see the other Celestial Wolf, Sköll, speeding down on his sister. But the gold wolf was nowhere in sight.

Bil tugged on Mani's sleeve, snapping him out of his stupor. He glanced around and saw Sol scowling at him.

"Why didn't you finish the job?" She rebuked. "If I hadn't shown up and destroyed those remaining tree fragments, millions of mortals would have perished because of your negligence."

A twinge of guilt tweaked Mani's conscience. But the all-consuming confusion at this inconceivable turn of events supplanted his shame.

"Sköll and Hati are gone," he stammered. "They chased us across the heavens for ages, and now they just...vanished?"

Sol lowered her bow and scanned the horizon. "They've been gone for some time. I didn't notice until a few minutes ago. I spun around, prepared to fire another arrow at Sköll, only to discover my pursuer was nowhere in sight. Then I noticed that branch falling."

433

Mani sat down for the first time in years as a tsunami of emotions washed over him: confusion, joy, intrigue, and worry. "Why would they stop chasing us after all this time?"

Sol pointed at Yggdrasil's trunk looming above them. "My best guess is they found easier prey and switched targets. That branch didn't fall by chance. Judging from the bite marks I spotted on the jagged end, Sköll and Hati chewed it free from the World Tree as they chased after something."

Mani swallowed. "Or *someone*."

"Don't you realize what this means, brother?" Sol asked. "We're finally free. What should we do?"

Mani gazed up at Yggdrasil's canopy with his pupilless, silver eyes. "What we always wished to do."

SAMPLE CHAPTER 2:
Dragon's Dream

Hunger and avarice coiled around the dragon's belly as he stirred awake.

Gold coins and trinkets clinked off his body as he rose, tensed his muscles, and stretched. He moved his head and swept his gaze past his large, golden bed to the cave floor. His eyes glinted with fierce pride in the dim light as he surveyed his hoard—a dazzling array of gold, silver, gemstones, and precious treasures scattered everywhere.

But having surveyed his hoard, his mood suddenly soured. Tips of stalagmites were still visible over the top of the hoard, even though the treasure was piled quite high. He let out a deep, frustrated sigh, his eyes narrowing in displeasure, similar to how a lord would react upon seeing patches of debris and bones scattered across the corners of his castle.

"I should stretch my wings a bit, fly, and pilfer more plunder to rectify this," he muttered, his voice rumbling throughout the cave. "It's past time I filled my belly with flesh along the way."

He raised his massive head and extended his wings, emerging from the mound of treasure. Rivers of coins, necklaces, and rings trickled off his back and wings as he stretched.

The dragon trekked across his hoard, careful not to crush any precious treasures beneath his massive bulk. The warm gold and metal gave way to cold stone as he headed toward the exit. Stalagmites and stalactites adorned the mouth of his grotto, making the cave resemble a yawning beast.

The stars high above twinkled like the jewels in his hoard, meaning it was still the dead of night. And there was no moon in this night sky.

Good, he smiled. *It'll be more fun if I catch them by surprise before dawn.*

Before the dragon spread his wings, he surveyed the desolate landscape for any hint of intruders. The starlight only dimly illuminated the vast, desolate wasteland stretching for miles in every direction, but his keen eyes picked out every detail of the barren land.

Petrified tree trunks jutted from the ground like the bones of a long-dead leviathan; their gnarled forms a cruel echo of the flora that had once reigned here. The soil was a sickly black-purplish hue, devoid of life and littered with the intact skeletons of birds, rabbits, foxes, and other critters that had foolishly wandered into his territory. The sand around the entrance of his lair had fused into glass, a testament to the intense heat that radiated from his body. Putrid purple mist hovered a few feet above the fetid ground, just waiting for him to ignite them with the slightest spark.

He sniffed the chilly night air, smelling nothing but poisonous vapor and death. Satisfied no thieves would threaten his fortune while he was away, he extended his wings, dashed forward, and took to the air with a mighty leap.

As he soared into the night sky, the dragon glanced down at the world below. Craters pockmarked the land, remnants of his previous rampages and battles with potential thieves and aspiring dragon slayers. He surveyed the horizon, seeing nothing but ruin and desolation as far as his keen eyes could see.

The dragon felt no remorse for the destruction he had wrought over the years as he sailed over the ruined terrain. This land was his kingdom, and the ruined landscape and toxic clouds served as an unspoken warning to any who dared to enter, dared to try and take his life or treasure—a clear warning to stay away.

Soon, though, the blasted hellscape gave way to a barren field dotted with plants that had sprouted, flowers and even trees. Then, verdant landscapes passed beneath him. A few deer and goats grazed through these parts, but no humans; there wasn't a single village within a hundred leagues of his kingdom. He'd made sure of that years ago.

As he soared beneath the clouds, the dragon pondered whom to visit. The nearest villages within an hour's flight from his lair offered meager pickings. Most of the few remaining nomad shepherds, brave or mad enough to raise their flocks nearby, had barely a single copper to their names. He remembered when one foolish shepherd tried to pay him off with "treasure" in exchange for sparing his flock. When all he gave was a paltry sack of copper coins, the dragon burned him alive along with his flock and family and razed the entire land for leagues around.

In recent years, he'd begun implementing a cruel type of tax policy. As long as shepherds paid him off and surrendered most of their livestock, he'd spare their lives, though he might come again and burn them if he got bored. One farmer audaciously called him an oath breaker. But what do dragons care about honoring promises made to lowly maggots?

"Too easy," the dragon decided. "I want a *real* conquest and a feast worthy of my time."

He racked his brain. As he sailed over a mountain, he recalled a fishing village he'd had the sense to spare a century ago when he first made his lair. It was a tiny settlement, but it had grown over the years into a walled town with stone walls and a harbor.

The dragon bared his teeth and stuck his meaty tongue out the side of his mouth as he imagined all the ships that passed through it. Ships meant trade, and trade meant money. And those stone walls meant they had something worth defending.

That settled it. He turned and flew west. It should have taken hours to arrive at the settlement, yet he made the trip in seconds. He found that peculiar, but didn't question it as he circled in the sky, eagerly gazed at the settlement far below.

He could no longer call it a settlement as it had grown into a formidable walled harbor town. It resembled a ringfort, covering a mile in diameter. The city was well-fortified, with a sturdy gate and several watchtowers along the cobblestone walls. A few sleepy guards manned the ramparts, peering out into the darkness with barely concealed boredom.

The harbor brimmed with longships, hinting at a bustling trade and fishing industry. The ringfort housed many wooden houses, each with a thatched roof and small garden. In the center of the ringfort rose a huge wooden longhouse, presumably the leader's home.

The dragon couldn't contain its laughter. "They built the walls out of stone, but constructed the rest of the city of wood? Fools! They're making this too easy!"

He swooped higher and disappeared into a bank of clouds to mask his approach. Then, the dragon descended from the heavens like a thunderbolt, belching fire and setting the longhouse's roof ablaze before vanishing back into the sky.

As flames engulfed the roof, the once peaceful village descended into chaos. The commotion jolted the sleepy watchmen awake, and they screamed in surprise and terror as they scrambled to gather their weapons and armor. Horns blared, waking the people from their slumber and announcing danger. Panicked and disoriented, they scurried out of their homes like ants emerging from their mounds and dashed toward the longhouse, where they believed some enemy had infiltrated.

The dragon circled overhead, watching the chaos as the villagers rushed toward the burning longhouse, armed with swords, spears, and axes, and hastily gathered buckets of water to put out the flames and fend off any intruders who might have made it inside. He smiled smugly as he listened to them scream and panic, wondering if their sworn enemies had somehow infiltrated them. They had no clue what or who they were dealing with.

I'll let them marinate in fear a little longer, the dragon decided. *It won't be long now before they're trapped.*

He waited until the whole town assembled around the longhouse, waiting for their imagined intruders to appear. But to their shock, the only people who emerged from the burning building were a man wearing an ash-covered tunic and two children. Based on the townsfolk's whispering, the dragon inferred that this must be the jarl of this settlement. He cradled a woman with a blackened face in his hands. As he called for help and raised his head to the heavens, wailing for the gods to save his wife, his keen eyes spotted the dragon sailing overhead. Fear overwhelmed him as he dropped his wife and pointed to the dragon. Everyone's eyes went skyward.

Too late for that, the dragon thought. *You're all right where I want you.* He folded his wings and swooped toward the harbor. He flapped his wings again to slow his descent and unleashed a torrent of flames from his mouth, setting the anchored ships and harbor ablaze.

Seeing their harbor transformed into a sea of flames terrified the townspeople. They scattered in all directions, screaming as they desperately sought sanctuary from the dragon's wrath. A few warriors found their courage and fired arrows at the dragon. One arrow struck his side, but bounced harmlessly off his reddish-black scales.

Disgust and disappointment swelled within the dragon as he bellowed, "Is this the best you can do?!"

That challenge melted whatever courage these "warriors" still had. They dropped their weapons and joined the others, fleeing toward the walls.

"There's no escape now!" Circling the ringfort, the dragon spewed purplish gas from its mouth. The gas dissolved the earth as soon as it hit the ground. A few people who had slipped past the walls died instantly, their flesh sizzling and melting.

The townspeople and "warriors" stopped in their tracks, watching as the dragon enveloped the walls with the purplish gas. Once he finished creating his ring of death, he swooped over the town and unleashed a single fireball at the gas, igniting it and turning the land around the ringfort into a sea of flames.

What fun, he thought.

The destruction eradicated whatever courage or defiance the inhabitants still had, plunging every soul in the ringfort into the iciest depths of fear. They ran about in a panic like ants seeking refuge from a flood. Most ran screaming as the dragon swooped down and landed on the blazing longhouse. A couple of "warriors" grabbed spears and pointed them dumbly at the drake as they quivered from a distance, but the dragon ignored them. Why would a dragon care what the ants at his feet are doing? His attention was fixated on the longhouse.

He'd been careful not to damage it too severely with his initial attack. Longhouses were the homes of jarls and kings, where most of the wealth was likely stored. He whipped the blazing roof off the longhouse with a crack of his tail. The roof splintered into burning pieces and soared through the air before landing on the roofs of other houses, which soon caught fire. The inhabitants screamed even louder, but the dragon was oblivious to it as he tore apart the walls and examined its prize like a child unwrapping a bundled gift.

As he peered inside, his excitement melted into disappointment when he saw only a few rugs, swords, tapestries, and many scrolls.

"That's it?!" He seethed. "A settlement this big, and *this* is all you've got?!"

The dragon's anger reached a boiling point as he turned and belched out a torrent of flame, setting a quarter of the town alight. The fire spread rapidly and consumed everything in its path, and the dragon could feel the heat of his own breath radiating back at him. But as he prepared to burn the rest of the ringfort to ash, he heard distinctive clicking footsteps drawing near amid the flames and destruction.

He peered over and saw someone in armor with a spear charging toward him. The dragon recognized him as the jarl he had spotted earlier, but he didn't pay that any mind as his eyes fell upon the gold chains glimmering on his chest. The jarl wore a glittering gold hauberk, and the dragon's mood improved as he realized coming here wasn't such a waste of energy after all.

This was the type of challenge he had been waiting for, with a prize to boot. The dragon spread his wings and let out a deafening roar, ready to duel this jarl and claim his golden prize.

It proved a disappointment, just like everything else about this town. The jarl's spear splintered against the dragon's hide as it reared up its arm and brought it down upon the jarl's chest, crushing him against the ground. The jarl's entire ribcage shattered beneath the dragon's weight as he coughed up a mist of blood. Yet the dragon didn't mind how abruptly the duel had ended as he gazed at the glittering hauberk with wonder.

"You humans were holding out on me!" The dragon chortled. "Seems coming here really was worth the effort. Now, how will we get this beauty off you? Should I cremate you while you're still wearing it and scatter your ashes to the four corners? Rip you into pieces with my talons? So hard to choose!"

Before he could decide, another voice pierced through the chaos and death, shouting, "You can't have that!"

The dragon looked up, curious about who had the stones to stand against him. His eyes narrowed as he realized it wasn't a man but a girl. She appeared to be only seventeen years old, yet she was a fearsome-looking woman, even with the mewling child in her arms. Her sharp, amber eyes gleamed with courage and defiance in the firelight.

As the dragon studied her, a voice whispered in his head, *"Don't hurt her!"*

The dragon frowned, unsure of who had spoken, but the voice fell silent as the girl shouted, "You cannot have that armor! It was a gift from the dwarves, passed down in our family for generations. I won't let you claim it."

"'A gift from the dwarves,' eh?" The dragon licked its scaly lips. "All the more reason for me to take it. I have a far better claim to it than any human in this realm."

"I'll not let you!" The girl shouted.

"Ylva..." the jarl gasped. "Don't...!"

Amused, the dragon looked down at the jarl, who was already on the cusp of death yet still clinging to life. "Are they your children, puny jarl? Good! You can watch them die screaming!"

"You'll leave disappointed!" Ylva refused. "I'm not afraid of you!"

The dragon stuck out its meaty pink tongue and licked its scaly lips. "Then you'll perish braver than most!"

As the dragon arched its neck back like a crossbow and lunged, Sigurd woke up screaming. Initially, his cries were filled with horror, but they turned into screams of anguish as his wounds flared up, leaving him moaning hoarsely.

"Everything all right back there?"

Sigurd's eyes cracked open, and he beheld a giant squirrel's head peering over its shoulder at him. It made him think he was still dreaming until he felt the soft fur against his back and remembered that he and his companions were getting carried up the World Tree by Ratatoskr, the messenger of Yggdrasil.

As Sigurd shifted his weight, he felt the plush fur of the tail beneath his head, and it brought him a sense of comfort from the nightmare he'd endured. He took several ragged breaths before sitting up as far as he could manage and gazing around, taking in the majestic sight of the World Tree's trunk towering above him. He noticed his brother, Sinfjotli, and the gods Magni and Modi sitting nearby, looking worriedly at him.

"I had a horrific nightmare, Ratatoskr." Sigurd admitted.

He wished that was all it was. But that dream felt too real, almost as if he were reliving a memory. But whose?

A grim idea flashed through Sigurd's mind as he glanced down at his chest. He examined his golden hauberk, still damaged from their recent battle in Niflheim. Running his sprained fingers over the dents and punctures, a wave of phantom pain surged through him as he recalled the moment Fornjót punched him and shattered it. What terrified him more was that the hauberk resembled the one he had seen the jarl wearing in his dream. The vision felt too real, and he couldn't shake off the feeling it was a memory. If that was the case, there was only one person it could belong to.

Fafnir. Sigurd shivered at the thought of his old foe. He gained his chainmail shirt and frightening helmet from the dragon's treasure long ago. But that wasn't *all* he had gained from the greedy dragon. Magni and Modi claimed he inherited Fafnir's power and appearance by eating his heart and undergoing the Trial of Svarblood. And Sinfjotli believed Sigurd also inherited Fafnir's spirit. The dragon might still live within him even now.

Was I the one dreaming, or was he? Sigurd shuddered. *He even takes control of my dreams. As I grow weaker, he becomes stronger. Will he supplant me entirely?*

Sigurd closed his eyes. No. That was impossible, given the state of his body. Even if Fafnir was alive within him, his body was far too damaged to be of use. He'd perish long before the drake ever had the chance to seize control...assuming he *was* living within Sigurd.

"That aside, did you have a good rest?" Modi asked hopefully.

Sigurd shook his head as much as he could with his injured neck. "Not for lack of trying on your part."

The back of Sigurd's skull still throbbed. Through the dim fog of pain, Sigurd recalled wailing about the pain and pleading to his godly companions to grant him rest. Modi complied and tapped the back of Sigurd's skull, knocking him out. He'd promised to be gentle, but it felt as if he'd bashed Sigurd's skull in with his warhammer.

Still, Sigurd considered that a fair tradeoff. The Apple of Idun that his companions fed him in the Valley of Corpses barely held his body together as it healed his injuries at a snail's pace. But it also energized him, preventing him from falling asleep and forcing him to endure the throbbing pain of shattered bones, mangled organs, and countless other injuries.

Sigurd almost cracked a smile at the cruel irony. The very thing keeping him alive, mending his body, and dulling the pain also prevented him from escaping that pain.

He squeezed his eyes shut. He never realized how much he took sleep for granted until this ride up the World Tree. To him, sleep was much more than the body's natural way to recuperate, rest, and recharge. It was an escape from reality and pain. He didn't care if he endured another nightmare. He was already living in one inside this broken body, plagued by immobility and pain.

"It's a shame you didn't wake up sooner." Sinfjotli said. "We just finished passing through Midgard."

Midgard? Home! Sigurd shifted his gaze forward, searching for any trace of his home realm amid Yggdrasil's trunk.

Modi pointed a meaty finger toward Ratatoskr's raised tail. "It's right below us."

Sigurd looked at Sinfjotli, then shifted his gaze toward the edge of Ratatoskr's tail.

Nodding, Sinfjotli helped Sigurd crawled to the edge of Ratatoskr's tail and peered over.

Sigurd's eyes widened as he stared at the giant blue-green sphere below them nestled amid Yggdrasil's trunk.

The oceans shimmered in a deep bluish hue, more vibrant than the largest and most precious sapphires. With his superhuman vision, he could discern the continents' facets in sharp detail. The closest landmass was a vast white continent encased in ice, reminiscent of Niflheim's icy plains. Further south, three landmasses formed a breathtaking vista of forests, plains, and mountains. Their rolling hills and lush forests formed a patchwork of greenery, interspersed with sparkling rivers and shimmering lakes.

As Sigurd stared at his old home world, his eyes drifted to Yggdrasil's ash-white trunk. The World Tree's trunk passed straight through Midgard, like a blue apple that had been skewered by an arrow. But the trunk seemed translucent where it touched Midgard's soil.

"Shame I missed it," Sigurd muttered "Once Sinfjotli dragged him back onto his spot on Ratatoskr's raised tail "Must've been quite the experience passing through the realm."

"You wouldn't have been able to see anything," Magni informed. "Yggdrasil and Midgard exist on separate plains of existence. And our grandfather made sure that mortals can't perceive Yggdrasil and Midgard simultaneously. Sinfjotli can tell you. The moment Ratatoskr touched Midgard, he fell into a trance and didn't—"

Suddenly, the temperature skyrocketed as a light appeared. The air became thinner as the heat increased, scorching Sigurd's skin and forcing him to squint. Heat waves pulsed through the air, making it harder to breathe.

"Oh, dear!" Ratatoskr muttered. "Seems Sol has chosen a different route to flee today."

Sinfjotli furrowed his brow. "What are you—?"

The Kistfuskare suddenly sprang to life. Its metal helmet coiled around Sinfjotli's exposed head like a snake and encased him in metal, a clear warning that he was in danger.

"I'd turn away if I were you," Magni warned as Sinfjotli and Sigurd looked around expectantly.

Then, the air exploded with galloping hooves, followed by a deep, feminine voice shouting, "Forward!"

As Sigurd craned his neck towards the sound, the glowing ball streaking towards them almost blinded him. He'd had the sense to squint his eyes shut, allowing him to make out some details before the brightness overwhelmed him. A chariot pulled by two horses was speeding towards them, dragging something hellishly bright behind it. The glare was so intense that Sigurd had to turn his head away and squeeze his eyes shut, though it pained him to do both. As the chariot rushed past them, creating a rush of hot wind, the shining object singed Ratatoskr's fur and set the nearest branches ablaze.

When the intense heat cooled, Sigurd slowly opened his eyes and got a better look at the chariot speeding off into the distance at an inexorable speed. The chariot was barely visible amidst a blurry streak of gold and red. Sigurd could scarcely make out the details of the horses pulling it, their manes and tails trailing behind them like flames.

The chariot vanished as quickly as it appeared, speeding ahead until it was a blurry dot on the horizon. The sun trailed after it, casting its light and warmth across the world below.

Sinfjotli gulped. "Was that...?"

"Sol racing across the heavens in the Sun Chariot," Modi confirmed. "But you shouldn't let your guard down yet. The real danger hasn't passed us."

Sigurd furrowed his singed eyebrows. "Wha...?"

A mighty howl pierced through the air. It was so loud that the World Tree's trunk trembled as if experiencing another earthquake. Ratatoskr, ever the dutiful guide, jumped to a nearby branch to ensure nobody fell off his back until the shaking passed.

As Ratatoskr leaped back on the trunk with everyone resting on his raised tail, they scrambled to the edge and peered downwards. Sprinting after the sun like a bat out of Helheim was a colossal wolf with bright orange eyes that glowed like hot coals and a fiery gold coat with a faint stripe of black fur running between his eyes and nose. Scars ran across his chest and back, from which streaks of orange light radiated and trailed behind him like a comet's tail as he raced after the sun.

Sinfjotli managed the first words, "So, that's Sköll."

Sigurd swallowed hard. He had heard many tales of Sköll and his brother Hati, who would chase the sun and moon until Ragnarök. However, he never envisioned that one of the Celestial Wolves would appear so radiant.

Suddenly, the Celestial Wolf stopped dead in its tracks, letting the sun race further away. The light trail behind him faded as the wolf sniffed the air and turned towards them. Even though they were hundreds of miles apart, Sigurd could feel the wolf's smoldering gaze as Sköll curled his lips back.

"W-What's he doing?" Sinfjotli stammered.

"Shifting targets," Modi muttered as the Celestial Wolf reared his head back, howled balefully, and charged.

"Magni and Modi, hold tight to your friends and me!" Ratatoskr warned in a grave tone. "I like you guys, but I won't waste time scrambling after you if someone loses their grip."

Thor's sons had only several heartbeats to grab Sigurd and Sinfjotli and cling to Ratatoskr's fur as the squirrel tossed caution to the wind and scrambled up Yggdrasil with Sköll hot on their heels.

---◈✦◈---

SAMPLE CHAPTER 3:
HOWLING PURSUIT

"What did we do to deserve this?!" Sinfjotli exclaimed as he clutched Ratatoskr's fur as the giant squirrel scrambled up the World Tree.

The wind whipped past them like a shrieking widow as the squirrel darted among Yggdrasil's gnarled limbs and leapfrogged across the branches, desperate to escape their pursuer.

Between jumps, Sinfjotli stole a glance at his companions. Modi grasped Ratatoskr's fur for dear life, while Magni could only afford to clutch his soft fur in one hand while holding Sigurd in the other.

He had no choice about that, as there was no way Sigurd could cling to the squirrel in his battered state. Even if Sigurd wasn't half-dead from his injuries, there was no way he could keep his grip as Ratatoskr sprinted, turned, and jumped. The squirrel moved so much that Sinfjotli had to order the Coffin Cheater to keep hold of the squirrel's body, as there was no way he could keep his grip through strength alone.

Ratatoskr couldn't afford to be considerate of his passengers with a Celestial Wolf on his heels. As he dashed into a clump of branches, the mighty wolf Sköll trailed after them, his snarls echoing through Yggdrasil's ancient branches.

Their only tactical advantage was Ratatoskr's smaller size, which let him squeeze between Yggdrasil's thick branches and maneuver through leaves the size of castles and islands. But try as he might, he could not outrun the Celestial Wolf destined to devour the sun.

"Why is Sköll chasing us like a bat out of Helheim?" Modi questioned after Ratatoskr leaped into a thicket of branches. "We did nothing to goad him into doing this."

Sigurd coughed, forcing himself to speak. "It has less to do with...what we've done...and more with...who we are."

Sinfjotli glanced at his half-brother, who was peering over Magni's left shoulder as the god of strength clutched him tightly to his chest while keeping hold of Ratatoskr's fur. Sigurd's serpentine pupils were dilated, and thick veins bulged around his eye sockets, meaning he was using his clairvoyance as he stared at the gold wolf racing toward them.

Sigurd grimaced as the Sköll drew nearer. But it wasn't from pain, more like...disgust.

"What can you see?" Magni ventured.

"Hunger," Sigurd grimaced. "Sköll's heart is... overflowing with desire and... murderous intent. But...beneath it all...I can see he's excited. The way... a champion... feels when a new ...cha-challenge comes along. Or how... Sinfjotli... looked at me during... our duel in Helheim."

"You think that's why he's chasing us?" Modi speculated. "Maybe he got bored chasing the sun and wants easier prey."

"You're wrong about that!" Sinfjotli shouted.

Before he could elaborate, Ratatoskr jerked to a stop, pressed his legs low against the branch, and jumped.

Sköll blazed beneath the rising squirrel like a comet, scorching the ash-white branch and rocketing away from Yggdrasil as the squirrel grabbed a higher branch.

Ratatoskr scrambled onto the branch and dashed into a tangled thicket of branches as Sköll veered around and barreled toward them like a hawk zeroing in on a rabbit. The surrounding air heated like a furnace as his golden paws galloped across the void, propelling him like a missile at the thicket.

Seven seconds before impact, Ratatoskr emerged from the top of the thicket and unexpectedly jumped toward the Celestial Wolf. Sköll's orange eyes widened as the squirrel landed on his back, and then springboarded off his golden fur.

As Ratatoskr sailed toward a higher branch, Sköll crashed into the thicket, causing an explosion of heat and branches, sending twigs the size of mountains flying in every direction.

The squirrel didn't bother making a clever quip or checking the devastation as he scrambled toward the trunk and scurried higher. Sköll's howl echoed like thunder as he burst from the debris. Ratatoskr ignored the piercing howl and kept scurrying.

Meanwhile, Magni climbed closer to Sinfjotli. "What did you mean before? How was Modi and Sigurd's theory wrong?"

Sinfjotli bit his lip. "It's more accurate to say that's only half the story. Yes, Sköll felt bored before he sensed us, but that's not the sole reason he's chasing us. It's because he hates us!"

Magni narrowed his eyes. "Wha...oh shit! Modi!"

A twig the size of an island was hurtling toward them from above. Sinfjotli figured Sköll must have sent it flying or knocked it loose when he slammed into the thicket.

"On it!" The god of strength inched up Ratatoskr's fur, summoned his war hammer to his hand while standing on the squirrel's left shoulder, and leaped ahead toward the giant falling twig.

Electricity crackled as Modi heaved his war hammer at the colossal twig. The impact echoed through the air like a thunderclap as the stick exploded into a shower of splinters and wood chips the size of houses that rained then down on Ratatoskr and his three passengers.

Sinfjotli, Magni, and Sigurd struggled to hold on to the squirrel's fur as debris pelted them from above. Each impact threatened to knock them loose, but they held on with grim determination. The Coffin Cheater's gauntlets seemed to drill into the squirrel's fur, anchoring Sinfjotli in place. Horse-sized woodchips slammed against his back. Magni's fingers were white-knuckled as he held on and shielded Sigurd with his body from the onslaught.

Modi landed on Ratatoskr's shoulder as the last wooden shards scattered below. He holstered his weapon and held on as the squirrel continued his mad dash up the World Tree. Once Ratatoskr reached a steady pace, the god of courage scrambled closer and scrutinized Sinfjotli.

"How can you tell Sköll hates us?"

"Sköll keeps spewing out profanities and threats of doom with every breath, vowing to take revenge on 'Týr's relatives.'" Sinfjotli explained.

Everyone's eyes widened.

"Y-You...understand what Sköll...is saying?" Sigurd questioned. "How?"

Sinfjotli rolled his eyes. "Have you forgotten that I'm a full-fledged wolf, despite appearances? You can communicate with birds. Why's it unnatural that I can communicate with those wolves?"

Sigurd blinked in astonishment, hinting that it had never even crossed his mind. He opened his mouth, but Modi spoke before Sigurd could answer Sinfjotli's rhetorical question.

"Hang on," the god of courage muttered. "Did you say 'wolves?' *Plural?*"

Sinfjotli nodded. "Sköll isn't our only problem."

Two more giant twigs plummeted past them. This time, they were certain it wasn't from the tremors Sköll created as he raced after them.

Another giant wolf appeared, racing down Yggdrasil's trunk from above. This one looked like Sköll's opposite with deep blue eyes, black fur, a gray stripe running down his forehead, and fresh scars across his chest and back from which blue light radiated. But his eyes looked just as ravenous as Sköll's.

Sinfjotli immediately deduced this was Hati, the second Celestial Wolf, who chased the moon across the heavens. He also realized the wolf had raced ahead from the other side of the World Tree and was waiting to ambush them from above.

Looking back at the Sköll sprinting up the World Tree after them, Sinfjotli realized the Celestial Wolves were as crafty as they were gargantuan. Sköll kept them distracted to mask Hati's approach from above, allowing them to set up a masterful pincer attack. They'd nab Ratatoskr even if he veered left or right.

But the squirrel was crafty, too. Rather than change directions, the squirrel kept scurrying toward Hati. As the Celestial Wolves zeroed in, Ratatoskr crouched as low as he could against the World Tree, then pushed himself off the trunk.

The giant wolves narrowly missed the tip of Ratatoskr's tail by twenty feet before they zipped past each other as the squirrel began free-falling. Sinfjotli's face buried against the squirrel's red fur as the air pressure slammed against his back as Ratatoskr plummeted back-first.

Ratatoskr twisted his body around and warned everyone to hold on tight as he extended his limbs. A thick, furry membrane appeared between his front and back legs. Soon, they were no longer falling, but gliding like an albatross. The Messenger Squirrel had used all his accumulated momentum and the air draft slamming against his belly to sail away from the World Tree.

Sinfjotli let out an uneasy breath as he relished the exhilarating feeling. This was the second time he'd experienced flying. The first was in Helheim when Baldur's dragon, Twilight, carried them from his ship to the City of the Lost. But this felt more magical. The wind lapped against them, carrying the scent of vibrant leaves and ozone. Midgard and the other realms twinkled below and above them like stars. For a moment, he was tempted to let go of Ratatoskr, extend his arms, and relish everything.

But they weren't safe yet. The Celestial Wolves' black and gold paws raced across empty air as they left Yggdrasil and pursued the five of them.

"Those two don't know how to quit," Magni grumbled.

"Why would they?" Modi muttered. "Poor Sol and Mani get pursued every day and night by those two. This chase is nothing but a pleasant distraction compared to that."

"Don't underestimate me," Ratatoskr warned. "Sol and Mani must also fulfill their duties circling Midgard while the wolves chase them. I'm not restrained by that kind of responsibility. I can take far more liberties than those two deities."

The squirrel veered to the left and sailed back toward Yggdrasil, aiming for a huge thicket of tangled branches.

These boughs were much larger than the twigs they'd passed on their way from Midgard. Sinfjotli realized they had reached a higher level of Yggdrasil, where branches were more abundant. That would afford them more hiding spots and obstacles to throw in the wolves' path.

But would they make it? Sinfjotli glanced over his shoulder, expecting to see the Celestial Wolves hot on their heels. But Sköll and Hati were nowhere in sight.

They hadn't vanished. They'd merely shifted tactics. As Ratatoskr turned his body nighty degrees to sail closer to the World Tree, Sinfjotli spotted Hati racing after them from below. Peering over his right shoulder, he spied Sköll sprinting overhead.

He admired their foes' ingenuity. The Celestial Wolves planned to snare them in another pincer attack. Sköll would fall upon them like an eagle swooping on a rabbit while Hati raced toward them like a shark lunging at an unsuspecting seal pup from below. If they both struck simultaneously, Ratatoskr would get ripped to shreds.

Fortunately, the squirrel reached the thicket before the wolves executed their plan. Everything descended into pitch darkness as Ratatoskr sailed through an opening in the leaves and landed on the branch. Sinfjotli could barely see a thing as Ratatoskr resumed sprinting the second his paws touched the bark. The leaves above them bloated out all light sources, but Ratatoskr knew where he was going as he navigated the twisting dark.

And the wolves knew where Ratatoskr was, too. An opening appeared in the thicket above as Sköll's snout bit through the leaves. Hati's paws appeared and swiped uselessly at Ratatoskr as he scurried past.

The wolves continued appearing periodically through the canopy, trying to reach them. But their size kept them from squeezing into the thicket. Also, these branches were much stronger than the twigs on Yggdrasil's lower echelons that. No matter how the wolves howled, clawed, and bit, they couldn't break these boughs.

"No wolf can hope to catch a squirrel in a tree." Ratatoskr boasted. "We're in my domain now!"

"For now," Modi cautioned. "Sköll and Hati never give up a hunt. They'll fall upon us the second we emerge from this thicket."

"And if we remain in one place for too long, they'll eventually claw through and reach us," Sinfjotli added.

"Like I said, we're in my territory now," Ratatoskr reiterated as he squeezed between two ash-white branches. "I know these branches like the back of my tail. I've got the topographical advantage here, not them."

His words didn't assuage them. But they felt content knowing they were safe for the nonce.

As Sköll clawed an opening in the thicket above, letting light illuminate the thicket, Modi inched closer to Sinfjotli.

"Before Hati showed up, you mentioned Sköll howled that he'll take vengeance on Týr's relatives," the god of courage recalled. "What does our uncle have to do with this?"

"Sköll and Hati are Garm's older brothers, right?" Sinfjotli checked. "Well, Garm abhors Týr for imprisoning his father, Fenrir. He said as much to Sigurd and me back in Helheim. Garm also despised us simply because we had a drop of Odin's blood in our veins, which made us Týr's kin in his eyes. It seems his older brothers are cut from the same cloth. They loathe Týr and all his relatives for imprisoning their father. The difference is Garm was chained to Gnipa Cave, which kept him from ripping us to shreds. But nothing is stopping Sköll and Hati from chasing us."

"But Sköll and Hati didn't attack Modi and me when we traveled down Yggdrasil's trunk in our father's chariot on our way to Svartalfheim," Magni highlighted. "Why would they care now?"

"Probably because there's a bunch of Odin's descendants clumped together." Sinfjotli guessed. "Sköll, Hati, and Garm automatically deem anyone with even a drop of Odin's blood in their veins as relatives of Týr, and thus their sworn enemy. Two of Odin's grandsons and two distant descendants clumped together on Ratatoskr's back would get their attention. It'd be like a hunter carting two freshly slain and bleeding stags and rabbits on his back through the woods, drawing the attention of every ravenous predator in the forest."

"That's a far-fetched but sound argument," Modi concurred as he worriedly glanced at Hati's paw appearing from below. "It seems their hatred for Uncle Týr and anyone related to him is far more intense than their desire to devour the sun and moon."

"This has been a fascinating symposium, but you can't lose focus," Ratatoskr warned. "We're about to run out of cover and emerge in the open."

The branches and leaves before them parted sporadically, letting light shine through. It'd be a beautiful sight if they weren't so desperate.

As Sinfjotli clutched Ratatoskr's red fur tighter, he heard the Celestial Wolves barking at each other. But unlike his companions, he could understand them.

<Ratatoskr scurries around like a rat in a house!> Sköll seethed.

<There's little difference between the two species, brother.> Hati agreed. <If not for the tail, they'd look alike. They even taste similar. Remember the rats in Asgard?>

<How could I? It's been so long since we've eaten anything. The moon and sun are the ultimate prize, yet always out of our reach.>

<I don't even feel hungry anymore. But Týr's kin should remedy that.>

<This game of wolf and squirrel bores me. Let's employ *that* tactic.>

Sinfjotli's eyes widened. "Careful, Ratatoskr! They're about to try something!"

"No shit!" Ratatoskr scoffed. "Brace yourselves!"

Time seemed to slow down as Ratatoskr emerged through the giant green leaves and leaped toward Yggdrasil's trunk. Sinfjotli expected one wolf to be waiting near the trunk or lash out at them. But nothing...

Suddenly, the wolves howled. As Ratatoskr landed on the trunk, the Celestial Wolves sped towards them from either side. They missed and struck the giant branch, tearing through the bark like arrows through fire.

With a sickening crack, the continent-sized branch broke off from the trunk, sending millions of tons of leaves, twigs, and debris plummeting.

Like eagles zeroing in on a rabbit, the Celestial Wolves veered around, racing after Ratatoskr as he jumped off the trunk and leapfrogged across other branches, always keeping close to the trunk in case he needed to make another break.

"Holy shit!" Modi exclaimed. "They tore off one of Yggdrasil's branches!"

Sinfjotli frowned, not sensing the danger. "Is...is that supposed to be impossible?"

"Not at this level of the World Tree!" Magni stressed. "Yggdrasil's branches become incomprehensibly stronger the higher up the trunk you get. We couldn't even put a dent in the tree's canopy. Yet they...!"

Sigurd coughed. "It...it's because...they hit it...as one..."

Sinfjotli climbed closer. "What do you mean?"

He wasn't sure why he asked. Sigurd could barely speak, and this was no time for a conversation. Maybe it was for his own sake. He wanted... *needed* to take his mind off Sköll and Hati, who were lapping at their heels.

Sigurd took a dozen ragged breaths, then elaborated. "An object is...likelier to break if you strike it from... opposite directions. An acrobatic wanderer...from the southeast...showed me how to break a sword with... mere knives by striking it from both sides. You could even... cut a rippling flag if you pull it off right. But... you have to hit it with... exact timing and energy." He glanced past Magni at the wolves. "For them to achieve it is truly remarkable."

Sinfjotli glanced at the debris falling toward Midgard. His eyes widened with concern. "Will everyone in Midgard be all right? What happens if all those branches crash into—"

"Worry about yourself foremost," Ratatoskr urged as he leaped off another branch. "Think about anything else now, and we're dead!"

Sinfjotli squeezed his eyes shut. The squirrel was right. They couldn't afford to concern themselves with anything else.

But did they have to keep feeling this helpless? He wore a magical suit of armor. Sigurd (despite his critical condition) was a dragon in the guise of a man. And they had two gods on their side! Couldn't...

"Sorry, Sinfjotli," Modi apologized. "This is above our pay grade."

Sinfjotli shot him a look. "Reading my mind?"

"Hearing your prayers." Modi corrected. "Believe me, I'd love to bash them with everything I have, but it wouldn't—"

"—You're Aesir!" Sinfjotli interrupted. "The protectors of the Nine Realms! Surely you..."

"Inspect Sköll and Hati," Magni urged, though it sounded more like an order.

Sinfjotli peered over his shoulder at the black and gold wolves, leaving behind orange and blue light streaks as they raced through open air after them.

"See those arrows and wounds peppered across their bodies?" Magni pointed. "Those are from Sol and Mani taking potshots at the wolves as they get chased across the heavens. Those two Vanir deities are powerful enough to raze an entire continent, and all their arrows do is annoy their pursuers. Do you think Modi and I can succeed where the goddess of the sun and god of the moon have failed for thousands of years?"

"Horseshit." Sigurd coughed.

Magni looked at him. "Come again."

"Horseshit," Sigurd wheezed a little louder, pushing himself to lisp out the words. "For the gods of strength and courage, you have... a ton of excuses not to fight. I don't have that option. Every moment, Sinfjotli and I must live... knowing Hel is looming over our shoulders, waiting for us to die and drag us back to the underworld. But we keep going! Look at me! I'm a broken mess, and it's taking everything I have to say this, but I'm still willing to fight those wolves. What's your excuse?"

Magni narrowed his eyes as his aura glowed brighter. Sinfjotli's ears popped as the god flexed his power, and he feared Sigurd had pushed him too far. But when Magni shoved Sigurd into Sinfjotli's arms, he realized the rage was directed at himself and Modi.

"Fighting the Celestial Wolves puts far more than our lives at stake," Magni grumbled as he summoned his greatsword. "But you're right about one thing: that's no excuse not to act."

"Couldn't agree more," Modi concurred, summoning his war hammer.

Ratatoskr didn't share their courage. "You're both dead if you take one step off my back and literally throw yourself at the wolves."

"Who said anything about disembarking?" Modi stood. "We just need to create distance between us and them."

"Is there anything Sigurd and I can do to help?" Sinfjotli ventured.

The gods didn't reply. Sinfjotli's ears popped as Modi and Magni closed their eyes and concentrated. The air temperature plummeted, and frost crystals formed on Ratatoskr's fur. A mighty gale slammed against them. Turning forward, Sinfjotli discovered it came from an enormous vortex swirling between two colossal branches. Lightning zapped from the clouds, striking the branches as the vortex unloaded a torrent of hail.

Sinfjotli whistled. "Nicely done!"

"It'd be... easier if... we were creating this in Midgard or... the other realms..." Magni groaned, his muscles spasming from the strain. "But this...will suffice."

"Are you kidding?" Ratatoskr balked. "We're up against the Celestial Wolves! A thundercloud can't deter them!"

"It's not... supposed to..." Modi admitted. "It's just...a smokescreen to mask our next move."

Ratatoskr lowered his head and hopped off another branch toward the thunderhead. "You dolts better have a good plan."

"You won't like it," Magni promised under his breath.

The giant squirrel flashed his yellowed teeth in a sneer, but reluctantly hopped toward the vortex, the Celestial Wolves hot on his heels.

As they drew closer, the air crackled with electricity and boomed with thunder. The wind intensified, pulling at their matted hair and ragged clothes as the sharp scent of ozone filled their nostrils. Soon, the hail fell upon them in punishing sheets, forcing Sinfjotli to shield Sigurd with his body as they entered the vortex. The wind roared so loud it made Sinfjotli's ears ring.

Then everything quieted. Looking around at the swirling walls of clouds, Sinfjotli realized they were in the center of the vortex.

"Now for step two!" Modi announced as he hefted his war hammer. "Ratatoskr, flip onto your back, extend your membranes, and brace yourself. This will probably hurt."

The squirrel muttered a curse under his breath, but did as he was told. As he flipped, Sköll and Hati burst through the thunderhead...right into the path of the two gods on the squirrel's back. Magni and Modi swung their weapons, shouting, "Landvinningur himins!"

Sinfjotli vaguely recalled this was the same attack that once brought Fornjót to one knee as the Coffin Cheater whirled to life and drilled itself into Ratatoskr's fur and the skin beneath to prevent him and Sigurd from sailing away as the gods unleashed their power.

Click here to continue reading or scan the QR Code below:

APPENDIX

HOUSE VOLSUNG

Boasting descent from the youngest son of Odin and Frigga, the Volsung family is one of the few mortal families in Midgard that can truly trace their lineage to the All-Father. They have been kings, conquers, avengers, and heroes. But above all else, they were warriors who carved their names into the annals of Midgard's history. Thanks to Sigurd and Sinfjotli, their story isn't finished yet.

SIGURD SNAKE EYES (slain by Guttorm but resurrected in Helheim),

—his horse, GRANI, roaming free in Midgard,

—his father, [SIGMUND],[1] perished in battle against Lyngvi's forces

—his mother, [HJORDIS], perished in battle against her brother-in-law, Yngvi,

—his children:

——by his paramour, BRYNHILD:

———ASLAUG,

——by his wife, GUDRUN:

———SVANHILD, saved by Freyja and became a valkyrie,

---

1. Regular brackets] indicate a valiant death and the character became Einherjar.

————{SIGMUND},[2] slain by GUTTORM,

—his half-brothers:

——SINFJOTLI, by his aunt SIGNY (poisoned by his stepmother but resurrected in Helheim),

——[HELGI] HUNDINGSBANE by his stepmother BORGHILD,

———his wife, [SIGRÚN], who perished in the Volsungs' last stand,

——[HÁMUNDR] by his stepmother BORGHILD, who perished in the Volsungs' last stand,

—his other kin:

——his aunt, {SIGNY} who died by suicide,

———her children by her husband, SIGGEIR the Beast:

————{RAGR}, her first son, killed by Sigmund at Signy's behest,

————{REKKR}, her second son, killed by Sigmund at Signy's behest,

————{AURORA}, her only daughter, killed by Sinfjotli at Signy's behest,

————{HANSEL}, her fourth son, killed by Sinfjotli at Signy's behest,

———by her brother, SIGMUND:

————SINFJOTLI, her third son,

—his uncles:

——[GRÍPIR], a hermit gifted with prophetic visions, perished alongside his sister in battle,

——{ARNE the SWIFT}, devoured by Siggeir's mother,

——{COLDBORN BLOOD AXE}, devoured by Siggeir's mother,

——{FRODE the WISE}, devoured by Siggeir's mother,

——{GERALD the DEVOTE}, devoured by Siggeir's mother,

——{HALVARD SQUINT-EYE}, devoured by Siggeir's mother,

——{JERRIK the UNDYING}, devoured by Siggeir's mother,

---

2. {Angled brackets} indicate a character is deceased and possibly ended up in Helheim.

——{ORWIG the PROTECTOR}, devoured by Siggeir's mother,

——{THURMOND the MIGHTY}, devoured by Siggeir's mother,

——{ULF the BLOODLETTER}, devoured by Siggeir's mother,

———his maternal grandfather, [EYLIMI], killed by Hávard,

———his paternal grandfather, [VÖLSUNG], killed by Siggeir,

———his paternal grandmother, HLJOD the Valkyrie,

————his great-grandfather, [RERIR the STERN], who died fighting,

————his great-grandmother, {BRENDA} who died in childbirth,

—————his ancestor, [SIGI, called THE MAVERICK AESIR], who died slaying countless men.

HOUSE GJUKUNG

An ancient dynasty that ruled over the Burgundians in the land of eternal mist, they played a pivotal role in Sigurd's final days in Midgard. Sigurd's arrival brought great fortune and prosperity to their lands. But after his death, they met a horrific, bloody end at the hands of Atli of the Huns.

{GUDRUN} who committed suicide,

—her father, {GJUKI}, the King of Burgundians who reigned until being slain by Atli's forces,

—her mother, {GRIMHILD}, who was tortured to death by Atli's forces,

—her siblings:

——{GUNNAR}, executed by Atli,

———his first wife, BRYNHILD,

———his second wife, {GLAUMVOR},

——{HAGEN} brutally slain by Atli,

——{GUTTORM} slain by Sigurd.

—her children:

——by her first husband, {SIGURD}:

———SVANHILD, allegedly trampled to death by Jormunrek's horses, but was actually saved by Freyja and became a valkyrie

———{SIGMUND}, killed by Guttorm,

——by her second husband, {ATLI} of the Huns:

———{ERNAK}, killed by his mother,

———{EITEL}, killed by his mother,

——by her third husband, JONAKR:

———[SORLI] killed by Jormunrek's men,

———[HAMDIR] killed by Jormunrek's men,

———[ERP] killed by Jormunrek's men.

THE AESIR

The gods who created Midgard continue to keep watch over it and the other Nine Realms from Asgard. After the All-Father, Odin, and his brothers, Hoenir and Vé, slew the primordial giant Ymir and fashioned Midgard from his corpse, he and his descendants continue to protect their creation and maintain the stability of the other realms.

ODIN the All-Father, King of Asgard and Chief of the Aesir,

—his pet ravens:

——HUGINN,

——MUNINN,

—his pet wolves:

——GERI

——FREKI

—by his wife, FRIGGA, the goddess of marriage, family, and motherhood:

——{BALDUR}, the god of goodness, joy, light, and forgiveness, who Hodr accidentally killed,

———his son by Nanna, FORSETI,

———{LÉTTFETI}, his horse,

———{TWILIGHT}, his pet dragon,

——{HODR}, the god of darkness and winter, killed by Vali,

——HERMONDR, the messenger of the gods,

——[SIGI], the Maverick Aesir, perished fighting and became Einherjar,

—by the Jotun, GUNNLQÐ:

——BRAGI, the god of poetry,

—by the Jotun, FJÖRGYN:

——THOR, the god of thunder,

———by the Jotun, JARNSAXA:

————MAGNI, the god of strength,

———by his wife, SIF:

————MODI, the god of courage,

————THRÚD, a valkyrie and the goddess of trees, flowers, and grass,

———TANNGRISNIR and TANNGNJÓSTR, his goats,

—by the Jotun, GRIDR:

——VIDAR, the god of vengeance,

—by the nine Jotun mothers, ANGEYJA, ATLA, EISTLA, EYRGJAFA, IMDR, GJALP, GREIP, JARNSAXA, and ULFRUN:

——HEIMDALL, Watchman of the Gods and Guardian of humanity,

—by the Jotun, HRÓÐR:

——TÝR, the god of war and justice,

—Odin's brothers:

——HOENIR, the god of silence, spirituality, and silence who gifted the first humans, Askr and Embla, with their wit and sense of touch and smell, and later became the temporary regent of the Vanir after the bloody Aesir-Vanir War,

——{VÉ}, the god of fertility and sensuality who granted the first humans, Askr and Embla, their outward appearances, speech, taste, hearing, and sight,

—Odin's Allies:

——The NORNS:

———URÐR,

———SKULD,

———VERÐANDI,

——SKADI, the goddess of the hunt and winter,

———her servant, [BREDI], an Einherjar whom Sigi killed

——ANDHRÍMNIR, the chef of the gods,

——AEGIR, the god of alcohol and tides,

———his wife, RÁN, goddess of the depths.

——the EINHERJAR of Valhalla.

---◦✦◦---

THE VANIR

The other major family of the gods, the Vanir once battled the Aesir in a bloody war. They were the only race in the Nine Realms to force the Aesir to capitulate after many lives were lost in the violent Aesir-Vanir War. They now monitor the Nine Realms alongside the Aesir as equals. Living in Vanaheim and sometimes Alfheim, the Vanir protect the natural world and receive half of those who perish bravely in battle.

NJÖRD, the god of the sea and former leader of the Vanir,

—his children:

——FREYJA, the goddess of love and war, the current leader of the Vanir, and equal to Odin,

———her daughters

————by her husband OTTR:

—————HNOSS,

—————GERSEMI,

————by IWALDI:

—————SIGYN, the goddess of fidelity,

——FREYR, the god of magic, harvest, and fertility and the ruler of Alfheim,

—SOL, the goddess of the sun, who flees in a chariot from the wolf, Sköll,

—MANI, the god of the moon, who flees in a chariot from the wolf, Hati,

—NANNA, the goddess of cooking, joy, and peace,

—IDUN, the goddess of youth, spring, and rejuvenation,

—DELLINGER, the god of the dawn,

—by his wife, NOTT, the goddess of the night:

——DAGR, the god of day.

THE DWARVES OF SVARTALFHEIM

The dwarves are the Aesir's oldest allies, whom Odin created from maggots feasting on Ymir's corpse. Tracing their descent from the first dwarf, Ivaldi, they are hailed as the greatest smiths and craftsmen in the Nine Realms who created Mjolnir, Draupnir, Gullinbursti, and Gungnir. Their contact with humans in Midgard is rare, but always consequential.

IVALDI, The King of Svartalfheim and Father of the Dwarves,

—MÓTSIGNIR, the Bear of Svartalfheim,

—BILLINGR,

—DÁINN,

—DURINN,

—DÚRNIR,

—GANDALF,

—DVALINN,

—{HREIDMAR}, murdered by his son, Fafnir,

——{OTTR}, a shapeshifter Loki, Odin, and Hoenir accidentally killed,

——{FAFNIR}, who transformed into a dragon and was famously killed by Sigurd,

——{REGIN}, Sigurd's mentor and foster father, who he later killed in premeditated self-defense,

—{LITR}, Baldur's companion who got kicked into his funerary pyre by Thor and now keeps the Hringhorni in order and builds homes for the righteous,

—ANDVARI, a shapeshifting dwarf whose treasure Loki swiped to pay a weregild to Hreidmar,

THE GUARDIANS OF NIÐAVELLIR, who drained Kvasir of his blood to create the Mead of Poetry:

—Fjalar,

—Galar,

—THE HULDRA BROTHERS who crafted Mjolnir, Draupnir, and Freyr's boar, Gullinbursti:

——BROK,

——SINDRI.

THE JÖTNAR:

The inhabitants of Jotunheim, who trace their descent to the beginning of the world, the Jötnar, or frost giants, are the Aesir's oldest enemies. The fates of the two races have been intertwined for as long as time has turned: by blood, marriage, and their eternal feud, which will culminate in Ragnarök. Giants possess ancient treasure, magic, and knowledge older than the gods and have been as instrumental in shaping the history of the realms as the Aesir.

{YMIR}, the first being, whom all giants, gods, and beasts trace descent from, was mother and father to all before being slain by Odin, Hoenir, and Vé, who molded his flesh and blood into Midgard,

—FORNJÓT the Destroyer,

——his son KÁRI, King of the Clouds,

——his son AEGIR, Jotun of the Waves,

——his son, BERGELMIR, the ancestor of all other frost giants,

—SUTTUNGR, the giant king who acquired the Mead of Poetry,

——his daughter, GUNNLQÐ,

—HYRROKIN, the giantess who launched Baldur's funeral ship, the Hringhorni, out to sea,

—{FÁRBAUTI}, the father of Loki by his wife, the goddess {LAUFEY},

—SVARBLOOD the Skin-changer, who taught humanity how to attain the form and power of beasts,

—{THIAZI}, the shapeshifter who kidnaped Idun and later became a draug,

——his daughter, SKADI, who became the goddess of the hunt and winter.

LOKI's PROGENY

Loki, the most infamous of the gods, was the son of the goddess Laufey and the giant Farbauti, who became Odin's blood brother. No god in the Norse Pantheon was more notorious or wily than the god of tricksters. Sometimes, he was the Aesir's greatest ally, at other moments, the worst thorn in their side, and later their worst betrayer after he orchestrated Baldur's murder. Yet Loki's descendants were just as infamous and reviled as him. All endured tragic fates, and many became the Aesir's worst enemies, destined to battle the gods at Ragnarök.

LOKI

—by his lover Angrboda:

——HEL, goddess of death and Queen of the Underworld,

——MÓÐGUÐR, the Guardian of Helheim who ensures no one living enters the underworld,

———her horse, HELHEST,

——FENRIR, the wolf destined to battle Odin at Ragnarök,

———by Odin's pet wolves, GERI and FREKI,

————SKÖLL, the Celestial Wolf who chases the sun across the heavens,

————HATI, the Celestial Wolf who chases the moon across the heavens,

————GARM, the Hound of Helheim who ensures no soul may leave Helheim unless his aunt allows it,

——JÖRMUNGANDR, the World Serpent who is so large he encircles the entirety of Midgard and bites his tail. Destined to battle Thor at Ragnarök,

—by his wife, SIGYN:

——VALI,

——{NARFI},

—by the stallion SVANDILFARI (while Loki was in the form of a mare),

——SLEIPNIR, the eight-legged mount of Odin who carries the All-Father on journeys throughout the Nine Realms.

‐◦✦◦‐

HELHEIM'S DRAUGS

T he mightiest entities in the underworld, subordinate only to Hel, Garm, and Móðguðr, Helheim's draugs are among the fiercest foes imaginable. With semi-invincibility, unique abilities, and inconceivable power, they are the mightiest enemies one could face. Only monarchs or generals have the potential to join their ranks. Some were the blackest of villains. Others became corrupted upon their death. Yet all now burn with hatred for the Aesir and their allies.

—SIGGIER the Beast,

—KING DURRAN,

—DONG ZHOU,

—QUEEN TAMARA,

—GOLIATH,

—KING PORUS of Paurava,

—THIAZI,

—YUE FEI,

—GENERAL ANTONY,

—AGAMEMNON,

—ALLANT,

—GUTTORM,

Former Draugs

—{ATLI} of the Huns (demoted and sent to the Valley of Corpses after losing a brutal duel to Guttorm),

—{SIGGIER} the Beast, eaten by Garm.

Other Notable Houses and Legendary Figures

THE VALKYRIES

The valkyries are the winged female warriors who serve Freyja and Odin. They scour battlefields to choose the slain worthy of a place in Valhalla or Fólkvangr and dispatch any restless spirits to Helheim. They are some of the Aesir's most formidable warriors and the bane of the undead.

—BRYNHILD,
——her brother, {ATLI}, killed by Merikh,
——her mother, {THORA}, who drowned at sea,
——her father, {BUTHLI}, executed by Merikh,
—SVANHILD,
—SIGRÚN,
—HLJOD,
—THRÚD.

HOUSE HUNDING

An ancient house that survived the bloody Battle of Frekastein, they later defeated Sigmund and his army, destroyed Hunaland, and almost extirpated the Volsung bloodline. Under their king, Lyngvi the Lusty, many ancient families and kingdoms were brutally razed. They were eventually brought to justice, and their bloodline was extirpated by Sigmund's youngest son, Sigurd the Dragonslayer.

{LYGNVI the Lusty,} the king who brought the Volsungs to their knees, brutally executed by Sigurd,

—his many sons by countless women, all slain by Sigurd during his war of vengeance,

—his father, {HUNDING}, slain by Helgi,

—his older brothers:

——{ÁLFR}, slain by Helgi,

——{EYIÓLF}, slain by Helgi,

——{HJÖRVARD}, slain by Helgi,

—his twin brother {HÁVARD}, the general of army, killed by Sigmund,

—his nephews, called {THE SONS of HUNDING}, all slain by Sigurd.

The Three Eagles:

—GULLINKAMBI the Golden,

—FJALAR,

—HRÆSVELGR the Corpse Eater.

RATATOSKR, the Messenger Squirrel who travels down Yggdrasil relaying messages between Nidhogg and Gullinkambi,

NIDHOGG, the dragon of the apocalypse who gnaws on Yggdrasil's root,

HOUSE YNGLING

The oldest and mightiest Scandinavian dynasty. Their prince and future king, Alf, rescued and married Hjordis after Sigmund perished fighting Lyngvi's army and raised Sigurd as his stepson.

King ALF,

—his father, {HJALPREK},

—his twin brother, {YNGVI},
—his first wife, [HJORDIS],
—his second wife, THORA,

{HÖGNE}, King of Östergötland, who perished at Frekastein,
—his daughter, [SIGRÚN], who became a valkyrie
—his son, {DAGR},

{GRANMAR}, King of Södermanland, who perished at Frekastein,
—his son {HOTHBRODD}, who perished at Frekastein,

{JORMUNREK} the King of the Goth, mutilated and slain by Gudrun's last three sons,
—his son, {Randver}, executed for treason,
—his advisor, {BIKKI}, killed by Gudrun's last three sons,

{MERIKH}, brutally slain by Brynhild,

VOLUND the SMITH, an elven smith who forged the cursed sword Mimung,

SURTR, the King of Muspelheim and leader of the fire giants.

—◈✦◈—

THE NINE REALMS:

The Nine Realms, a group of vastly distant worlds spread across Yggdrasil's branches and roots, are home to many races and untold wonders. Few can travel between the realms; even fewer dare to journey beyond their home realms. The Nine Realms offer the ultimate challenge to those with nothing left to lose and everything to gain.

ASGARD, the home of the Aesir,

VANAHEIM, the home of the Vanir,

ALFHEIM, the home of the elves,

SVARTALHEIM, the home of the dwarves,

MIDGARD, the mortal realm,

JOTUNHEIM, the home of the frost giants,

NIFLHEIM, the realm of eternal frost

HELHEIM, the realm of the dishonorable dead,

MUSPELHEIM, the realm of the fire giants.

ALSO BY ALEX

ABOUT THE AUTHOR

A lex E. Martin is an epic fantasy storyteller and lover of Norse Mythology. Born in the Northeast United States, Alex is an avid explorer, fencer, aspiring chef, dog lover, gamer, and world traveler with an insatiable thirst for adventure.

Learn more at https://sites.google.com/view/alex-e-martin/home or scan the QR Code Below: